MW00658639

playing HARD

Perfection SAGA

BOOK ONE

BETH PELLINO-DUDZIC

My 3 Girls
PUBLISHING

Playing Hard
Perfection Series Book One
Published by My 3 Girls Publishing LLC

Copyright © 2024 by Beth Pellino-Dudzic. All rights reserved.

No part of this book may be reproduced in any form or by any mechanical means, including information storage and retrieval systems without permission in writing from the publisher/author, except by a reviewer who may quote passages in a review.

All images, logos, quotes, and trademarks included in this book are subject to use according to trademark and copyright laws of the United States of America.

ISBN: 979-8-9896803-0-6
FICTION / Romance / Contemporary

Cover and Interior design by Victoria Wolf, wolfdesignandmarketing.com, copyright owned by My 3 Girls Publishing LLC.

This is a work of fiction. Names, characters, businesses, places, events and incidents are either the products of the author's imagination or used in a fictitious manner. Any resemblance to actual persons, living or dead, or actual events is purely coincidental.

All rights reserved by My 3 Girls Publishing LLC.
Printed in the United States of America.

My 3 Girls
PUBLISHING

To my family: my husband, Ron, my three beautiful daughters,
Ashley, Chelsea, and Kara, and my new addition Penelope June.
To my brother Michael, who we lost way too early.
I know he gave me the strength to write this book.

THE FAMILY

GINA RICCI WADED through the crowd at the St. Mary's College Preparatory High School graduation, class of 1972. Her parents, Mario and Francesca (Franny), and her brothers, Frankie and Ant, were out there somewhere. She turned to see who was tapping her on the shoulder. It was her cousin Mario. He hated that name and chose to go by Rio instead. He had just graduated from Chaminade high school, another Manhasset Catholic school. He pointed toward the family and pulled Gina through the crowd. Being so close in age and growing up together, they were more than cousins; they were best friends.

Gina saw her father. "There's my princess. We've been looking for you. We have over a hundred people coming to the fucking house. Your mother and I have lots to do. We're done here. Get your ass moving."

Franny was a true old-country Italian wife who maintained some old-fashioned ideals. "Gina, please hurry and do what your father wants. You'll see your friends at the party."

Gina lagged behind her parents as they started walking to the parking lot. "I'll catch a ride with Rio. Don't worry, I'll be there. I need to chill anyway."

Gina was looking for her best friend, Liz Richards. She wanted to say goodbye. Liz was leaving right after the ceremony to go to Europe with her parents. Her father was a well-known lawyer in Manhattan, and her mother was an ER doctor at Stony Brook Eastern Long Island Hospital.

Although nobody dared to mess with Liz and Gina, they weren't mean girls, just a little wild. They cut school frequently to go to Manhattan, just a few stops away on the Long Island Railroad. Once they even took an Amtrak train to a concert in Philadelphia, and their parents were never the wiser.

There she was. Gina hugged Liz and told her, "I'm going to miss you the most."

Rio was waiting. "Let's go and get out of here fast."

The two girls wouldn't see each other again for years. They had no idea how much their lives would change in the meantime.

Ricci was a well-known name in Long Island. Gina's grandfather, Mario Senior, was a large man with thick salt-and-pepper hair. He was always dressed in a suit when he wasn't tending to his beloved tomato plants. Mario Senior loved his grandchildren, who he considered to be his most treasured assets. Maybe because he knew the family business was in good hands. Grandpa was a generous and loving man who enjoyed life, laughed a lot, and was gregarious. He loved listening to Jimmy Roselli albums and singing classic Italian songs. The Ricci grandchildren loved him unconditionally. There was a dark side to him though that the grandchildren never saw. Very rarely did he let the veil slip. Then Mario Senior was cold as steel, and his sons needed to take care of business.

Their grandmother, Angelina, was a plump woman with silver-gray hair and the bluest of eyes. She was born in Italy where Mario met her on one of his "business" trips. Grandma said it was love at first sight.

Angelina was an excellent cook. Gina, her mom, and her Aunt Deidre helped. Gina always helped her cook for the holidays. Franny and Deidre weren't the best cooks and only feigned interest in baking, but Gina took to it immediately. She knew how to make pinoles, ricotta cheesecakes, and cannoli. Gina could even cook all the Christmas Eve favorites for the Italian American tradition, the Feast of the Seven Fishes.

Being the only female grandchild, her grandparents doted on her. When they both passed away too soon, Gina was crushed. Grandpa died two years ago in his office from a massive coronary. Angelina died ten short months later. The family said it was because she missed her husband so much, she couldn't go on without him. Both funerals had more than 200 attendees. Off-duty police officers worked the streets, which had to be closed off around the church to accommodate the crowd.

Their sons, Mario Junior and Antonio (Tony) had been running Ricci Construction and Development for ten years. Ricci Construction had office and apartment buildings in Manhattan, Queens, and Brooklyn. Strip malls all over Long Island, New Jersey, and Westchester County each brought in millions more, along with renovation work on business parks and apartments. The development side of the business was booming with land purchases at cheap prices and the right influence to get any zoning changes they needed to make. Ricci Construction and Development was a legit business, but the family also had less than legitimate endeavors. The brothers, plainly speaking, were very successful "wise guys."

Growing up, the "M" word was never, ever, *ever* used in their home. Gina's father Mario preached, "nothing that happens in this house is ever discussed outside of this house." Gina thought that was a little extreme. After all, why would anything that happened at home be interesting to her friends anyway?

Franny and Aunt Deidre had hired help. Serena practically raised Frankie, Gina, and Ant from a young age. She cooked, cleaned, and tried to give the children a real-world perspective of growing up—the "do's and don'ts" of being a decent human being.

Aunt Deidre was a striking, statuesque, African American former model. She was invited to many functions. Mae helped Deidre with cooking and cleaning, watched Rio, and kept track of Deidre's busy calendar, which was filled with gallery openings, parties, and luncheons.

The four Ricci kids grew up in a world of privilege, but would they all take advantage of what was given? Frankie was being groomed to join the Ricci business, no pretense that he was going to college. He was ready to "do it all" for Dad. Gina and Rio were different, their paths about to take a much different turn . . . not even their parents could imagine what would happen over the next ten years. Ant was still too young to see which path he would choose. But Gina and Rio were in the unfamiliar territory of having to prove themselves.

RIO'S BAND

RIO OPENED THE DOOR to his new black BMW 5 Series. It was the first year they were produced and it had all the upgrades— black leather interior and the best audio system available. Zero to sixty in 9.7 seconds. Gina hopped in the passenger seat and the two sat for a minute before Rio started the engine so they could finish the joint they were smoking. Gina lit up one of her Sobranie pastel cigarettes.

"Hey man, seriously, you're smoking a cigarette in my new car. It's going to stink up my ride. A joint is different. Oh, Gina, you suck."

"Oh, I'm so sorry." Gina didn't give a shit what he thought.

"I give it to you Rio, this is some graduation gift your parents gave you. I should be so lucky."

Rio looked at her with disbelief. "Hey man, you don't think your parents are giving you a car for graduation. They gave Frankie that red Trans Am. I'm sure you're getting some kind of ride."

"Well, I'm not my brother, heir apparent of Ricci Construction and Development," she whined. "I can't handle going to this motherfucking lame-ass party our parents are having. It's all their friends and associates." Gina gave air quotes to the word 'associates.' "What has it to do with us?" Gina was pissed as she rolled another joint.

"Go with it. We know this shit isn't for us. Did you even invite any of your friends?" Rio was mellow as usual.

"Who the fuck am I going to invite? I only have three real friends—Liz, Susan, and Angela. Oh yeah, and of course their parents." Gina was ramping up; she needed that joint. "Don't ruin my buzz, okay? Turn the radio on so we can forget about the shit show we are about to walk into. Did you invite any friends to this phony display?"

"Yeah, a few." Rio took a hit and then laughed. "I have some of my band friends coming."

"Wait, what? You have a band?!" Gina was clearly pissed to just be finding this out now.

"Look, it's not a real band, but it could be someday, probably soon," Rio explained, sounding more hopeful than positive.

"When were you going to tell me about this double life you have? I'm hurt . . . everyone else only wants to be my friend to get close to Frankie or to say that they know me. All those St. Mary girls are a bunch of bitches. Put the radio on, let's listen to music while we ride in this bitchin' car."

Rio's dial was already set to New York 95.5 WPLJ. It was the standard rock fare—Stones, Elton John, mostly Top 40.

"Rio seriously, put on WNEW. They have the good stuff, progressive music—Yes, Jethro Tull, Deep Purple, Moody Blues, Traffic, Pink Floyd. Progressive rock is a different sound than this typical crap. It's also great music to listen to when you're high. WNEW plays a whole side of an album. Who does that? It's super cool. I'm shocked you don't listen to it, especially since you are in a *band*." Gina felt a little cooler than Rio at that moment.

"Look, I love the guitar and you can't get more pumping rock and roll than the Stones and shit. When did you become a connoisseur of rock and roll?"

Gina smirked. "Man, you're so cool, I thought you would . . . you know what? Forget it. I'm still pissed at the band thing. I mean super fucking pissed that you would not share that with me. You suck. I love you, but you suck."

Rio slowed the car as a stone wall came into view. Over six feet tall, it surrounded the property and thick shrubbery and shrouded any view of the massive estate from the street. He stopped at the front gate and punched in the code.

"Don't go all the way up to the main house. Park at the carriage house so we can smoke another joint before getting bombarded with all those os. I can't stand it."

"We'd have to walk all the way up to the house. I have a change of clothes with me. It's fucking annoying when you do this. It's hot." Rio was pissed.

"Rio, do it. I don't want to make a grand entrance. I want to ease into it, please. I want to go through the garage undetected. If you drive your car, they will bombard us. Let's sneak in on foot."

"You know you're a real spoiled bitch."

Gina smirked. "Thank you. I accept that."

Rio turned left, drove 500 feet, and idled the car in front of the carriage house while they finished another joint. The ground level garages held equipment for the gardeners. Over them was a two-bedroom apartment with a large living room, fireplace, and brand-new kitchen.

After Gina flicked the roach out the window, Rio put the Beemer back into gear and headed up the winding driveway. The grass looked golf course perfect. There were weeping willow trees in the front yard and under each willow was a huge bed of brightly colored flowers. The driveway circled in front of the stone and brick Tudor home situated on four acres in the exclusive waterfront area in Manhasset, facing the Long Island Sound.

Two glass and wrought iron doors that Franny found at an estate sale in England served as the front entrance of the eight-bedroom house. The doors opened into a foyer with marble flooring and a crystal chandelier. A large, round glass table, always graced with a vase of fresh flowers, sat in the middle of the foyer.

Rio followed the drive around to the back so he and Gina could sneak in through the garage entrance and run upstairs to get dressed.

He ditched into the extra bedroom next to Gina's, his room when he was at her house.

Gina walked into her room and noticed her mother had laid out the outfit she wanted her to wear. It was a floral print dress with trumpet sleeves and a pleated skirt. The tags from Bloomingdale's were still on it and Gina thought the $250 price tag was nuts. She had bought a boho crochet maxi dress to wear. She decided to go with her mother's choice, only because she liked it better. It would go nicely with the pink platform shoes she bought. She sat at her vanity and reapplied her makeup, making it a little bit more edgy. She tried to straighten her hair using a blow-dryer and thick brush.

Rio gave a quick tap on the door and walked into the room. He was dressed in black jeans and a white silk shirt with half of the buttons undone.

Gina couldn't contain her amusement. "So, are you trying to impress a girl with that outfit? Or did your parents arrange for a record producer to show up?"

"There you go again, you are being more than a bitch . . . you're more of you know . . .that C word."

"Okay you look good, very good. I'm fucking with you."

They were on their way downstairs when they heard footsteps coming up fast.

It was Franny. "There you are. Everyone is waiting to see you. This is a party for both of you. Make your presence known and thank everyone for coming. You're being very rude right now."

Gina's disdain for her mother was evident. "Sure Mom. I'll make sure I am a perfect daughter, saying hello to all your friends. I bet there are eight people I know."

"Don't be ridiculous. The Shapiros are here, Angela and her parents, and the Rothsteins—Susan and her parents."

"Why would you invite the Shapiros? I broke up with David a month ago. Why would I want to see him? It's done." Gina had dated David Shapiro from the summer before her junior year until a month before graduation. David's father was the family dentist with an extremely profitable practice in Manhasset. David was cute with curly light-brown hair, green eyes, and a muscular build; he was a swimmer for Manhasset High School. Their relationship was a good one. He was kind and considerate, taking Gina skiing in Vermont over Christmas break, and to Fort Lauderdale for spring break. They even rented a cabin in the Poconos with a heart-shaped bathtub. Gina thought it was so romantic of him.

David was not the first guy she had sex with, but she was *his* first. Their lovemaking was simple and perfunctory, meaning they did a standard repertoire of early love sex.

Gina's first was a total mistake. She was at one of her favorite clubs, Lion's Den, and a roadie for the band chatted her up. She couldn't believe he found her interesting at all. Gina portrayed herself to be older. In her mind she was average. The guy's name was Dane. He had long hair, a biker type. He invited her to his van to smoke a joint. In a few minutes there was a lot of making out, deep-throat kissing, then shirts came off and, before she knew it, he undid her pants. She was way out of her league with this twenty-five-year-old, but she went with it. She never understood why songs used the line, "It feels like the first time," because the first time hurts like a bitch.

The relationship ended after a couple of months when she walked into a bar and saw Dane chatting up another girl. She hated men with their two-timing attitudes, assholes. She strode up to him, spit in his face, and walked out. Let him explain that to his floozy!"

Gina broke up with David when he got accepted to Princeton premed. She hoped she was going to the University of Miami, and they would drift off as boyfriend/girlfriend, so she ended it. She told him she cared deeply for him, but a long-distance romance was unfair. It was a high school love affair anyway.

Gina choked back some angry tears. "Thanks, Mom, for making this awkward party even more awkward. I swear you never hear me when I try to have a conversation with you. If you did you would have known this wasn't cool."

"Rio, would you help me with this mess over here? You're the only one she seems to listen to anymore."

"Gina, get your ass downstairs now before your father decides to look for you. I swear you're f'ing exasperating." Franny turned and floated gracefully down the stairs.

Rio tried to calm Gina. "Come on Gina, let's do this. You're still buzzed right? We smoked two joints, you should be good. Let's divide and conquer. I'll keep David off your scent, promise."

The house was buzzing with people and conversations, a Ricci party extraordinaire. Serving stations of seafood, prime rib, and pasta were spaced throughout the dining room, covered with black tablecloths and skirts of gold and silver. Massive candelabras carried the theme of silver and gold. The dessert table looked like a combination of an Italian bakery and a Godiva chocolate display at Bloomingdale's. There were three fully loaded bars—one in the house, one in the rose garden, and one by the pool.

Twenty tables decorated with black, white, silver, and gold were spread across the veranda. Balloon bouquets graced every table along with floral arrangements of white roses, hydrangeas, and lilies of the valley. There were gold and silver candles on the tables. The pool was decorated with floating flowers and candles.

Franny really outdid herself with this party; there wasn't one area of the backyard that wasn't decorated. It was a wonderland of flowers, food, and people.

Aunt Deidre looked beautiful in a colorful caftan that one of her designer friends made for her specifically for her son's graduation party.

Her husband, Uncle Tony, was laughing with some of the Ricci Construction guys, Vinny and Sal. They were in charge of making sure all projects were completed on time. It was Frankie's job to drive to each site, making sure all materials were delivered correctly. He reported directly to his father, so if there was a screwup, Mario was the next person to check out the job site.

As Gina and Rio reached the bottom of the stairs, there was a thunder of clapping and congratulations. Every person there had known them since they were christened, and now they were all grown up, going to college.

"I'm getting a drink, and my parents can't say a thing. Let's go cuz." Gina walked up to the bar and asked for two Rum and Cokes. "At least we can be high and drunk at the same time."

Mario caught his daughter's eye and walked over swiftly with an ear-to-ear smile. "There's my princess . . . what took you so fucking long? You two were smoking that shit again? Say hello to the Shapiros, the Rothsteins, and what the hell is Angela's last name again?"

Gina was pissy. "It's Smith, Dad. It's a hard name to remember."

"Listen, go around and thank everyone, and I mean *everyone*, for coming to your party. Have class Gina and do the right thing for Christ's sake."

Gina looked to her right to see Rio getting the same lecture from *his* father.

Mario was no nonsense and cursed so much it became an adjective, noun, and verb. He was a very handsome, muscular man; tall with light-brown hair and blue eyes. Like a better version of the actor Ray Liotta. He was totally in charge of his family, maybe. He expected his three children to adhere to the script he wanted them to live.

Francesca Angelone Ricci was the perfect Italian wife; she made sure the household ran to Mario's liking. She was attractive, with frosted-brown hair, brown eyes, and high cheek bones. Her makeup was always impeccable, even if she was walking the dog or going to the grocery store. She had a manicure every week. She wasn't super thin or fat; she was voluptuous. She bought her clothes at boutiques on Manhasset's Miracle Mile and Saks Fifth Avenue. Only the best for Franny. Gina believed her parents were truly in love, but love she thought should be more.

Frankie (Frances) was a clone of his father. Six feet, two inches, Frankie wore his dark hair slicked back like his father. A tough guy. A gym rat. He was always ready to take care of any ass kicking his father needed. He could have any girl he wanted, and he had many. He was learning the Ricci family business, especially the art of befriending the people he needed to work a deal with.

Ant was the youngest, born eight years after Gina. He had the sweetest nature of the three siblings. His looks were a combination of Mario and Franny. Ant had a cerebral nature. He was a deep thinker who loved puzzles and games like Risk. Ant loved Gina, she always protected him from Frankie and from her parents. Gina used to love taking care of Ant when he was a baby. Mario didn't understand how Ant had such a gentle nature. Whenever their father admonished Ant, Gina came to his rescue. The difference in Gina and Ant's age was noticeable. When Gina asked Franny about having another baby so long after she was born, Franny's answer was expected. "God makes those decisions and blessed us with another child. It's God and Mother Mary at work." Gina didn't get a straight answer. Ant was most likely a mistake, something went wrong with their birth control. Gina laughed because Ant was a great younger brother.

Gina was a petite girl, standing at five feet, two inches tall. She frequently dyed her chestnut-brown shoulder length hair, hating every iteration, returning quickly to her natural color. She was born with the Italian olive skin but did not inherit the beautiful blue eyes of her father and grandmother. She had big brown eyes with long lashes and perfect thick eyebrows. Although a striking looking girl, she would describe herself as "average," always thinking she could lose another five pounds.

Gina's closets were exploding with the latest fashions, thanks to her frequent shopping trips with Franny and visits to the mall with her friends. Gina never did without.

Gina was more interested in having fun than focusing on her grades. She maintained a B average without putting in much effort. She wasn't willing to put in the work. She realized way too late the colleges she wanted to get into expected excellence and even her father couldn't get her accepted.

Tony was much softer than his brother Mario. He could easily order some poor sap to have his ass fucked up, but he did it in a way that he had no choice. You made him do it.

Unlike Mario, who married the "perfect Italian wife," Uncle Tony married a statuesque African American model. Her artistic nature was apparent in the way she dressed. Fashion designers were thrilled when she visited their salons and chose to wear their clothes. Gina loved talking to Aunt Deidre, who always gave gentle advice without any judgments.

Rio came by his exotic looks naturally, with long, thick ringlets of dark-brown hair. He oozed a sweet sex appeal in his faded blue jeans, tank tops, and band T-shirts. He was the cool guy everyone wanted to know.

Deidre exposed Rio to the arts from an early age with any type of music lesson that interested him. He had been playing guitar and piano since he was ten years old. Deidre honored her son's passion and encouraged him to follow a path in music. Uncle Tony and Aunt Deidre used their connections to ensure Rio was accepted into NYU's music program. Not even an audition. It pays to be a Ricci sometimes.

Gina and Rio had started going to the rock clubs all over Long Island when they were sixteen years old. Rio already had a full beard and Gina carried herself with an unquestionable confidence. In 1972 the drinking age was eighteen. Gina and Rio were already eighteen when they graduated.

Gina wanted to go to college at the University of Miami, partly to get away from her family. She dreamed of a career in finance. Why not be a kick-ass *Fortune* 500 bitch babe? She could be iconic. Miami was known for partying, a great football team, and warm weather.

Unfortunately, that was not in her father's plan. No daughter of his was going to school 2,500 miles away to study finance. He hated accountants, "those scumbags," looking at his businesses. He had his own way of doing finances; no daughter of his would be in that asshole category.

Mario and Franny had arranged for Gina's acceptance to the Fashion Institute of Technology (FIT) for Interior Design in New York City. They envisioned a future where she would expand Franny's business and someday take over. Gina could be a very filthy-mouth bitch and told her parents how fucked up their plan was, to no avail. Mario reminded her he was in charge.

Gina only had two good friends at the party—Susan and Angela. She alienated most of her classmates with her language, looks, and obvious wealth. Gina's friends came from wealthy families. Most of the girls at St. Mary's were members of the church, an automatic acceptance. She didn't care. *Assholes.* Susan and Angela came over and proceeded to give her the rundown of good-looking guys at the party. For Gina, the problem was they were all Italian guys, sons of her father's friends.

"You know what . . . you two can have your pick of any guy here, except for my brother Frankie; he's a dick. I'm not into Italian guys. They want to own you, tell you what to do, and they cheat on you. I hate cheaters. There is nothing more disgusting than a cheater. I live in a household of Italian men. No thank you."

Gina kissed each girl and gave them a big hug. "But come on, have fun, I love you guys. You're my best friends. Now go ahead and find some men."

When Gina turned around, David was standing there. "Hey Gina, you look fantastic. I heard you weren't going to Miami. So, FIT down in the city?"

"Yeah, that's what my parents want."

"You know . . . we could . . . well . . . see each other on the weekends. Or you could come down to Princeton," he suggested hopefully.

Gina looked at David with a sympathetic smile. "David . . . I really think it's best that we keep things the way they are. You're premed; you'll have no time for me and I'm walking on another path. I'm happy to be your friend, always."

David nodded silently and turned away, hurt but putting on a good face. She didn't see him for the rest of the party. Gina did say hello and hugged his parents, though—Ben and Adele. Ben was, after all, her dentist.

Time flew by while she said hello to her parents' friends. Rio was doing the same to make sure the Ricci family held their esteemed position in the Manhasset social scene.

Out of nowhere, Mario's voice boomed over a microphone. "Hey, everyone, hope you're having a real good fucking time here eating and drinking all our alcohol. Ha ha ha. I'm messin' with you. Could everyone come around to the front of the house? Gina, come over here with me; let's walk together."

Rio was laughing as he whispered in Gina's ear, "This is your ride, you spoiled bitch."

"For my beautiful princess—she should have a beautiful ride." Mario enlisted Frankie to drive around the circular driveway in a red Mercedes-Benz 350SL convertible and stopped in front of Gina. The crowd applauded, and Gina felt embarrassed, but that didn't stop her from jumping behind the wheel and running her hand along the leather upholstery in admiration.

As the evening wound down, a huge cannoli cake was rolled out. "Congratulations on your Graduation, Gina and Rio" was written in icing. Uncle Tony gave a little speech on what special work both Gina and Rio would do in the coming years. The party started to break up around eleven thirty. Gina, Rio, Frankie, Susan, and Angela were still drinking. The caterers started to break down the party, which meant the bars were closed.

Frankie stood up and took a set of keys out of his pocket. Gina knew they were the keys to the pool house, which had a stocked bar and fridge full of beer. The five of them strolled down to the pool and Ant ran after them. "I want to come. Mom and Dad don't care if I'm down here."

Frankie began to protest, but Gina was more accommodating to her little brother. "Sure Ant, hang out with the cool kids. But no telling Mom and Dad what's going on. If you do, I'll kick your ass, okay?"

As they sauntered down to the pool, a gorgeous girl with porcelain skin and long black hair tagged after them. She had bright red lips and wore a skintight black mini dress. No one knew who she was. She introduced herself as Dawn West, the daughter of one of Aunt Deidre's socialite friends. "I'm not sure where my parents are, can I hang with you guys for a while?"

Gina thought Rio's eyes would fall out of his face. He was taking her all in, and even stumbled on his words, "Umm, yeah sure . . . umm it's cool. I bet your parents are with mine. They are either here or at my house, a few houses away. I can take you there or I'll call my parents. Frankie, there's a phone in the pool house, yeah?"

"Rio, have at it man; bring back some beers while you're at it too." Frankie was being uncharacteristically friendly.

With a phone call, Dawn's parents were found at Rio's house. "I'll take you over at my house, my car is . . . my car is down the driveway a bit. I hope you don't mind walking." Rio sneered at Gina. "I need to leave anyway; I'm meeting with some friends tomorrow."

Gina jumped up and grabbed Rio by the hair. "Are you having some sort of band thing going on? If so, I want to come. Please. I want to check out this secret you have been keeping from me."

Rio caved. "Yeah, okay Gina, if you drive me to my car in that new Mercedes of yours."

Gina sighed heavily. "Fine. But if I fuck it up because I drank too much, it's on you."

Dawn had to sit on Rio's lap as Gina drove down to his car. She wondered if he was getting excited by Dawn sitting on his lap. Probably. "What time tomorrow?" Gina asked Rio.

"Everyone is coming to my house at one, so you can sleep late, princess." Rio's sarcasm was sickening.

Gina pulled her Mercedes up to the BMW and couldn't resist. "Hey, get home safely you two." Rio drove off, giving Gina the finger. She laughed so hard, maybe she *was* a little drunk.

When Gina got back to the pool house, Susan and Angela were getting ready to leave. "Do you need a ride?" Susan assured Gina that she was fine to drive home.

Ant fell asleep on a chaise lounge and Frankie picked him up. The party was over.

Frankie turned to Gina, "That Dawn was a knockout. I hope Rio gets a piece of that."

"You know Frankie, you are disgusting; you always have sex on your mind." But Gina was thinking the same thing. She would find out tomorrow.

Mario was still up having a scotch in the informal living room when the kids entered through the French doors. "Oh, there's my children. Have a good time by the pool? Enjoy the pool house bar? Frankie, next time you raid the bar, I'll make you replace everything you take, capisce? Gina, thank you for being somewhat social to the guests tonight. I haven't heard a thank you yet for your gift."

Neither Frankie nor Gina had the energy to give their father shit. A simple "thank you" and "it won't happen again" was the only thing they could muster up. Frankie dropped Ant onto his bed, took his shoes off, then went to his own room and shut the door.

Gina dragged herself up to her room, stripped off her clothes, and threw on an oversized Led Zeppelin 1972 concert T-shirt. Exhausted, she fell asleep immediately. Her last thoughts were about tomorrow and Rio's band.

The next morning, the smell of bacon, hash browns, and Serena's homemade biscuits drifted up through the house. The smell was like an alarm clock going off. Gina was a little hungover but would never let anyone know how shitty she felt. Serena set the table for five, as she usually did. She never knew if Mario and Franny would join the three Ricci children for breakfast. Franny came down perfectly made up—beautiful as always. The last one down was Mario, already dressed in his golf clothes.

"When is your tee time, honey?" Franny asked.

"In about thirty minutes. I should make it in time. Gina, your mother is going to talk to you about your summer plans, and I want you to pay attention. It's not a request. You don't have a choice, okay?" With that her father left the house.

"Mom, what the hell is he talking about? I have no choice about what exactly? This sounds like a blow job."

"Gina! Watch your language, do we need your filthy mouth first thing in the morning? What your father is talking about—I want you to work in the office to help me this summer. Kind of get you acquainted with some interior design tips and terminology before you head to FIT." Franny was firm and was hoping Gina would see this as an opportunity.

"When you say the office, do you mean here at home or the Ricci building on Northern?" Ricci Construction and Franny's business, Elite Interior Design, were in an otherwise empty recently remodeled office building on Northern Boulevard in the heart of the Miracle Mile in Manhasset. Mario would walk clients over to Franny to have her touch put on any renovation, making money on both sides of the work. Aunt Deidre worked at Elite too. She had a flair for the modern aesthetic. It was a win/win.

"Gina, of course the Northern Boulevard office. Why would I want you to work here? You need to experience a real workplace. Situations can come up and you need to know how to handle those issues. Don't give me any crap. What else do you have planned for this summer? Your father and I gave you a car so you can drive to work. I need four hours a day from you. It will save me from hiring a part-time worker."

Gina was pissed off. Again, her parents were planning her life. "So let me get this straight, four hours a day, and I don't get paid either?"

"Gina, seriously you have a wonderful, generous allowance along with a credit card that you use profusely. Four hours a day is not the end of the world. Jesus, be a little respectful here."

"Can I pick the four hours that I work at least?" she pleaded with her mother.

"We'll figure it out. You have until after the Fourth of July weekend.

Then I expect you for four hours a day. We will also go shopping so you have the proper office wardrobe. That should make you happy, shopping for new clothes. I'm off to a charity breakfast meeting, not sure when I'll be back. Serena is in charge." Franny threw kisses in the air and left.

Serena waited for Franny to leave and spoke to Gina in her heavy Italian accent. "You . . . my dear Gina. You don't realize how much you have. And you behave badly. Spoiled. Didn't I teach you to appreciate your lives?"

Gina groaned. "I know. You're right Serena, but I don't like my life planned out by them. I have my own dreams, but it doesn't matter, I will find a way to do what I want."

"Well, Gina, welcome to my world," came a male voice.

Gina was so angry; she had completely forgotten Frankie was in the room. "You don't realize how good you will have it working for Mom and Dad." He was half mocking her, but he really did love the amount of control he had working for them.

Gina grabbed a biscuit and ran upstairs. She had plenty of time to get showered, do her hair and makeup, and ride over to Rio's. She wondered what happened with Dawn West, and exactly who the other guys in his band were. Little did she know how this meeting with Rio's band was about to change her life.

Gina dressed in a pair of hip hugger blue jeans and a white lace tank top. She thought they showed off her figure well. She straightened her hair with the blow-dryer and hairbrush, which took forever. She looked at a recent *Cosmopolitan* magazine for makeup tips. *Cosmo* was the rage with its racy sex advice and great tutorials on how to do your own makeover. Gina followed the instructions to make her eyes look bigger and bolder and how to make her lips full and desirable. She didn't know why she was making a big deal of going to her cousin's house.

Gina grabbed her keys, ran downstairs, said goodbye to Serena, and told her she would be at her aunt and uncle's. She left her house at twelve fifteen so she could get there early; she liked hanging out with Aunt Deidre.

She was easy to talk to and exceptionally intuitive. It seemed like she knew what Gina was thinking before she blurted it out.

She got in her brand-new Benz and was still shocked she got this prime car. The weather was in the high eighties, so she decided to put the top down. She took a deep breath and realized this was the first time she was going to drive her car. Not just down the driveway like last night.

Five minutes later, she pulled into the long driveway of the ultra-modern house. As she parked, she noticed a car she didn't recognize. Must be these new friends of Rio's, the band. But the car seemed too nice for some guys trying to put a band together.

She knocked on the door and let herself in. Deidre and Tony were seated in the living room with two other people. Her Aunt stood up and welcomed her. "Gina, I would love to introduce you to my friends Inez and Paul West. They own a gallery in Manhattan. I adore it. I think you met their daughter Dawn last night."

So, the Wests were overnight guests. *Did Rio get with Dawn last night?* It would have been a perfect scenario for him to do so.

"If you're looking for your cousin, he's already downstairs waiting for some friends to come over for their first band practice. I'm so excited for him." Aunt Deidre was bursting with pride. "Did you eat breakfast or maybe lunch?"

"Aunt Deidre, I'm good. You know Serena. She had breakfast ready early but thank you. It's nice to meet you, Mr. and Mrs. West. I hope you enjoyed the party last night and thank you for sharing my graduation with us." Gina could be polite when necessary.

"We loved the party. Thank you so much Gina. It was nice to finally meet your parents."

Going downstairs to Rio's lair she saw her cousin setting up his guitar and amps. Dawn was sitting on a beanbag chair, wearing pink bell-bottoms with a wild floral top. Bitch looked great by doing nothing. Gina hated those girls. St. Mary's was filled with them.

"Hey, you made it . . . early even. I think maybe you're more excited than me." Rio was weird.

"Well, you know I had to be here for whatever this secret band thing is. Hi Dawn, did you have a nice evening last night?" Gina didn't really care. She was hoping Dawn would give a "tell" whether she slept with her cousin.

Dawn gave nothing away. "I had a very nice time, thank you."

Rio excused himself and went into his bedroom to get something, and Gina followed him. "So . . . I was wondering . . . Did you have a nice time with Dawn last night? Was it special?"

"Well, bitch face, it so happens that Dawn is only fifteen going on sixteen in August. So yeah, I wouldn't touch that, ever. Shame on you for thinking the worst, but I should have expected that from you."

"Okay, I apologize. How would I know that she was so young? I mean she definitely looks much older. Is she hanging out with us or is she leaving soon? It doesn't matter. I wanted to know if I had to entertain her while you practiced." Gina was trying to make up for her faux pas. They were still in his bedroom when he heard a noise; it sounded like "the band" was making its way into the house.

Before Rio could answer, four guys came through the sliding glass doors of Rio's sanctuary. Gina scoped them out to see if she knew any of them. She didn't and wondered where her cousin had met them. Rio obviously played guitar, but what did these guys play?

It didn't take long before the mystery became clear. Rich played drums. Rio had a complete drum kit in his music room. Jeff Wainright played bass and sang lead vocals. Eric played rhythm guitar, and Craig played keyboards. *Strange*, Gina thought Rio was a highly accomplished keyboard player in his own right. She then realized that Rio couldn't play both, he loved the guitar. So, he chose to add a keyboardist.

They were all dressed in shitty looking jeans and band T-shirts. Jeff wore a Led Zeppelin North American Tour T-shirt. Eric wore a Jeff Beck

T-shirt. Rich wore a Sticky Fingers Rolling Stones shirt. Craig wore a Yes Fragile T-shirt.

They settled into the music room and Rio introduced them to Dawn—behind her back he used the wave off sign so they knew she was off limits—too young. Then he introduced Gina as his cousin.

Everybody settled in and Rio gave each band member a set list of seven songs he wanted to play. They would go through them all at once, like they were onstage. Gina peeked at the set list and was surprised that The Who made it on the list.

"Good Times Bad Times" – Led Zeppelin
"All Right Now" – Free
"American Woman" – The Guess Who
"All the Young Dudes" – Mott the Hoople
"Baba O'Riley" – The Who
"Stay With Me" – Rod Stewart and Faces
"Angie" – Rolling Stones

It was the first time they had all played together. Rich counted the band in on the sticks . . . "One, two, three, four." The bass and guitar started the beginning of "Good Times Bad Times." Gina was impressed by her cousin's guitar work and the drums sounded great, keeping the rhythm going. Why was Gina so enthralled by the band? She wondered, *maybe I could sing? I have a good voice.*

CHANGING COURSE

AFTER THE FOURTH OF JULY BREAK, Gina had to report to her mother's office. Her job was to pick up samples from vendors. After Franny's approval, Gina would drop them off at the clients' home or office. There was a lot of driving, but if this is what Franny wanted her to do, it was a piece of cake. Every now and then Franny would tell Gina the aesthetic the client wanted and test her on the best options she would propose. After work each day, Gina would race to Rio's for band practice.

She was already envisioning herself as the singer. Jeff was a great bass player, but not strong as a vocalist. She thought the more she showed up, the better her chances were of injecting herself into the band.

One night, during the fourth week of practice, Jeff was struggling with the vocals and Gina asked if she could sing one or two of the songs. Rio looked at her like she was nuts, but when she started singing, Rio was surprised.

"Gina, who knew that a bitch like you could sing?"

She coolly replied, "Rio, I can do many things well."

He rolled his eyes.

All through July and part of August, Gina spent most of her time at Rio's practicing. She was doing something she liked and thought she might be able to do it well. Jeff was secretly relieved to give up vocals because he knew he wasn't that great at it.

Gina felt torn. She had to keep up the pretense that she loved working with her mother, and in a few weeks, she had to go to new student orientation at FIT. Rio was lucky. He was looking forward to attending NYU. Who wouldn't, in the heart of Greenwich Village?

In mid-August, Franny gave Gina a Long Island Railroad monthly commuter ticket, which she would use every day back and forth from the city. Gina looked at Rio. "I know you're excited about going to school but I'm sure I'll hate it. All those wannabe models, fashion merchandising girls, it's like I'm back at St. Mary's."

Rio shook his head. "Gina, you always find the worst situation for yourself. Honestly, you may like it."

"No Rio, I decided. I'm going through the motions, but what I really want is to sing with your band."

"Whoa, Gina. I haven't decided if I want you to sing with us."

Gina looked through him. "Rio, Jeff is great at playing bass, but his vocals suck, and you know it. How cool would it be for you to have a female lead? I don't want to sing chick songs. I want to sing what guys sing. Come on, that would be cool, and you know it. I can do this and do it well."

Rio looked at her. "Well, we both have to go to school and worry about the band later."

Gina wasn't happy with that answer, but she would take it for now. The two cousins commuted together every day. On Thursdays and Fridays Rio had band practice, and Gina was at every one.

Aunt Deidre came to listen one night and pulled Gina aside. "If you want to be a professional singer, I have a friend who can train you. He usually works with Broadway singers, but I'll call. He'll take you; I promise."

During the week, Gina had to endure classes on color theory and math. She never thought she would need math for interior design but quickly found out she had to calculate the square footage of the interiors. Gina was hating it already and she was only two months in.

Rio, although attending one of the finest schools in the US, was equally dissatisfied. He didn't realize he would be studying History of Music and taking freshman requirements. He thought he would be learning how to write music.

Aunt Deidre came through with an appointment for Gina to meet the voice coach, Simon Beauvaux. She was running late and as she raced through the door, the only person she saw was a drag queen. Gina asked politely, "I'm looking for Simon?"

He clucked his tongue, "Young lady, you are late. If you weren't Deidre's niece, I would throw you out. I'm Simon. I need to go to my other job soon, but I have a few minutes to work with you." Simon quickly had her do drills and scales to find her range.

Gina loved working with Simon every Thursday afternoon—at three sharp. Simon was flamboyant and proud of it. Gina learned so much from him and loved his stories about being a drag queen. He promised he would get her ready to sing. Before Thanksgiving break, Gina and Rio started cutting classes and ended up back in Manhasset, practicing. Gina was studying every inflection of the songs they were singing.

Thanksgiving was a big Ricci family affair. Gina got home and started racing up the stairs when Franny stopped her, "Gina, why am I seeing that you haven't attended classes in the last three weeks? What have you been doing?"

Gina had to come up with something quick, so she told her mother the truth. "Well if you must know, I have been singing with Rio's band. I like it. I think I'm good at it. You and Dad chose FIT for me; I didn't get to decide on anything, so now I am."

"Gina! You can't do that for a *living*! You need to go back to school." Franny was shocked.

Gina started up the stairs. "Mom, I'm not having this discussion with you now."

Franny followed Gina up the stairs. "Gina, this is not what your father and I planned for you. You need to go back to FIT. I hear Rio hasn't been attending school either. You think you are going to become big music stars?"

Gina retorted, "Yes, I do. We are good. Why is it that Aunt Deidre is so supportive, and you can't understand that I'm good at doing this? This is what happens Mom when you try to plan out your daughter's life. Guess what? I am rebelling. I'm not going back to that school with stuck-up chicks. Sorry not doing it."

Franny announced, "We will have a discussion with your father, then we will see how this shakes out Gina."

Mario came home and sat down with both Franny and Gina. Franny had tried to shield Mario from this news, but now it was something that had to be discussed. Gina explained to her father that this was truly something she wanted to pursue, and she wouldn't be forced into something she didn't want to do.

Mario listened to Gina. "Princess, I don't agree with this at all, but I will give you eighteen months to make it work. If you don't, you go back to school."

Gina did not like a time limit. The club scene was hard to break into. She was determined to use the time to show her father that she was going to be successful. If she needed to, she would work her father to extend her time frame.

Rio had no issues with his parents understanding his passion for music. Aunt Deidre wanted him to see it all the way through. Uncle Tony gave in to what his wife saw for their son's success. Rio was lucky.

One night sitting by the pool at Rio's house, both Gina and Rio decided they did not want to have the name of Ricci attached to a budding music career. They would never know if their talent or name got them the exposure they craved. Gina looked at where they were sitting. "Hey, how about Poole, with an "e" at the end. So, while high, they decided to call themselves Poole.

ENTITLED

IT WAS FRIDAY AFTER BAND PRACTICE when Gina remembered she needed to talk to Rio about going to the football game. Gina and Rio made it a habit of taking tickets for any game they wanted—baseball, hockey, basketball and football—from the Ricci season ticket folder. They planned to go to the football game on Sunday. "We need to go to Northern and pick up the tickets."

Gina grinned. "Absofuckinglutely. The best game of the year. Let's go now. Hopefully, the fathers won't be there."

The Riccis had season tickets for both football teams, baseball, hockey, and basketball. No one ever used them, so Rio and Gina took the best games. Gina looked in the folder where they were usually kept. "Rio the tickets are gone, what the—"

"Hey Gina, looking for these?" Frankie walked into the room holding four tickets in his hands. "You know these tickets are for us to give to clients, not for Gina Ricci's personal use."

Gina tried to grab the tickets. "Screw you, Frankie. I have had those seats for the last two years."

Frankie couldn't resist. "Well spoiled bitch, you don't have them this year."

Mario walked in. "What the hell is going on?"

Frankie loved it. "Your spoiled brat daughter wants the tickets to Sunday's game, but I promised them to the Phelps. We are doing their building."

"Your brother is correct; those tickets are for clients, not you two."

"I'm not leaving until Rio and I get tickets to that game," Gina responded petulantly.

Mario caved immediately and started making phone calls. Within minutes he scored two tickets to the game.

Frankie was angry. "She gets whatever she wants. You're a spoiled bitch."

Mario stopped the drama. "Enough! Everyone is happy. Stop."

Gina bragged to Rio. "Who cares how we got them? We got 'em."

BAND BEGINS

GINA AND RIO DECIDED to audition for the Tri-State band circuit. If you wanted to play the clubs, especially in Long Island, you needed to go through Sammy and Nadine Gold, who booked most of the acts in the clubs. Sammy was the negotiator, Nadine followed with notebooks on the bands. They knew the Golds would only get them booked into low-rate clubs, but it would be a start. They also knew they took a percentage off the top. For Rio and Gina, it wasn't an issue; they had family money, but how dedicated were the other band members? They would find out.

After a brief discussion with the rest of the band, everyone agreed—they were in. This informal group of friends playing in Rio's basement was a band now and needed a name. After throwing ideas around for an hour, they decided on Vision Skye, Gina's idea. Next, they would need professional pictures taken.

Rio was hoping to get Sammy Gold to his rehearsal studio. Sammy was a tough businessman. If Vision Skye could get an audition, Rio thought Sammy would sign them. It took a few phone calls to get the receptionist to leave a message for Sammy, but when the Golds recognized the address of the rehearsal space was in a wealthy suburb, they were intrigued and agreed to come the following week.

Rio's professional setup, with the best instruments and expensive sound system, impressed the Golds. Sammy asked them to play a set for him. He was even more intrigued when he saw the lead singer was a girl.

After three songs Sammy told them to stop. Not only could they play decently, but they also had a schtick—Gina was a female lead singer. That would appeal to club owners. Both men and women would be interested in watching a female lead. There was money to be made with them.

"I'll start you in some local bars with a Thursday, Friday, or Saturday spot. I need to get good feedback before I can book you in the smaller clubs in Long Island."

For three months Vision Skye played the bars two nights a week and hated it because people were eating and talking during their performances. Sammy must have gotten the feedback he was looking for because he started getting them booked in the smaller Long Island clubs. They were starting to get a following. Gina attracted a lot of male followers and females who wanted to be like her. Sammy told Gina point blank, "You need to sell your sex appeal. Make the audience want you." He already knew Rio was a phenomenal guitar player and had his own sex appeal. He was a rock star in the making.

They played the circuit for a year, dragging their equipment around in a van that Uncle Tony provided. Vision Skye wanted to play in the bigger clubs. They saw themselves as the next band to ascend the club scene and they were getting close. They needed a break.

They got a break when a band scheduled to play at one of the larger clubs backed out at the last minute. Sammy booked Vision Skye and told them, "You make a good showing, and I'll book you better clubs."

It was worth the 15 percent the Golds took off the top for the chance to move up the club scene. Vision Skye soon became one of Long Island's favorite bands.

UNEXPECTED MEETING

IT WAS A YEAR AND HALF since Vision Skye started playing the Tri-State rock club scene. The eighteen-month deadline her father imposed proved to be to Gina's advantage. They were getting a following, mostly chicks wanting to meet the seductive Rio. Gina thought it was funny to see all those groupies wanting to say hello and give their phone numbers to her cousin.

Gina's popularity came from singing all the popular hits, not the "girl songs." She made friends with other bands. Her favorite was The Thirst, getting close to a few band members and some of the roadies. Stevie, The Thirst keyboardist wore his brown hair short and sported Elvis Costello glasses. They played a progressive type of music and pulled a large group of guys who followed them around and girls trying to date them. Gina would go see the band when she wasn't performing.

Gina liked hanging out on the side of the stage watching the maestro of keyboards do his show. She kept his Rum and Cokes within reach for him to chug between songs. When the set was over, they walked out to Gina's Benz and smoked a couple of joints. They would talk about life, not just music. Stevie had a pleasing soft voice and always had a humorous way of asking a question, which made Gina feel at ease. Stevie often asked, "Gina my love, you have everything a man would want; why have you not found someone? I mean someone who excites you. Because we know that's what we all need, darling." Stevie felt he needed to tell her, "Sweet Gina, one of my bandmates is super interested in you. I don't know if it's a fit. Wanted you to know that he has his eye on you, my dear. What will you do with that information, Gina?"

Gina sighed. "Stevie, I know who you are talking about. We've had brief discussions. I can tell if someone is interested. But I know he has a girlfriend. Look, I'm number one. I'm never a number two or someone's sidepiece. So . . . I guess I'm not interested."

Stevie replied with his humor, "Yes Gina, you are number one, nobody's number two. I respect that my sweet female lead singer."

Gina had both male and female hangers-on by this point and detested them; she would rather be alone than hang out with those losers. Tuesday nights in the summer, Gina would make the long thirty-to-forty-minute drive to Glen Island Casino in New Rochelle. The main room featured two stages and downstairs there was a small room for up-and-coming bands. She hoped that the Golds would soon book Vision Skye into that room.

Rio decided he would take the ride with her one particularly hot July night. Gina was positively clear in what she was about to say to Rio. "Listen, you and I are going together and we're leaving together. You realize some random fan will recognize you and try to take you home. Don't do that to me; I wouldn't do that to you."

Rio laughed at her comment. "Gina, I think you hate men. There's not been one guy that you have given a micro-spec of a chance. What exactly are you waiting for?"

"I don't know. I haven't met him yet. He must be someone different, someone who gets me hot. How's that? You like that answer? I haven't met that person. It's hard to find a man doing what we do and not think they are interested in something else. Do you get it? Probably not, you're a guy, its fine for you to have a woman in every bar we play. It's not that way for me. I'm picky. I want something more. I'll know when it happens."

"I want you to know Gina, you are a stunning, sexy woman and men want to bed your ass down. I get it . . . you are looking for someone more permanent, where us disgusting guys will take a one-night stand in a minute."

"What makes you think I haven't had random one-night stands? You think I'm dead? I'm not interested in having bad sex. One-night stands are like, shake the tree a little and then leave me alone. It's not even good sex, so why bother. I want that passionate kind of love. So, that's that. Look, let's have a good time, see Stevie do his thing, and work the room a little. I'm still hoping that we can book a place like Glen Island. If not there, since the summer is only a month away from being over, then The Sunset in Garden City. It's a big club with two stages. We need to try to arrange a meeting with the agency. I want to be a headliner, not a fill-in band when the bigger bands book up the better clubs. We're playing clubs that aren't dives but not what we deserve—at least not now. Our following grows every weekend; we deserve more."

Gina drove through the paid parking lot at Glen Island and straight to where the bands and trucks parked. She motioned to the attendant by the cones to move them aside as she said, "Hey, we're friends of the band, can we park here?" He must have recognized her and Rio because he let them roll past with a wave. Gina pulled into two spots and straddled them so her Benz wouldn't get dinged by some asshole.

Rio and Gina walked past the line of people waiting to get in and said to the bouncer, "Poole. We're on the guest list." Rio was wearing leather pants, a graphic T-shirt, black boots, and sunglasses. Gina was wearing a long white crochet dress that clung to her body, clearly showing her lace panties. With that, she paired beige Candie's platform shoes. Her hair had light-blonde highlights, her face was made to look seductive, and her skin was bronzed by the sun. That was another advantage of living on the Ricci estate—hanging out by the pool.

The pair oozed rock and roll.

Gina owned the room. Every man watched her walk to where The Thirst had their stage set.

She saw Josh, one of the roadies. They were friends now, but there had been a brief moment when they tried to be something more. He turned out to be more like a big brother, better than her own prick brother Frankie. Josh came over and gave her a kiss on the cheek.

Gina was glad to see him. "Hey pal, how's it going? Working hard tonight for the headline band?"

"You are dressed to kill, Gina. You look amazing . . . well dare I say it, exceptionally sexy tonight." Josh always had something nice to say.

Two big arms enveloped her from behind. It was Stevie. He was a master showman and her best friend on the circuit, and The Thirst was always the headline act. The Tri-State area club scene was a grind—dirty floors, dirty bathrooms, and a lot of drunk people.

Stevie was overwhelmed by Gina's appearance this evening. "Well, look at you, let me see you . . . you look fabulous. Any reason?"

"If I was dressing for someone or something special you would be the first to know." Gina gave a small laugh at the compliment. She never handled them well, always feeling no more than just average.

Rio waved at Matt Payne, the guitarist for The Thirst. He was also a great musician. Rio and Matt had formed a friendship over Rio's extensive collection of vintage guitars and new guitar techniques that they played around with in Rio's studio. Gina liked him because he was a talented musician and a good guy.

"Hello Matt, how you doing? Is that girlfriend of yours here tonight?" Gina always made it a point of being friendly with the girlfriends. This way there was never a misunderstanding that she was interested in their man. She was simply a friend.

"No, sorry Gina. She isn't here tonight. But the question is, who are *you* meeting tonight?" Matt couldn't help but check her out.

"Yeah, sorry guys, nothing special here tonight. Who's going on first?

Do we know the band?" Gina laughed at the absurdity that she would meet anybody at Glen Island that she didn't know already. But she was more interested in who was playing second stage. Something that she hoped Vision Skye would ascend to.

"It's a band from Canada of all places! Wonder why they came here and not the LA music scene. Well, we are all looking for the same thing, right? A record deal." Stevie was accurate in that assessment. That's what they all were looking for.

"So, hey, I'm thirsty, going to get a drink, you coming Gina?" Gina sensed Rio wanted to talk.

Rio was pissed at the idea that a band he didn't know was playing in their coveted spot. But Vision Skye had not gotten to that level yet. "Can you believe the agency signed a band from Canada and they are playing here? That's like band jumping. What kind of following can they have?"

Rio and Gina got their drinks. Gina instructed Rio, "So, listen, if we see Sammy and Nadine Gold, we need to speak to them. Let's divide and conquer. That's the mission for tonight. If the Golds are here, they might not want to conduct business. But I dressed this way for a reason. To show them we are top-tier talent. I mean, you are, Rio. I'm the average one. A record guy would want to replace me anyway. Although I do have a superb rock voice.

"Gina, have you looked around? Every guy here hasn't stopped checking you out. You're hot. You have what it takes. We need more exposure. Stop it. You're a beautiful woman. Everyone gets it but you. Now stop. I saw some of our Long Island fans here tonight. You good?" Rio was afraid to leave her but after all Gina was a woman and one who had a big mouth, she'll be fine.

The lights were starting to slowly dim, and the house music stopped. That meant the first band was about to take the stage. Gina positioned herself with not one, but two Rum and Cokes at a table by the windows at the back of the room. Some guy came up to her before she even sat down and she wasted no time in informing him, "Leave me alone. Fuck off. Thank you very much."

The emcee introduced the band as Stanley Park. The drummer started a melodic rhythm. The lead singer and guitarist came onstage next. The singer had wavy, dirty-blond hair to his shoulders and facial hair like he hadn't shaved. He was tall with long arms and legs, but not skinny, with the softest, bluest eyes, not the cool steel-blue eyes of her father. He was wearing a shirt from some bar in Canada, sneakers, and impossibly tight jeans. She was mesmerized by him; he was a perfect specimen of a man. She couldn't take her eyes off this man. She stared, feeling something she never had before. She was sexually stimulated by watching him. Like a vibrator made her feel, but more intense. They played three songs and, afterward, introduced themselves individually. His voice was soft but had that hard rock edge. His name was Trevor McNaughton.

Gina felt naked, like everyone in the club could see she was entranced by this guy. She didn't want to stand up for fear everyone could see her raw erotic being, her lust for him. She was totally sexually overcharged.

Gina finally noticed Rio had taken a seat at the table. "Gina, I have never seen you like this . . . you are so attracted to this guy. I bet you couldn't even name the first three songs they performed. They have original music, which puts them on a fast track for a record deal. But seriously, Gina—"

"Stop it Rio. I feel like you're looking right through me . . . that you can feel everything I'm feeling now. I don't like it. You can see how I'm lusting for him. I can't trust myself. This feeling of being so stimulated by the look of this man."

Stanley Park finished the last song of their first set and walked off the stage. Gina was antsy. "Let's go get another drink. I have to use the ladies room too."

Rio went to get the drinks while Gina headed for the ladies room. As she was opening the door to leave, she collided with Trevor McNaughton. His eyes were more beautiful up close. Everything was better up close.

"I'm sorry. I almost knocked you over." His voice was even softer and sweeter. He moved her out of the way of the door and touched the small of her back. Another vibrator moment. His touch set her skin on fire. Trevor was headed in the same direction and began to pass their table as Rio showed up with their drinks. Trevor stopped and said, "I know you, you're Rio Poole . . . word is you have an unbelievable vintage ax collection and a studio."

Trevor turned to Gina, who was a step behind him. "You must be Gina Poole; wait, are you two a couple?"

Gina was tongue-tied, staring at someone she had been fantasizing about a moment before. She finally stammered, "Oh God no. We're cousins."

Rio stepped in. "Yeah, I'm really happy to share and show fellow players what I've got. Anytime. Where do you live?"

"I've been here seven months and I'm still trying to figure out where things are. The band has rented a house in Franklin Square. Is that far from you?" He was talking to Rio but staring at Gina. She returned the stare.

"No man, its only fifteen minutes, twenty if you catch the lights. You're super close. Hey, I see some people I know; I'll be back in . . . a few?" Rio wanted to remove himself from whatever was about to happen between Gina and Trevor.

Trevor waited for Rio to walk out of earshot. "I could see you, through all the smoke and people walking around, I could see you." Trevor's eyes looking into Gina's eyes. They were mesmerized by each other. Gina felt that Trevor could certainly see how she was lusting for him, and Trevor could not look away from Gina and how inviting she was.

"I'm flattered that you noticed me. I don't know what to say to you. I was watching you also." *Why is this man was so intoxicating?* "So, Canada . . . I have to ask, is there a wife or a girlfriend back there?"

"I am most definitely unattached. I am the guy who ruins relationships; I drink too much, do too much cocaine, have a few DUIs, and other legal issues in the past. I am the guy who sabotages any relationship I have." Trevor was honest for sure.

Gina Poole, the woman who always knew what to say at every moment, was speechless. She didn't care that he drank too much or even the coke. It's not like she hadn't had her moments with both. There was an awkward pause in their conversation.

Trevor changed the subject back to her. "How could I not see you? That dress is so sexy, and you in it . . . are too much for a man to look away. Can you hang out until our second set ends?" The club had two bands playing. Each band played two sets, and in between, the house music came on for the next band to take the stage. Stanley Park did their first set and had one more to play.

Gina finally felt a little more herself. "Sure. I can . . . I'd be happy to." She realized she was missing Stevie and The Thirst play; she wasn't in her usual spot on the side of the stage. She felt bad, but Stevie would understand. She knew their usual set lists, they did mix things up, but it wouldn't be anything she hadn't heard before.

Trevor took her hands in his and made her promise she wouldn't leave. How could she leave now? "Of course not. You don't go back on for what, fifteen or twenty minutes? I can give you a ride later if you like. Did you drive?" The lights came on in the large room, which meant The Thirst was done and the club music came on. Stanley Park would be playing their second and last set of the night.

"Is there anything you don't know, Gina Poole? I would love a ride. The band has only one car that we all drive. That sounds extremely intriguing. Let me get out of this shirt, I'm sweaty, sorry." Trevor looked apologetic.

"No go, I'll find my table in the back." Gina was tingling with the idea of what could be, and how their meeting was going to go. *Was he playing a game? No, he made a point to say he saw me.*

Rio walked up with a girl on each arm.

Gina pulled him away from the girls. "What are you doing? You know those girls are underage right? I need to talk to you. Did you see the Golds?

I can't believe they didn't show. Remember when I said we come together, we leave together? I may not be able to do that."

"Good for you. A little piece for Gina. Don't worry; those two girls are eighteen. They don't live far. I'll have them drop me off."

"Are you nuts? Then they'll know where you live. Do you want them to come around to your house? And don't use that term with me, I'm not 'getting a piece.' I am going to give him a ride, don't know where that's going to go. But I finally see a man I have some sort of connection with. Don't deflate my confidence. I'm feeling uncharacteristically nervous and unsure of myself."

"I'm sorry. I want you to have what you want; you obviously feel some connection with this guy Trevor. I've never once in my life seen you so raw. It's okay for you to allow yourself to be a little vulnerable. Let your emotions take you. As far as my ride, I will let you in on my secret. I have a trick. I leave a car at the Ricci building and drive home from there. No one knows. I must see which girl wins or maybe I'll get both. You sure you're good? Because I'm leaving now. We will deal with the Gold situation tomorrow. Love you."

"Hey, you know you're a piece of work. A ménage a trois, really? I can't . . . You do whatever, but please don't give me a recap." Gina was laughing, but also thought, *It's so easy for guys.*

Gina sat in the back and listened to Stanley Park. They did a couple of covers, and their original music had an edgy personal feel to it. Was Trevor bearing his soul? If so, there was a lot of heartache and damage there.

Stanley Park finished their set and left the stage. Gina sat waiting. *Is Trevor coming back?* Was this another musician playing nice to blow her off? No, it can't be—they had an instant connection. She didn't imagine that. She was also dying for a cigarette.

She knew that The Thirst would be getting ready to perform their last set of the evening. She went over and saw Stevie and Matt. "Hey guys, not sure if I'm staying for your last set so I wanted to say goodbye." She kissed them both on the cheek and gave them each a big hug. "Love you guys." Gina adored their friendship. And why not? They were the marquee band on the circuit. You keep friends like that.

She walked out to the balcony, which ran across the large room and lit up one of her Sobranie Cocktail cigarettes. She stood on the balcony contemplating what her next move would be. She felt a gentle touch on her shoulder. It was him—Trevor. A quiver ran up her back.

"I was looking for you. I thought you left me here. What's that you got there? Is that a cigarette?"

Gina had a schoolgirl-like smile. "Yes, I like them. They're different, Russian. And strong. Why, do you want one?"

"Sure, I'll try one of Gina Poole's pastel-colored cigarettes. You definitely like to be different and noticeable; I'm not saying that in a bad way, so you know." Trevor took the cigarette and started smoking. "I'm waiting for Ian, my drummer, to get paid and we can leave. I need to get my guitars off the stage. I have three vintage guitars and don't want anyone walking off with them. It shouldn't be more than twenty or thirty minutes. Are you cool with that?"

Real Gina came out. "I can wait, as long as I get the reward."

A smile rose on Trevor's face and his soft blue eyes were searing into Gina's soul.

Trevor walked away. She finished her cigarette and lit up another one, waiting, the anticipation of what might be . . . she tried to get her libido to calm down, but another cigarette wasn't going to help that.

A cool breeze came through from the Long Island Sound. Across the Sound was her parents' home. She wondered where her house was, but she knew she was too far north to see the massive Ricci estate. She panicked a bit. *If I take him to my place, how do I explain my house, my life?* A life she was hoping to put behind her. She was now hit with the music bug, and she would see it through to wherever it led her. The Thirst was playing a Zeppelin tune; she loved it when they played "Kashmir."

She went back inside and sat down. Some drunk asshole tried to join her. Did she really have to contend with another dumbass that wouldn't leave her alone? "Listen motherfucker, get away from me and don't even try to talk to me, leave me alone." She hated dealing with the drunken men at the end of the night, but it was par for the course in this type of atmosphere.

"Well why would you wear a see-through dress if you weren't looking to get laid, huh?" He stunk of alcohol and as far as she could tell was the typical guido.

"Look you prick. I told you to get the fuck out of my face, my space. I know all the bouncers. They will throw you the fuck out of here and I'll make sure they never let you back in this place. Do you like that?" Gina was fired up; she didn't want anything interfering with her mood. She turned her head to look away from the drunk and Trevor was standing there with three guitar cases.

"We can go now. Is he bothering you?"

" Oh . . . yeah, I get it. You're a chick with the band. So sorry to bother you. You band chicks think you're so fucking awesome, don't you?" This guy had something coming to him.

Gina grabbed his shirt. "Guess what asshole? I have my own band. I'm not some pick up, just so you fucking know."

She turned her attention back to Trevor, who was laughing, not worried that she couldn't take care of herself. His teeth were so white. *Is there anything wrong with this guy?*

She picked up one of the guitar cases to help him. "I parked in the band lot so we're close. I hope these guitars fit in my car, it's kind of small." Gina would get those guitars in her Benz no matter what.

The drunk guy staggered away and they walked out the back door. "Here we are. The red one. This is me."

"You have a Benz 350SL? I know you didn't get this from playing gigs. Who are you exactly Gina Poole? You're beautiful and intriguing at the same time."

"Well, Trevor McNaughton, you are about to find out who I am, and it gets better than this. I promise."

Gina was a tease, getting into a sexy seductress role. They packed two of the guitars in the small trunk and placed the last one behind the front seat. The space was small but Gina was determined.

They climbed in and Gina searched for small talk. "So, what kind of guitars do you have? Are they collectibles or special? I don't know that much, just what Rio tells me."

Trevor was proud to expand. "I have a 1968 black Fender Stratocaster Relic, a Gibson Les Paul 1968 Black Beauty, and a Fender Custom Shop 1964 Telecaster Journeyman. I searched for each of them and was able to find someone who didn't know what they had."

"I'm guessing they're worth more than you paid, clever and savvy of you. Okay, let's go. You live in Franklin Square, close to Northern Boulevard? I want to know the best way to go." Gina was hoping he would suggest maybe not going to Franklin Square. She lit up another cigarette and offered one to Trevor. "Or I can make another suggestion; if you're interested . . . we can always go to my place . . . it isn't that far from your place. I have no roommates at least." Gina felt uncomfortable and insecure right now.

"That sounds like that would make for an interesting evening. I think I would like to get to know you better." Trevor placed his hand on her cheek and traced his finger down her neck.

She shivered. His touch was light and gentle. Luckily, they hadn't yet left the parking lot when he touched her, or she would have been distracted for sure. She pushed his hair behind his ear, leaned in, and kissed his cheek softly. He turned to her, and she kissed his neck. He smelled good, probably put a little cologne on before he changed.

They looked at each other, rubbed their noses and fell into a deep passionate kiss. It was an electric jolt for Gina. She broke away from the kiss for a moment. "How do you expect me to drive now? I promise . . . we will continue this . . . at my place. One more kiss."

Trevor ran his fingers through her hair and pulled her as close to him as he could in the car, giving her a wonderful deep kiss, and whispered in her ear, "I can't wait to see what's next."

Gina had to control her passion to drive home. She put the radio on. Maybe music would be a good distraction. It worked for a while as they drove over the Throgs Neck Bridge. Trevor rested his arm over her seat. Her excitement was in overdrive; she wanted to get home. Gina pulled into the private drive of the beachfront home.

Trevor sat up and asked, "Where are we now? This is some expensive real estate. You live here? Gina Poole who are you?" Gina punched in the code to open the gate.

"Okay, let me first explain, this is my parent's estate. I live here in the carriage house. My father thought I was too disruptive coming home at three a.m. after a gig. My mother redecorated it for me, and I beat my older brother to this sweet place. We can take the guitars inside, but I promise you that they are a hundred percent safe in the car. This house has a highly sophisticated security system. I understand if you want them near you."

Trevor sat for a moment and looked all around him since the automatic lights turned on once they hit the driveway. Gina took the guitar out from the small area behind the front seats. Then she opened the trunk. "Come this way. It's one flight of stairs."

Trevor followed Gina upstairs. She closed the door and turned on the soft lights of her apartment. Two-toned shag area rugs covered wide plank pine floors. A denim-covered sofa, two oversized chairs, and a rustic pine coffee table filled the living room. Knotty pine built-in bookcases surrounded an old stone fireplace. A round table and six chairs sat in the middle of a modern kitchen open to the living room.

Trevor set his guitars on the floor and looked around. "This is *your* place, right? We aren't breaking in somewhere?"

Gina replied, "Yes, this is my place. Is it a turnoff for you?"

She walked up to this beautiful man, swept his hair from his face, and started kissing him softly on the lips. She looked into his eyes. "Tell me I'm crazy. I'm wanting this to happen, no hesitation."

Trevor started kissing her neck and slowly started unbuttoning her white crochet dress. Gina kicked off her shoes. He started kissing her shoulders and moved to her breasts. The dress fell to the ground, leaving her in a pair of white lace underwear.

Gina lifted his head up, pulled off his shirt, and unbuckled his belt. They explored each other with their hands. Trevor slid his hand inside her white lace underwear. She had gotten his pants to slide down, revealing he was a boxer guy. They stood together fondling and kissing each other.

Gina took him by the hand and led him to her bedroom. They stripped off their remaining clothing and fell into her king-sized bed. She marveled at his perfect penis; it was the nicest thing she could have been given. They touched each other like they had been lovers for years. Trevor got on top of her and kissed her neck, working his way down between her legs. He took his time using his tongue in a gratifying and knowledgeable way. It didn't take long for Gina to climax, thinking, *This is what no man has ever done for me.* She returned the favor, kissing every bit of what he had between his legs. He pulled her up to him. They stared into each other's eyes as Trevor eased his way into her and they started moving in a slow rhythm.

Gina rolled him over and straddled him. She knew they were both on the edge of a huge finish. Trevor sat up and they moved together. It was for Gina sweet and tender lovemaking. Trevor found her breasts again, which excited Gina even more. She lifted his head to her and told him, "Don't hold back," as she exploded into her second orgasm of the evening.

They fell back on the bed and stared at each other. She loved his eyes and his long hair; she kept sweeping it away from his face. Who was going to speak first and what would be said?

Her fear was that Trevor did this often and she was just one of many.

"Gina, I never expected anything like this to happen to me tonight. You have something that a man would never quit."

Gina was holding him tight. "I'm not sure what you're saying . . . I don't think there could be a man who could ever replace you. It was instant, like an explosion. But tonight is the first night we met. How can this be . . . I'm not sure what's happening . . . I do know I don't want to stop whatever this is. We are two singers in two different bands, how would that work?"

Trevor was sitting up in bed now, exposing that gorgeous body of his. "G, we will make it happen. We will play our gigs and come back either here or my place. What were you thinking?"

"As long as this is real, we will make it work. Honestly, I prefer us coming here as opposed to Stanley Park's bunk house. Did you call me G?"

"Yeah. My name for you, personal; something between us."

"I like it. I like it a lot."

Neither of them was tired, the adrenaline of emotions keeping them up. "Want a cigarette? I heard a cigarette after sex tastes better." Gina fumbled for the cigarettes in her nightstand.

"That might be true, not sure if we are seeing the situation the same way. Is this just sex for you?" Trevor looked slightly hurt.

"Well, what should I say to you without sounding completely crazy? I fell in love ten minutes after seeing you. It's true . . . but I'm totally afraid of rejection. One night of incredible lovemaking, does that tie us together? Do I want the answer to be yes? Of course. You now hold all the cards. I'm not used to being this vulnerable." Did she just ruin this good thing? Why couldn't she let it play out and not say what she said? That would scare most men away for sure.

"G, I found you . . . I found you. I am lucky, a man who has many faults and can find a woman as desirable as you. I'm willing to see how far we can go." He tousled her long hair and started kissing her. They made love again and finally fell asleep.

MOVING FORWARD

THE SUN WAS SHINING through the floral chintz drapes. Gina knew it had to be around ten a.m. She shot up, getting untangled from Trevor's arms and legs wrapped around her. She started the coffee and went into the bathroom to wash off last night's makeup. Trevor followed her into the bathroom and peed.

"Morning, look at you, no makeup. You're still beautiful." He kissed her neck.

"I made coffee. Are you hungry? I can make eggs, waffles, whatever you want. I'm quite a good cook." Gina slipped into her bathrobe hanging on the bathroom door. "If you would like I have a bathrobe you can use." She handed him a thick terrycloth robe she had picked up on one of the family trips to Italy. It was too big for her but fit Trevor perfectly. Was everything going to be this perfect?

Trevor and G, sitting at the table drinking coffee like it had been their routine for years. She lit up a cigarette and handed one to Trevor. "So, we aren't booked on a steady gig for Wednesdays yet. Rio will want to practice. What's your Wednesday look like? You booked?"

"Yeah, the Golds have us booked on Wednesdays at this club out here on the Island. Sound check is at seven."

"You're lucky, the Golds are bullshitting us around. We need more exposure, we have some big clubs but not enough. We are regularly booked on Thursday, Friday, and Saturdays. We do have a following, mostly Long Islanders who know we're from here. It's a good thing I don't have to make a living on what we get paid." Gina felt like Vision Skye wasn't a real contender.

"Why don't you come to my gig tonight? I'll go to your practice, and you come to my gig."

"Sure. I'll tell Rio I'll be a few minutes late. He won't care. He only lives five houses down the street. You'll enjoy his guitar collection and the little studio he has set up."

"I need to get some clean clothes. Can we swing by . . . what did you call it, a bunk house?" Trevor laughed.

"Yeah. Can I ask you a question? Why New York and not LA?" Gina felt she might not like the answer.

"It's simple, LA is a crowded scene, lots of bands. In New York, you have a better chance to be seen by some A&R rep. You know that those A&R guys from the record labels are always scouting out talent in the club scene. Does that make you feel better or worse?" Trevor looked at her with his beautiful eyes. "G, stop worrying about things we can't control. You and Rio are after the same thing, correct?" Gina knew that the A&R reps were the Artists and Repertoire people who were the ones who scouted the clubs for new, promising talent to sign for their record label.

Yes, he was correct, and that could separate a fast explosive relationship, cause tensions, being in two different bands. Gina decided not to worry about what was ahead.

After finishing their breakfast of Belgian waffles and bacon, Gina decided it was time for a shower. "I have a rather large shower. You can join me or be that smelly musician people always talk about."

Trevor happily followed her, getting clean and dirty at the same time as they made love in the shower.

It was getting late. She should have been at Rio's house. *Fuck it, I'll come late, and he'll know why.* They packed the guitars into the Benz and headed down to Rio's. Gina entered the code and the gate opened. She drove down the long driveway to Uncle Tony and Aunt Deidre's house and pulled around back where Rio had a separate entrance to his downstairs compound.

Trevor shook his head and asked, "Who are you people?"

Gina knew she would soon have to give full disclosure on the family dynamic. Gina walked in with an apologetic voice and a glowing smile. "Sorry man, I'm late."

Rio winked at her. "Cool, cool . . . hey Trevor, right? I'm glad to see you man. Feel free to check out my ax collection. I have some vintage guitars and some new ones. Let me know if you want to play one; I can hook it up. So, should we start with the first part of the set?"

All of Vision Skye was already at Rio's. Gina introduced Trevor to the band—Rich as their drummer, Craig, Vision Skye's keyboard player, Eric, rhythm guitar, and Jeff, their bass player. Trevor said, "Hi, nice meeting fellow musicians."

Gina asserted herself. "Rio, I think we need to retire 'Angie.' I'm singing a love song about a chick. Can I make some additions or suggestions? I was thinking of adding, 'I Saw the Light' and maybe even 'Can't Get Enough' or 'Feel Like Makin' Love.' Give me something here. I'm open but we need to add music to our set list."

Rio responded, "I get it. We need to refresh. Lots of the bands on the circuit are dressing in chick clothes, face paint . . . the gimmick. That prick Sammy Gold keeps giving us shit about it. Our gimmick is Gina, so we need to showcase that. Okay, I know all three songs. Rick, you're the drummer, count us in." Rio was ready to add these songs and more.

"Wait, Rio, what song are we playing first? I'm confused."

Gina thought Rich was a mediocre drummer. He would miss key drum riffs. He was so average, which coming from Gina was a statement since she considered herself average. Craig could fumble his way with the keyboards, but then Eric on rhythm guitar would occasionally miss his mark. How would they ever get a wider audience if these guys didn't get their shit together? However, Jeff was an excellent bass player, maybe not a lead vocalist, but he played a mean bass.

"So, this is the deal. Everyone needs to figure out these five songs. I'm adding the two more songs. And guess what? I want to play them tomorrow night at the Canyon. So go home and drill this shit into your head. Practice is over ."

Everyone left to hopefully practice the songs that were added. Rio was pissed. Other than Jeff, Gina, and himself, Vision Skye was mediocre. He knew something would need to change. He was happy all the others left, leaving him, Gina, and Trevor at Rio's practice area.

Trevor was walking around, thinking about Rio's displeasure of some of the band members and offered up some of his wisdom. "Rio, if these guys are missing it, you may have to replace them. There's always someone on the sideline waiting. You have to think of your ability to get a record company to love every member of your band. There are no friends when you think of a bigger picture." Trevor was right. Are those guys holding Vision Skye down? Is that why Sammy and Nadine keep putting them in B clubs? Probably.

Rio was interested in this new coupling of Trevor and Gina. "So, what's going on you two? I'm guessing a nice evening. Not prying man, seriously, but I don't think I have ever seen Gina so mellow. Kidding again. No, really, you guys seem like together, after one night. It had to be some night." Rio was nervously laughing; he didn't know what the hell to say to them. It was like the two had a magic wand waved over them and they were a team.

Gina responded, "Rio, sometimes things are just meant to happen and it's perfect." Trevor smiled with Gina's response. He was equally taken with her.

Trevor was impressed with Rio's setup. "Hey, have you ever actually thought of recording music in your studio? It's sweet. Maybe one afternoon you and I can jam together. It might spark some music writing. After all, the more original music you have, the more record companies will be interested in you."

Gina was impressed by Trevor's interest in Rio. "I think that's a great idea. I hope you let me listen. Who knows? Maybe I can add some lyrics to whatever music you write."

Trevor grabbed her waist. "I wouldn't have it any other way. But if you're cool with it, could I ask my drummer to come? Ian is a close friend from Vancouver and is a phenomenal drummer."

Rio was mellow. "Yeah, man, I would love to play with a great drummer since I'm disappointed with Rich. I don't think he is a true musician; just a guy who likes playing drums for fun."

Trevor added, "Do you like your sound guy? That makes a difference . . . a good mixer can make you sound better."

"Our guy, Kirk, is mediocre. I have to tell him how I want things during sound check. It's annoying; he should know his job. But he is mediocre like the rest of the band, except Jeff.

"Hey, Rio, would you like to come to my gig tonight? We're playing in Levittown, not far. I'm taking G, why not come? The Golds might be there. They make the rounds Wednesdays to check out the crowds, you know, if the bands are a right fit for the club . . . you know the drill." Trevor hoped it might make Rio feel better.

Rio liked the idea. "Yeah, I could be talked into coming."

Gina was disgusted. "Well, since band practice was a total wash, let's get something to eat."

Rio suggested, "Hey, let's take my car; we can't fit three people and three guitars in that Mercedes."

"Brilliant observation Rio. Let's go to the diner, it's easier. I can't think of any other restaurant now." Gina knew a diner was always the answer when you didn't know where to eat. They had everything you could want to eat.

BAND ISSUES

THEY GOT TO THE CLUB EARLY so the stage could be set up, mostly the roadies' job, but Trevor had a particular way of setting up his amps and lining up his guitars. He gave Gina a big hug and kiss. "I'll see you after the first set is over, beautiful lady."

Gina had chosen a black-and-gold mini dress. It was somewhat see-through, so she wore a lacy black bra underneath. She added black patent leather platform shoes with gold bows. Her bronze skin looked more intense with her wardrobe choice.

Rio and Gina enjoyed Stanley Park. The mix between covers and original music was tight. As they were sitting at the bar, they saw two unfortunately familiar faces—Sammy and Nadine Gold. Rio was the member of the band that dealt with the Golds regarding money and club bookings. He was preparing what to say to them and ran it past Gina. "Before we pounce, we need to have a plan, what do we want out of them aside from more gigs and better clubs?" Rio knew Gina would have her opinion.

Rio thought that was it, but Gina was more fixated. "I think we should tell them if we start to draw larger audiences and bigger clubs, we want to renegotiate our deal—the percentage we pay, and maybe even a piece of the door. I know it's bold and aggressive."

Rio was worried about issues with the other band members. "We need to get better. Let's go over there and get this over with."

The discussion with the Golds didn't get them everything, but it did get them bigger club venues. Now they were expected to produce in numbers. Sammy Gold was more interested in why Gina Poole was dressed sexier than usual. Nothing escapes that man.

Sammy surprised Gina. "So, Gina, a little birdie told me you and Trevor McNaughton of Stanley Park are an item. True? It would make for great buzz in the circuit you know. I'm tellin' you, the crowds at the clubs eat that shit up."

How could Sammy Gold know about something that happened twenty-four hours ago? He must have people scout out every club, every night to get dirt. Gina did not appreciate her brand-new relationship being anyone's business. That was a private matter; within time it would be exposed. *But seriously, twenty-four hours ago and this douche bag knows my business?* Gina was infuriated but had to pretend to like the Golds because they were their ticket to work.

Over the next two months Vision Skye played in the better clubs and their following grew. Gina had become a much more confident woman and was dressing sexier. She was in love and the only man who mattered was Trevor. She had morphed into the butterfly she knew she would be one day.

Trevor and Gina may have played different clubs on the same night, but they always went home to the carriage house. On nights that Gina wasn't working, she would show up for Trevor's last set. Some nights they would go to the Island Splash Diner with Trevor's best friend Ian White, and Gina began to develop a deep friendship with him. He was a powerful drummer and Gina thought he could rival The Thirst's drummer, Mike.

Gina loved hearing stories of the shit he and Trevor got into when they were younger, including some of the low points—drinking to excess, snorting way too much cocaine, the arrests for drunk driving, and being sent to juvenile detention. Ian brought up some of Trevor's old girlfriends who he said were batshit crazy. Gina was happy he was a good friend to Trevor and how they helped each other over those "bad moments." How could Gina not love this guy? He helped the man she cherished become a better man. Each of them helping each other—true friendship.

Ian was sweet to her and respected her relationship with Trevor. He was never jealous of Gina; he cared for her because she was Trevor's woman.

With his shoulder length hair, beard, and burly build, he would be attractive to the right woman. Gina knew Ian would find a good woman, not a groupie or gold digger, but a nice woman.

She was losing touch with Susan and Angela—the only real friends she had at St. Mary's. She didn't know where Liz was. Susan and Angela went on to college and things changed, but the girls would occasionally come to see the band during school breaks. She heard that Angela was engaged to her college boyfriend. Good for her. Gina wished the best for each of them. Her priority was Trevor first and the band second.

Some nights Rio would hang out at the diner with them. They would share the highs and lows of the evening and laugh at the absurdity of their lives. They smoked Sobranie cigarettes and a few joints to mellow out.

Gina and Trevor were spending every night together and every night ended in passionate lovemaking, which only got better and never boring. Some nights Gina stayed at the bunk house. She hated it and loved it at the same time. She would wake up and cook the entire house breakfast. Trevor and Ian loved watching Gina's domestic side.

However, not everything with Stanley Park was perfect. Their bassist, Jay, was starting to miss his bass lines, and Paul, their rhythm guitarist, wanted to go back to Canada. Like Vision Skye, some of Stanley Park's players were not good enough. They also didn't have that ambition to get a record deal. They wanted to go home.

There was a lot of backstabbing within all the bands in the circuit. Trevor and Gina tried to keep their dirty laundry well hidden. With all the business bullshit that went on, they trusted each other. Being in different bands meant they both had a posse of groupies. Trevor knew how much Gina hated groupies. She would give a wave to the guys who chanted obscenities, mostly telling her that they were available, as she left the stage and headed to the dressing room. But it was a life they both chose, hoping to get noticed. They would be in this together.

Stanley Park was always adding to their repertoire of original songs, which would get some hot shot A&R rep to come calling. Rio started writing original music and always looked for Gina's input on lyrics. She was happy to be able to contribute.

SECRETS

IT WAS A SUNDAY MORNING, the second week of October, and Trevor and Gina were hanging out in bed, working *The New York Times* crossword puzzle. They loved trying to do it when they were super stoned. On Sundays after the weekend gigs, they enjoyed just getting stoned. Gina put the paper down suddenly and looked up at Trevor. "I have to talk to you about my family. I'm afraid they might scare you away. I have been dreading this conversation but I—"

"G, I love you. Do you think I haven't heard the stories of you and Rio and the family you come from? It's not a secret. I will deal with whatever your family throws at me. I can take it because I take you and nothing will change that."

What he didn't tell her was he had a secret of his own that would be more disruptive than the Ricci family.

The phone rang, ending further discussion. Ian wanted to let Trevor know he had gotten a message from Sammy and Nadine Gold. The phone rang a second time and Gina thought maybe Sammy was trying to call her to get Gina and Trevor on the same call since he knew that they would be together. She didn't pick up the phone in case it was Sammy Gold. Rio took care of Vision Skye business, so why should she talk to him?

"Baby, what would Sammy want from both of us? It's weird, right?"

Trevor shook his head. "G, the best way to find out is to call him back."

Gina felt a bit nervous. "Ok, I'll call . . .

"Yeah, hi Nadine. It's Gina Poole—you called me?"

Nadine answered with, "Hold for Sammy."

Sammy knew about the love story between Gina and Trevor. He used their relationship to get a great show. He spoke with a creepy laugh, "Well, it's a funny thing since you and Trevor McNaughton are a couple. True? It would make for an extraordinary Halloween show on the last Thursday in October. It will be at The Sunset. It will be a packed room. How sweet would it be for both your bands to play on the same night?"

Gina held the phone against her chest, astonished at this opportunity, but she felt it was only to have a crowd see the two of them perform on different stages—like some window into their personal life. She answered Sammy. "Well, Rio is the one you should be talking to about scheduling any gigs, not me. And you would have to talk to Ian regarding Stanley Park. Why call me?"

Sammy Gold snickered, "I know Trevor is probably with you right now. Why don't you ask him?"

Gina was interested but would not give him an answer. "Well, Sammy, I would have to talk to Trevor, but you still need to talk to Rio and Ian. Or is this something that's already done—do we have a choice? My feeling is that you are backing us in a corner."

Sammy laughed at her audacity. "You talk to your boyfriend and have Rio and Ian call me." He hung up.

Trevor heard one side of the conversation. "Gina, what the hell is going on?" He hadn't called her Gina in months.

"Sammy Gold wants Vision Skye and Stanley Park to play at The Sunset on the last week in October, Thursday night. He thinks it's a great draw because of our relationship. He is making a mockery of our relationship, but if I'm being honest . . . it's not a totally horrible idea. But I will do whatever you feel is right. I don't want a bunch of drunk fuckers looking at us like a freak show. Our love for each other shouldn't be on display for every asshole at The Sunset's Halloween celebration."

Trevor needed answers. "I don't know what kind of shit he's pulling but let him talk to Ian and Rio. Don't worry baby, we'll be fine."

Gina had an idea. "If they want us to play the same night, why not give them what they want? We will sing a song together. I will have to really get my voice in shape, but you can sing anything. What do you think? It would have to be a cover. I wouldn't want to presume to sing one of your original songs. Besides, the crowd would want something they already know. Is that a terrible idea?"

"I like it and hate it at the same time. Screw all of them. Come here and let me devour you. And ditch that crossword puzzle."

A few hours later both Rio and Ian called, and they all decided to meet at the diner.

They sat in a booth away from other people. Rio started the conversation. "Man, this is a bunch of interesting shit here. I think we say yes and do it. Why the fuck not? It's a gig and it's only an issue because of you two. Otherwise, no one would care that Vision Skye and Stanley Park played at the same venue. It's only weird because the word is out on the two of you. I'm not judging man; I'm saying let's do this."

Ian added his perspective. "Rio's correct . . . they want to see a show and, unfortunately, it's how the crowd reacts to both of you. So, you play your set list and we do ours, no harm. But we ask for a percentage at the door. That should shake up Sammy a bit."

Trevor interjected. "G had an idea, but we need your input. Why don't we give them what they want, we sing a song together? Something the crowd would know. That would leave them talking."

Rio and Ian looked at each other. "We're in."

Gina went deeper. "I think we should combine bands a bit—Ian, Trevor, Rio, Jeff, and me. The best of each of our bands. It's a thought . . . what do you each think? One song."

Rio chirped in. "We can practice at my place. Do you think you can maneuver time away from your other bandmates?"

Ian was receptive. "We can make it work, but we have three weeks. Think we can get one song down and still hold our regular band practices?"

Trevor wrapped it up. "I can practice with G at home—with a guitar and vocals. You both are accomplished enough musicians to get through one song. G, do you have a song you're thinking of?"

"You know I do . . . it's a song I have been asking Rio to add to our playlist, The Who's 'Long Live Rock.'"

Rio jumped in, "You decided?"

Gina was excited. "Yes, because it talks about rock and roll and how your life is around the music. It's great. I love it, but you all need to like it too."

Trevor put his arm around Gina and said, "It's decided, we will start practicing tonight."

Ian liked the idea of merging the bands. Stanley Park had a serious problem looming. Trevor knew that he had to have a difficult conversation with Gina that would impact their relationship.

Trevor and Gina went home and listened to the song. Trevor started playing it acoustically and the two played around with harmonies. Gina had a lower register, which worked well with the song. Trevor had a much higher range—a rock star voice. The next day Rio had the merged group over at his house to knock the song out. He used his mixing board to get the right mix for the song. Rio didn't trust Vision Skye's sound man, Kirk, who had jumped around various bands before he landed with them. Rio never thought he got the right mix for the band; they may have to find someone better. Maybe Kevin, Stanley Park's soundman, could help.

Both bands had separate practices. Rio and Gina were concerned that maybe they were in over their heads a bit. Stanley Park's covers were spot on, and their original music was hard core rock and roll. It was too late to change much of Vision Skye's playlist, so they made sure the songs highlighted Gina's voice and Rio's awesome guitar skills.

BEGINNING OF PERFECTION

IT WAS SEVERAL WEEKS PRIOR to the Halloween show at The Sunset. Days were filled with long practice sessions, and both bands had three nights of club dates they needed to fulfill. Trevor and Gina went home to the carriage house exhausted every night. Gina found some old Black Beauties from the days when she and Rio were playing gigs, getting three hours of sleep, and pretending to go to school. Trevor did a few lines of coke to keep him going. The two rationalized the drugs would get them through the next week.

Both bands were ready . . . somewhat. Gina hadn't been nervous like this since her first gig when she had a bout of stage fright. She had been doing this for almost two years, but this night was different. She was playing on an opposite stage from the man she loved.

Gina and Trevor drove together to The Sunset on Thursday night, their Halloween show. Their roadies drove the trucks with the equipment and then set up the stages. Rio spent a lot of money on the best amps, new soundboard, and lights. It was time for Vision Skye to show they were a player in the Tri-State club scene.

Stanley Park had good equipment and an excellent sound man, Kevin. He relied on Trevor's great voice and guitar playing, easy to sound great.

Ian had made a name for himself as a premier drummer on the club scene. Another band had tried to poach him, but Trevor and Ian would never part ways.

Peter, the club owner, met them as they were unloading. He was a wannabe guitarist and loved music. He couldn't play well but owned the hottest club on Long Island. "I'm looking forward to a great night financially and musically. I'm glad we got to meet; you probably won't see me the rest of the night."

The rest of the band trickled in, walking over to their respective stages. Vision Skye did their sound check first. Rio was frustrated with Kirk—a lot of reverbs. Rio took over the mixing board to create the sound he was looking for. Gina stepped up to the microphone and sang a few lines. She was a little pitchy, she needed to work out her voice. When she sang a few lines, her voice sounded great. Trevor set up his guitars onstage the way he liked them, a different guitar for a different song.

It was two hours before the crowd of Halloween madness would descend on the club. The cover charge was ten dollars, and Rio and Ian negotiated a percentage of the door, setting a precedent for future dates. There were two dressing rooms, one for each band, but everyone agreed that they would give Trevor and Gina their own dressing room and both bands would take the other.

Gina decided to go along with the Halloween spirit and dress up in a red satin bustier, her breasts almost spilling out. She added a tulle skirt, red fishnet stockings, and ruby-red platform shoes. She teased and sprayed her hair big and wild with waves of brown and blonde. She went a bit harder on her makeup, making her look genuinely mature as hell.

Trevor wore skintight jeans, a music themed band T-shirt, and sneakers. No matter what he wore he looked phenomenal—to Gina at least, and that's all that mattered. There would be a ton of hangers-on, and she would deal with them.

The club music started playing, which meant that the door was open, and people were filtering in the club. The girls wore slutty costumes and the guys dressed as pirates or bums.

Trevor and Gina left their dressing room and found Rio and Ian at the bar.

Ian said, "Time for a little liquid courage. This place is going to be packed. There's a line out the door and probably seventy-five people already in the club."

Gina agreed. "You're right, I need a little liquid courage. I'll take a double shot of rum please."

Trevor gave Gina a disapproving stare. A first.

Ian handed the double shot to Gina.

Gina said, "Thanks mates. I'll have another."

Rio was laughing. "There you go girl, pound it down, you need to be loose tonight. What are you supposed to be? A seductive wench?"

Gina laughed. "You know Rio, I don't know what this is as long as I'm a sexy bitch up there singing, and that's all I care about."

Trevor bolted a shot of Jack Daniels and pulled Gina to the side. "G, baby, what are you doing? I saw you take two Valium. You're going to pass out if you don't watch it." He leaned down and kissed her head. "Go out there and kick some ass, you seductive wench."

Gina offered up a smile and a kiss. "I have a high tolerance, I'll be fine. Love you."

Rio announced, "We have ten minutes."

When he turned around, some pussycat was all over him, shrieking above the club music, "Remember me? Remember me?"

Rio was cool. "Yeah sweetheart, I remember you. Enjoy the show."

Gina asked the guys, "Do I have time for a cigarette?"

"Go ahead," Rio replied. "We will keep them waiting, build up some anticipation."

Gina headed out the back door and Trevor went with her. The bouncer at the door looked familiar, but Gina couldn't remember where she knew him from.

He looked at her and said, "Gina Ricci! How the fuck are you? I'm Sal, a friend of your brother Frankie. I've been to your house." Sal was a big guy, balding, wearing a Yankee hat, and had a stomach hanging so far over his belt he hadn't seen his feet in years.

She gave a nod of recognition, but she didn't know who he was. He was, after all, Frankie's friend, and she never associated with his friends.

Trevor then stepped out and took out two cigarettes. "You okay? Right, look at me. You're fine, go out there and kill it. I'm sure the Gold's will show up tonight. Slay it baby."

Gina felt confident now.

The band was standing by the stage and Rio was jumping around, full of energy, "Here we go . . ."

Gina walked onstage and looked at the largest audience she ever played. "Hello Sunset. Happy Almost Halloween! My name is Gina Poole, and we are Vision Skye. Ready to party?!!!"

The band started with "Can't Get Enough," then went into a classic "After Midnight." The club was rocking. By the time they finished their first set, the crowd was roaring. The light show Rio added was an exciting new element.

Soon the obscenities from the men in the crowd began. "Show us your tits!" "Let me sleep with you, wench!" This is the part Gina hated but she knew it was coming since half the bar was drunk already.

Vision Skye finished their set, and the lights came on. Gina exited the stage and headed toward the dressing room. Trevor was leaning against the wall talking to a leggy blonde. She walked up and placed her arm through Trevor's.

Gina tried to be calm. "Hi, how's it going?" She said to the girl. "I'm sorry, your name is . . .?"

The disappointed fan walked away.

"A little jealous, huh? G, I was getting rid of her. You don't have to—"

"Yes, I do. You know I hate groupies."

Trevor laughed and turned to head down the hall toward the stage, blowing a kiss to Gina along the way.

Stanley Park opened with Zeppelin and slid into The Who. Then they went into their originals. Trevor was such a talented song writer; Gina hoped that someday they could write something together. The crowd loved Stanley Park, and Gina believed they were on their way to great things. Did that include her, she wondered.

While both bands were in the dressing room, Gina, Rio, Jeff, Ian and Trevor went into the dressing room that Gina and Trevor were using. They all were figuring out when they would fit in Trevor and Gina's duo. Gina realized, "Oh, shit, this song could use keyboards." Craig was not a strong enough keyboard player, especially for The Who. Rio was, but he was playing rhythm guitar to Trevor's lead. Gina thought, *Crap, crap, maybe we shouldn't play the song. If the Gold's are here, it will be a major drawback for Vision Skye.*

As if scripted, a familiar face walked into the dressing room; it was Stevie, the keyboardist from The Thirst.

"Hi. Happy to see me? I came to check you out."

Gina was shocked. "You're not playing tonight? I thought you were booked months ago."

"Well, we were until Mike got the flu, so no can do." Stevie seemed a little disappointed. "Aren't you happy to see me?"

Gina hugged him. "You have no idea . . . can you help us out?"

"What is it you need me to do?"

Trevor interjected, "We need an amazing keyboard player; we need you." Gina said, "We need a great keyboard player that isn't Craig. The other band members have no idea we're doing this. They won't know until we take the stage."

"Get me a couple of Rum and Cokes, and I'm good. What am I playing?"

Eric, Craig, Rich, and Kirk from Vision Skye were dumbfounded when they found out they weren't playing. Eric was incensed. "When the hell did you five find the time? Leave us out, no discussion, nothing. Rio, you and Gina suck. I guess Gina's boyfriend has more say in our band than we do."

Craig didn't really seem to care, especially once he saw Stevie. He knew there was no way he was playing. Most of the members of Vision Skye acted angry, but realistically none of them looked at Vision Skye as a career. It was more of a hobby. However, Rich looked at Rio, "Dude, you know what? I should quit right now, but I need the cash tonight. So, you have your special little group asshole."

Jay and Paul from Stanley Park didn't care as much. It was like they were going through the motions. They wanted to go back to Canada anyway. But they were pissed at the suddenness of it. Paul yelled at Trevor. "What the fuck? When were we going to find out?"

Gina looked at them and boldly said, "Right now."

At the end of Vision Skye's set, Ian walked over to the drums, Jeff grabbed his bass, Trevor and Rio picked up their guitars, and Stevie strode up onstage with a thunderous round of applause. Gina took the stage and shouted, "This is what you came for . . . me, Gina Poole, and the man I love, Trevor McNaughton!"

The song started and the crowd, well they were drunk, but they loved the foreplay between Gina and Trevor more than their singing. The closeness of their singing, a kiss in between choruses, the way they looked at each other. They were now solidified as the "it couple" for the Tri-State area club scene. Gina and Trevor may be in different bands, but it didn't matter. Seeing their onstage chemistry dashed away any ideas for many women in the crowd that Trevor was available. Men thinking they might have had a chance with the siren that was Gina Poole saw otherwise.

The Sunset gig wrapped up at three in the morning. Ian, Jeff, Rio, Stevie, Trevor, and Gina felt energized after the show and headed to the Island Splash Diner. They also didn't mind their share of the door that night. No one saw Sammy and Nadine, but it didn't mean there wasn't someone spying for them. It was a success, and they kind of got a win over the Golds. Sammy Gold thought it was a great maneuver, putting Gina and Trevor playing the same night. It was a win for everyone, except the members of Vision Skye and Stanley Park who were on the side. Sammy thought there would be a dynamic between the two lead singers, it would make club goers want to see both or either band. They did see two people in love singing together.

Stevie had a bunch of circuit gossip. God love him, he knew everyone's business. "So, I heard Hustle found some guy with money to manage them, then the band got new outfits, booked recording time—and in three weeks, fired their drummer, bass player, and guitarist. What a way to say, 'Thank you, you're out.'"

And they aren't the only ones. Temptation got rid of their keyboard player and lead singer. Ouch. I mean their vocals weren't great, but you changed the face of your band. I'm sure there will be more movement as the ousted folks find places in other bands. There is no job security in music."

"Stevie, The Thirst won't change. You all have been friends forever," Gina replied.

"And, what now for you five . . . do you become a band? I think that's something you all should be considering." Stevie was heartfelt in his response.

Ian started to speak, "Well, we first need to—"

Trevor cut him off immediately. Gina noticed a stare between them. *Were they keeping a secret? Is Trevor keeping a secret from me?*

Times were about to get difficult, sorrowful, and painful. They say love conquers all . . . it's about to be tested.

UNEXPECTED PROBLEMS

HOLIDAYS AT THE RICCI HOUSEHOLD were a major event. Mario and Franny expected all their children to be present—no questions, you better be there. Uncle Tony, Aunt Deidre, and Rio were also expected. Mario sometimes invited a friend or another family, especially if there was a business deal involved.

On Thanksgiving, the house was decorated with enough orange twinkle lights to rival the trees at Tavern on the Green in Central Park and beautifully carved pumpkins sat on the entryway. The interior smelled like cloves, oranges, and pumpkin pie. Every conceivable type of Thanksgiving themed figurine graced the tables and shelves—pumpkins, cornucopia, pilgrims, and turkeys.

Serena did most of the cooking. A thirty-pound turkey, green beans, squash, stuffing, corn muffins, and mashed potatoes with special ingredients that even Gina couldn't get out of her. She also made the best pumpkin and pecan pies. Gina thought she cooked an excellent Thanksgiving, considering she was an Italian woman from Naples with no real knowledge of the holiday. Yet she mastered the holiday of Thanksgiving for the Ricci family.

Ironically, Franny, who did not like to cook, would make baked ziti, meatballs, and antipasto platters. Gina's job was to make apple pies, ricotta cheesecakes, and pignoli cookies as taught to her by her Nonna, who hoped she would hand the recipes down to *her* grandchildren one day. Gina treasured those memories of her.

This Thanksgiving and Christmas would have a new component: Trevor. Gina had not been to her parents' house in the six months since she met Trevor. For someone who was from Vancouver, Canada, had he ever met a man like Mario? Probably not. She was afraid her father was going to scare Trevor away. Trevor said he knew who she was, but did he really? Even she didn't know everything about her family and there were things she never wanted to know. Her father and mother tried to plan her life, but she rebelled and never thought for a second about the path she walked down. She traveled it with her cousin, so that should count for something. She worked with family.

How would Mario receive Trevor? He wasn't Italian and wasn't even American. He wore jeans, T-shirts, boots, or sneakers. He had long hair and facial hair.

He was a musician. It was okay for Rio to be a musician; after all he was Uncle Tony's problem. Gina could hear Mario, "He doesn't shave, and what's up with that long hair? He's got a problem." It would never be enough for her father to tell him she loved Trevor more than anything she could ever imagine. And why isn't it enough? Her parents loved each other. She needed to talk to Trevor about what to expect. And of course, there was Frankie. She couldn't stand her brother most of the time and could not find any favorable or redeeming qualities about him. He would be equally critical of Trevor. *How dare they!*

Her father had to be aware that Gina was living in the carriage house with some guy. Mario watched the camera footage every night. He would see them coming and going, so he knew. Gina's head was spinning. She was anxious. Maybe she needed to refill her Valium prescription. Her father would also hate her new look and would tell her she looked like a whore. But she was a sexy siren now. How do you win? *I will win. I will live the life, the dream, with Trevor.* At the same time, she felt Trevor was keeping something from her, something big. She was frightened and it made her uncharacteristically insecure.

Gina started baking two days before Thanksgiving. She had already finished three ricotta cheesecakes and had pignoli cookies in the oven. She was peeling apples for pie when Trevor came home. She had the spices measured out in a bowl and had already made the pie crust.

"Hey, G, what smells so good?" Trevor took a deep breath.

"Hey, baby. I'm cooking desserts. Are you okay? You look worried. What's going on? I mean, we haven't made love in days. Did I do some—"

"G, stop. You have done nothing wrong. I love you. But I do have a major problem that you and I need to talk about."

Her heart dropped and tears began streaming down her face.

Trevor was firm. "We aren't going to discuss this until after Thanksgiving. Let's get your father and family over with. I know you have anxiety about me meeting them, but I don't. What can he do?"

"I'm not sure. It depends on what you're going to drop on me." Gina was in full-blown panic. "Oh, shit my cookies . . . fuck's sake. Thank God they aren't burnt. I'm going to make my apple pie. If you don't want to talk, fine. Go write your music."

Gina was pissed. She used her words like claws to swipe Trevor.

"What the hell, Gina? Why are you acting so childish?"

"Excuse me. What did you say to me? Childish? Really! You're holding back, and I'm childish." Gina was half crying half yelling, she was out of sorts, and this was their first fight. *Thanksgiving is two days away and now he starts a fight with me.*

Trevor looked at her with wet eyes. "Look, Gina. Can we stop? I never meant to do this now. Let's conquer your parents and I promise you. I will . . . I need to talk to you about stuff. It doesn't change anything, okay? So, no more Valium, no more being anxious."

Gina sobbing, "I can't bear to lose you and I feel like something is standing in the middle of us, please don't . . . I love you."

She kept repeating the same words. Trevor stroked her hair and told her things would work out. It wasn't reassuring, but it was something she had to hold onto. She remembered the discussion at the diner. Whatever Trevor was afraid of, Ian also felt it was an issue. Gina had to clear her head and get ready to be interrogated by her family.

That night the two of them sat in bed and watched TV. It was football season, which meant Gina had to watch every College Bowl game and all the pro games too.

She turned to Trevor and started touching him. She wanted him.

He looked at her. "I'm not sure I can right now . . ."

"Let me try." She continued to stroke him and was finally able to get him hard. She ran her fingers through his hair, which was getting longer. She kissed him deeply and passionately. She climbed on top of him, never breaking eye contact. "Baby, I love you. I need you right now. I want you right now." Gina ripped off her clothes. She wanted him bad and was determined to show him how much. After she took her clothes off, she stripped him. First she pulled off his shirt and then his pants. She noticed he chose not to wear underwear. Gina continued to slowly work her body into his. It took Gina to be in control of him. He rolled her on her back. It took a few moments, and he was finished. He was done faster than normal.

Gina nestled into Trevor's arms, and he kissed her gently on her neck and cheek. "Gina, always remember I love you . . . I found you. It will always be this way. I found you, through all this bullshit, remember."

They sat up in bed and resumed watching the game. Gina was ecstatic her team was winning. She took a joint and a cigarette from the nightstand and lit them both. They fell asleep early—probably smoked way too much weed.

The next morning Gina got up earlier than usual. She promised Serena she would drop off the desserts she made. Her first step back into the Ricci family dynamic. Trevor got up when he smelled coffee and walked into the kitchen naked. It was hard to contain that primal lust she had for him every time she saw him naked. "Baby, I need to drop off all these desserts at the house. Can I make you breakfast?"

"G, I know you're a great cook, but can I have just eggs and bacon?"

She kissed him on the lips. "Anything you want. Hey, have you had band practice lately? I haven't heard you talk about it."

Trevor was somewhat evasive. "We are only doing two weekends between now and Christmas. Ian and I think we need to take some time to write more original material."

"How are the guys surviving in the bunk house without money coming in?" *Where was the money coming from for them to live?*

"We have a reserve . . . plus honestly G, me living here has saved them money. I don't really pay for anything. Except for new strings . . . stuff like that."

Gina was concerned. "Is this an issue between us? I never wanted you to feel we weren't equals here. I can't help what my family situation is; I thought it was good for us to not worry about money. Money breaks up couples. Well, since we're talking about money, it's about time I tell you this before Thanksgiving because it might come up. My Poppa Ricci set up trust funds for his four grandchildren, and when we turn twenty-one, we are allowed to have access to the fund. Rio and I turn twenty-one soon after the New Year so we will have . . . Oh God, I don't know how to say this, but I'm going to say it. The trust fund is worth five million dollars." This in some weird way made Gina embarrassed. "Does that put you off in any way?"

Trevor smiled. "I'm glad you told me; your father might think I'm a gold digger. You never mentioned it before, so how can this make a difference now? You're silly. Although there might be a situation soon I could use your help with."

There it is again; he alluded to some issue . . . *What could it be?*

"I'll find out after Thanksgiving," he promised.

Gina went into the shower while Trevor ate breakfast. She had just rinsed her hair when he joined her. He turned her face to the wall and entered her from behind. She loved how the water poured over her face and the sensation of the water dripping from his hair onto her back. Wet bodies made their lovemaking so easy. That's why she loved Trevor McNaughton, he surprised her, excited her, and how simple . . . by showing her how much he really did love her.

Gina got dressed in a pair of jeans and a cashmere sweater. It was November in New York and cold. She started packing a basket with all of her baked goods.

"Trev, what are you up to today? You need to take the Benz? I can take the walk of hell to my parents' house."

"If you don't mind, I was going to pick up Ian and possibly go to Rio's."

"Oh, wow didn't realize you all got together, but cool. Maybe you should invite Ian to the fiasco tomorrow. Warn him what he's walking into. I'll have Franny set another place. Kisses, I'm going to leave, see you later."

Why were Ian, Rio, and Trevor meeting? Strange. It hurt Gina to be excluded. She thought it was shitty of them to treat her that way. Why wasn't she included? *What the hell is going on?*

Gina walked up the driveway to her parents' house, which had been landscaped with orange, yellow, and red mums. Franny had the gardeners freshen the flowers every season.

Gina opened the heavy glass and wrought iron door and instantly smelled cloves, oranges, and pumpkin spice. Serena walked toward the door, "Princess Gina! What do you have there?"

Gina laughed. "The usual desserts that you always have me make. You're silly." She kissed her cheek. "Is my mother around?" Gina was apprehensive to see her mother. Gina walked through the wide foyer down the hall to the kitchen and found her mother looking stunning and well-put together, as usual.

"Well, well, it's my long-lost daughter, the rock star. How are you, Gina Annamarie? You look good, it's a pity you don't have time for us anymore."

Gina took a long breath. "Mom, we're not doing this, please. I'm here, and Trevor and I will be here tomorrow for Thanksgiving. But if you are going to be dismissive, I may have to rethink the Ricci ritual."

Franny was extremely direct. "Gina, your father and I are looking forward to meeting this man who you claim to be in love with. He has been living on our property for five months and we haven't seen you in about six months. We look forward to meeting him, Gina."

Gina pleaded, "Can you be happy for me? And I need you to be respectful to Trevor. I would think having someone who truly loves me would make you happy, or accepting, or treat me with something other than ridicule."

"You are correct. I haven't met your Trevor. Your father and I only see him on the security tapes. You have allowed someone we don't know into our secure home. Since nothing bad has happened, I'm assuming he is a decent fellow. I will tell you, your father may not be as gentle with you as I am."

Gina laughed. "You think you're being gentle, Mom? You're being a bitch if we are going to be real. I'm coming tomorrow to let you into my life, to let you see I'm doing well and I'm happy, successful. I'm sure Aunt Deidre will tell you how well our band is doing. Rio and I are successful, especially here in Long Island. Trevor's band is excellent. I wouldn't be surprised if a record company doesn't sign them soon. Can you be the adult in the room tomorrow? Dad will be testy at best and grill Trevor. He will pull his Italian machismo bullshit. Can you try to contain that, please? Mom, if you ever wanted to do anything for me, please restrain Dad."

Franny shrugged her shoulders. "Gina, can anyone control your father when he starts going down a path? Your Uncle Tony and Aunt Deidre could probably step in. They think Rio is a genius, so that makes you special, I guess." Franny looked lovingly at her daughter. "So, this man makes you happy? Are we planning a wedding soon?"

Gina shook her head. "Wedding, umm no, I mean . . . I hope one day, but we are so engrossed in our music careers. I never gave it that much thought to be honest. If he asked, yes, I would marry him in a minute."

"Can he support you, being a musician? Does he know about your inheritance?" Franny was concerned.

Gina was exasperated at her mother's direction of questions. She thought they would come from her father, or even dumbass Frankie. "Mom, I really would love to show Trevor that we are somewhat of a normal family, where we all love each other and are rooting for each other. Can we pretend for a day?"

"Gina, we *are* a loving family. We have never disowned you . . . even though we haven't seen you for six months. We've paid your bills, and you always have money available to you. Does that sound like parents who don't love their child? I think not. I will do my best to derail some of your father's line of fire, okay?

"Now, let me see those desserts. Wow, three cheesecakes, pignolis, and two apple pies. Good for you Gina. I don't know where you find the time with working at night like you and your Trevor do." Franny was a bit sarcastic.

"So, yeah, we're kind of taking a little break for the holidays. Oh, I almost forgot, you wouldn't mind setting one more place for Thanksgiving? For my friend Ian?"

"Of course not. Is he from Canada too?"

Gina stood in amazement. "Yes, he is . . . how did you find out that Trevor was from Canada?"

Franny looked at her deadpan. "Honey, your Aunt Deidre and Uncle Tony. You're so silly. Oh, so you won't be surprised, guess who Frankie is dating? I think it's serious. MaryAnn Fanelli. She went to St. Mary's with you, didn't she?"

Gina only vaguely remembered her; she was a class below her. Then it was coming clearer, yes . . . she remembered MaryAnn. Straight, long blonde hair. Hung out at Roosevelt Field Mall on the weekends. Worked at some cosmetic store. Wore a lot of makeup—the stereotypical Long Island Italian girl. The type Gina would never be friends with and now would probably have as a sister-in-law. Hopefully her mother was wrong.

"Gina, come help me pick out the linens for tomorrow." As her mother called her into the dining room, she heard the front door open.

"Well, look who's here, my princess who I never see anymore. Where's the guy? Or does he not want to show up in front of me?" Gina was hoping to stay long enough to appease her mother and avoid her father until tomorrow.

"Daddy, first, hello . . . second, the guy's name is Trevor, and I love him. Let's not do this, please. We will be here tomorrow and I'm hoping you will show him some respect. And please, no interrogation. Can you not? I want to be here, and I want you to want us here."

Mario looked at Gina. "I want my daughter here and I want to meet this man who is living with my daughter. You can understand why a father may want to give the guy the business. Maybe I'll like him Gina, but as your father, this man is living in my house."

Gina responded, "It's Thanksgiving. A day to give thanks. Can you try to understand that I love this man? That's something to be thankful for, at least for me."

Mario walked into the kitchen. "What's all this?"

Serena answered, "Gina, made all these desserts. I asked her to. She outdid herself, yes she did Mr. Mario."

"Gina, did you make Nonna's recipes? I haven't had these for years." He took a bite out of one of her pignolis . . . "Oh my, like my mother made. Did Nonna teach you this?"

"Yes, she tried to teach Mom and Aunt Deidre, but I guess they never mastered her art of cooking like I did."

Mario leaned over and kissed his daughter on the head. "Look princess, I can't guarantee I'm not going to give him a little once-over. But now listen, I'm going to try my best not to rattle this guy—who's sleeping with my daughter. Can you understand why a father may not like this guy who's being intimate with my daughter in my house?"

"Well, thank you for the promise of not making him feel so uncomfortable. However, I'm not sleeping in your house. I'm in the carriage house.

It feels like a million miles away from this house. I'll see you all tomorrow. Love you all, and I truly mean that. Hope you remember that tomorrow."

Mario warned her, "Oh Gina, your brother Frankie is bringing MaryAnn Fanelli for Thanksgiving. We think a wedding is coming soon. Great, isn't it?"

"Yeah, I heard, should be something. Where's Ant?"

"Ant is at the movies with his friends. I think there are girls there. Starting to venture into coed moviegoing," Franny answered.

"Make sure you wear something nice," Franny had to add.

FAMILY AND DEMONS

GINA ENJOYED WALKING in the fresh cool autumn air. She went into the house to get a joint and a cigarette then back outside to smoke them. She hadn't enjoyed sitting in the sun, smelling the fresh air for months. She smoked part of the joint, finished her cigarette, and then returned to her apartment to see what she had in the refrigerator for dinner.

She expected Trevor would be home fairly soon. She looked in the freezer and found meat to make meatballs; she had sauce and some linguine. There was wine in the wine fridge. She heard her car pull up, followed by another car. She looked out the window and saw Trevor, Ian, and Rio. She opened the door for them, trying to read their faces, looking for some sort of "tell."

"Hey, what's up with the party? Did I not get the invitation?" She wasn't expecting two other people for dinner.

Gina could tell Rio was high even though he thought his sunglasses would hide his red eyes. "Gina, what's going on? Have you been up to 'the big house' today?"

Ian seemed a tad uncomfortable. "Hey Gina, sorry you have unexpected company."

"Baby, everything go well with your parents?" Trevor leaned over with a kiss.

"Sure, it could have been worse. I'm still the princess, so I guess that's something. My father had my pignolis, and he remembered Nonna, my grandmother. Rio you remember when Nonna would bake, right?" She was testing to see how high he was.

"Yeah, it was cool." Rio's answer was weak.

Gina knew something was up. "It was cool. How high are you all? What exactly are you high on? Anyone? I guess you're hungry too."

Rio protested. "Come on Gina don't be that way. You can't say you didn't smoke a joint today."

"Trevor, you've been quiet. Why don't you tell me, and I'll make dinner." *My God, I sound like my mother.*

"We got carried away. We took some quaaludes and we're fucked up. I'm sorry. And we drank some." Trevor was waiting for Gina's disapproval.

"And the two of you drove here fucked up? You could have screwed up our cars and gotten into an accident. It's the fucking day before Thanksgiving and you decide to go rogue and get drunk and do quaaludes? Is this the beginning of your band? Let's all get fucked up and write music? And oh, let's not let Gina in on the secret. I'll call and get you whatever takeout you want. I'm not cooking. Excuse me." Gina stormed into the bedroom.

Rio yelled, "Gina, be cool man. It's not bad. No one talked about the bands, oh shit."

Ian said, "I'm actually hungry, what should we order?"

Rio was laughing, "Yeah, let's order some gyros from the Greek place."

Trevor walked into the bedroom and found Gina fuming. "Ok G, baby, I'm sorry. It's been a super-long time since I put myself in this situation and I'm sorry for hurting you."

"Trevor, I don't care if you fuck up once in a while. You told me you've had issues. I love you in spite of the fact you told me all that shit. But really, the night before Thanksgiving? When I have enough anxiety about my parents? Seriously. Do you care about what this means to me?"

Trevor crawled into the bed with her. "Please, please I need you now, more than ever. Let's go out there and wait for them to come down a bit, then go to bed."

From the other room, "Hey, Gina the Greek place is dropping off a shit ton of food, cool right? I got it, I have cash."

Oh, Rio, I want to kill you right now.

Gina and Trevor came out of the bedroom. Even though she was angry with Rio and Trevor, she didn't want Ian to feel more uncomfortable than he already was. She composed herself.

"So Ian, I want you to know that you're invited tomorrow to my parents' for Thanksgiving. I hope you can come."

"So, even cooler, Ian can stay at my place, and we'll come over. Cool, Ian, right?" Rio added.

"Sure guy, as long as I can take a shower and borrow a shirt." Ian could roll with anything.

The food arrived and Gina made it clear. "Rio take the food you want back to your place. Can you drive?"

Rio pretended he was fine. "Okay Gina, I got you. I'm good. I'll see you tomorrow."

"See ya." Gina slammed the door and stalked into the bedroom.

Trevor stripped off his clothes and was lying face down naked on the bed. He turned his head toward the door. "I know I really fucked up today. Come here. I want you to be next to me."

Gina knew this was the vulnerable guy who sabotaged relationships. He told her that the first night they met.

"I'm not mad. I'm worried about what's going on in your head. You need to be on your A game tomorrow." As Gina curled up next to him she smelled the alcohol on his breath.

"G, you're so arousing. Why do you love me so much? I'm a scumbag sometimes. I don't want to be that man for you."

Gina was loving, "So don't be that person. You don't have to be perfect . . . love me the best way you can. I'll always love you."

Trevor fell asleep, his head on her chest.

THANKSGIVING

MORNING CAME and Trevor had a slight hangover. Gina handed him a cup of coffee, brushed the hair away from his face, and kissed his forehead. "You good this morning?"

Trevor took a big sip of coffee. "Oh yeah, now I am. Keep the coffee coming. What time are we expected?"

Gina thought for a second. "Probably noon. The football games will be on; it's a big deal in my family. My father likes to see what the point spreads are—for obvious reasons. What are you wearing today?"

Trevor had a panicked look. "Babe, I don't have dress-up clothes; you know my wardrobe."

Gina looked at him appraisingly. "I don't want you to be someone different, but let's see what we got here." Gina rummaged through the closet. "Okay, this works. Black jeans, this plain white T-shirt, and this leather coat. Ding, you're good. See, the designer in me comes through."

Gina chose for herself a black skintight jersey dress. One of the more modest pieces in her wardrobe, it came down past her knees. She matched it with a pair of black satin platforms.

She went to the kitchen and got a second cup of coffee. Trevor was lying in bed and Gina noticed he was ready to go. She couldn't be more accommodating either. Trevor was the lover he always was—sweet, loving, and so incredibly sensuous, especially when he sang to her when they made love. She would giggle or sometimes sing with him. Back in sync, she knew this day would go well with the two of them as a united couple. Nothing, not even Mario Ricci, could divide them.

Gina and Trevor shared the bathroom, trying to look their best. Trevor shook out his long, dirty-blond hair and trimmed a bit of the hair on his face. Gina blow-dried her shoulder length hair, wavy and full. She was lucky she had beautiful thick hair, full of blonde highlights. She put her face on for the day, but sparingly. Just enough to show off her big eyes and perfect eyebrows.

Trevor looked at the soft leather jacket. It looked like a sport jacket but better. He looked at Gina and said, "G, this isn't my jacket. I don't own anything this expensive. Where did it come from?"

"I bought it a few weeks ago at Roosevelt Field. I saw it in one of the men's stores and thought to myself, *Trevor would look hot in this, I'm buying it.* So there, aren't I allowed to purchase something for you?"

"G, you can do anything you want for me. How do I look? Do I pass?"

Gina placed her hands on both sides of his face and planted a lingering kiss on his lips. "Baby, you look fantastic. I could eat you up."

"Can I count on that later?" he asked mischievously.

At noon Gina and Trevor drove her Benz to the circle in front of her parents' house. Uncle Tony and Aunt Deidre were already there. Gina turned to Trevor, "You ready for this?"

They entered the two-story foyer and Trevor's eyes widened. He followed self-consciously behind Gina as his shoes echoed on the marble tile floor. Trevor entered the dining room where a boardroom length beveled glass table was set with Lenox china, Waterford crystal, and decorated with white roses. Gina was sure Trevor had never seen such a lavish table setting.

Uncle Tony greeted them. "Gina, sweetheart, how are you?" He gave her a kiss and a big bear hug. Uncle Tony was three years younger than her father, but he was starting to gray first. Uncle Tony looked like her grandfather, a sweet memory for Gina.

"Uncle Tony, this is Trevor, and . . . wait, what are you doing? Why is this huge TV in Mom's formal dining room? She will freak out, and the piece of furniture it's sitting on . . . oh my God she's going to lose it."

Uncle Tony laughed. "Do you think for one minute I would do this without your mother saying it was okay? She would shoot me if I didn't clear it with her. I've already met Trevor."

Gina was surprised to hear this. Was Trevor spending more time at Rio's than she knew about?

Franny and Aunt Deidre entered the dining room together. Ricci women dressed for the holidays. Her mother was in a St. John's suit and Aunt Deidre looked stunning as always in a designer dress.

"Mom, Aunt Deidre, this is Trevor."

Franny spoke first. "Trevor, so nice to meet the gentleman who has taken our Gina away. I'm kidding of course. We are so happy to have you in our home. I can see why Gina is, well, so in love with you. What can I get you to drink? Scotch? Martini? Whatever you want."

Trevor was feeling a little uncomfortable but said, "I'll have a scotch neat, thank you."

Aunt Deidre gave Trevor a big hug. "Trevor, how are you? Good to see you again. Are you ready for this? Promise I'll save you if needed."

Gina looked around. "Where's Rio? Oh, and Ian?" Not here yet?"

Aunt Deidre smiled. "He is always late, you know that, but he should be here soon with your friend."

"Okay, Aunt Deidre, where is he? I need to get this over with—Dad and Frankie."

Trevor took the drink from Franny. "Trevor, if you need anything else, Serena is in the kitchen. She'll get it for you. Gina, your father is in the living room. I'm sure he can't wait to see you and Trevor."

Gina got a shiver up her back and led Trevor by the hand to the formal living room. Her father was sitting on the large silk sofa holding a glass of scotch, and Frankie was there with MaryAnn Fanelli. *Oh, damn, this is most likely serious—wedding, Italian wedding, ugly bridesmaid dresses serious—let me kill myself now.*

Mario stood up setting his drink on the end table. "So . . . you are the man who has taken away the princess?" He pounded Trevor on the shoulder. "Hey, I'm only kidding. Nice to meet you in person and not on security footage. No, really guy, I'm glad you're here. Apparently, you make my daughter happy, and how can a father be mad at that, right? You're a scotch man? Nice, I'll treat you to some of my good stuff later."

Trevor was in the bull's-eye and all he could say to Mario was, "Appreciate you having me here and I promise I'll take care of the princess. I do love your daughter."

Mario stared at him with steely blue eyes. "You better treat her well. Hey, this guy is all right. Sit down. This is Frankie, my son, Gina's brother. Oh, I'm sorry, and his girlfriend, MaryAnn."

Gina stepped up. "So, hi Frankie, how the hell have you been? I see you're busy now. Hi MaryAnn. How did you meet my brother?"

In her pretend soft voice, MaryAnn replied, "I saw him at this gym in Old Westbury, and we clicked. Then I remembered he was you brother. It's like I already knew him, you know?"

Gina laughed to herself, *Oh yeah, I know.* Gina wanted to throw up. MaryAnn was dressed in pink just like a doll. It made Gina gag a little in her mouth.

"Where's Ant? He still lives here, correct?"

"Hey, Gina, you're the only one who doesn't live here anymore." Frankie had to be an asshole. He was still pissed at Gina for taking the carriage house. But he had the pool house and used it frequently in the past; Gina actually caught him in the act. That image still creeps into her head, *disgusting*.

Almost on cue, Ant came into the room. "Gina! Oh my God you're here. You look pretty . . . is this your boyfriend?"

Gina looked at him sweetly, "Yes Ant, this is Trevor." As they exchanged hellos, a commotion stirred in the foyer. It was Rio and Ian, finally. Trevor has people he can relate to and relax with.

"Hey, everyone, I'm here. What's with the TV in the dining room? Football? Oh, cool. Who thought of that?"

Rio was high. Gina knew it.

Trevor finished his scotch and Rio jumped in. "Let's get another. Oh yeah, everybody, this is our friend Ian. He's a cool guy." No one ever reacts to Rio being Rio.

Ian was quiet. This was a lot for a guy from Vancouver to know how to handle all these Italians. Gina, Trevor, Rio, and Ian moved into the kitchen where the alcohol was. "Is everybody good here? I know it's a lot to take in, so I apologize now for anything said from this point on." Gina grimaced.

Franny began ushering everybody into the dining room. "Thanksgiving is ready, please take a seat."

Mario sat, of course, at the head of the table with Franny at the other end. Uncle Tony always sat on the right side of her father, Aunt Deidre next to him. Frankie sat on the other side of her father—the heir apparent waiting for his moment—*sickening*.

Franny motioned to Trevor. "Trevor, I would love it if you sat next to me. Gina, you sit next to your Trevor on this side. Who will lead us into grace today?"

Oh, shit. Gina forgot about all this religious stuff. *Please, please don't look at me.* MaryAnn Fanelli went for the brownie points. "Oh, I would be honored to say grace."

Gina shot Trevor and Rio a look like she was getting sick.

As dinner progressed, the football game became paramount. It was Dallas and Washington and Roger Staubach was hurt; the game became an exceptional contest.

Dinner was filled with chatter of how great this one was, how pretty this one was, and some dirty jokes told by her father. Rio talking about writing some original songs. Wait what, when? Where was Gina? An ass kicking will happen.

Serena cleared the dishes. Gina offered to help but she wouldn't hear of it. The guys moved into the family room. Gina walked over and sat next to Trevor and asked if he was okay. He said he and Ian were enjoying a "real Italian style dinner."

"Well guys, I'm going outside to smoke a cigarette." Gina was halfway out the door when Franny called her.

"Mom, I'm having a cigarette; you can come outside with me if you want."

Franny stepped outside with her, "Gina, don't forget to use the ashtrays that are out here. I used to find your cigarette butts all around the yard. So, I want to tell you . . . I like your Trevor. He's not the type I would have picked for you, but I see what you love about him. I wanted you to know that. Enjoy that kind of love. It only happens once in your life."

Gina looked at her mother. "I do love Trevor, Mom. He is the only man I have ever met who makes me feel special. This is my once-in-a-lifetime love. I just want you to know that he is my everything."

Franny nodded. "Finish your cigarette. I'm serving dessert." She turned quickly on her heels and went back in the house. Gina wished her mother would have responded to her comment of loving Trevor as much as she did.

Gina sat for a minute to collect herself. Never would she have thought those words would come out of Francesca Angelone Ricci. She lit up another cigarette and let out a deep sigh.

Trevor joined her a moment later. "I think I'm doing okay, right? Your mother sounded interested in Vancouver and the band. I didn't anticipate her being so interested."

Gina looked at him lovingly. "She thought you were perfect for me. I'm blown away, but in a good way." She leaned over and kissed him. "Do you want a cigarette . . ."

Rio and Ian came out. Rio said quietly, "Let's go smoke a joint; we can go by the pool."

Gina stood up. "My mother is getting ready to serve dessert. You go ahead Rio." Trevor took Gina's hand as they walked through the French doors. The desserts were displayed on the dining room table. When Ant saw the pignolis, he exclaimed, "Oh Serena, you made my favorite cookie."

Serena turned around and said, "That was your sister who made them Ant. Thank her."

Ant was twelve years old but still came over and hugged his sister.

Frankie was fixated on the TV. "Can you fucking believe Dallas is going to win this game with Staubach out? Shit."

Gina was ready to leave. She whispered to Trevor, "I'm done, can we leave now?"

The best words of the evening were, "Sure baby. Anything you want."

Gina and Trevor were saying their goodbyes when Rio caught them. "Hey man, you guys leaving? Let's continue the party."

Gina looked at Rio, shaking her head. "Yeah, not tonight. I'm exhausted by being here. But you and I need to talk, band stuff you know, remember Vision Skye?"

There was a look between all three of the band guys; something was going on and Gina was on the outside.

FINDING OUT THE TRUTH

GINA AND TREVOR DROVE BACK to the carriage house. She was a little perturbed but didn't want to ruin a comfortable evening with her man.

They walked into the house and turned on a few lights. Gina pulled her dress off as she walked in, exposing a black bustier. She flipped off her shoes.

Trevor followed, laid out the leather jacket neatly on the chaise lounge in their bedroom, and took off his jeans. He walked over to Gina. "Remember when you said you were going to eat me up? I've been thinking of it all day. Come here."

Gina sat next to him and started kissing his neck and then traced her finger around his mouth. "Yeah, baby I will . . . I want to make you happy. But let me ask you, how come neither Stanley Park nor Vision Skye has many gigs coming up? Is it that you and Rio are going to form a band on your own? I mean, I keep wondering, all those looks between the three of you, something's going on." She worked her way down his stomach, tracing his body with her finger. Next, she pulled off his boxers. "See, I come through with what I promise . . ."

Trevor knew what she was doing and would give him the pleasure he craved.

But she was smart; she knew something was up and she wouldn't let it go. It would have to wait until the pleasure reached a climax.

As Trevor unhooked the bustier, Gina begged him, "Take me now."

After they sated their sexual appetites, Gina lit up a cigarette and handed one to Trevor. "When the fuck are you going to tell me what is going on with the music, band, and any other shit I should know? Why would you keep me out? I know it's something big . . . drop it on me, I can take it. I'm out, right? You three are going to form your own band. I know I'm the weak link here, but I thought you would have enough respect for me—"

Trevor stopped her. "G, it's not like that. There *is* something I'm keeping from you though. I was hoping to wait a couple of days, but you seem hell-bent on knowing now, so I'm going to tell you. It will upset you, but we're working on a solution, okay. So, when I tell you, try to remember we are working on a solution."

"For Christ's sake Trevor! I sucked your cock and made love to you, and you're dancing around this situation. Really, you don't trust me at this point of our relationship?"

"That's not fair to put our intimate life in the middle of this discussion, seriously. Can I have a cigarette, please? All right, get ready." Trevor took a deep drag on his cigarette and continued. "Stanley Park got notice two weeks ago that we need to go back to Canada; our visas are going to be void by December thirtieth. We got the wrong visas. We didn't know if we would be staying longer than the six months, the amount of time for a visitor visa, and then Sammy Gold extended it for another six months. But that's it. We have to get a work visa where someone sponsors the band. But other than Kevin, our sound guy, Ian, and I, we want to and need to come back. The rest of the band is fine with going back to Canada. I know that with Rio, Jeff, and *you*, we could have a real power band. We need to get back legally. So, baby, I'm sorry, I'll need to leave you"

Gina was stunned. "You . . . you what!?! You need to leave me? Are you kidding me right now? How long Trevor? A year, months? So you can forget me. Be real with me Trevor. How long?"

Trevor was afraid of her response. "Maybe six to eight weeks. Hopefully it doesn't take longer. You know I don't want to leave you, but if I don't go, they'll deport me. I may not be able to get back to the US. So that is the big secret. I've been dreading this."

Gina hid her face. Trevor took her hands away from her face, and she was sobbing violently.

"You see G, I knew this would be bad . . ."

Crying now hysterically, "I knew that this would be bad, but not that you have to leave me . . . to go back to Canada, on the other side of the country, and leave me, leave me . . . I can't process this . . . and Rio knows this before me. I think now, I was fun while you were here; you have no reason to stay. What was I? A fuck toy of yours, to only go back and find some Canadian bitch to take my place?"

She was wildly out of control. Gina felt every emotion. She started to have a panic attack and went for her Valium, muttering, "No, this can't be real. This can't be real." She started chain-smoking and hyperventilating. "I'm going to be all alone. What do I do without you? I can't understand. I don't want to understand." Gina ran into the kitchen, took a plate out of the cabinet, and smashed it on the floor. "You see that Trevor? That's what you have done to my heart, my spirit, everything."

"Gina, damn it, that's not true and you know it. What the fuck? I know I can be awful when I drink, but I never held back my love for you. And if you stop and think about it, you know it in your heart, we're supposed to be together, for a lifetime. I told you I found you . . . found you, above others. Please, please, we can get through this. You're the toughest woman I know."

Trevor was now crying with Gina. A God-awful period of time for two people who were destined to be together forever. It took an hour before the crying stopped. At that point it was a headache and there were no more tears.

Gina was still sniffling and struggled to find her voice. "How is Rio involved? What can he do to help? What can I do? I'll move there. I'll move there right now. I'll start packing. The idea of being here without you is like a knife in my heart." She started sobbing again.

Trevor tried to reason with Gina. "Listen our future is here, to get a record deal and make great music. It has to start here. We will reform the band and perform mostly original music, a few covers. I don't think that can happen in Vancouver. Please, you know this. You can't wait for me for eight weeks? I waited years to find someone like you . . . please wait . . . for . . . me." Trevor had tears down his cheeks.

They fell into each other's arms, exhausted by the emotion of it all. Somehow, this would work out. It had to. Lying in bed, Gina had a thought, "You will be here for Christmas, and you'll be gone for New Year's. Great way to bring in the New Year. How could 1975 be a good year?"

WORKING IT OUT

THE NEXT MORNING, Trevor and Gina were emotionally spent. They lay in bed wrapped in each other's arms. Hours passed before a word was said. Gina broke the silence. "I want Rio and Ian to come over. I want to talk about these options you mentioned. I want the answer. I don't want to go on maybes. Let's brainstorm the fuck out of this mess. I can hold on. I can. It will take every bit of my soul, but I promise I will be waiting. I'll be strong. I'm not sure how I will do it. We do have Christmas . . ." Gina started to get choked up again.

"Yes, G we have Christmas, and it will be the first of many, promise."

Trevor knelt down beside the bed. "I promise, it's the first of many . . . so many we might forget that it's Christmas as we're old and feeble."

Gina summoned a slight grin, hoping that was the truth. She got up to take a shower. As she let the hot water flow over her body, Trevor came in. "You don't mind if I join you, right?"

"Trevor let's pretend everything is normal. You never ask. Come in like we're fine. We have thirty-one days of we're fine."

When they finished, Gina put her robe on and a towel around her hair, then threw a robe at Trevor. She walked up and tussled his hair. Trevor hated the bathrobe Gina gave him. He was more comfortable lounging around in his boxers.

Gina announced, "It's time to call Rio and Ian. They are probably together."

"I'll call in a little; can we have coffee and your fantastic Belgian waffles first?"

"Of course, I feel like having one also. Give me about fifteen minutes, and coffee is ready now."

The phone rang as they finished eating. It was Sammy Gold.

"Sammy. What can I do for you?" There was snark evident in Gina's voice.

Gold was screaming into the phone. "I would like to know why Vision Skye and Stanley Park aren't taking any work. None at all."

"Well, to be honest, we're taking the month of December off, since as you know Stanley Park has to renew a visa. Yeah, it's a visa situation that you totally were informed about. So, I don't feel like working until Stanley Park is back from Canada. How do you like that? We aren't pulling out of any gigs. We aren't taking anything until everything gets squared away. That's all I need to say."

Sammy Gold was screaming, "Let me talk to Trevor!"

Trevor shook his head vehemently *no*.

"He doesn't want to talk, so I'm going to hang up and I will talk to you when we are ready to play."

She hung up the phone, then picked it up again and dialed Rio's number. She got his answering machine and left a message. "It's Gina. I know everything, and I would like you and Ian to come over so we can talk about solutions."

Rio and Ian were a bit shocked that Trevor had told Gina so soon, but it made sense. It gave her more time to digest what was about to happen.

Rio called back and wanted to bring Kevin, their sound man. "He wants in, and we need to bring Jeff in."

"That's fine; bring whoever, as long as we get something accomplished." Gina hung up.

Within an hour all the participants were at the carriage house. When Rio walked in, he hugged Gina. "I'm sorry I couldn't tell you sooner, I promised."

"Well Rio, there are a lot of promises going around here. I don't like to be minimized. Understand? Don't ever do that to me again." Gina felt hurt by her cousin's betrayal.

Rio laid it all out. "So, this is the situation. Stanley Park has to go back; there is no question there. I will keep the rent going in the house in Franklin Square so there is a place for them to come back to. We need to get a sponsor, someone who can put the band on their payroll. It has to be a job that can't be done by someone here in the US. The band would fall into that category. We need to find that sponsor and get the visa process fast tracked. We need to come up with who that person could be. Even with a sponsor it may take a few weeks to get all the paperwork done. Gina, you have any questions?"

"Rio, have you been reading up on this? You seem to know quite a bit on the subject."

"I have talked to an immigration lawyer; we can retain him if necessary."

Gina was flustered with lawyer talk. "Where is everyone going to stay in Canada?" She was more interested in where Trevor was landing.

Trevor calmed her. "Babe, I'll be staying with my father. He lives alone, so I'll hang out with him for a while."

Ian stepped up next. "There's a little family cabin I can stay in, and Kevin will stay with me."

"Sounds like everything is all set up nicely." Gina's voice was dripping with sarcasm. "What about the music? How is that being handled? Rio, have you disbanded Vision Skye?"

Rio shook his head. "Yeah, I told Rich, Craig, Kirk, and Eric—it's done. Jeff is all in."

Gina asked, "Is everyone going to be writing music while there is downtime?" Gina was eager to see how this would be handled. She had written some lyrics, but she didn't have any music background; she could only contribute the words.

This was Trevor's area of expertise. "I have some things in the works, nothing put all together, and Rio has the same."

"So, when we are brought back together, we should have some solid songs in the works. That should send Sammy Gold over the edge," Gina said with a smirk.

Ian added, "We can't use either of the band names; it has to be something new, a rebrand."

Various names were floated about for what seemed like hours. Nothing was resonating with one person. Everyone had all suggested wild-ass names. Then Gina asked each of the guys, "In one word, what do you think would be a great band name?"

Suggestions were wildly varied, all over the place: Beats, Sober, Soundcheck, Pump, Rhythm, and Mixed. No one agreed, lots of arguing. They couldn't agree on any one of the names offered up.

They seemed to come to an impasse. Gina asked, "What word would describe our style of music? Beside it being a hard rock band, what would you want it to be?"

Rio came up with "Kick-Ass," which Gina dismissed immediately. "We aren't calling ourselves Kick-Ass. It sounds like that's something we would do. What word then would describe bringing our two bands together as one?"

Jeff came up with "Unity." That was also rejected because the meaning could be misconstrued.

Finally, Gina landed on the idea of "Perfection." She explained that since the bands were comingled, it brought together the best of each band; they were a perfect mix of both bands. The music that was being written, they were writing true to their hard rock presence, which was perfect. Gina thought out loud, "We don't want to use Perfect, it's too simplistic. Our goal is to create Perfection. I think Perfection hits all of our desires as a band. To create music which is perfection."

It was also how Gina saw her relationship with Trevor, that was Perfection.

Rio looked at everyone. "Look, I get where Gina is going with this. I personally don't have an issue with it. God knows us dudes can't think of anything that isn't guy driven and we do have a female lead. We need to appease women also. I'm good with Perfection."

Ian and Kevin didn't care where they landed as long as they landed somewhere. Although Kevin did add that the sound equipment that Rio had was a sound engineer's idea of perfection. Jeff rolled his eyes a bit. He thought it was prissy, but he would go with it. Trevor looked at Gina knowing it meant more to her than just the music. He knew that she felt her life with him and the band was Perfection. He advocated that Perfection be the name.

Gina walked outside for another cigarette break so she could clear her head. She felt these guys needed to get their heads out of their asses. Finding a name for a band shouldn't be that hard.

Trevor came outside and joined her. "We think Perfection should be the name. The visa problem is too much for you, isn't it? I tried to make this as easy as I could."

"The only way you could do that is for it to go away, or become born an American citizen. Even if we got married you would still probably have to go back." Gina took three pills from her pocket and said, "Baby don't lecture me about the pills; my anxiety is off the charts. Let's go back inside. If they want to go out to eat, I'd rather stay home. If you want to go, I'm fine with it."

"No, I'm not leaving you, until . . . I have until the thirtieth."

Gina's eyes started to tear. That date became too real.

TIME FLIES

THE WEEKS BETWEEN THANKSGIVING and Christmas went by quickly.

The evenings with Trevor became so much more important to Gina. It was like a clock ticking to leaving town. She had already bought her immediate family their Christmas gifts, but she still had Serena, Uncle Tony, and Aunt Deidre to shop for. Rio would be a problem, but she had an idea. What was she going to get Trevor? She wished she could get him a visa, but that was out of her control. She decided on a distressed leather bomber jacket she had seen in Brooks Brothers.

She called the Ricci family jeweler, Pepe Notori, and asked him to make a tiny replica of Trevor's Les Paul guitar to hang from a thick gold chain. On the back of the guitar she had engraved, "G loves T 4 ever." Getting Rio something similar would be a sentimental gift for him. She had it engraved "Rio my brother, G." That should pull at his heartstrings.

Gina started wrapping the gifts for her family, using the finest wrapping paper and ribbon. She tied an ornament on top of each gift to match the recipient's personality. She found a rolling pin for Serena, a distinguished-dressed woman for her mother, and a Monopoly game for Ant. She also found two guitars that she hid from Trevor. It was difficult to find something for her father, but she did find a work desk that would suit Mario well.

Trevor was watching her. "I never saw anyone be so meticulous about wrapping a gift. I learn something every day about you. Can I help at all?"

"Sure. There are tags next to the roll of wrapping paper. I'll call out a name and you write it on the tag. Easy."

Trevor laughed. "That's a tough job."

His handwriting was magnificent, which struck Gina as strange, since his set lists were scribbled. He was always a happy surprise.

Christmas Eve was the next day. Gina was on edge; only five days left together for, well, she didn't know how long. It was snowing lightly making the property look like a Christmas card. Trevor and Gina took the phone off the hook and snuggled in their soft, cozy bed.

"Trevor, I want you to know . . . I can't go on without you in my life. I know it sounds dramatic, but from that first time I saw you, I knew I had to have you. Please don't forget me." Gina started sobbing.

"G, this is a setback, not the end. You know that. I'm only taking one of my guitars and leaving the other three here with you. You know I'll be back. Please don't cry . . . I might lose it."

Gina stared into his beautiful blue eyes and played with his long blond curls. "I want to look at you like this, so I'll have this picture in my mind."

She rolled on top of him, not necessarily to make love to him but to feel his body against hers. "I love this, feeling you so close to me. I can smell you, feel you, and look . . . those calluses on your fingers. I want to take you all in."

"G, can I make love to you now, so you can take that in too?" They made love all night and then Christmas Eve was upon them.

The Ricci estate looked like it should be in a Christmas magazine, white lights were strung through the trees and shrubs. Huge wreaths and gold ribbons hung from every window and door. There was an eighteen-foot balsam fir decorated with white, silver, and gold in the foyer. Every room on the first floor had a differently decorated Christmas tree. Franny always went with a traditional Christmas theme that would be found on Fifth

Avenue in Manhattan—beautiful and classy, nothing whimsical. She was married to that look with no deviation.

In the dining room was a sideboard filled with the Feast of the Seven Fishes, an Italian American tradition that was never missed. There was baccala, fried calamari, fried scallops, linguine with white clam sauce, scungilli salad, lobster, and shrimp cocktail. This feast was prepared by a caterer. Franny wasn't about preparing all the seven fishes, not her style. Of course, there was lasagna, meatballs, antipasto platter, and lots of traditional Italian desserts including cannoli, Gina's favorite. Poor Trevor, this guy from Vancouver, getting initiated into the most loved Italian American Christmas tradition.

Franny wore a beautiful red sequin cocktail dress. Mario was in slacks and a Christmas-themed shirt that Franny made him wear. Ant wore black slacks and an "off-color" themed Christmas sweater. Serena wore the same outfit every year, an empire dress with Christmas trees all over it. Frankie was wearing a suit and MaryAnn was wearing a frilly black dress. She looked like she was going to prom, not Christmas dinner.

Gina and Trevor drove to the front of the house, making a few trips to the car for the Christmas gifts and Gina's pignoli cookies. "Babe, are you going to be able to handle a bunch of drunken Italians tonight? Anything is possible and anything can be said. I think Frankie is going to propose to MaryAnn." Gina stuck her fingers down her throat pretending to throw up.

"Your drunken Italian family isn't any different than the drunks at the clubs we play," Trevor laughed.

As they reached the door, Rio got out of his car, wearing his usual black jeans, some artsy type of shirt, and his trademark sunglasses. "Hey, you two have been MIA. What gives?"

Gina gave him a look of disbelief. "Are you kidding?"

Rio went back to his car and took a joint out. "You want to smoke a joint before we go inside?"

Gina put the gifts down on the front stairs. "Sure, but we smoke in your car, not here by the front door. Are you crazy?"

They got in the car and Rio lit the joint, "Oh, hey Trevor, here, I have something for you; it's your ticket for the thirtieth. I got you, Ian, and Kevin first class, cool right? The other two guys are going coach, they're not coming back. It's an open-ended return, so we can book it when everything is resolved. I dropped off the tickets at the Franklin Square house for everybody."

Gina glared at Rio. "Did you have to do that now, seriously? You have no idea how that hurts; you do that in front of me?"

Rio was matter-of-fact about what he had done. "Gina, you know this is happening, you can't run away from it. At least I got them first class."

"You know what? You're an asshole. I'm going inside."

Gina flounced out of the car, wearing a clingy gold taffeta dress. When she entered the house, she was met by Ant, who was happy to see her. Gina always made Christmas special for him. She felt bad that she hadn't spent any time with him over the last six months. "Hi bro, you doing good? Are Mom and Dad driving you nuts?"

Ant laughed. "They are so drunk they have no idea what's going on. Guess what? The Fanellis are coming over later. I betcha Frankie is going to get engaged. What do you think?"

Gina groaned. "You know Ant, you are probably correct, and that sucks for all of us. Can you imagine what this wedding will be like?" A twinge of jealousy hit her. Why MaryAnn and not her? Although she and Trevor never really discussed marriage, she felt eventually it would happen. Maybe when they got a record deal. At this point she knew nothing about her future.

Her Mother came around the corner. "Merry Christmas, Gina! Why so sad, princess?"

Gina whispered, "Nothing. I will tell you later, in a quiet moment. I should let you know what is happening." Tears were forming in her eyes.

"Gina, should we talk now? You're trembling. What's going on?"

"Mom, I would like to talk, but please can it wait?"

The front door opened and Rio, Trevor, Uncle Tony, and Aunt Deidre walked in. She looked amazing in a beige, silk long-sleeved body-hugging dress.

"Hello everyone, we made the long commute. The house looks beautiful as always Franny." Aunt Deidre was the fun one. Franny was too serious.

Aunt Deidre threw a look at Gina, like she knew. Of course, Rio was the one who got the tickets.

Gina walked into the kitchen to see Serena. "Hi Serena, everything looks wonderful as always."

Serena grabbed her face. "Thank you, my beautiful princess. Merry Christmas. Oh, you brought the pignolis. Aren't you precious." Gina turned and there he was, her father. "Merry Christmas, Dad."

"Princess, you okay? I can always tell when something's bothering you."

"You know Dad, the holidays are stressful."

Mario had a scotch in his hand. "Where is that man of yours? Oh, there he is. Scotch, Trevor? Let's walk in the other room. I have the good stuff in there. Where's that nephew and brother of mine? Jesus . . . I shouldn't say that we are celebrating his birth." Trevor looked confused. Mario was taking him into his private office, the place few privileged people were invited to. Mario motioned for Rio and Uncle Tony to follow Trevor started to think,. "what kind of bloody hell is going on?"

Gina preferred the family room. It was less pretentious. Aunt Deidre sat next to her and grabbed her hand and kissed it. "Gina love . . . I know what's going on. Why pretend? You must be heartbroken; this Christmas is not a happy one for you. Rio and Uncle Tony are thinking of everything they can. Your uncle hired that immigration attorney. Everyone is trying their best. For you and Rio, he thinks that this band can get a record deal. I know separation hurts. I spent a month in Paris when I was modeling, and I was away from your uncle. I was in the City of Love, and it felt nothing like it." Aunt Deidre hugged her tightly.

Gina had tears running down her face. "Excuse me Aunt Deidre. I need to fix my makeup. I appreciate you. You understand." Gina went upstairs to her old bedroom, looking at her life before Trevor. She would never come back to "the big house." She sorted through her vanity and found some of her Chanel makeup and decided she would take all of it back home with her.

On the other side of the house Mario poured a generous amount of scotch for the men. "Can someone tell me what the fuck is going on? I can see that my daughter, well, she looks like she's having some sort of a breakdown. What the Christ sakes? I did it again, sorry Jesus. Someone better start talking real fucking fast . . . Tony why don't you tell me first, and Trevor, you're next. If you hurt my daughter, you and I have an issue, a big one. I trusted my daughter with you."

Uncle Tony jumped in. "Listen Mario, we have an issue. It has to do with visas. Trevor and the other guys have a visitor visa, which is good for only six months, and that guy, you know that talent agency guy? He extended it for another six months, but they have to go back. We need to try to get them a work visa. Someone has to sponsor the band. I got a guy, an immigration attorney. Hopefully, we can find a sponsor—"

Mario interjected, "Fuck me, Tony. Can't Ricci Construction or Ricci Inc. do it? Find out what the hell we have to do, Jesus. And you? You are planning on coming back to my daughter? I'll break your fucking fingers if you hurt her."

Rio jumped in. "Uncle Mario, no stop. Trevor, can I speak for you? Gina and Trevor love each other. He's not going to do that, and if you break his fingers, you'll screw me over and Gina too. He's my writing partner, we're going to make it, and so will Gina. Please listen to reason here."

Mario took a sip of his scotch. "Let me hear from you, Trevor. You have not said a blessed word."

Trevor was not afraid of Mario's threats; he realized that he would be in his life forever, so he better deal with him. "Mr. Ricci, do you think for one moment I want to leave Gina and everything that could be here? No, I don't fucking want to leave, but I also don't want to get deported and not be able to come back. I'm asking for a little compassion for both of us. You don't think it hurts me to leave Gina? She's my one. I found her. I found her and I'm not going to walk away. So, do whatever. I don't care but I'm coming home to her. So, yeah, we'll get it straightened out."

Mario poured another scotch. "We say nothing to the women, nothing. Let's get this shit done. My daughter is hurting and all this getting the band signed is the next thing that has to happen."

There it was. Trevor now saw why Gina wanted to distance herself from this family, why she and Rio changed their names. But people knew the world they came from and why they were chasing a far different dream than the families they were born into.

In the dining room, people had started eating. Franny asked Mario where he had had been. "It was nothing, a bunch of guys sharing a scotch." Trevor looked a touch shaken when he reached Gina.

Gina looked concerned. "Where were you? Sure you're good, baby? Seriously?"

Trevor stood up tall. "I'm good, you? Let's get wasted."

Gina laughed for the first time during the evening. "Wasted, huh? Yes, I'm in, but you still didn't tell me—"

"I had a scotch with your father, Uncle Tony, and Rio, that's all."

The doorbell rang and Franny answered the door. "Well how wonderful to see you! Welcome to our home. Mario, hon, the Fanellis are here."

Mario had known Pasquel Fanelli for years. He was a plumber in Manhasset with a great reputation. Mario ushered them into the dining room. "It's all good. Let's get some of this food."

Franny encouraged the family and guests to gather in the living room. Once everyone was assembled, Frankie, extremely sure of himself, got down on his knee and proposed to MaryAnn, handing her a four-carat marquis diamond.

MaryAnn pretended to be surprised and, fake crying, squealed "Yes, yes, I'll marry you." The Fanellis were there, so Gina felt this was clearly a staged event. Even though her parents hinted it was probably coming, Gina thought, *what a farce*.

However, Mario cheered, Franny cried, and everyone started giving their congratulations. Gina couldn't swallow her food. She went outside to smoke a cigarette and Trevor followed.

"Cigarette?" Gina offered Trevor. "Well, he did it and now it's going to be a huge Italian wedding. I hope I'm not in her wedding party and have to wear some tacky-ass dress. Fuck, fuck, fuck. I can only hope you're back by then."

Trevor reassured her, "I'll be back. But promise me, when the time comes and we marry, we elope to Vegas." She kissed him softly on the lips and told him, "Whatever you want works for me."

The evening was winding down and gifts were exchanged. Gina's parents gave her what she always wanted—money. She was a saver, other than spending money on food, weed, and cigarettes. Cashmere sweaters and designer bags were nice but only money mattered to her.

Gina and Trevor got home, stripped off their clothes and threw them around without a care. Gina put on her lacy underwear and one of Trevor's T-shirts. It smelled like him, and she wanted to take in every breath of him. They sat on the floor while Trevor took out his guitar and played bits of music he was trying to string together as a song. He started singing "Gimme Shelter." His voice was smooth. Gina had a much lower range so definitely couldn't hit the high notes of the background singer in the original version. Trevor told her how to use her low range to harmonize with him, while sounding strong. It took a few tries until she got it.

They played it several times and started laughing, "Can you imagine if this was our first record?" Gina asked. Stranger things happen in the music world. It was past midnight, so it was Christmas morning and Gina got excited. She went into the bedroom and told Trevor not to follow her. She put on a red lacy lingerie set and pulled several wrapped boxes out of the closet for Trevor. She wanted this moment, their first Christmas, to be as perfect as it could be, considering. Gina called, "Trevor, come here,

Santa came, come. Come get your gifts. They are all waiting for you in the bedroom. Come quick. Hold on, wait." Gina put her robe on and took a pitcher of spiked eggnog and glasses out of the fridge. She smiled, "Okay, now Santa brought you gifts, but he wants us to drink this also."

Gina gave him several cashmere sweaters so he would be warm in Vancouver. She gave him the leather bomber jacket. This way he would look badass as a lead singer. She bought him an acoustic guitar that he was always eyeing in magazines.

"G, my God, how did you know? I've wanted this since I started playing." Tears trickled down his cheeks. "I don't deserve this much; I never had this extravagant a Christmas in my life." He leaned over and gave her one of the kisses she loved—the soft tender kisses, where he would come back three or four times. Her favorite thing was to brush his hair away from his face while he kissed her.

"I have one more gift. I'm not sure you will like it, but here, I had it specially made."

Trevor opened the box and saw the gold replica of his Les Paul guitar. He turned it over and read the inscription. "G, I love it all. I love you. You pay such close attention to all the details of my life. I want to spend our time doing what we did tonight—singing together and laughing, and planning what we want in life."

"I want the same. You are my everything. All I need is to make my own way . . . with you."

Trevor looked nervous. "I have something for you. I wrote it down, but I thought I would play it for you first." He took the acoustic guitar out of the case and spent a few minutes tuning it. "I wrote you a song for your Christmas present. It's about me seeing you that first night. I was able to look through the crowd, with all the craziness, smoke, and drunkenness, and I found you. That's what I named the song: 'Found You.' It's the first song I want our new band to record. This song about us will live on forever if we record it and you'll always know that it was written for you."

Found You

I'm a singer, I play my guitar every night,
Every night the same as before, but tonight I
Looked across the room, with its smoke and noise
And people who didn't listen to the words
I was singing, and across the room by the
Window filled with stars I saw you
Found you, found you
I hope for the rest of my life
Found you, do you think you could find me?
So many before, but never could be you
Found you
I hope my crazy life doesn't distract you
I've been someone who has fallen into
Different troubles of the world
I couldn't imagine any other woman could be more
Attractive, no one could have your class your smile
Found you, found you
I hope for the rest of my life
Found you, do you think you could find me?
So many before, but never could be you
I've made mistakes, many, I haven't been a perfect
Man, but today I might be lucky to have
A woman like you, who will love me as I am
Found you, found you
I hope for the rest of my life
Found you, do you think you could find me?

"You wrote that about me? Us? I can't put into words how I'm feeling right now. It's beautiful. I couldn't think of any better gift you could have given me." Gina reached over and pulled him close. She rubbed her nose to his and stared into his blue eyes and kissed him. All the horrible events about to take place, for a moment, didn't matter. He wrote this beautiful song for her; it would always be her song, their song.

Trevor let out a sigh. "I haven't written the parts for you yet; we sing it together. I'm still working out harmonizing. I think it will start off soft and slow and then the last choruses will be rocking. What do you think?"

Gina didn't know anything about writing music like Trevor and Rio did. "You are the music writer. If I can sing with you, that's all I need. This could be the song that makes Perfection a real band. I'm so honored and amazed you wrote this about us. So, we can never split up you hear me?"

Trevor gave her a handwritten copy of the words, written on a gold piece of paper with his excellent penmanship. "Here, you have the original. One day we will frame it and hang it in our own home."

Gina sat in his lap, playing with his long hair, which always turned her on. She whispered in his ear, "I love you. I love you and you did, you . . . found me." In five days, Trevor was taking a flight from JFK to Vancouver. "Don't you have one more gift to give me?"

Trevor looked perplexed for a moment, then realized where she was going. He lifted her up and carried her over his shoulder and threw her onto the bed. "Is that what you were talking about?"

Gina gave him a sultry look and raised up her elbows. "Yes, but I want you to be rough with me. Take me hard and don't ask me if you're hurting me because I want it that way."

Trevor was a bit hesitant. "You're going to be sorry you said that."

SOLUTIONS

THE NEXT MORNING Gina and Trevor were still deciding if they wanted to join Christmas dinner or hide away for the next couple of days. Around ten o'clock, the phone rang. Gina had a feeling it might be her mother telling her what time Christmas dinner was being served. She was afraid to answer. She didn't know if she wanted to share the precious moments she had left with Trevor. She made herself answer, and it *was* Franny.

"Hi, Mom. What's up? Is it about dinner?"

"Your Father and I decided we are going to have Christmas brunch. Serena is cooking up a storm, even lobster omelets. Isn't that wonderful? And of course, mimosas. You and Trevor don't have a choice, it's just us. I like your Trevor, Gina. Gina, it would be nice to be able to spend more time with him. He is part of our family now. I expect to see the both of you."

Gina was confused. "When you say 'us,' do you mean me and Trevor? Or are you talking about the whole family? You're confusing me."

Franny explained that Frankie was going to the Fanellis' for Christmas dinner because of their engagement. "So, I thought you and Trevor, Dad, Ant, and I could have brunch. It will let you out of dinner."

Gina sighed, "What time were you thinking?"

Franny said, "I'm thinking noon."

Gina covered the receiver and whispered to Trevor who was still groggy from sleep. "My parents want us to go over for brunch. If we do that, we're out for dinner."

Gina was waiting for Trevor's answer, "What do you think?"

Gina repeated herself and Trevor yawned loudly. "Yeah, sure, why not. Do we need to get dressed up?"

"Mom, we don't have to dress in Christmas finery, do we? Can we come in jeans? You know, be casual?"

"Gina, darling, I don't care what you two wear. Come. But don't come in your pajamas."

"No worries, Mom. We will be wearing clothes, not pajamas."

Gina strode over to the kitchen and put the coffee on. She walked into the bathroom and looked at her face. She had slept in her makeup again and started giving her face an exfoliating wash. Trevor stepped into the bathroom and peed. Everything was so normal. But in five days the worst thing for Gina was going to happen.

Gina walked into the bedroom and handed Trevor his coffee and sat down next to him with her coffee in hand. "Thank you for last night. The song was incredible. I'm still taken by the words. I really hope we eventually get a record deal. I also want to thank you for being rough. It was so sexy to see you like that. You make rough, sexy. I have to take a shower now, so finish your coffee and get your ass in there with me."

"Damn, Gina. You're a demanding woman. I'll be there in a minute." Trevor smiled.

Trevor wore a Zeppelin concert T-shirt and one of the knees of his jeans had a rip. It was a fashion statement. Gina was not sure Franny would think that way, but she thought it was cool. She wore a new beige cashmere sweater with pearl collar that her aunt gave her. *It's a little dressy*, Gina thought.

"Should we walk? It snowed last night, it might be fun. Wear the bomber jacket, please. You will look like a lead singer for sure."

Trevor put the jacket on and looked in the mirror. "I do look badass, don't I?" That's what Gina wanted him to be—a man who dressed and oozed rock star.

"Yeah, you do, but your ass belongs to me, Mr. Badass."

The two of them walked up the long driveway, throwing snow at each other, laughing as they approached the door.

Franny greeted them at the door. "Having fun?"

"Hi Mom. When have you ever greeted people at the door like this? I can count on my fingers."

"Come in you two love birds. It's sweet." Franny smiled.

Gina's head was on a swivel. *Who is this lady? Not the mother I grew up with. Something's up. That's why she planned a brunch.*

Franny motioned them into the sunroom off the kitchen, "I thought we would be casual and take in the festive scenery."

Mario entered the room, scotch in hand, "Trevor, let me get you a scotch. You don't want those, what are they called Franny? Mimosas? It's a woman's drink, not a man's."

Trevor nodded. It was early even for him to drink scotch. There was a time when he would finish a bottle of whiskey by ten o'clock a.m. Gina hadn't seen that man yet.

Gina chirped, "How nice you decided to do this instead of another dinner. This is much better. Where's Ant? Is he coming down?"

"Yes of course, sweetheart. However, your father and I wanted to talk to the two of you about this situation. It sounds difficult, but maybe not so much. If we as a family sponsor Trevor and the other gentlemen, I don't know how long this would take, but I think we could try to work out something. Gina, is this what you were going to talk to me about last night? Poor darling, I don't like seeing you so sad, especially when we can help."

"Mom, I found out Thanksgiving night, the night before you met Trevor. Why would I think this was something you would help with? Please don't misunderstand. I'm extremely appreciative that you and Dad are willing to help. If you didn't offer, I'm sure I would have spiraled out of control. We have so many dreams—being together, recording music, forging our path, even though you may think we're crazy."

Mario stood up. "Gina, this is definitely not what your mother and I had in mind for your livelihood. However, you have always been our child who did something different. So, why would I expect you to do anything else? As long as this guy here promises that he will protect you. You understand me, Trevor?"

Trevor was wondering about the whole conversation. He felt like it was target practice. He put down his drink. "I would never let anything happen to Gina. I believe we can be something special. This kind of lifestyle is a tough one. Even when you think you're great, there are other people who control if you have it or not. I believe we have something special. It's going to take hard work and a lot of rejection, but we are strong, especially when we are together. That's the best I can give you, and the fact that I love your daughter. That's what I have to offer. I am also humbled that you are willing to help with the visa. I can't begin to tell you how thankful I am."

Serena walked in. "Merry Christmas. Come eat some of this food—bacon, sausage, waffles, lobster omelets, fruit salad."

Ant came into the room grinning. "Isn't this great? Brunch instead of dinner. Mom and Dad are going to the Fanellis' for dinner."

Gina couldn't hold her tongue, as usual. "Oh, I see, discussing wedding plans already. They got engaged last night. I give it to MaryAnn she is locking down Frankie quickly. Can I say one thing about this? And I'm serious. Please discourage her from having me in her wedding party. I don't want to wear an ugly bridesmaid dress. I think I'll wretch."

"Gina, I don't like to hear that. It's your brother. MaryAnn lacks a fashion sense. I mean the way she dresses—phew, it's terrible. The Fanellis can't afford the type of wedding that a Ricci deserves, so we will help pay for some of the costs. Does that assuage your concerns?"

Gina flippantly responded, "Not really. Let's eat this delicious food Serena prepared and I can get hammered drinking mimosas."

Trevor leaned over to Gina. "Remember what I said. We're eloping."

Ant poured himself an oversized portion of the mimosas. "This orange juice is bad."

"It's orange juice with champagne Ant," Gina informed him. "Join us in getting drunk."

Gina spit out a mouthful of mimosa, spraying Ant in the face. "Sorry, bro." laughing her ass off.

It was a colder walk back to the carriage house than when they left. Trevor walked into the apartment and asked about the stone fireplace. "Does this work or is it for show?"

"I'm sure it works. Why? Do you know how to make a fire? I sure as hell don't."

Trevor opened the flue, then walked outside and found wood stacked on the other side of the carriage house. Within minutes, he had a fire started.

Gina yelled from the bedroom. "Oh my God Trevor, something's burning."

"Come out here. I started a fire. There's plenty of wood outside. How about we spend the next couple of days sitting by the fire. That's the image I want to have when I go to sleep and you're not there."

Gina walked into the living room, kneeled on the carpet, and began crawling on all fours. "I can't take how fucking sexy you are, driving me mad. I'll get some pillows and the duvet from the bed and bring them out here by the fire." She got up and returned with the pillows and duvet. "It's still Christmas; we should put on Christmas music."

Trevor shook his head. "I hate Christmas music. How about classical?"

"Sure, fine. I'm good with that. Are we staying dressed or are you going to be naked for the duration? I want to know."

Trevor flung his hair back and grinned, "Gina Ricci Poole, you are a dirty woman. You are always trying to find ways to be naked. I like it."

Gina performed a strip tease, then relieved Trevor of every stitch of clothing. The heat from the fire felt good, and they stared at it lying there together. Gina asked about the times Trevor mentioned he got into trouble and had issues with drinking. He never went into detail, but she wanted to probe a little. Nothing would change.

She touched Trevor's face. "You've now had a real dose of my family. But you never talk about *your* family."

Trevor nodded, "I realized I haven't shared anything about my family situation. It's not fair to you."

Gina then asked, "Is there a reason? I want to know about your life back in Canada. You said you would be staying with your father."

"Yes, it's where I grew up, so it's the only place for me to go. My father won't care, he doesn't care about much honestly."

Gina had noticed Trevor never spoke about his mother. "Is your mom alive? I'm not trying to hurt you by asking."

Trevor's voice cracked as he responded, "My mother died in a car accident when I was thirteen. I'll just say that event changed my life forever. She slid off an icy road into an embankment and died. It's the reason my father is the way he is."

Gina had no idea about the sadness in his life. She needed to ask, "And the drinking? How bad was it? Did you take pills too?"

Trevor knew he had to share these things with Gina, but it was difficult for him. "After my mother died, it was just my father and me. He checked out. He worked long hours. I was lost. I hated everything about my life. I was left home alone, so I got in trouble. I started drinking at thirteen. When I got older, I stopped going to school and started stealing alcohol—mostly whiskey, but whatever I could get away with. My friends and I would drink all day, get stinking fucking drunk. I was probably drunk every day for three or four years. And I got high on whatever I could get my hands on. Then a friend of mine started bringing us pills, mostly downers, so with the alcohol, I was shit-faced all the time. My father did what he could, but he would have his three or four beers and fall asleep. I got three drunk driving citations. They were going to suspend my license, but my father talked them out of it because I needed to drive for work. That was half ass because all I wanted to do was play guitar. My father gave me one when my mother died, hoping I wasn't going off the deep end, which I did anyway. He couldn't handle me sometimes, and when I got caught by the police for any reason, I went to juvenile detention. I have a drinking issue. I try not to indulge too much because it might set me off. Those demons are always waiting to come out. I need to watch myself and need you to help me not fall."

Gina was a bit shell-shocked but tried not to show it. "Trevor, my love, I don't know what to say. You were so young, so many issues. Your father didn't get you help? That makes me sad. "I know there were women before me. Is all this the reason why none of your relationships stuck?"

"Baby, I was unable to keep myself straight. The women, you know I was a dick. Women see you drunk and shit, they start getting on your case. Some of them were nice, pretty girls but I didn't treat them right. Or I would talk to them very cruelly and even cheat on a few. That is never good, so lots of messy situations. Ian helped by directing me to music, playing guitar, and I discovered I had a pretty good voice. I found some solace in music; we played parties and raunchy bars. Some agent saw us and told us that we needed to leave Vancouver and go to LA or New York. We chose New York because it has a big club circuit. What else do you want or need to know?"

She placed her hand on his cheek, "My sweet, handsome man. I'm sorry for everything. I bitch about my life, but you have a lot of pain, even demons. I know now to make sure you never go down that hole of despair. I don't want there to be things we don't know about each other. I'm glad you shared this with me, I can't believe you went through such a horrible childhood. You know my deal. I'm glad you let me in. I'm not judging you. I want the next level of you, especially because you're going back there, hopefully for not too long. It sounds like it won't be a happy homecoming. I wish you didn't have to go back. I won't be there to give you the love that you so need."

Trevor added, "I'm glad I told you about all my demons and what my life was like, so you know what my weaknesses are. I've seen everything in your world. I've lived in this place for the last six months and never talked about myself. That stuff doesn't matter anymore. I'm here with you . . . and I'm a different person. I finally understand what love is about and that it's good, no excellent."

They lay by the fire for hours, adding logs so it wouldn't go out.

They looked to the future and talked about how they both wanted it to play out. Play a couple of years in better clubs, get a following on their original music, get a record deal, pump out music, go on tour. They would be together, no long tour dates apart. Buy a beautiful apartment in Manhattan. Gina could have a few babies. It was a lovely picture they painted.

Gina looked up at Trevor. "Baby, we have made lots of promises to each other, but I need to tell you, I hate cheaters and I hate groupies. I don't ever want to see a bunch of groupies at any of our shows. And if you ever want to cheat on me, don't."

"I promise Gina, I won't." Trevor loved her.

BEING APART

IT WAS THE DAY BEFORE Trevor's flight. Rio had already volunteered to drive to JFK, because there was no way Gina was going to be able to drive in the state she was in. She would lose it when Trevor went through the doors to the international flights he would walk through alone. Leaving Gina outside those doors. Rio was afraid he would have to pick her up off the floor while she screamed. Gina was putting on a good face for everyone; she believed her father and Uncle Tony would get the proper paperwork done. She had to hope; hope was all she had.

Trevor started getting his things together and realized he didn't have a suitcase. Gina went to her old bedroom and found a big black suitcase. Once Trevor started placing his clothes in the suitcase, Gina lost it. She took his clothes out as he put them in.

"I need to take *some* clothes with me. I'm leaving guitars and my records, everything that means something to me. I'm leaving them with you. Stop. You know I have to do this."

"Please take off that shirt; I want to have your smell. I want to sleep with it every night. I won't change the sheets. I need to smell you with me." Gina was choking out the words between sobs. Tomorrow she would be coming back here alone.

Trevor pleaded, "Please don't cry the whole time our last night together. Wouldn't you like to spend it another way? I want to leave you loving me."

They went to bed that night, savoring every inch of each other. Gina stayed awake all night, watching Trevor sleep, taking in every bit of his face, his hair, his chest. As morning approached the dagger went deep into her heart. Rio would come early because of the traffic on the Long Island Expressway. Trevor showered, got dressed, and begged Gina to try to be calm, to no avail.

Rio showed up somber; he knew there was no way to get around Gina today. He would have to "manage her." He walked up the stairs, almost like he was walking into jail, slow with a heavy foot. When he knocked at the door, Trevor answered. Rio asked, "Is she bad? Don't answer. I know already."

Gina looked wrecked. She hadn't slept or showered.

Rio was firm with her. "No Gina. Go take a quick shower. You're not going out like that."

She didn't have the strength to argue and went back inside to take a quick shower and get dressed.

Trevor sat up front while Gina lay down in the back seat, half asleep—a zombie. Rio found parking at the Air Canada terminal. They grabbed the luggage out of the trunk and walked silently through the automatic doors to the terminal. The rest of Stanley Park took two cabs to JFK. Since only Ian and Kevin would be returning, they went in one. The other ousted members took all their belongings and got in the other cab.

Trevor couldn't check in until he went through the doors leading to international flights. Rio gave Trevor a hug. "Hey man, I'll be in touch every couple of days to let you know how things are progressing. Safe flight."

Trevor squeezed Rio's shoulder. "Take care of Gina for me."

Rio backed away to let Gina and Trevor have a minute alone. "G, don't cry. I love you, you know that it will be okay. Baby, please. I'll get to see my father."

Gina through her tears said, "Don't call me, I'll call you. This way your dad doesn't have to pay the phone bill."

"Alright, but I'll call you when I get there."

After one last kiss, Trevor walked through the doors that led to the international flights.

Gina leaned on Rio and broke down. He tried hard to console her, but it was no use. Rio didn't have the words to make anything better. "Gina, you need to walk to the car. Can you do that, please?" Rio was able to get her to the parking lot and into the car. She would release an occasional sob, but she was doing her best to hold it together.

Tomorrow was New Year's Eve. The traffic was heavy on the Long Island Expressway. Rio said to Gina, "Hey, you want to smoke a joint? It might help."

"No, I don't want to smoke a fucking joint. Damn Rio, I can't think straight as it is." Thank goodness the airport was only twenty minutes from their houses.

Rio pulled into a fast-food place. "I'm starving, I need food. Can I get you something? You should eat something."

Gina looked over at him with mascara streaks running down her face. "Coffee, I want coffee."

Once they got their food, Rio pulled into a space to eat. He handed Gina her coffee and noticed she popped four Valium. "Gina, seriously, you need to watch how many pills you're taking. I'm now officially concerned about what you are going to do to yourself."

Gina snapped back. "Don't judge me. I'll be fine. Do you honestly think I would do something to hurt myself when I'm looking forward to a lifetime with someone, the band? Why would I hurt myself? That's stupid."

"I'm sorry. I'm worried, that's all. We all have a lot to gain. It will happen, I promise you."

"Well Rio, a lot of promises have been made. I'll leave it at that," Gina snapped back.

Rio punched in the code at the Ricci estate and drove to the carriage house. Gina managed to walk up the stairs to the little apartment she shared with Trevor. Rio was behind her, watching as she opened the door. She went in and walked around the living room, touching Trevor's guitar cases, his records. She went into the bedroom, picked up his T-shirt and smelled it. She closed her eyes and smelled the shirt again.

"Gina, you all right?"

"It smells like him. I think I want to be alone." She put her face in his shirt and started sobbing. Rio kissed her head. "I'll give you space. You need to work this out."

Rio left Gina in her misery and drove up to his aunt and uncle's house. Aunt Franny would want to know Gina's state of mind. Rio walked through the front door and Serena came to see who it was. "Oh Rio, so nice to see you. Can I get you something?"

"No thank you, Serena. I'm here to see Aunt Franny."

Serena announced, "She's coming now, Rio."

Franny walked through the foyer with fabric swatches in her hand. One look at Rio and she knew. "Rio, is it princess?"

"Aunt Franny, she's a mess. I can't get through to her. Maybe you should go see her."

Franny gave Rio a hug. "Thank you for taking her to the airport. She would never have been able to drive back. Give me a moment." Franny walked back to her office. She thought of her daughter, raw and emotional, and started to cry. She let herself have a few tears, then got her coat and keys. Rio was still in the hallway. "Rio, I'll go to her. Thank you again, I know you love her."

Franny told Serena, "If Mr. Mario comes home, tell him I went out."

Serena nodded her head in acknowledgment.

Rio walked out with his aunt. "Rio, if you're free tomorrow, come over for a drink; it is New Year's Eve. We can at least toast for a good year."

"Yeah, Aunt Franny, I'll stop by. See you tomorrow."

Franny got into her car and drove down to the carriage house. This was a new moment for Franny. She loved her children but consoling them always fell to Serena. She was the warm one who made everything better. Franny was a working woman; she was busy. She and Mario entertained clients. Their lives were filled with obligations; consoling her children was not one of them. She knew she had to walk into that apartment and be there for her daughter but had no idea of the words to use. She opened the door and saw Gina sitting on the floor holding two of Trevor's T-shirts, classical music playing.

"Gina, I'm here my princess. I'm so sorry." She knelt down next to Gina on the floor and raised Gina's tear-streaked face up to hers. She placed her head in her lap and stroked her hair. "Gina, let it all out. Take your time, I'm not going anywhere."

When her crying finally stopped, Gina asked her mother, "Why are you here?"

"Gina, you're my daughter and you're hurting. When you hurt, I hurt with you. I didn't do enough of that when the three of you needed me, but I'm here for you now. Your father and uncle are working for a solution to bring your Trevor back as quickly as possible. I'll be here until you cry it all out. You have to have faith, Gina. You remember in school they taught you about faith? If you believe, God will hear you. God has a plan for all of us, and he has one for you and Trevor. Lean on your faith, Gina. Now, let's make some chamomile tea. I know there is some here."

Gina got up and walked to the table while her mother put the kettle on. Gina had never realized how devoted to the Catholic church her mother was. She was always doing charity work at St. Mary's. Her mother loved that church and was one of their biggest donors. The kettle whistled, and Franny poured two cups of tea.

"Mom, I appreciate you coming here. I don't know what to do all alone. You said it's temporary. I hope so. My life plan is Trevor, the band, and making it to the big time. I never thought my life would lead to this, but it's what I want."

"Tomorrow is New Year's Eve. I think you should come up to the house. We aren't doing much, having your aunt and uncle over for a lovely dinner, a few cocktails. I know Ant would love to spend time with you. Rio said he would come for a drink. You need to get out of this place for a night. Please say yes, we would all love to welcome 1975 with you." Franny tried to make it sound like a good time.

Gina didn't want to be alone either. Maybe seeing Ant would be a distraction. They could play some stupid board game or watch the ball drop. She would watch Dick Clark's New Year's Rockin' Eve. They always had some band lip syncing to a popular song. "You know what Mom? Yes, I'll come. I'll even spend the night in my old bedroom. I probably have things in there that I forgot about, or I can actually use. Yes, yes, I would like that. I'll need to call Trevor sometime in the evening."

"Wonderful Gina. Knowing that, I think I can leave now. Kiss your mother."

Gina gave her mother a kiss and a hug. "Thank you. It's good to know I have a place to go, and it's still home. What is Serena making for dinner?"

"Oh Gina, how silly you are. You know she always makes chateaubriand with those special potatoes. I'm sure it will all be exquisite. Your father is probably wondering where I wandered off to."

With that Franny left. Gina was interested in what treasures she still had in her room, and one in particular. Gina went for a shower, sad she would be taking it alone. Trevor would not be walking in, no lovemaking, just a shower.

She got out of the shower, put on her bathrobe, and wrapped her hair in a towel. She started watching the clock. It had been a good eight hours since Trevor boarded his plane. Gina started thinking, certainly Trevor's plane should have just landed. She wondered when he would call, to hear his voice. Maybe he was catching up with his father. She had to stop thinking the worst; he would call. Gina settled on the couch and turned on the TV. She found a College Bowl game and turned the sound down. She called

Rio. Maybe he was with some girl. There were always girls who wanted to be around him. Like Trevor, he had that star quality. He was as excellent a musician as Trevor. Their band would certainly have something that a record company would want to sign. Rio picked up.

"Hey, umm I'm sorry for today, being so emotional. I've wound down a bit. My mother said you were going to stop by tomorrow."

"Gina, it's cool. I get it. Your man went away. You two are tight, but maybe use some of that pain to write some lyrics. It could make for a great song. People identify with pain."

"Sounds like an idea. So, you're stopping by tomorrow. What's up? No date?" Gina feigned interest.

"You're funny. I actually double-booked dates, and you know what? They knew each other, so they both backed out and called me a prick. I deserve it. Maybe after, I'll check out one of the clubs. I don't suppose you would want to go?"

"That's a big negative for me. Plus, it will be fun spending time with Ant. Are you coming for dinner? You should. Serena is making chateaubriand and those potatoes we all like and she won't give anyone the recipe."

"Maybe. I need to see what pops up, you know?"

"Yes, I know, Rio . . . your lengthy list of ladies, whatever. I'll see you tomorrow. Do you have weed? I checked my stash and I'm out. I have one joint to get me through tonight."

"No worries there. See you tomorrow." Gina hung up the phone and turned back to the TV—the Gator Bowl, Auburn vs. Texas. She was going for Auburn. She actually thought of going to school in Alabama if Miami didn't work out. That went to hell.

She was dozing when the phone rang. "Hello? Trev, is it you?"

"Yes, baby it's me. How are you doing? I know that's a stupid question. I'm an ass."

"Well, I spent most of the day crying my eyes out. Rio couldn't take it anymore, so I think he asked my mother to come down. Unbelievable.

Franny came down and let me cry, then made me tea, and told me it's God's plan for us to be together. She was trying. She has never been the one to be a consoler, but she did it.

"How's your father? Happy to see you?"

"I guess so. I had to tell him about the whole situation with the visa. Don't think he exactly got it. I told him about you, how much I loved you and had to go back. He said, 'She must be some woman, to love a fucked-up guy like you.' So that was nice. You love me even if I'm a fucked dude, right?"

"I love you always. I missed you in the shower tonight. I miss seeing you and it's not even a day. I hope this process won't take long. I didn't even realize that tomorrow is New Year's Eve, did you?"

"I didn't either until I drove back from the airport and saw Happy New Year's signs in the local bars. I'm not about celebrating. I'll probably write some songs. I can't imagine you doing anything."

"I'm going to my parents' house for dinner. I'll hang out with Ant and watch football and the ball drop. At least I won't be alone. Remember, I'll call you at my time at twelve and then I'll call you at your time, to wish you Happy New Year."

"Gina, that's three a.m. your time! That's nuts. Don't."

"Shhhh. I want to be the first to wish you happy 1975. I think it will be a great year for us."

"Listen baby, I don't want to stay on the phone too long. It's an international call."

"I get it. That's why I'll call you every night. Twelve thirty a.m. my time, nine thirty your time. Trevor, I love you so much."

"I love you more. Go to bed thinking of the dirtiest thing we ever did . . . I love you."

Click.

Gina fell asleep on the couch, thinking of the day they bought a copy of the *Kama Sutra*. They both wanted to try as many sexual positions as possible, every position in one night. She remembered them looking at the book and staying up all night experimenting. They both used body oil that when you used it made your skin warm. Of course it was used on the most sensitive parts of their bodies. It took their lovemaking to an extremely heightened level. Gina could remember at least six different positions; she was amazed they got in that many. And she also remembered having so many orgasms it was heaven.

The next morning Gina woke up on the sofa and turned on the pregame shows. She put on a pot of coffee, remembering she only had to make enough for herself. She decided Rio was correct. She should put her pain in lyrics. She needed to contribute, and words were the only thing. She rummaged in the other bedroom closet and found her FIT notebooks. She started chain-smoking and writing random thoughts . . .

Untitled (Waiting)

Today my heart breaks in pieces bit by bit
People say it will go away,
I disagree
They say a love like ours is so special and time will heal
But time stands still when you're alone and what you feel
Is time doesn't understand the pain, it doesn't go away
But everyone tells you it will go away
I disagre,
The only thing to cure my pain is when I hold you, touch you
Smell you, then the pain will slide away and to love you
Love you always and that I will agree

It needed to be reworked but she would show it to Rio. The lyrics were so personal. Maybe she would wait for Trevor to come home, and they could work on it together. They were a team in their personal life and musically. She would write more, but not today. It was New Year's Eve after all. She would get dressed and go up to her parents' house, hang out with her brother, and look through her old room.

SEPARATION

HER MOTHER HADN'T MENTIONED Frankie and MaryAnn. She hoped they had planned to be somewhere other than the Ricci home. Gina jumped in the shower and washed her hair again. It was out of control.

She would talk to her father about this situation and how it was being managed. He would be honest. Her mother didn't say to dress formally, so she put on her favorite comfortable jeans, another cashmere sweater, and boots.

It was thirty-one degrees outside, so she would drive up to the house. She could hear the football game when she walked in and her father cursing every time a play didn't go the way he wanted. She went directly to the kitchen and saw Serena.

"How are we today, princess? Feeling any better? That's silly, probably not."

"Serena, I'm managing, that's the best I can do. I love you for asking. Did you make those potatoes? That's why I decided to come," she laughed.

"Of course I did. And I still won't give you the recipe."

Gina peeked into the family room. "Hi Daddy. Hi Ant. Getting pissed at the games?"

"Ehh, same shit every year. Some piece of shit team beats the favorite. How are you, princess? Can I get you a drink?"

"Do you have martinis already mixed?"

"You know I do, hold on."

"Hey Ant, I thought maybe we could play a board game later, but not Risk. That takes too long."

"Sure, Gina let's do that. Are you okay? Mom and Dad said you were upset that Trevor had to leave. I'm sorry. I don't want to see you hurting."

Gina punched his arm. "Thanks bro. I appreciate it, means a lot. Speaking of brothers, where is the newly engaged Frankie?"

"Him and MaryAnn are going to some fancy party in the city."

"Yeah, sounds right. MaryAnn has big eyes, only the best. What a bitch. I hate her." Gina was disgusted.

Mario handed Gina a martini in a chilled glass. "Sit down princess. I want to talk to you about Trevor's situation."

"Am I going to be upset?"

"No. Your uncle talked to that fucking immigration lawyer. You know I hate lawyers. Anyway, he said Ricci Inc., not Construction, could sponsor, but your Uncle Tony would be named manager. In name only of course. I mean, what the hell? He doesn't know how to manage a band. But then he could say these guys have a special skill set. He also suggested that Rio, you, and that guy Jeff join the American Federation of Musicians. There is a Canadian Federation. You should tell Trevor and that other guy . . . What's his name? It starts with an I or something. Anyway, it will establish you all as musicians. We will have this lawyer find a lawyer in Vancouver he can work with and move things along. You get me?"

"It sounds great. I don't know what to say but thank you Daddy. This means everything. Do we know how long?"

"It's up to the guy in Canada to push it through. Of course, we will tell him it needs to be expedited. But we will apply a little pressure, you got me?"

"Clearly, Daddy. I think I will enjoy this martini now. It will go down a little smoother."

Franny walked in. "Gina, you *are* spending the night, correct? It will be fun. Dinner will be ready soon. I guess I should have a cocktail." Franny picked up the martini shaker and poured herself drink.

Uncle Tony, Aunt Deidre, and Rio walked into the family room. Gina couldn't wait to tell Rio about the visa situation, but he probably knew already. Everyone settled in around the TV, watching the Sugar Bowl. Gina didn't care who won; she hated both teams. Serena gave them a five-minute warning for dinner. Gina took the opportunity to go outside in the freezing weather to have a smoke, and asked Rio to join her.

As they stood on the patio, Rio asked, "Do you want to smoke a joint? No one will notice. I also have your stash. I'll give it to you after dinner, cool?"

"Yeah, Rio, it's cool." Gina needed that stash.

Rio wanted Gina to know, "I'm sure you are aware of what's going on with the visa situation."

Gina responded, "Yes, I just spoke to my father and he told me the strategy."

Rio remained optimistic. "My dad said he has it under control, but Gina, keep in mind we don't know the timeline. It could happen next week, or it can happen six weeks from now."

"Rio, I understand that, but you realize that I feel like a part of me is gone. Mom said I need to have faith. I have faith it won't be an extended period of time; it can't be. I miss him."

"Try to be patient. I have a huge stake in this too. It's about putting the right band together. I want it to happen now, start playing gigs again. I'm getting some really cool sounds together. I can't wait for Trevor to come back too."

"I finished my cigarette. Where's the joint? Light it up already." Gina was antsy.

Everyone sat and enjoyed a tasty dinner and, for once, a relaxing conversation. Gina and Rio played board games with Ant and goofed around like they did when they were kids.

Later, Gina had a mission to check out her old room. She knew there were items in there she would want. Franny handed out Christmas crackers she had left over. The pops, the silly hats, the toys, and everyone read their jokes. Gina turned on Dick Clark's Rockin' Eve. The ball drop was coming soon and some band was playing. She said to Rio that Perfection would never lip sync. They would sing live. It was two minutes until midnight. She had to call Trevor. She excused herself, walked upstairs to her old bedroom, and turned on the TV. She dialed Trevor's number. It rang three times, and he picked it up. "Hi G, is this you? You cut it close."

"Hi, my love . . . miss you. I'm here at my parents'. Rio showed up. It's been a low-key New Year's. If I'm not with you, I guess this is the next best place. I have some news about the visa situation. It sounds promising."

"Yeah, I heard. Rio called me and told me the news. Now we wait."

"Hold on. Rio called you. He could have let me talk to you. Why did he go behind my back?"

"Gina, stop. Rio has a stake in this too. Having your uncle listed as manager, it's kind of funny don't you think?"

"Not really. You need to have the Ricci name to push this through. I'm pissed at Rio. Hold on . . . the countdown . . . Happy New Year 1975. It's going to be our year. I wrote some words that could be a song. I'm not sharing it with anyone but you. I'll show you when you're home. So you have an image, I took my shower and of course thought of you, your hands all over me, and the hot times. You know what I'm talking about—your dirty fantasies."

"Stop. You're making me very horny right now. Damn you woman. Even talking to you about this makes me hard. Gina you're a witch."

"As long as I can get you hard by talking to you, it makes me happy and miss you more. I feel bad for you when you come home. We're locking the door, taking the phone off the hook, and enjoying each other, in every way possible. I'll go and set an alarm for three a.m. to call you back and wish you Happy New Year in Vancouver. You take care of that hard penis of yours and I'll be thinking about it."

"Gina, we're going to be fine. This is more positive than I thought. All right, I guess I'll talk to you later, you crazy bitch."

"You know you love it. I'm kissing you . . ."

Gina set her alarm and hoped she wouldn't sleep through it. She ran downstairs quickly to say goodbye to her aunt and uncle. Before he could leave, Gina pulled Rio into the living room. "Hey, motherfucker, if there is news regarding this visa bullshit, you let me talk to Trevor. You went behind my back. Don't ever do that again. I know you're antsy to make music, but when it comes to Trevor, it goes through me."

"Gina, you better step the fuck back a little. It might be your relationship, but this is my future. You forget we're in this together. You don't have to have this tight grip on Trevor. We all know you're territorial with him. My advice, loosen up Gina. One day you might have to share him with thousands of people."

"Back off Rio, but I hear you."

"You better. The band takes off, both of you will be the desire of thousands."

Gina reminded Rio. "My stash? Did you give it to me?"

"In your purse downstairs. And you're welcome."

Maybe she was too hard on him. She would apologize tomorrow. He had a point; it was his future also. But to say that she was territorial, that's wrong. She did not like the comment about having to share Trevor with thousands of women. She said goodnight to her parents and rushed upstairs to her room.

Gina started going through the antique dresser drawers and found some nice underwear, sweaters, and some vintage sixties peasant blouses she had forgotten about. She walked into her closet and was reminded she had quite a wardrobe. She started packing the clothes in suitcases. She looked at her cosmetics vanity and couldn't believe she hadn't taken all the expensive makeup she bought at Bloomingdale's. But there was still something that eluded her, and she definitely knew she had it. Where could it be? She searched her nightstands, and in one drawer, there it was, wrapped in a nightgown. Her vibrator. Every girl needs one.

Gina woke up at three a.m. and called Trevor back to wish him Happy New Year. She promised to call him next day. She had a surprise for him, something she would use until he came home. A girl's got to do what she has to.

A NEW SENSATION

AFTER A FANTASTIC BREAKFAST courtesy of Serena, Gina packed up her car with the suitcases. Franny looked on with amazement that she had so much still at the house.

Gina finished carrying her things into the carriage house and put a football game on the TV. She opened her refrigerator and realized she needed to go grocery shopping.

She found an A&P that was miraculously open on New Year's Day and spent $250.00 on groceries. That should last awhile.

Once she got back to the carriage house, she popped some popcorn and watched the games as she unpacked her suitcases. She hung up the dresses her mother had bought for her at Lord & Taylor, Saks, and Ralph Lauren. Some of the price tags were still on them. Jesus, Franny spent a lot of money on Gina's clothes.

She found the one item that she was most interested in . . . her vibrator. She was waiting for the time to call Trevor. She would make sure to take care of him even though he was 2,900 miles away.

She made a quiche lorraine for dinner, so she could have it again tomorrow. Then she indulged in eating a tub of coffee flavored Häagen Dazs. She hadn't been eating well for weeks and had lost a little weight. She would take her diet seriously when they started playing again. She needed to be stage weight and Sammy Gold would tell her to lose weight if he felt she was carrying an extra five to ten pounds.

It was twelve thirty. Gina undressed and slipped into her bed. She hadn't changed the sheets; they still smelled like him. She plugged in the vibrator and called Trevor. She used her very sultry voice, "Hi baby, how are you?"

She turned on the vibrator and started stimulating herself. "I've been thinking of you."

"I think of you every hour. Last night I thought a lot about you."

"Yeah, was it sexy?"

"Yes, of course it was. You got me hard. What was I going to do? What's that noise? It sounds like humming."

"Well, I found an old toy and I'm using it while I talk to you."

"Is that a vibrator? Are you masturbating while you talk to me?"

"Yes, talk to me, Trev. Talk to me, so I'm thinking of you, right now between my legs. Talk to me. That's all I need."

"You're so hot right now you are turning me on."

"Trevor . . . talk to me like you were right here. Why don't you join me? You know you want to . . . we can be together. Come on . . . I'm almost there. You need to catch up."

"Gina, I could eat you up right now . . ."

"Baby, in my mind you are already doing that . . ."

"Oh, God . . . you . . . bitch." Trevor breathing heavily.

"Give me a minute and I'll be right there."

The line became silent on both ends.

"I think we should do this every night until you come home. Any complaints?"

"Not from me . . ."

"I love you Trevor and can't wait until it's the real thing. Good night my love, love you always."

The lovers stuck to their bedtime ritual for the next month. Gina was relieved somewhat that at least they were still connecting sexually. She never took for granted that Trevor was hot and women were attracted to him on and off the stage. She felt she always needed to take care of his needs.

PASSING TIME

RIO AND JEFF WERE PUTTING TOGETHER some guitar and bass parts for songs. Gina came over to see what they were working on. Rio asked Gina, "Hey, are you doing your homework? Writing lyrics?"

"As a matter of fact, I did I have lyrics for a song, but I wanted to show it to Trevor before I brought it to the group."

"Gina, that's great! If you have something, bring it to the group. We work together, remember? Rio was a bit exasperated.

"All right, I'll bring it tomorrow, maybe."

The three of them were playing some cover music and Gina was singing along. She hadn't sung anything in a while, only "Gimme Shelter" with Trevor by the fireplace. She needed to get her voice back into singing mode—practicing the mouth exercises Simon Beauvaux had taught her, getting her singing range on track.

Rio wanted to go out. "The Thirst is playing in Hauppauge. Want to go, Gina? It will be good for people to see us out."

"I agree. We should do it, but can we be back by twelve thirty? That's when I call Trevor."

"He would be okay if you went out and we got some fan exposure. He would be all about it."

"Listen Rio, if you can't guarantee you can bring me back here, let's take two cars. You'll probably meet some adoring fan anyway."

"Gina we are going out to do recon, for fans to see us out. We need to make sure people know we're still in the game. I'm not interested in meeting an adoring fan, okay."

Gina asked, "It's been over two weeks, have we heard from the lawyer? How are things progressing? I feel left out of the loop on this."

Rio simply told her, "It's being handled. Who knows, maybe another couple of weeks if we're lucky. Chill, it's going to happen, have patience. Which I know you have none. So, are we going tonight?"

"Sure, but I'm taking my car, so let's go out and eat early. What club is in Hauppauge. Is it new?"

"Sort of. It used to be The Surfer Club; now it's Island Stop, new owner most likely. It must be up and coming, The Thirst wouldn't play a dive bar." Rio still knew the club dirt.

Gina shared her musings. "We should start taking inventory on the clubs we want to play when Perfection is ready. No more shit bars. Sammy can suck it! We will be better than that. Where would you like to go to eat?"

"I'm feeling some seafood, like crab legs. We can go to the Shore House. It's ten minutes from here."

"Alright, I shall leave you both, so I can become Gina Poole. Meet me at my house . . . what time is it? Four thirty? Let's do six."

Gina hadn't been out and about since Trevor left. She felt guilty that she shouldn't go, but she was looking forward to seeing Stevie, Matt, and Josh. There were questions and rumors about what happened to Vision Skye and Stanley Park. Tonight would be a good opportunity to get the buzz going about the new band.

Gina rummaged through her closet and discovered a pair of skintight black leather pants she didn't know she had. She found a soft form-fitting leather shirt and a pair of black boots. She looked like she was going onstage. Makeup done and hair straightened, she was ready. She looked in the mirror and thought Trevor would hate her getting dressed up without him. Gina, Rio, and Jeff needed to be seen, show the fans that they will back with a different band.

At six o'clock precisely, Rio and Jeff pulled up to the carriage house. They came up the stairs and walked in while Gina was still primping.

"I'll be right out. Do you have a joint we can smoke before we go?"

Rio laughed, "I was going to say the same thing. Come out already. I'm sure you look great."

"Pass that joint, suckers."

Rio looked Gina up and down. "Looks like you're dressing for a purpose. I know it's not a man. So, what gives Gina?"

"Like you said, there may be fans of Vision Skye there. We need to let them know we are forming a new band. Got to play the part, and yes, so you know, I feel extremely guilty going out like this without Trevor."

Jeff, who normally didn't have much to say, reassured her. "I don't think Trevor would hate you spreading the word about Perfection."

"Okay guys, let's go eat and then conquer the club."

They got to the Shore House and ordered food before getting to the club.

Rio ordered a shit ton of crab legs. Gina went with a lobster because they shelled them; she didn't want all that juice getting on her outfit. They finished dinner, got in their cars, and headed to Island Stop.

There was a line outside the club and the bouncers were collecting a cover charge. Gina skipped the line and walked right up to the door. "My name is on the list." Stevie always put her name on the list. She swaggered through the crowd, Rio and Jeff following behind.

"You know Sammy Gold could be here tonight. Gina, you need to work him."

"No fucking way. He probably wouldn't talk to me anyway because I didn't let him talk to Trevor, and he was pissed that we didn't play any gigs in December. So, I'm out. Rio, he loves your ass, so you talk to him. Besides

I think you know more than I do about the visa situation. So, you deal with that prick Gold. I'm not."

Gina looked around the club and saw Josh checking the cords onstage. She worked her way over to him. "Hey, you, what's going on?"

"Gina Poole. Well, hey, look at you. Come over and give me a hug."

"Sure, I needed to get out. You know about the visa crap, right?"

Josh said, heartfelt, "Sure, everybody does. How are you doing?"

"I miss him terribly. I know he'll be back soon. I even feel guilty about being here. Got to make a presence so people don't forget us. Once we reunite, we will be a power group. I have a lot of things to be happy about." Gina lit up a cigarette and gave Josh a hug. "Thank you for always being a good friend. I don't think I say that enough to you. I do adore our friendship." She then gave him a hug that lasted a bit longer. She had tears in her eyes.

She started looking for Stevie and saw him swamped by the usual club goers. They think they are Stevie's best friend. It's the group that follows The Thirst around; you can't blow them off. But Gina pushed through. "What ya doing man?"

Stevie said a quick "Thanks and see ya later" to his admirers.

"First, how are you with Trevor in Canada? And, what's up with the outfit? You vixen. And thank you for saving me."

Gina laughed. "Let's go get you your Rum and Cokes first. Yes, I am missing him, but he'll be home soon. Listen, you know, between us, Vision Skye and Stanley Park are forming a new band. It will be a power band. I'm kind of here to make sure we're seen. You know the bit, it's a game, but I'm playing."

"That sounds great. Good for you. A couple singing leads, that will be something different." Stevie seemed genuinely interested.

"I'm excited about it. Oh, I think it's time for you to take the stage. Take this drink and I'll bring the other."

Gina sat on the side of the stage near Stevie where she always had in the past. She checked her watch constantly. She didn't want to be late for her call and planned to leave after the first set.

Rio and Jeff were already high as they walked up to her. Gina told Rio, "I'm leaving after this set. Did you find out anything?"

Rio laughed. "Hey man, people coming up to us, 'When you going to play?' I said real soon. Oh fuck, yeah guess who's here? Sammy and Nadine. And Sammy is walking this way."

Gina wanted to make a quit exit, but it was too late; he had spotted them. Gina came face to face with Sammy. "I'm leaving Sammy. Talk to Rio."

Sammy smiled. "I'm good Gina. I can't wait to see this new band Rio and Trevor are putting together. Two excellent guitarists and a couple that are leads, should be interesting."

"Well, you can come to one of our practices and see how good we really are."

With that exchange Gina was out. As she was leaving, a few fans called out her name. It was nice to be recognized and she wondered if she would always enjoy the attention. She would find out in the years to come—maybe not.

She drove home listening to the radio and smoking cigarettes. The drive only took thirty minutes, leaving her plenty of time to get ready for her call with Trevor. God how she loved that man. She wasn't going to tell Trevor she went to a club. It wasn't a big lie, but she wasn't sure how happy he would be with her dressed all sexy, without him.

She washed her face, got a couple of crackers, and set up their sex time. She wondered what was going on with that damn visa. At twelve thirty precisely, Gina dialed Trevor's number.

"Who am I talking with at this time of night? I bet she's some sexy bitch. Hi baby. How was your day?"

"I hung out with Rio and Jeff. They were going over some new guitar riffs. Rio said he can't wait for you to come back so you can start working on songs. He told me to start writing lyrics. I said I had something but wanted to wait for you first. He told me I should bring it forward now."

Trevor agreed with Rio. "Although I do appreciate you waiting for me, you should bring it to him. Why not? I'm glad you got out and saw Rio. You know you need to get out more Gina. I hate the idea of you sitting in the house."

"Well, I went out to eat with the guys and got a drink. So, my first baby step, but seriously Trevor, it's not the same going out without you . . . I feel lost, like I'm missing a limb or something. It's not right. But I love youuuu . . . are you ready to get hot?"

"Baby, can we just talk tonight? I love the hot sex over the phone, but I miss hearing you talk, hearing your voice speaking, about well . . . anything. I miss your voice."

"I'll talk all night if you want me to. I'll critique the restaurant we went to; I'll never go again. Rio had a shit ton of crab legs. He looked like a child eating them. It was fairly entertaining, butter all over his fingers. I had a lobster, shelled of course. I don't want to work for my food, and I had a salad. I've lost five pounds since you left. I guess another five and I'll be good for the stage."

"You looked perfect when I left. Please don't get too skinny. I love your curves. I love your body as is."

"I'll take note then. I still think another five pounds won't hurt. After eating we went to some local bar, had a drink, and I came home. Waiting to call you. My exciting night. What have you been doing? Have you seen Ian?"

"He came by the other night with Kevin. They're worried about the visas. I told them we will be good, relax. Like I try to tell you. Sometime soon the Golds need to be called and told about the new band."

"I think Rio is putting that out into the world. I bet Sammy already knows and will bounce at the chance. But we need to ask for a better deal. Seriously. Why not ask for something like The Thirst? We're going to kill it. You and Rio on guitar. You are both amazing. Then we have the "schtick or the something different" that Sammy loves—you and I singing lead vocals together, people eat that shit up. I will tell you it's also letting people see a little into our world. We can sing together, but everyone will see our love displayed onstage. Do you know what I mean? Letting a veil down, exposing our personal life."

"G, you knew that if we did this together, we were going to put a piece of our lives out there. There's no way for us to sing a love song or any song without showing a piece of our lives. It wouldn't be authentic. We are a couple and that's what people will want to see. It's sexy for them."

Gina agreed. "I get it. I don't want the veil to drop too far. I want to keep the best part of our life private. People don't need to know everything."

"It's not like we're letting them into our bedroom."

"I will let you take the lead on that. I want us to be dynamic together. I miss you so much and this sucks."

"I know, it does blow. We will make up for lost time, I promise. It's getting late for you. Go to sleep and dream big."

"I'll try. That's the best I can do. Loving you."

Gina went to bed that night unsatisfied. She started to analyze everything Trevor said. *Does he really miss me? What will happen to our relationship once the band starts up again?* It was going to be a totally new dynamic, and she was afraid. Maybe her mother was right, "Lean on your faith." Her faith was Trevor. He would never break the trust and the promises. He couldn't. Gina still had a strange feeling she couldn't exactly pin down. *What is it?*

GETS HER VOICE

THE NEXT DAY SHE REALIZED that Rio was right; she was going to give him lyrics. *I'm one-fifth of this band and I'm going to contribute, not sit back and let the rest of the band dictate the direction.* She deserved a voice. Her lyrics were her contribution and she wanted to be able to voice her opinion. She shouldn't be sitting home while Rio and Jeff were putting music together. She would go over there with the one song she had written. Now she knew she needed to spend more time writing.

Gina showered and grabbed some coffee and a bagel. Then took off to Rio's. Of course, she didn't need to be invited over, she would show up. When she got to Rio's house, it was quiet downstairs. Certainly, Jeff should have been there by now, but his car wasn't there. No worries. She let herself in and called out Rio's name. She heard movement in his bedroom. *Oh my God.* She might have walked into something. She called him one more time, staying away from his bedroom. "Rio I'm sorry. I didn't realize you had company, I'll leave."

Rio came stumbling out of his bedroom, pulling the door closed behind him. "No Gina, please don't. I've been trying to get her to leave. All she does is talk about what a great guitarist I am, blah, blah."

Gina gave Rio a smug look. "Umhmm. Well, that's what happens when you take a bar chick home with you. She's a star fucker. The clubs are filled with them and the general bar sluts. Which one did you take home?"

"I can't fucking tell."

Gina laughed at his ignorance. "Listen. Be a gentleman, no matter what. Give her a cup of coffee and then send her on her way. That's it. I'll go see Aunt Deidre for a few minutes and then I'll come down and say we have a meeting. You need to be more discriminating in who you bring home, bro. Remember a cup of coffee, so you don't look like a dick."

"I'll ring the house phone upstairs when I'm ready. Thanks Gina."

Gina walked around the front of the house, knocked once, and walked in.

Mae, the housekeeper, greeted her at the door. "Hello, Miss Gina, I haven't seen you in a while. Are you looking for Miss Deidre?"

"Yes. I am going to work with Rio but thought I would come up and say hello first."

"She's in the kitchen. Go in."

"Thanks Mae." Gina walked into the kitchen and found Aunt Deidre dressed in designer jeans and a crisp Brooks Brothers shirt.

"Gina, honey, how are you? I'm sure you're missing your Trevor. Uncle Tony is in touch with the right people. Hopefully he will be home soon, and you all can start making music together. I think you are going to be a hit, I really do. Coffee?"

"I should come here more often before going downstairs to see Rio. I appreciate your words. Aunt Deidre, when you were modeling in Paris and away from Uncle Tony, did you ever feel like you were growing apart, or felt like your relationship wasn't as strong as you thought it was?"

"I thought the distance would make our love stronger. I never doubted your uncle. Push those thoughts away Gina. Trevor wouldn't want to come back here if he wasn't sure he wanted to be with you. I like Trevor; he seems very happy with you. You are a very attractive woman, but I know you don't see what everyone else does. I'm always here for you to talk to . . . hold on, the phone is ringing."

"That's odd. Rio called to say it was safe to come downstairs. He wasn't alone when you got here, was he? He needs to find a decent girl, not these bar . . ."

"Aunt Deidre, they are called star fuckers. I don't want him involved with that either, but he's a guy and the girls want him. I'll use whatever persuasion I have. How's that?"

Aunt Deidre gave her a hug and a kiss, then sent her downstairs. Gina was hoping she didn't have to see the girl. As she got to the door, Rio was sending her off. She recognized Gina and said, "I know you. You're in Rio's band. Cool."

"Yeah, he's my cousin and it's our band. Thank you for remembering me, bye."

She got into some Chevy Malibu or something, so she wasn't on Rio's level.

Gina whispered, "Now close the fucking door already. I'm not sure what that was, but I'm going with bar slut. You need to up your dating game. You shouldn't be picking up chicks at these bars."

Rio astutely reminded Gina, "Didn't you meet Trevor at a bar?"

"Oh, you shithead. I'm in a band and I ran into him. Totally different. It was a bar, but we were equals. I don't know why I'm justifying my relationship to you, especially after what I saw leave here. I'm here to work. I have lyrics for one song, but I would like to work with your music, and I'll try to write lyrics around it. Can we give it a try?"

"Finally, Gina. Thank you."

The two of them worked for hours, Gina listening to the music and getting a feeling for what kind of song she could write—this is a kick-ass song, get off your ass and dance, love song, sad song. They were starting to put pieces together. Jeff came over later and worked on the bass riffs he liked, adding another dimension. They worked until ten o'clock and decided to go to the Island Splash Diner.

They talked about all the good work they had put into the music. Now Gina felt like she was a contributor. She could even have her name on the song rights if they were to record. Time had slipped by quickly when Gina noticed it was eleven forty-five. She needed to go home and call Trevor. She said her goodbyes and drove off.

JEALOUSY

AT TWELVE THIRTY ON THE DOT, Gina called Trevor's number, but a different voice answered the phone. *Did I dial the wrong number*?

She said to the unfamiliar voice, "I'm sorry, I think I dialed the wrong number."

"Is this Gina? I'm Trevor's Dad. Nice to talk to you. I have heard so much about you from Trevor. Unfortunately, he's not home. He went out with some of his mates."

"Oh, ok . . .umm do you know when he'll be back?"

"Wish I did. I know these mates, it might be a long night."

Gina was fuming but had to keep a lid on it for Trevor's Dad. "Well, I'm glad he said nice things about me Mr. McNaughton."

"Call me Shawn. Maybe one day you'll visit Vancouver."

"I would love to meet you. Could you let him know I called and whenever he can it would be nice for him to return my call? Thank you so much, Shawn, it was good speaking with you."

Gina's jealousy went wildly out of control with conjecture. *Did he finally decide to find someone to keep him company while he was out of my purview?* Gina went to bed angry and was still fuming when she woke up. Trevor hadn't called back.

Gina was hanging a by a thread, jealousy raging. She thought of every horrible thing Trevor could have been doing. Granted, she had gone out to a club, dressed to be noticed, but never did she have a thought that another man could ever replace Trevor. The last time they spoke he didn't want to play their sex game. Was that a sign?

She took the phone off the hook. She didn't want to talk Trevor for fear of what she would say to him. She sulked and didn't leave the house. She played every sad song in their album collection . . . and cried. For two days, she played all the scenarios in her head. What did the other woman look like? Or maybe there were several. How long had this been going on?

Rio had been calling her but got the constant busy signal since the phone was off the hook. On the third day, Rio drove to the carriage house and pounded on the door, "Gina, I know you're in there. Open the door, please, we have to talk."

After a few minutes, Gina unlocked the door and returned to the sofa.

"Gina, what the hell is wrong with you?" Rio walked in and took a look around. What a mess. Gina was in a ratty shirt and sweatpants, her hair greasy and limp. Ashtrays overflowing. Dirty tissues all over the floor. Dishes in the sink. He strode to the coffee table and put the phone back on the hook. "Nobody knows what the hell is happening. Trevor has called me three times. He told me he went out with some friends and missed your call, and you haven't called him back. What gives Gina? Are you mad he went out and wasn't there for your call?"

Gina was ready with ammunition. "I don't want to talk with Trevor. He missed my call. I never miss a call no matter where I am, he always comes first. I feel the distance has changed our relationship and not for the good. He's home. I thought this was his home, but obviously, I was wrong. I'm crushed, so leave me alone."

"You went to the club all dressed up like some sort of sex kitten and you're pissed he went out? Are you that fucking jealous? Bitch, get over yourself. I have never seen this side of you; it's not attractive."

"Did you tell him I went to the club and how I was dressed? Because

I didn't tell him. Did you open your fucking mouth Rio? I swear I'll break your motherfucking fingers. Stay out of my personal business."

"Gina, you're a crazy bitch right now. There's a guy in Vancouver wondering what he did. You're really this upset about him going out? Get your shit together. We have a band to think about. You are so selfish. I can't believe you, you're sabotaging your relationship and our band. I won't let you do that because you're jealous."

Gina had a rational moment, the only one in the last three days. She hadn't heard Trevor's explanation, and she should at least hear him out.

"So, I should call him. Will he even be home?"

"Gina, call him, please. I'm stuck in the middle of this, and it's stupid and fucking crazy."

Gina cried on Rio's shoulder. "I love him and I'm afraid of losing him. This visa thing seems like it will never get fixed."

"Gina, call Trevor, please. Don't cry to me. Talk to him. This isn't a big deal."

Gina drew a deep breath and looked at the phone, trying to figure out what time it was in Vancouver. It's ten thirty in the morning in New York, so seven thirty there is too early. She was afraid, but she was also strong. This was a blip in the relationship. She was being ridiculous. But Rio had to leave for her to make this call.

"Rio. I'll call but I would rather be alone when I do it. Can you understand that?"

"I'll leave but promise you'll hear him out. There's nothing wrong. It's all in your head. I'll leave now."

Gina wouldn't let herself sabotage their relationship. She dialed the number, and Trevor answered on the first ring.

"Gina! What the fuck is going on? Are you seriously that mad that I wasn't home when you called? It was one night, going to a pub with friends. I lost track of time. What's the problem? What did you think I was doing?"

"I'm sorry. I was insanely jealous. Why, I don't know; maybe because we haven't seen each other for almost six weeks?"

"You seriously think I would do something to fuck up our relationship? Is that the kind of trust you have in me, really? Please tell me you're not that jealous, it doesn't suit you."

"I've been trying to keep busy and write music with Rio. But you are always in my head. This not knowing when the visa is coming seems endless. I'm sure there are women coming on to you, you're so damn sexy, and I wouldn't blame them."

"Gina, you need to realize there's always going to be women, its rock and roll, like there will be men who will want you. I'm the man who gets to take that sexy woman home, every night."

Yes, there were women at the pub and some of my friends were talking to them and even invited them to the table. That was their thing not mine. Please baby, we will have a lifetime of people trying to get in our way. You need to be tough and not let those people into your head and into our lives."

"You're right. I'm so sorry. Please forgive me for being an insanely jealous bitch. I never wanted anything this stupid to happen. I was wrong. There, I said it. I was wrong and stupid." Gina waited anxiously to see if Trevor would accept her apology.

"I was waiting to ask you this, but I think now it's time. Will you get on a plane and come to Vancouver?"

"Yes, yes! I'll be on a plane tomorrow. Is your father okay with me coming?"

"Would I ask you to come if it was an issue? Baby, get on the plane."

"I'll call a travel agency and book a ticket. I'll call you as soon as I know my flight. I have to look for my passport. But now I can't wait to see you, knowing tomorrow I can touch you, smell you . . . okay, let me call. I love you. I truly do. Is it cold there, what should I bring to wear?"

"Pack warm and casual. I'll wait for your flight information. Love you more Gina, always love you, found you, baby."

VANCOUVER AND SURPRISE

GINA CALLED THE TRAVEL AGENCY and bought a first-class ticket. She would need Rio to drive her to the airport. After their conversation she was sure that wouldn't be an issue. She would also need to tell her parents.

She called Rio. "Hey, umm I talked to Trevor and I'm flying to Vancouver tomorrow. Can you take me to JFK?"

"Thank God. Yes, I'll be happy to take you. Honestly, it's the best news you could have told me."

She called Trevor and gave him the information for her flight. In twenty-four hours, she would be in Vancouver to see Trevor's world. The excitement washed over her in a wave.

Gina emptied the ashtrays and started tidying the house. She went to her closet, looked through her sweaters, jeans, and jackets and started packing. Once she got that sorted out, she took a shower. She made coffee and drove up the driveway to her parents' house. She hoped her mom was home. She walked through the door. "Serena, are you here?" She walked into the kitchen knowing Serena would be cooking.

"Princess, everything okay?"

"Yeah, is Mom around?"

"No, she's at the office. Can I help?"

"I'm going to Vancouver tomorrow! I'll swing by the office so I can tell both Mom and Dad." She kissed Serena goodbye and drove to her parents' offices.

Gina greeted the receptionist. "Hello Misty. I'm here to see my mother. She free?"

Gina didn't wait for her to answer, but instead walked directly into Franny's office.

"Gina, darling, what brings you here?"

"I'm going to Vancouver tomorrow to see Trevor. Don't try to talk me out of it."

Her mother smiled. "I think it's a good idea actually. It will make you happy."

Mario, hearing her voice, walked in. "What gives princess? News?"

"Yes, I'm going to Vancouver to see Trevor. He asked me to come, so I'm going."

"Well, it's about time you went out there."

Gina did not expect that reaction from her parents. "I don't know how long I'll be, but I wanted you to know so you didn't think I did something to myself or something crazy." She kissed her parents and told them she would let them know when she would be back.

Franny and Mario looked at each other, like they knew something that Gina didn't know.

Gina returned home and put her suitcases by the door. She turned on the TV, hoping that she could get some sleep. She tossed and turned, smoked a few cigarettes. She thought of taking a Valium but was afraid she would oversleep. As soon as morning broke, she made coffee, ate a bagel, and went into the shower. She dressed casually but had to make her hair and makeup perfect.

Rio showed up on time. She looked at him like she couldn't contain her excitement. Rio spoke first. "This is the smartest decision you have made in a couple of days. I mean it when I say I'm happy you're going."

"Thank you, Rio. I'm sorry I was a lunatic the other day. You didn't deserve it and I shouldn't have said the things I said to you. Can you forgive me?"

"Gina, I know how much you have been missing Trevor, and any little thing that you feel that's off, you react to it. You know he loves you, but you question it? I can forgive you but promise me we won't have a conversation like we had the other day. I love you too. I will have your back, okay? We're cool."

During the drive to the airport, Rio reminded her, "I want a couple of songs written by you two when you get back. I think you will be inspired." Rio found a parking spot and walked Gina into the terminal.

Gina continued their conversation. "Inspired, sure. I will be more than inspired."

Rio walked her to the door that led to the international flights. "Okay, this is where I leave you. I know you will be in good hands on the other side. Call me if you two come up with some good music."

"Will do. I hope I get inspired by Vancouver. Kiss me goodbye."

He gave her a bear hug and kissed her on her cheek. "Love you, Gina Poole. Go get your man."

The doors opened and an agent went through all her suitcases, which pissed off Gina. What could they be looking for? But she wasn't going to let that ruin her excitement. When she got to the gate, they had already started boarding. She walked on the plane and took 4B, an aisle seat. She sat back and took two Valium, which she washed down with a glass of champagne.

First-class passengers were served chateaubriand with new potatoes and a touch of caviar, and for dessert—hot fudge sundaes. Gina wished she could have enjoyed the food, but she was too excited to eat. Every hour seemed like two. Was this plane ever going to land? She got a pad out of her new Pucci bag and started writing her feelings down, maybe a song?

Hours passed and she felt the plane starting to descend. She looked out the window, at the waterfront of Vancouver. Gina knew she was getting closer. Thirty minutes later the plane touched down on the tarmac. Trevor would be waiting outside the doors that led from Customs.

REUNITED

GINA RAN OFF THE JETWAY to the terminal. She showed her passport and answered she was there for a holiday. The officer stamped her passport and told Gina to enjoy her time in Vancouver.

God it was taking forever to get her luggage. She finally saw her suitcases and yanked them off the carousel.

The automatic doors opened and standing on the other side was that beautiful man she loved. She ran to him, leaving her suitcases on the floor behind her. Trevor swung her around and couldn't stop kissing her—her hair, her neck, and then her lips. Gina ran her fingers through his wavy, long blond hair.

He spoke first. "Oh G, I missed you so much. Let's get your suitcases and get out of here."

"Trevor, you look beautiful. I love you so much." They walked through the terminal linking arms and dragging the suitcases. Trevor threw the suitcases in the trunk, and they drove off, Gina next to him on the bench seat, holding hands.

Gina noticed the skyscrapers and asked, "Your father lives downtown?"

"I have a surprise for you. We aren't going to my father's house for the next two nights. We have hotel reservations downtown with an incredible water view. There's so much to see. I want to show you what my world is like. Although, I didn't grow up the way you did. We will stay a few days with my father too."

"I have to admit I wasn't expecting this. How special."

Trevor pulled up to the hotel and gave the keys to the valet. They headed to the front desk. Trevor was in command now. "I have a reservation. The name is McNaughton."

"Yes, Mr. and Mrs. McNaughton. We have a beautiful water view room for you. And you requested a smoking room, correct?"

"Yes, I did."

"Okay, I just need a credit card and I'll have the bellman take your luggage to room 1104. Here are your keys. I hope you enjoy your stay. If you need anything, please contact our concierge."

"Trev, baby, this is an expensive hotel. I would have been happy at some shitty motel to be alone with you."

"G, no worries, okay? I want to make the next two nights here memorable, something we will always look back on. Okay? So, no worries."

They followed the bellman with Gina's luggage. Trevor had that duffle again. This was going to be special. Trevor opened the door to a king-sized bed, sitting area, mini bar, and a beautiful water view.

"Trevor, this is beautiful. I love you for thinking of this."

"Did you notice the nightstand?" Sitting there was a chilled bottle of champagne and her favorite flowers, hydrangeas. Trevor stepped behind Gina and pulled her close to him. She could feel he was hard. She wanted to linger and feel his hard penis against her. He started kissing her neck, an automatic turn-on for Gina. He turned her around to face him. She placed her hands on his face, pulled his hair around his ears, and kissed him, soft light kisses all over his face. She traced her finger to his lips and kissed him softly at first. Then she couldn't resist going in for a hungry kiss of wanting him, deep long kisses. She slid his shirt off and kissed his chest, that perfect manly chest, the right everything. She pulled off her own sweater and jeans and stood there in ivory lace lingerie. Trevor picked her up and dropped her on the bed. They wanted to enjoy this moment—no rushing, this was a reunion, no hurry. Gina reached down and undid his jeans and stripped him naked. She glided her hands around his body remembering how he felt, his arms, his shoulders. She grabbed his hard penis. She wanted it badly, but she didn't want it yet.

They stared at each other and kissed in a frenzy. Trevor started working his way down between her legs. She thought he was a master at the guitar—but this, he was a maestro. She couldn't contain her pleasure and cried out in overwhelming release. Waves came over her and she arched her back, running her fingers through his hair.

She returned the favor, getting him excited but leaving him on the edge. She wanted him inside her; he rolled her over and got on top. She wrapped her legs around him like a vise. She wanted all of him. He played the slow game, teasing her. They didn't speak, their expressions saying what words couldn't—the pleasure, the love, and the love they saw in each other.

Gina begged, "Take me now. Do me hard."

Trevor didn't last too much longer after that. She stroked his hair when they finished. This was heaven. No words could ever describe this type of love.

"Babe, no one could ever replace you, ever."

Trevor turned to her. "You want a glass of champagne and a cigarette; you have your funny pastel cigarettes?"

"Of course I do. Yes, champagne would be wonderful. I love the flowers. I love everything right now; the world is back to normal."

Trevor filled the two glasses, spilling some champagne.

"You know, this is such a treat. We never really went anywhere except the carriage house. I feel like this is a holiday, as you Canadians say."

"Gina, you realize if the band makes it, or when we make it, this would be our life—hotels in different cities, people trying to find out where the band is staying, all the shit that comes with touring. Are you ready for that when it happens?"

"We will be together, so I will be ready for it. Are you doubting my dedication to the band?"

"No, not at all but our lives will be out there for public viewing."

Gina was defiant. "We don't need to let them all the way in; we discussed this already. If we have children, we need to protect their privacy."

"When that happens, we won't let anything interfere with our children. Totally different subject, anyone talk to Sammy Gold yet?"

"Rio said he would handle it but not until you got back to New York. There's no power band without you there. You and Rio are the power, Ian's a great drummer, and Jeff plays a mean bass. Then there's me, the weakest link."

"People will come to see us sing together. They probably will walk away thinking, 'They must fuck a lot.'"

"Trevor, oh God, you're probably right. It's sort of voyeurism thinking that they could imagine us making love. Well, I'll take it if it gets us a record deal. How's that? Bet you didn't think those words would leave my mouth."

"Bring that mouth over here." He kissed her hungrily. Gina sat on top of him and took command—Trevor liked that. They moved together rhythmically like playing music, but they were playing each other. Trevor sat up, held her back, and whispered to her, telling her how much she was making him crazy, and of course how much he loved her. They fell back to bed satiated by their lovemaking.

"Did you bring *The New York Times* crossword puzzle?" Trevor asked.

"Babe seriously, I had no time to think about that. You told me to come, and I was on the next plane. I don't even know what I packed."

"I thought we would get room service. I don't want to leave this room tonight. Maybe tomorrow we will go around shopping and then for a walk tomorrow night and see the lights downtown. You good with that?"

Gina replied happily, "This is your plan. I'm going with whatever you want. Let me see that room service menu, I'm starving. I didn't eat on the plane, I was way too excited. Well, I had a little bit of a hot fudge sundae."

Gina chose the Grand Chef's salad and Trevor had a steak, baked potato, and salad. Trevor knew she loved carrot cake and added one to his order, along with a nice cabernet. Gina was wondering if this was getting expensive, but she knew not to push. They put on the complimentary bathrobes and let the waiter set up the table when he arrived.

"Hope you enjoy your dinner Mr. and Mrs. McNaughton." Gina loved the way that sounded, but no rushing, they have the band to establish first. They ate, drank, and laughed. They had missed this interplay with each other, laughing at stupid things. There would no band talk tonight.

Trevor rolled the table outside the room. He wanted Gina all to himself for the entire evening. The next morning, they woke up and went to a restaurant in the lobby for breakfast. They enjoyed breakfast and Trevor said, "Let's shower and go for that walk. I want to show you this incredible place. I think you are really going to enjoy it."

"I'm excited to see the sites." Gina walked into a generously sized bathroom, with marble double sinks, and dropped her robe. "I'm getting in the shower now, don't know what you're doing."

"Did you think I forgot?" Trevor washed Gina's back and slid his hand further down, pressed her against the shower glass, and took her from behind.

Now showered and dressed, Gina was excited to see where Trevor was going to take her. They exited the elevators arm in arm. They walked a little farther to Stanley Park. Gina never imagined it was an actual place. "Oh Trevor, I need to go in and look around."

"It's a huge park, but we will walk awhile."

"Babe, this is the best thing we could have done. It's beautiful here, I love it."

Trevor reminded her, "Remember, we need to go back to New York if we want to see A&R guys. We have a band to reorganize, and we need to start playing gigs. But I'm happy you're enjoying it."

They walked around hand in hand for an hour. Gina wanted to do a little shopping. He let her walk in and out of stores looking at clothes and enjoying every minute. They found a little bistro and had dinner. Once back in their room, they snuggled up. Gina loved the lights of NYC, however seeing the lights around the water in Vancouver was breathtaking. After a long day they fell fast asleep.

When morning came, Gina woke up thinking, *Is this real? Are we really here together? This isn't a dream.* She ordered a continental breakfast from room service, then returned to bed where she nestled under Trevor's arm as he slept.

When he awoke, he murmured, "Hey baby. Good morning. Did you sleep like this all night?"

Gina loved every minute of their time, wondering how long it would last. The visa issue still needed to be addressed. She pushed that thought away.

There was a knock at the door. Gina put on her bathrobe to let the waiter wheel in the breakfast cart.

"We have coffee and some muffins, toast, and croissants," Gina announced as she poured the coffees. They sat down to breakfast, drunk on the lovemaking from the night before.

Trevor looked at Gina in the morning light streaming through the window. "You look beautiful in the morning with no makeup—natural."

"You know how to make me feel beautiful. I'm just average. There are so many beautiful women out there, I wish I was one, but I'm me."

"You know, men think about attributes in a woman other than beauty; it's who the person is as an individual, kind, giving. I keep telling you, you are more than beautiful. You're sexy, the kind of woman a man wants to take home and make love to."

Gina took the compliment. "As long as *you* feel that way, I could give a shit about other men."

After another round of lovemaking, they showered and dressed. Gina had a long leather trench coat and Trevor wore the bomber jacket Gina had given him for Christmas. Before they headed back out, Trevor said he needed to make a stop while they were on their walk. As they strolled the streets, Gina ran in and out of some more little boutiques and Vancouver attractions. Gina noticed Trevor checking his watch constantly.

"You're preoccupied with the time. Is there something wrong?"

"No, I have a three o'clock appointment at a solicitor's office. That's the stop I mentioned. I don't want to be late. Maybe we should start walking."

They stopped in front of a high-rise and Trevor checked the piece of paper he had scribbled the address on. They entered, took the elevator to the seventh floor, and walked into Smythe and Carter Attorneys at Law. Trevor informed the receptionist he had an appointment with Douglas Carter. A few moments later, a handsome balding man stepped into the lobby and greeted them, "Mr. McNaughton, hello, I'm Douglas Carter. Please follow me."

Trevor and Gina sat down. "Mr. McNaughton, I have the completed paperwork and work visas for you, Ian White, Kevin Moore, and Brian Mayfield. Mr. Antonio Ricci has sponsored you for work in the entertainment industry. Everything is all legal and you're set to enter the United States as soon as possible."

Gina blinked and blinked again. Was she hearing this correctly? Mr. Carter handed Trevor a large envelope with the visa paperwork. Gina sat silently, still not believing what she heard. "Excuse me, are you saying Trevor can leave anytime?"

"Yes, that is correct. I'm sorry, I didn't catch your name."

"My name is Gina Ricci Poole; my uncle is Antonio Ricci."

They all shook hands and said their goodbyes. As they got back on the elevator Trevor said to her, "I wanted you here so you knew as soon as I got the paperwork. You're happy, we're going home."

Gina was stunned. "I'm shocked and happy. My parents said something strange when I left, and I couldn't process it. And Rio told me to 'go get your man.' Did they know?"

"Yes, but don't be mad at everybody; they all wanted you here with me when I got the paperwork."

Gina started to cry, "I'm not mad, I'm overjoyed. Do we get to go home together?"

"Yes, of course. I thought we would stay a few days so you could meet my father."

"Oh my God, yes, yes. I'm the happiest woman. I thought you made me happy yesterday, but now I'm in shock."

"We can start our life together now. You ready for the roller coaster?"

"I can handle anything with you. Let's kill it and get that fucking deal. By the way, who is that other guy Mr. Carter mentioned? Brian something."

"Mayfield. Yeah, he's just an old friend who in the interim will act like a manager, but he's not one."

Something about Trevor's response felt evasive to her. Gina thought it was suspicious how this guy was pushed through at the last minute with no previous mention to her. He could be trouble. If she only knew how much, she would have ripped up his visa right there.

Gina was still glowing from the past thirty-six hours, being with her man and then getting the visas. "Trevor let's celebrate. Everything is perfection. I don't want to waste a moment of this time together. When we get back, there will be a lot of work and late nights, but better clubs. Does the hotel have a rooftop bar? Or what's the fanciest restaurant here? I want to do something real special."

"Sure. There are fancy French restaurants or steak houses. But do you really want to do that when we can celebrate alone and have privacy? We won't have a lot of that when we go back."

"Hmm, let me see, the privacy sounds spectacular. We can order from room service, and I can watch Canadian TV."

"We do get US stations you know."

"What's the fun in that? Do you promise to be naked?"

"Whatever you want."

As they entered the lobby of the hotel the desk clerk waved Trevor over. "Mr. McNaughton, you have a telegram."

Trevor read the message on yellow paper aloud to Gina. "Hi love birds. We have a date with Sammy Gold ten days from today. Come home ready to work on some music. Love, Rio."

"We'll have to leave in three days. The tickets Rio got us were open-ended. So, all we will need is to book seats.

"Hold up my love. We fly first class. Not that I don't love Ian, but they fly coach even though their tickets were originally first class. I have to tell Rio to get a bigger car. None of this is a problem."

They ordered bacon cheeseburgers with poutine and beer from the room service menu. Gina had bought candles at one of the charming stores she had visited earlier in the day. She lit them and set them around the bathtub which she filled with relaxing lavender bubble bath. She got in and called out to Trevor, "Hey baby, there's something in the bathroom. Can you kill it?"

He walked in and shook his head when he saw her.

"Get in with me. This is our last night before we go to your father's house. Let's enjoy, sexy, sexy time."

"The food is going to come soon."

"It can wait, this can't. Take those clothes off and get in here."

Trevor dutifully stripped down and stepped into the piping hot suds.

"Damn Gina, it's hot in here."

"It's about to get hotter." She wrapped her legs around him. "Do you have anything to say now?" She brought his head toward her heart. "I will remember these days as our special time together. No one can take this memory or ever split us apart. Remember this always."

The water was slippery and made it easy to maneuver two bodies in a tub. "See baby, now you smell great too."

They ate dinner, watched TV, and laughed. Gina had her pastel cigarettes and a joint for them to smoke.

Gina was nervous about meeting Trevor's father, Shawn. Would he like her—the woman who kept his son on the East Coast of the US? Gina's head was on Trevor's chest. "What if your dad doesn't like me?"

"Don't worry Gina; I'm not all that close to him."

GINA'S TIME WITH SHAWN

THE NEXT MORNING, they drove thirty minutes north to a suburban town with modest, cute houses. Trevor pulled into the driveway of a blue rancher. Gina thought, *What must he think of my lifestyle?* Her life was over the top compared to where Trevor came from. He got her things out of the car, and she held onto him like a life preserver.

Shawn came to the door. "Oh, there you are. I thought you might have changed your mind about bringing this young lady here." He turned his attention to Gina and smiled. "We talked on the phone. I'm Shawn."

Gina saw where Trevor got his blue eyes. She reached out to hug Shawn. "Thank you so much for having me in your home. I appreciate it."

Trevor moved past his dad, carrying the suitcases. Gina panicked for a second. Were they allowed to sleep together? She never thought of that. But Trevor put their suitcases in a bedroom with a double bed. There were guitar magazines on the nightstand and rock posters on the walls, definitely his old bedroom. She whispered softly, "Are we staying in here together?"

Trevor laughed, "Yes, G, there are no illusions in my father's eyes that we don't sleep together. It's not a king-sized bed like you're used to, but I think we can manage. But you can't get loud. Know what I mean?"

"Yeah, noted."

They sat in the well-used living room, not like the one at her house, which more closely resembled a showroom. "You have a very homey house, Shawn. I hope you let me help out. I'm actually a good cook."

"Are you, eh? Good to know. What do you like to cook?"

"Everything, actually give me a list, and I'll make it."

"Even Italian food?"

Gina boasted, "Especially Italian."

"Well, looks like my son found a winner this time."

Gina let that statement go.

"I made beef stew, you like that?"

"I will like whatever you give me."

Trevor told his dad, "I got the visa. We are leaving in three days to go back to New York."

"Well Trev, you got to do what you went there for, play music."

"Yes, G . . . I mean Gina and I have a lot of work to do, but we plan on getting a record deal."

Shawn questioned Gina. "Tell me, do you like this kind of work?"

"I do. It lets you be free and when you are good you feel it from the crowd; you want more. It's crazy I guess."

Shawn interrupted her, "No, you *should* feel that way about your work. Are you into gardening?"

"The house I come from has gardens all over—beautiful roses, peonies, and hydrangeas. It's breathtaking in the summer."

"Who takes care of the garden, you?"

Gina was embarrassed, "Oh, no, we have gardeners. Has Trevor told you about my family?"

"He said they were rich, extraordinarily rich."

"Yes, that's true. I hope that doesn't change your mind about me."

"Gina, let's sit and eat, okay?"

"Of course."

Trevor had barely spoken a word to his father since they entered the house.

Gina whispered to him, "Are you okay? You haven't said a word."

"I admit it's strange having you here at this house."

"Like my parents are easy? I'm enjoying your Dad. I hate calling him Shawn, though. It's weird. But he didn't want me to call him Mr. McNaughton. Give me a place to land the plane."

"Baby, you figure that one out. I'm getting a beer." A subtle change in demeanor came over Trevor. Did he not get along with his father?

Gina sat with the two of them at the dining room table. "This is nice. Dinners at my parents' house are always so formal. I enjoy a more relaxed environment like this. If you would like, Shawn . . . Okay I can't keep calling you Shawn. If it's not Mr. McNaughton, can I go out on a limb and call you . . . Dad?"

Trevor spit out his beer.

"I'm not trying to be presumptuous. I'm used to calling people an auntie or uncle, that kind of more personal salutation. Trevor, are you upset with me?"

"Baby, I'm enjoying this show."

Gina was totally confused by that comment.

Trevor added, "Dad so you know, when the day comes that we get married, we're eloping to Vegas. No one will know until we want them to know."

"You do what you want son; you always have. I'm going to watch TV."

Gina was trying to be helpful. "I'll be happy to clean up and if you give me a list, I can go to the grocery store and buy groceries for an Italian dinner. What would you like?"

"Can you make Italian food like the Italian Kitchen Restaurant? Meatballs and lasagna?"

"I can make Gina Ricci meatballs and lasagna, which is a hundred percent better, I promise."

"There you go."

Gina finished cleaning up the kitchen and looked for containers to place the leftover stew.

"Are you mad at me? I'm trying to be cordial to your dad."

"He eats and drinks a few beers and he's done; it's always been that way. I didn't want you to expect much."

"I'm trying to make a connection with him."

Trevor pulled her into the bedroom and closed the door. "I know you're trying so hard, but he's been like this is since my mother died. He doesn't say much and when he does, he's precise and direct. That's why I got so horribly mental and messed up."

Gina wanted to know, "Was this the way your room was your entire childhood? I love it. We can sleep in this small bed and snuggle up."

There was a knock on the door.

"Trevor, your mates are here."

"Wait what, who's here?" Gina wasn't expecting Trevor's mates tonight.

"It's probably Ian, Kevin, and Brian."

So, I get the chance to meet the mysterious Brian, she thought.

Trevor walked out dragging Gina. "Hey guys, look who I convinced to come to Vancouver."

"Gina, hey . . ." Ian and Kevin gave her a tight hug, "Are you ready to make music in a few days? Rio has some ideas in the works. He's just waiting on you."

"Gina, hi, I'm Brian Mayfield. I guess I can fill in as manager of the band."

"Hello, Brian. Well I am pretty sure my Uncle Tony is listed as manager of the band until we find a legitimate manager with some record company associations. So why are you really coming? Want to visit New York? I guess it's not a visit because we got you a visa, so you're planning to stay in the States?"

"I want to help you get further along . . . you know, help Trevor in whatever way possible."

"Appreciate it Brian. The band and I are totally capable of helping Trevor in whatever way necessary. Do you write music? Now that would be helpful."

Trevor looked at Gina, taken aback by her hostility toward Brian.

Trevor offered everybody a beer. Ian and Kevin asked questions about the band. Gina mentioned she wrote what could be a song; she needed help, and then added she wrote some ideas when she was on the plane coming to Vancouver, but she wanted Trevor to see them first.

Ian and Kevin set the empty bottles down and declared that they were leaving. "You two get some downtime together before the crazy shit starts to happen." Brian followed them out the door.

Gina was happy to meet them but was also happy she could be alone with Trevor in his old room.

Trevor shut the door. "G, you were fairly hostile to my friend Brian. You never met him before. What's up?"

"Baby, I'm sorry, but if I get a bad feeling from someone, I can't hide it. I definitely get a bad feeling from your friend. I'm sorry."

"Gina, you worry too much. We are fine, and not one person can get in between us. Let's to go my room and snuggle."

"Let me wash my face. I'll be right there."

"I love this bed. Did you lose your virginity here?"

"Yes. I actually did. It was so awkward."

"Well, you worked those awkward parts out."

They spooned together, watched TV, and had a little something extra before they went to sleep. Trevor begged Gina to not be so loud and put his hand over her mouth as a joke.

Next morning, Gina and Trevor made breakfast, then got ready to go to the grocery store. Gina asked, "How far is the nearest grocery store?"

Trevor looked at her and laughed, "G, we have a few grocery stores close. We aren't in the middle of nowhere. Come on and let's get you cooking."

They drove ten minutes to the grocery store. *This is the domestic experience I want with Trevor.* She felt good.

Gina got a cart and went right to the meat section looking for ground beef and pork to make meatballs. She found the meat counter and looked puzzled. "Trevor, everything is metric, what do I do? I skipped that part of Chemistry where we converted our system to metric. I feel like an idiot. I should have paid attention in high school."

"How much do you want?"

Gina made a face. "I guess a pound of each. I'm going to have this problem with the entire store?"

"Yes, you're in Canada. Didn't the Ricci family travel all around the place, like Europe?"

"You're being silly. Of course we did. But why would I pay attention to that shit? Everything was done for us. Now, I do know my way around a grocery store, but not seeing pounds and ounces is throwing me off. Help me."

Trevor took the grocery cart. "Read me your list."

"Ok, meat, we got. Cheeses, parsley, basil, lasagna noodles. We should get a nice bottle of red wine and I'll make a cheesecake. I even remembered a springform pan."

"G, this seems like a lot of work, you don't have . . ."

Gina shook her head. "Listen, I promised your father I would cook Italian food. Let me do this, please. I feel like maybe we can have a little connection. I mean, when will we see him again? Not for a while. We have a steep, formidable mountain to climb. Now let's hurry if I'm making homemade sauce it's got to cook for a while."

"If you want wine, we need to go the liquor store, only place we can get it."

Gina went in by herself and found the wine her father always ordered. It was $50.00 a bottle and she bought two.

They walked into the house and Gina exclaimed, "Phew, let's get cooking. Why don't you take your guitar out and start playing? It will be soothing while I cook." She kissed Trevor on his lips and wiped the lipstick off his mouth. Even that simple act was sensual.

Gina was happy to be doing something useful and having her man there. Like life was this simple, it was beautiful. She took the cheesecake out and made the sauce. She had her Italian dishes prepared. Trevor played some music she knew, and one piece she had never heard before. She wondered if it was the music for "Found You." It was beautiful. Gina was in a state of euphoria—how sweet this moment was—for her, for Trevor, and to be able to share it with his father.

The doorbell rang. Gina's face went sour when she saw Brian Mayfield walk in the door. She knew something was wrong here but couldn't put it into words. She didn't like him but didn't know why. It was a vibe. She was fairly good at judging people. She had an intuitive nature, which told her Brian Mayfield was going to be a problem.

Brian walked in like he belonged there. Maybe he knew Trevor longer, but certainly not as intimately as Gina. "Something smells really good. Who's cooking?"

Gina chimed in. "I am. I promised Trevor's dad I would cook an Italian meal for him. You know, a family dinner."

Gina could feel what was about to happen. She was hoping Trevor wouldn't do it after she told him how she felt about Brian, but there it was.

Trevor said it. "Stay for dinner. I know G will make too much anyway."

Gina shot Trevor a look she never thought she would give him—Mean Girl Italian with daggers and venom.

This was their moment with Shawn, and she had bought that expensive wine. Why waste it on this guy?

Trevor felt her stare piercing through him and dragged her back to the bedroom to talk in private. "G, it's fine. You're a better woman. Maybe he'll grow on you. It's dinner, and my dad has known Brian for years. I'll make sure he leaves early." Trevor saw the tears Gina was holding back.

She sniffled. "Oh God, I want to make you fucking happy. If this makes you happy, then I'll endure this intrusion. Only because it makes you happy."

Trevor leaned over and kissed her, and they walked back into the kitchen.

"Hey, Brian, I'm the luckiest man in the world to have this woman."

Brian couldn't say anything. Trevor had declared his feelings for Gina, and that seemed to be the way it would be. Gina was holding all the cards for the moment, but Brian was playing the long game. Gina didn't know that, but her feelings about Brian Mayfield would prove to be correct.

Shawn McNaughton returned home from work, saw the table set, and could smell the food cooking.

Gina thought she saw a small smile. "So, what do think? Better than Italian Kitchen? I made Italian cheesy bread and salad. I hope you like cheesecake. I made one for dessert."

"Gina, I don't know what to say. I haven't had this type of cooking in a while. Thank you, you love my son too much."

Gina smiled at him. "I do love him, but I wanted to make *you* happy tonight. So please relax. Here's a glass of wine. I'll serve dinner in a minute. Brian, why don't you sit here?" It was a small table, and he would be right there in any conversation. Gina decided she would observe rather than speak unless someone asked her a question. She would watch Brian.

Shawn talked about his day at work and Brian seemed genuinely interested. They had known each other a long time. *Maybe* he was decent.

Trevor kept an eye on Gina, knowing at any time she could come up with her direct line of questions.

Gina and the three men ate, and *Dad* was over the moon with the food, which he said was way better than Italian Kitchen. He even told Trevor, "Don't mess this up. You should marry this woman."

Gina smiled. "Thank you for the compliment. It's appreciated. Like Trevor said, when we get married no one will know until we decide to tell people."

She thought Brian was going to choke. If only.

Brian spoke directly to Gina. "This is delicious, and I appreciate you having me here, at Trevor's. Is there anything you can't do? Because this guy here is crazy about you."

Gina smiled. "Brian, I can't write music . . . I can sing well, and I can write lyrics. That will be my contribution to the band, and oh yeah,

I'm a badass bitch onstage. So that's what I can't do and what I can do. Unfortunate, but that's my limitation."

Trevor threw her a look she knew. *Settle down Gina.*

She got it. "Anyone want another glass of wine?" She was trying hard to be the hostess that Franny would want her to be. But it's hard when you know that someone is trying to interfere with your life. Gina cleared the table and served dessert.

Brian lingered. However, Trevor gave the excuse he was tired, and they had a busy day tomorrow. It was, after all, their last day in Vancouver. She hoped they could spend it alone with Trevor's Dad who had taken the day off of work. Brian said his goodbyes and asked how they were going to the airport.

Gina chimed in. "I got us a limo. Too many people and suitcases, so you're going to the airport first class."

"Hey, cool. I'll see you both then."

Gina washed the dishes and was putting leftovers away in the containers she had bought at the store that afternoon. Trevor walked behind Gina at the sink, put his arms around her waist, and whispered, "Thank you for everything. I know it's not what you expected and I'm sorry for that. But you reminded me once again why I love you."

She turned around, put his beautiful blond curls behind his ears and whispered, "I'll do anything that makes you happy. Always remember that, for you, anything." She kissed him in a sweet long kiss. "Let me clean this up. You're starting to get me going if you know what I mean."

He did.

Shawn was watching TV and called out from his recliner, "Thank you Gina, for making this guy a wonderful meal and making this son of mine happy. You two should go and relax."

Trevor took that as a hint for them to be able to go to his bedroom.

Gina put on one of Trevor's old concert band T-shirts she found in his dresser. Trevor stripped down to his boxers. They laid down in his bed, smoked a joint and a cigarette. Gina pulled out a bag of potato chips. She was dying for them after that joint. They got sleepy and spooned for a while. When she felt Trevor was ready to go, she whispered, "Are we doing this?"

The answer was yes, and they fell asleep content.

The next morning Gina called the airlines. Gina, Trevor, Ian, and Kevin had open-ended tickets. They just needed to get their seat assignments. Trevor and Gina had their first-class seats, and since Ian and Kevin flew out first class and were going back coach, the money went for Brian Mayfield's seat. Gina went into the kitchen and made coffee, French toast, and bacon for breakfast. Trevor stumbled out in his boxers and kissed Gina on the head. Shawn came out dressed. When he saw that Gina had made breakfast, he told her she was spoiling him. While eating, Shawn asked Gina if she would like to see his vegetable garden.

"I would love to see it."

Shawn took her to the backyard, the boundary lined by an old split-rail fence. In the center was a perfectly square plot, filled with seedlings; it was still a little too cold.

"What are these? They smell wonderful."

Shawn told Gina they were herbs and explained what each one was. Gina grew up with beautiful plants but never asked what anything was or how they were planted. When they got back home, she would ask the gardeners to clear a patch of dirt so she could start her own herb garden. The smell of the basil, oregano, and lavender was so aromatic. She must have her own herb garden.

It was a wistful day, the last day with Trevor's dad. Gina felt they had made a sweet connection with the dinner and her interest in the garden. "Dad . . . I want you to know how much I love your son. I know he has faults. I know about his drinking and the demons that go with that. I accept him for his faults and love him because of them. I will try my best to always keep him safe. The life we are building has many pitfalls; it's the life we choose to pursue. I know you may not understand this life of music, and we don't know what to expect either. We need to try. Love will keep us from the hazards, or I like to believe it will. Please trust me, I won't let him fall down."

Shawn looked at her for a moment, then grabbed her hand. "Gina, I don't worry about your devotion to Trevor. I can see you love him deeply and I believe he loves you back the same way. Trevor will lose his way sometimes. He always does. Are you strong enough to carry that? Do you have that much love for him, to love blindly when he messes it all up?"

"Yes, yes, I do. When we get settled, I would love for you to come to New York. I hope you take me up on it one day." She leaned over and kissed him on the cheek. "I would like to take you out for dinner tonight, anywhere. We can drive to downtown Vancouver. Any restaurant you want to try?"

"There's a cute little bistro fifteen minutes away. I thought about going but being alone, I never did."

Gina was happy. "Well, that's set, we're going. Do we need reservations? Don't worry, I will take care of it."

She spent a good part of the late morning and lunchtime with Shawn. Later, she walked inside and sat next to Trevor as he was playing his guitar. "Hey Babe, I told your father we would take him out tonight, being it's our last night here."

"Gina, I love you, but my dad isn't the sweet man you think he is. Remember, I was left alone for a good part of my life after my mother died. I got into trouble because he wasn't there. Our relationship is complicated. I see he likes you, so I won't interfere. We'll go out tonight but know I can't wait to get on that plane tomorrow."

"I understand your relationship is complicated. I want to have part of your past, the good parts, and connect your past to our future. No matter what you did in the past, I support you, so you will never fall back on those demons. I'm certainly not without my faults, but damn, I take you the way you are, no questions." She laid her head is his lap. "Play for me. I love hearing your fingers on the strings."

Trevor played for two hours as Gina lay there listening to the beautiful music coming from his guitar. He kept playing the same music from the other day. "Babe, what is that song? I don't recognize it."

"Something I'm working on . . . soon we'll flush it out with Rio and Jeff."

"Well, I should show you something I wrote on the plane. I was feeling many emotions. Let me show you . . ."

(Waiting)

Today is the day, I look at your face; see your blue eyes and your handsome face

Wondered, how lucky can I be to love you.

I flew many miles but never a journey to far to see you, to be with you

To tell you that I love you for lifetime

You're so easy to love, so easy to love, how can love be this simple

But never a journey to far to see you no matter how

Many miles, never to far, so many miles to be next to where you are.

"I had an idea, and you guys have to refine it. I write what I feel. I'm probably not that good at it."

"G, you wrote this about me?"

"Yeah, you're the only man I am in love with."

He put down his guitar, leaned over, and kissed her. "Come here you beautiful woman. I want to show you how much I love you. I love the idea you thought about writing a song for me. I want to show you how you are *my everything.*

"I would like that too."

Gina made the dinner reservation for six thirty since they all had to get up early in the morning. They enjoyed themselves and each shared a little bit about themselves over their meal.

Shawn looked at Trevor and told him he hoped that things would take off for his band and that he would settle down.

Trevor told him he appreciated his support, and that was the best they both could do.

PAYING DUES AND MAKING THE CUT

MORNING CAME. Time to fly home to New York. Gina was happy they would get to continue their life back at the carriage house, although she enjoyed Vancouver and hoped she would return soon. The limo came to pick up Trevor and Gina first. Everyone else was supposed to meet at Ian's, then off to the airport. They pulled up at the little cabin where Ian and Kevin were staying. Brian had three oversized suitcases. Clearly, he expected to stay a long time.

Five passengers in the limo and four of them were critical to the new band. Gina still had to figure out how Brian Mayfield fit into the picture of Perfection. She would come to realize he was her worst nightmare.

Trevor and Gina were perfectly comfortable in first class. Champagne flowed for Gina and Trevor enjoyed a beer. They were served a hot meal, cooked in the galley, with cookies and ice cream for dessert. Hard work was definitely on Gina's mind. They wanted to be headliners, get some traction in the club circuit, and build their name. It might take a year or so. She was ready and knew everyone else was too. The biggest prize for Gina was having Trevor back home, knowing he wouldn't have to worry about visa issues anymore. Gina snuggled up against him. She was happy. No, she was more. She was ecstatic to have him next to her again. No one could break that bond, although she knew with any kind of fame there would always be someone who would try to interfere. She didn't realize it would be an internal threat.

Gina looked up at Trevor. "I love you, babe. I'm so happy we're going home together."

"I can't wait to be back at the carriage house. It's home."

"What's Brian going to do when we get back to New York?"

"G, don't worry about him. It's not a problem."

"If you say so. Will he be living at the Franklin Square house?"

"Yeah, sure. Rio has been a tremendous help keeping up with the rent on the house,"Trevor admitted.

"Rio is going to expect us at his house tomorrow, you realize that. We have about a week before Sammy Gold wants to audition us. I honestly think he wants to rank us; he can't seriously want us to audition."

"We play Sammy's game. Then we make our demands and see where it gets us. He's an asshole. We all know that but we need him so we can play the better clubs. I'm not worried, are you? I have a few songs I wrote, and Rio has his. We'll still have to play some covers. That is what the people at the clubs want to hear."

Gina was thinking out loud. "Do we sing off each other, or sing a cover together? I'm not sure how that is going to work out."

"We will figure it out when we decide on what covers we play. Anything original, we arrange ourselves. It's all good. Don't worry about what we play yet. We're good."

Gina snuggled back under Trevor's arm and pulled up the blanket and fell asleep. She woke about an hour away from JFK. She didn't expect to see Brian in the aisle, crouched down, talking to Trevor. She was still groggy and couldn't hear what he was saying, probably a good thing. Then a flight attendant shagged him out of first class and told him he needed to go back to his seat; the plane was starting to descend. Gina sat back, with a smile. *Brian, you were thwarted by the airline.*

Gina jolted up. She realized that Trevor and the rest of the guys were going to use those work visas for the first time; she hoped everything was in order. *Shit, why didn't I think about this sooner?* There was nothing to do at this point. She felt the pressure of the plane descending fairly quickly—and there it was—"The City" for people who live in New York. For people not from New York, it was "Manhattan." Nothing else compared to that beautiful skyline. Gina felt calm, *my home, this place, New York. We will make our mark here.*

Gina always carried an oversized purse when traveling. She pulled down her large purse from the overhead while Trevor blocked the crowds of passengers waiting to disembark. Gina grabbed his hand, "Let's get to customs now before we have to wait on line."

They were taken quickly and answered a few questions. Then "Welcome to New York." She thought, *You idiot. You see I live here.* But knew better than to talk to a customs agent that way. He looked over Trevor's documents and handed them back with no issue.

They walked to the luggage carousel. "Trevor, we will wait for the rest of the guys here while they get their luggage." It took Ian, Kevin, and Brian twenty minutes to get through the customs line. By that time, the luggage started to come out. Brian needed one of those carts since he had three suitcases.

The automatic doors opened and, standing there dressed all in black with his signature sunglasses, was Rio. Gina walked up to him and gave him a hug. "You're nuts. Why did you come here? I thought there was a limo waiting."

"Yeah, Gina, there is, but I had to take the ride to see these fucking guys." Rio felt that the vision was now in focus.

"Hey man, it's so good you're back." He gave Trevor a hug and high-fived Ian and Kevin.

He noticed Brian Mayfield and took out his hand. "Hey, I don't know you man. What's your name?"

"I'm Brian Mayfield. I'm going to help manage the band."

Rio shook his head. "Hey, my dad is the manager on record, but I'm sure we can find something for you to do, like we need roadies. You can hire us four really good roadies. I'm sick of setting up my own shit. There you go Brian, you have a gig."

Gina smirked. Serves him right, saying he was a manager.

The limo was parked right outside the arrival doors.

Trevor and Gina sat next to each other. Rio sat on the other side of Trevor; he wanted to talk a little band business. The rest of the group sat across from them. Gina asked Ian and Kevin, "So how do you feel about going back to Franklin Square? Is it weird to be back here?"

Ian laughed. "Actually, I'm thrilled. I can't wait to take a long, hot shower."

Kevin echoed Ian's comments.

Gina added, "And then order some good New York pizza."

Brian looked puzzled. "The pizza is good here?"

Gina laughed out loud, hard, "You're kidding me, right? It's the only place for pizza. Whoa! How did you not know that?"

Rio had an announcement for Perfection. "Okay, we have one week before the Golds come. We're good but need to show them *how* good. So tomorrow, we should work on covers first, and then gradually add our original stuff, which we will work on this week too. Is everyone good with the plan?"

BACK HOME

TRAFFIC WAS HORRIBLE but they made it to Franklin Square sooner than they thought. The limo driver placed the suitcases in the driveway. Rio handed the house keys to Ian. "Cool guys. See you tomorrow."

A few minutes later, the limo pulled away with Rio, Gina, and Trevor.

Rio looked at Gina and Trevor. "You guys look happy. It's good, right? You guys are all good?"

"Rio, yes, we're all good. We can't wait to get home. Don't get me wrong, I totally enjoyed Vancouver. It was beautiful, you should really go. But I think Trevor and I are happy to be in our little cocoon."

"Gina, we get a record deal and it takes off, North American tour baby."

"Okay Rio let's conquer Sammy Gold first. Then we'll worry about the tour. I'm so tired. We lost three hours, so I'm beat. Maybe we should order pizza?" Gina suggested.

Trevor was excited. "I'll bring all three of my guitars to get the sound right. Hey, G, whatever you want, it's all good with me."

The limo approached the gate of the Ricci estate. Nothing had changed. Gina was gone for six days but it seemed like so much longer. Rio punched in the code and the limo pulled up to Gina's much loved carriage house. Rio got out with them. "No worries, I'm not going up. My car is parked here.

You two are home now. Remember, eleven o'clock a.m."

Gina and Trevor walked up the flight of stairs and opened the door. She noticed covered dishes on the dining room table. It was fettuccine alfredo with shrimp and Serena's antipasto salad, and there was a note, "Welcome Home Gina & Trevor, Love Mom & Dad."

"Wow, I feel special. All I want to do is rip these clothes off, wash my face, then eat."

"I'm right behind you. Let's see who gets to the table first." Trevor had an unfair advantage—pants and shirt off, boxers.

"I see you. No fair. I have to wash my face and shit. Start eating. I'll be right out." Gina washed her face, brushed her hair, fluffed it out, and wore one of Trevor's T-shirts over lace underwear.

"Look at you, Gina Poole. You look so good . . ."

"That you could eat me up, yes? Eat your dinner and we'll discuss dessert later."

"It feels good to be back here. This place is where we started, it's special."

"Oh, Trev, you're being sentimental. I love it. I love my life right now, it's perfect. I can't wait to get into that cloud of a bed we have and cuddle up to you and feel normal."

They finished dinner, packed up leftovers, cleaned up, locked the door, and went to the bedroom. They got under the comfy duvet and smoked a joint and a Sobranie.

"Trev, you're not going to believe I'm saying this, but I'm tired. Can I save your dessert for maybe the morning?"

"You're a funny lady. Yes, I love lying here together, smoking your funny cigarettes, and falling asleep next to you."

Gina ran her fingers through his long, beautiful blond hair. "Trevor McNaughton, I will never leave you. Ever. You're my heart always. Good night my baby." Gina fell asleep instantly. Trevor followed after her.

HARD WORK

THE ALARM WENT OFF AT NINE. Gina turned it off, got up, and made coffee. She had a feeling it might be hard to get Trevor up, so she brought him coffee. "Good morning. Ready to start Perfection?"

"Oh G, this coffee is fantastic. Yes, I've been waiting for this for a long time, and we are finally doing it."

Gina sat next to him on the bed. "Yeah, I would have never thought this four years ago, but now I can't imagine my life without music." Gina snaked her way up Trevor's body and stopped halfway. "I'll have a little of this with my morning coffee if you don't mind."

"No, I don't mind a bit." Trevor and Gina were definitely a passionate and loving couple. They looked like that couple, and their mannerisms with each other were very intentional and intimate. There was no way the audience could not catch that magnetism. If they were going to do covers, she wanted to make sure there was something absolutely racy in the song, something she could play off of Trevor. After all, they both were lead singers. She was okay if Trevor took the lead and she sang harmony.

She thought of a few songs she wanted to sex up. If the record companies wanted that extra, she was happy to provide it.

After breakfast, they headed over to Rio's. He had the amps and microphones all set up, even Ian's drums.

"Hey, you two are the first. I definitely thought you would be late. How does it feel to be back, Trevor?"

"Oh man, so good. There is an energy in New York. You feel it."

Gina was already in work mode. "Listen, if we are going to do some covers, I want to use the sex factor to play off Trevor. Like if we sang 'Can't Get Enough' or 'Houses of the Holy.' How about 'All Right Now,' 'I Just Want to Make Love to You,' some Stones, let's pump up the sex."

"Damn Gina, you were the one who said you didn't want your relationship so exposed and now you basically want to dry hump Trevor onstage?"

"Rio, you're ridiculous. I want to give them what they want. Trevor and I playing off each other or singing together. Is that a problem? I know the original music is a focus, but the club circuit wants to hear music that they know. We have to figure it out. Trev, what are your thoughts?"

"I want to concentrate on our own music. But I get what you're saying. We do have to pick out covers and sprinkle our own material in. We have to show any A&R person we have enough of our own shit to record a demo. We have to do both, unfortunately. Rio, any covers we do should show off your lead guitar playing, and we can switch, where I play lead. Are you in sync with that idea? Where are the guys? They're late."

"Trevor . . . this guy Brian. He doesn't really think he's our manager, does he? On paper my father is, but sometime soon we need to get a real manager who deals with the money and club owners, and Sammy Gold. When we take off, we need someone who has a wide range of management experience. Who is he to you again?"

Trevor looked resigned in his answer. "Look, you're right. He has no experience in music at all, but he can get roadies, make sure equipment is maintained, shit like that. He's an old friend, that's all. I thought I would give him something to be a part of, that's it. He has to prove himself. But it's funny, my lady over here doesn't trust him at all."

Ian and Kevin arrived then, and Jeff came in after. Brian lingered outside for a minute. He had probably never seen a house like this one.

"Man, you guys are like thirty minutes late. We got some serious shit to cover." Rio wasn't going to let them slide.

They discussed the covers that should go on a set list. Gina added her favorites—"Long Distance Runaround," "Money," "Tuesday Afternoon." Those were more progressive for these guys, but Gina could carry off the lead with confidence. Collectively they made a list of fifteen covers they felt would show off Gina's voice and Trevor and Rio's guitar skills.

Now for the real work. Trevor had written four songs. Gina was surprised that the one he pushed was "Found You," the song he had written for her. Trevor played some chords and Rio added a bit more guitar. They started putting together a mix of music. Gina could only wait until the vocals were addressed. She had no idea how to write music. Trevor and Rio were brilliant, and they knew what key and chords would work. Gina was clueless until Trevor started to teach her how to harmonize with him. The band knew Gina could sing, her voice was sultry and she sang with feeling. She put her soul into every note. It captured you, her voice made singing male parts easier. She didn't have to try to sing those high soprano notes.

Rio had some ideas, which of course highlighted his and Trevor's guitar mastery. Ian was an excellent drummer. He and Jeff were a great combo. Kevin had the soundboard getting the right amount of bass, guitar, and vocals. He could accentuate each song with the right mix. Gina was bored since the band was working on bringing their ideas into one formulated song without vocals.

They worked for seven hours straight and decided to eat. It was funny, both Gina and Brian were on the sideline. The group elected to go to Island Splash Diner. Trevor and Gina got in the Benz. Rio drove Jeff and the rest of the guys took the car that was the old Stanley Park communal car.

As Trevor drove them to dinner, he asked, "G, I know you were bored but this is a process, and you will be a big part once we can put things together. You trust me, right?"

"Yes, of course I do. I want to know what I'm going to sing, and I need to get my voice back in shape. I haven't sung in over two months. Sammy Gold is going to be judging me the hardest. Although if I wear see-through clothing and show my tits, he will overlook my deficiencies."

"I'm not keen on you showing your tits off onstage. I would rather you dry hump me onstage." A grin came over Trevor's face. "Yeah, yeah ok, you drive me crazy."

They stayed at the diner for two hours and broke up for the night. Rio told the band to meet at the same time the next morning.

Trevor and Gina returned to their nice quiet little home. Gina started stripping immediately. After a long day, clothes felt confining.

Trevor laid down his guitars in the living room. "G, what are you doing? I know rehearsal didn't have you doing anything, but baby I promise you will be working hard. Why are you so quiet? You okay?"

She came out of the bathroom naked except for her lace underwear. "I don't know Trevor. Does it look like I'm upset at you right now?" She walked up to him, jostled his long blond hair, and pulled off his shirt. She maneuvered his jeans, then ripped off his boxers, then pushed him back on the bed. She leaned down and kissed him softly and sweetly. Her kisses started to make him hard. She peeled off the lace panties and straddled him. She kissed him on the lips, around his neck, smelling his hair and nuzzling his ears, gently kissing each one. She kissed his chest. She could tell she was driving him crazy by the moans he was making.

"What's the matter, baby? You want something more? I can give it to you. Tell me what you want."

"You know what I want. Take it."

"You mean take all of it?"

"Is this a new game you're playing? It's totally a tease . . . come on baby."

"You want me, and I want you more. Let me show you . . ." Gina took him inside her and took total control of his body. He begged her not to stop. And why would she? He was driving her insane with a primal passion. She tried to prolong the pleasure as long as possible, but he finished quickly.

Trevor was sweating. Tonight, she had whipped him into a frenzy of sexual pleasure. "God Gina, are you trying to drive me crazy? You always have some new way of driving me mad."

"Trev baby, I always want to leave you wanting more and will always keep you guessing all the different ways I will pleasure you. That's a promise." She kissed him as she dismounted him. She rolled a joint and lit a Sobranie. "Want a cigarette?"

"Yeah baby, thanks. You wore me out. I won't have a problem falling asleep tonight."

Gina finished her cigarette and kissed him goodnight. "Baby, I love you. Goodnight." They slept wrapped in each other's bodies. Tomorrow will be another day of practice. Maybe she'll get to sing something.

HARMONIZING AND WEDDING DATES

THE PERFECTION TEAM was at Rio's at eleven and then formed breakout groups. Rio wanted Gina to sing "Can't get Enough," but she would need Trevor. Jeff added a bass line.

They started the song and Gina got flustered, wanting them to start over. She started singing in her low voice. She added a little more emotion, and her attempt was passable. On the third attempt, she closed her eyes and envisioned the audience. She let loose and started dancing as she sang, her movements taking every beat of the song. It would make the audience get into the song. She stopped. "I need Trevor to sing with me, if I can't get enough of him, I need him to sing." When they sang together, it was absolute gold.

Rio stopped writing music and looked over. "Yeah man, that's it. Do it again Gina. Play up to your man. Trevor, let her go."

She revealed a part of herself Rio had never seen before—a sexual foreplay with a song and with Trevor. Rio thought this was going to be what sells in the clubs. People would want to follow Perfection just to see the show between Gina and Trevor, and Rio's great guitar licks. He asked Gina what song she wanted to try next.

"I would like to try 'Long Distance Runaround.'" Gina sang tentatively at first but nailed it on her second attempt. She knew what it was like—to be separated from the person you loved, it sucks.

Rio was amped, feeling like things were heating up. The rest of the afternoon was dedicated to serious music writing. Trevor wanted to finish "Found You," and he wanted to write Gina some harmonizing lines to his.

They worked until seven that evening. Brian had sat there with nothing to do. Rio mentioned that he wanted him to look for roadies, guys with experience. He gave Brian a few names to contact. He had to do *something*.

When Trevor and Gina got home that night, there was a message on their answering machine from Franny. "Hi princess and Trevor, it's Mom. I wanted you to know that Frankie and MaryAnn set their wedding date for June fourteenth. I know you were hoping that you would not be in the wedding party, but she wants you to be a bridesmaid. Of course, it will be at St. Mary's, but unfortunately the Fanellis are having the reception at one of those wedding factories in Huntington. It is not our family's way, but your father and I will contribute to make it nice. So, that's all. Hope to see you both soon. Bye for now."

Gina's face fell with disappointment. "Oh shit, I don't want to do this. She has no taste, and she'll have me in a cheesy dress like yellow or lavender. Ugh, you will have to go, you realize that. Which means we won't be able to work that Friday or Saturday."

"Don't worry about it. We need to concentrate on the music. We will deal with it."

THE GRIND

IT WAS THE SAME GRIND—rehearse, write music, and try to get a good bunch of covers. They needed to have it all set before Sammy and Nadine Gold came to see them on Tuesday. The band rehearsed until Saturday evening. Trevor and Rio wrote the music for "Found You," adding a background vocal for Gina.

Sunday was a day off before their audition. Franny had invited Trevor and Gina for brunch. When they entered the house, Franny greeted them. "We haven't seen you two since you came back from Vancouver. What have you been doing?"

Gina had to explain. "Mom, we're rehearsing since the band is technically a new band. The agency that signs the talent for the Tri-State area needs to audition us. Which is silly because Trevor and Rio are extremely talented. We have had to write some of our own music. We have been working hard to get the music tight. We want to play bigger clubs and have a schedule for gigs."

"Well, it sounds like a lot of work for you both, but this is what you wanted, correct?"

Trevor answered, "Yes, Mrs. Ricci, it's what we have been working for. We believe it will pay off."

"That's wonderful news. Come into the sunroom. I have it all set for the family." To contrast the dark February landscape, Franny had set the table in a completely white theme. White linens, white roses, and white tapers in the silver candelabras.

"Mom, when you say family, who's coming?"

"Your father, myself, you two, Ant, and I invited Aunt Deidre and Uncle Tony. Maybe Rio will come but I'm sure you have seen enough of him."

Mario entered the sunroom. "Is that my princess? Hello Trevor. Scotch neat. Here you go. You both dressed for the occasion. No matter, hey you both are here, happy right? After all that visa bullshit. Feds."

"Well Daddy, sorry we came in our jeans, but we have been working hard on our music."

Franny motioned for everyone to sit down and called Ant to come downstairs. The front door opened, and Aunt Deidre and Uncle Tony came through but not Rio. He probably had a hot date. He was so involved in the music, he needed a "slut break." Aunt Deidre came over to Trevor and Gina. "I've heard you practicing, you sound great. I love hearing you sing, both of you. This will mean so much in you taking the next step."

"Thank you, Aunt Deidre. We have a big day on Tuesday. Keep your fingers crossed."

The brunch consisted of Serena's quiches, bacon, sausage, shrimp salad, chicken salad, and homemade biscuits. The alcohol was flowing—mimosas, scotch, wine. That worried Gina slightly, knowing that Trevor had a problem, but it hadn't turned on any alarms yet. After two hours the couple decided it was time to go back to the carriage house; they would soon have a big day ahead of them. Gina did some laundry and made a shopping list, while Trevor practiced "Found You."

"Come here, G. Come and harmonize with me. I want to get this right."

She liked the way "Found You" sounded on the acoustic guitar; it made the whole song sweeter. Then Rio could come in with a big guitar solo. "I love it, sounds so much more like a love song."

"Come on and let's do *The New York Times* crossword puzzle together."

Gina slipped into Trevor's old Woodstock T-shirt, and he stripped down to his boxers. They lit a joint, smoked Sobranies, got close to finishing the puzzle, and did what they did most evenings—made love.

Sitting up in bed, Gina asked Trevor, "Are you nervous about what Sammy Gold is going to throw at us?"

"I'm not. We have a solid group of songs. Our originals are great and mixed with the right covers, we will kill it. Don't worry. Don't be nervous. You'll be fine, more than fine. Now let's get some sleep."

GOLDEN HOUR

THE MORNING OF THEIR AUDITION came and Gina got up and made a pot of coffee. She wanted to be fully awake for this audition. She woke up Trevor with coffee and the two of them speculated what would happen. Trevor wore his worn-out jeans and T-shirt, but Gina thought, *I'm going dress to kill.* She wore a short boho dress with billowing sleeves made of a sheer gauzy floral print and thigh-high boots.

They got to Rio's by ten o'clock, giving them time to tune guitars and bass and have Ian's drums set up the way he liked them. Their set list included two covers and two original songs: "Found You" and a classic rock song that Rio had written called "Punch the Night." Sammy and Nadine Gold arrived at eleven fifteen. Everyone exchanged pleasantries but they were there to judge this new band that had been created from Vision Skye and Stanley Park.

Sammy thought a different name would be better, but the band stood firm on the name; it was nonnegotiable. They started with "Can't get Enough," then "Found You" acoustic version, with Rio coming in with a hard guitar solo. The next song was "Saw the Light," which showcased Trevor and Gina together. They followed that with "Punch the Night." They were ready to play a few more covers when Sammy stopped them.

"I knew you would be a power band, but I needed to see how you worked together. It works. It's big. I'm placing you in a club on Monday, Wednesday, and Thursday. That's steady. On the weekends I am thinking of getting you dates in the A clubs."

Rio spoke up. "Sammy, sounds great, but we need to talk money. We have no problem with you getting your 10 percent as long as you're charging the club premium. We also want a percentage of the door with a guaranteed minimum. We know we will bring in the crowds. We still have a following from Vision Skye and Stanley Park."

Trevor spoke next. "At this point Sammy, we don't need to prove that we can bring people into the clubs, so the deal is what Rio laid out for you. You taking it? We would like to start playing as soon as possible."

Sammy accepted. "You have a deal. Let me get to my office and I'll let you know the clubs you will be playing Monday, Wednesday, and Thursday. You're telling me you're ready to perform right now?"

Rio jumped in. "Give us a week. We need to get a truck for our equipment. Do you have any names of roadies looking for work?"

Gina remained quiet, but was thinking, *What the hell? Brian Mayfield was asked to do this. It was his job, but he didn't know anybody in the Tri-State area club scene so how could he do the one task that was given to him? Sammy will come through with names.*

Sammy left with, "Like I said, I'll call you tomorrow with the clubs you will be performing at."

The whole band exhaled a sigh of relief. They had done it. They were a new player in the club circuit, and they could rival The Thirst. Ian looked amazed. "This calls for a party. We should go to the Franklin Square house and get beer and food and party."

Gina had remained quiet throughout the whole negotiation. "You guys are happy with this arrangement? Don't you think we should wait to see where he is putting us?"

Rio was shaking his head. "Gina, we got a deal where we are playing three nights a week. We will build a following. I think it's a good deal."

"Okay Rio. I trust you and Trevor. Hey, Brian, you need to talk to Sammy and get us four good roadies. Kevin, what do you need?"

"Listen Gina, four roadies who know how to set up amps, drums, and lights. I think I can train them."

"Cool, so Brian, call Sammy later and get at least six to eight names, and make sure Kevin is with you when you are having discussions with these guys. You wanted to be a *manager*, so do your job." Gina was pointed and calculated in what she said to Brian. She could not shake her feeling about this guy. He also reminded her of someone she couldn't place, but she was thinking about it constantly.

DEMONS FLY

A PARTY AT THE FRANKLIN SQUARE HOUSE. She had slept there a few times, but Trevor had moved into the carriage house quickly. "Okay guys, what do you want for this party?"

"Gina, if you can get a keg and some pizza, maybe some of those great Italian subs." Ian was such a cool guy and had simple tastes.

Gina laughed. "I'm sure I can find a place to do all that for us. We have a family friend who owns a restaurant. I'll ask him about a keg, but that's a lot of beer guys."

Ian laughed. "You remember Trevor and I are Canadian?"

Gina was not pleased about all that alcohol. Trevor had not shown her that side of himself, but she knew it was there. She did not want that demon to show up.

She used the phone at Rio's to place the order. Domenic would take care of her. He even told her where she could get the beer. She was afraid it wouldn't fit in the Benz. Domenic would deliver the food no problem, but the keg was something else.

Trevor and Gina got into the Benz. Trevor loved driving it, and Gina didn't care. They went to the liquor store to pick up the beer and asked what beer they could get in a keg. The clerk listed all the beers including a Canadian brand. Trevor got excited, so that was the one. The clerk glanced out the window and asked if the red Benz was their car, because there was no way a keg would fit. Once Gina gave her credit card, he noticed the name.

"Are you related to Mario Ricci?"

"I am. I'm his daughter."

"Oh, well no problem. Where are we delivering it to?"

Gina gave the address and was told the keg would be delivered in less than an hour. It pays to be a Ricci in Manhasset.

Meanwhile, Brian Mayfield had some other party favors he was working on. He spoke to Sammy and got the names of six out-of-work roadies who would love the work. It was up to him to follow through.

Gina was feeling awkward going to the old Stanley Park house. "Trev baby, it's weird going there. I mean, I remember in the beginning of our relationship I stayed there a few nights, but it's a guys' house."

"Should we have had it at the carriage house where your father would watch security footage? I don't think either one of us wants that. Besides, if they get shit-faced, they're home and can sleep it off."

"You're right as usual, but I'm the only woman there."

"Baby don't count on that. I'm sure there will be some ladies partying."

"Do you mean groupies or star fuckers?"

"Listen, Gina, whatever you want to call them, it doesn't affect us. Who cares what those guys do? We will hang out, then leave."

Gina hesitated, "Remember, you promised, I'm holding you to it."

They arrived at the house as Domenic was pulling up. There were already a lot of cars parked on the street. Gina showed Domenic to the kitchen and the dining room table where he laid out a spread. She thanked him and gave him a generous tip.

When Gina walked into the living room, there were four girls already hanging out. She turned around and went back to setting up the food.

Rio walked in. "Gina, I know you, you're upset that I called up some chicks. You know it's no big deal."

"Rio, I don't want to have anything to do with it. I don't feel like having conversations with these kinds of chicks. Maybe when you get a nice decent girl, I will feel different. Excuse me. You go have fun."

Gina found Trevor in his old bedroom, which Ian had taken over. "Gina, when I first came here, I thought, look I'm in a nice place here, going to make music, make my dream come true. I didn't count on meeting a woman, a woman who would change my life. I never thought I deserved a decent woman, but you're more than decent. Any man would want you, and why you picked me, I'll never know."

"My love, we picked each other that first night. I never look back, only forward to the life we want to build. Don't ever ask why I picked you; it was always going to be you." She kissed him, pushed back his hair, and held his face and kissed his forehead.

Trevor grabbed her hand and pulled her up. "We need to make some sort of presence."

When they walked into the living room, Ian handed her a plastic cup with beer. Gina wasn't a big beer drinker, but she would be a good team player and have the Canadian beer that Trevor was excited about. She was hungry, so she went to the table to make a plate. One of the "ladies" walked up to her and Gina thought, *Here it comes.*

"Hey, you're Gina Poole, right? Rio's cousin? What's it like singing in a band? I bet it's really cool."

Gina turned to her and answered, "You know, it's a job like anything else. It seems glamorous but it's hard work. So that's all I have to say."

Brian walked in the front door and went directly into his bedroom. Fifteen minutes later he came out holding a mirror loaded with cocaine. He started separating it into lines and offered it around. All the guys and some of the ladies took a hit. Gina did not like that Brian now brought something into the band's inner works. He turned to Trevor. "Come on guy, you used to go hard with this stuff. A little, it won't hurt. Come on—like the old days."

Trevor snorted two lines of coke. Gina sat back and watched him. *Are we really going down this road? Brian has brought big-time drinking and cocaine back into Trevor's life. The demons. What the fuck is he trying to do?*

When Brian got around to her, he asked her if she wanted to indulge. Absolutely not. Someone needed to drive home. She was growing angrier by the minute. The girls were coked out and hanging on Trevor, telling him was "sooo sexy." Gina was fuming. She grabbed another slice of pizza and sat in the kitchen, not wanting to watch the shit show Brian had created. Even Ian and Jeff were different. Coked out, they were rowdy and out of control. She wanted to leave. *If this is the way they party for just getting steady gigs, what the hell would happen if we truly made it? What would Brian Mayfield do then?*

Trevor was talking to Rio, who had one of the girls on his lap when Gina returned to the living room. Trevor and Rio knew that look. She was ready to blow. As fucked up as Trevor was, he knew it was time to leave. When they were halfway out the door, Brian grabbed Trevor.

"Trev seriously, you're leaving? This is your party. Come on, we still have lots of coke to do."

Trevor knew he was already fucked with Gina. He shook his head and told Brian to have fun, but he was out. Brian shot Gina a look, and she returned it with a 'fuck you' attitude. "Hey Brian . . ." When he turned around, she gave him the finger.

Gina got in the driver's seat and looked at Trevor. "You were telling me earlier how lucky you are to have me, and now you are so fucking high and drunk I can't believe you. You can't even look at me straight. What the fuck, Trev? We won a prize and at the first chance you all get drunk and high on cocaine like a bunch of fucking idiots. Is this what I need to worry about each time the band has something great happen?"

Trevor gazed glassy eyed out the windshield.

"Brian is a fucking scumbag. I do not like him. He has an agenda. I think he is using you to feel important. I don't know how far he'll go. I am livid with you right now. I have never been mad at you before like this. Tell me why you felt you needed to slide down that slope. Please give me an answer."

Trevor shook his head. "I don't have an answer. I know I fucked up. But you also know that I am quite capable of being that asshole guy. I told you that when I met you. I do not want to be that guy for you. I'm so sorry. Can you pull over? I think I might get sick."

"Fuck, Trevor. Really?" Gina pulled over and he stumbled onto the shoulder to vomit. He got back in the car smelling like beer and wretch. He kept apologizing as Gina drove home.

She parked the car. "Can you manage to walk up the stairs to our home?"

"Gina, stop please. How many times do I have to tell you I fucked up big?"

"Well, if I were you, I would go to bed."

"What are you going to do?" Trevor begged her, "Lay down with me, come on babe."

"Seriously, Trevor, you smell like vomit. Go clean yourself up. I don't want the bed stinking." He walked into the bathroom and turned on the shower.

Gina walked into the living room and got on the phone, knowing Rio would be useless the next day. They needed a truck for their equipment, so she called Uncle Tony. Since he was technically their manager, she asked for the favor of getting a box truck for the equipment. They would have three days of gigs at three different bars and then the weekends. He told her not to worry; he would find something in a week.

She returned to the bedroom and found Trevor with his hair damp, lying naked in the bed. He begged Gina to sit with him.

"Tell me why. Why did you do it? You know what it does to you, and now I got to see it firsthand. I do not like it. You are so much better than this. The man I love is not the guy I saw tonight. What kind of hold does Brian have over you?

"Forget about that asshole. I'll deal with him."

Trevor put his hand on her face. "Baby, please don't stop loving me cause I'm a fucked-up man. I'll be better. I won't do coke and I know how to regulate my drinking. You know that. Gina, please."

He was actually crying. Gina took his head in her lap and stroked his wet hair. "Trev, I love you. I don't want to see that person, snorting so much coke and drinking hard. I enjoy a good party, but not this. Promise, promise me you won't go overboard again."

He looked up at her with tears. "I promise, Gina. I won't be that guy. Love me."

"I don't think you can get hard right now. So how about I hold you for a while?"

She stroked his hair until he fell asleep. Gina loved this man even with his faults. She had hers too. She believed they would be fine. But she had to get rid of Brian Mayfield. How would she do it and who does he remind her of? It was driving her crazy.

The next morning, Gina called Rio and woke him up. "How the hell did you get home last night?"

Rio was a bit foggy. "Gina, I got home. What's that important?"

"Well, if you must know, your actions last night were unconscionable. Why would you let that asshole bring cocaine to the party? It's the beginning of a slippery slope. I won't let Perfection be one of those bands that self-destruct before we even begin. Sammy is supposed to call you today with our schedule and the clubs we're going to play. Did you forget that?"

"No, Gina. I did not. Stop being the fucking mother of us all. I'm waiting for his call."

"Let me know what the information is. By the way, I called your father to get us a truck for the equipment. We will have it sometime this week. You're welcome. Call me with the information."

TIME TO PLAY

SAMMY GOLD CALLED RIO with the schedule as promised. Three nights at three different clubs, plus weekend gigs.

Monday	The Stop	Roslyn
Wednesday	The Arena	New Rochelle
Thursday	Depot	Fort Lee, New Jersey

The plan was to play for six months and see what kind of following they could produce.

They were to start the following week, the beginning of March. The band practiced nonstop. Brian was only interested in getting drugs and procuring ladies. Gina knew she had to find a way to get rid of him. But how? He had to fuck up royally.

Monday, the first gig, three sets a night. The band started with four covers and then played "Punch the Night." They ended the set with more covers. The crowd loved them. The second set started with "Found You," the acoustic version. Trevor and Gina sang in beautiful harmony. They finished with Rio's song that had the killer guitar solo.

Even though the club goers liked their original music, it was the covers they loved, especially when Gina would move around the stage and sing with Trevor, sharing a microphone and a brief kiss.

Each club had a different crowd. They were known in Long Island, so when they played The Stop, it was their people. After all, Long Island was their home. People from high school showed up. They had a lot of Perfection groupies, girls who loved Rio, guys who wanted to be like Rio, faux guitarists, as Gina would say. Jeff always had friends who he knew from back in the day and of course his band of groupies. Ian was the guy who came offstage and went directly to the dressing room. He could not be bothered with groupies or aspiring drummers who wanted to know the best drums or cymbals. He just didn't want to engage.

Trevor and Gina had hangers-on, guys who wanted to talk guitars, and chicks that wanted to know where Gina got her clothes. She also knew that some of those skanks thought getting closer to her might let Gina's guard down and maybe they could get closer to Trevor. Yeah, like that would ever happen. Gina tried to keep her jealousy in check.

Every Monday, same drill, same people, and bigger crowds. They added more original music and people started singing along. The original music was taking off.

Wednesdays they played The Arena in New Rochelle, Westchester County. It was home of The Thirst. Perfection had a different music vibe, so they attracted a slightly different crowd. Lots of guys wanting to be musicians who played air guitars, and chicks who loved to dance by the stage, trying to get the attention of any guy in the band.

Gina noticed those Westchester girls had no shame in trying to get to the band. Rio was more than happy to indulge them. Same with Jeff. Ian went offstage into the dressing room. He was not interested in small talk with their fans. Gina thought he had morals where Rio and Jeff were musicians looking for the next best thing.

Trevor and Gina tried to be nice to the fans and thank them for liking their music. But there were two chicks who were constantly trying to push their way toward Trevor. Gina watched with a careful eye. One of the scantily clad females in the club tried to put Trevor in a compromising situation. She pushed her hip into Trevor's leg and boxed him in with her arms. He had nowhere to move without possibly giving this girl the idea that he was trying to make a move back. She was talking up close to his face. Trevor lifted one of her arms out of his way and excused himself. Gina watched it play out to its conclusion and saw Trevor remove himself from the situation.

Gina followed the girl into the ladies room and waited for her to come out of the stall. She held the restroom door closed so the girl couldn't escape. "Listen bitch. You stay far away from my man. That's right—*my* man. He's not interested, so stop making a fool of yourself because you will never be me, Gina Poole. If you ever want to walk through the doors of this club again, back the fuck off. You got me?"

Gina now had the reputation of a hot commodity onstage, but hotter if you tried to disrupt the Gina Poole/Trevor McNaughton duo. Gina liked being the badass on *and* offstage. Her jealousy was becoming a strong personality trait that would continue for years to come.

Thursdays was Depot in Fort Lee, New Jersey. Jersey crowds were a little rowdier, so the band played music that was more kick-ass. The regulars enjoyed the covers more so they could jump around to music they knew. But the original music . . . well, the crowd probably didn't know the difference. Depot patrons were heavy drinkers. Fights happened, chicks fighting. It was kind of entertaining from Perfection's point of view, standing up there and playing while the crowd entertained them. Rio and Jeff had their regular girls at Depot.

Trevor and Gina made it a point to get to know the bar owners and enjoyed listening to their stories of how the clubs originated. Getting in good with the owners was a ticket to getting booked for weekend gigs.

On the weekends, they played the top clubs on the circuit—The Sunset, Old Maid Pub, and Sailfish. Sometimes they would play on weekends at their Monday, Wednesday, and Thursday locations. Those weekends were totally obscene with women trying to get a piece of the band. Gina was vigilant. Trevor would come home and pull at least ten phone numbers out of his pockets from the star fuckers who thought they had a chance with him. Gina burned them in the ashtray. *Not too jealous, but don't take any chances.* Trevor was equally cautious about the attention men were giving Gina. After all, she dressed highly flashy and seductive. But it is a show. She would not let another man ever get that close.

It had been three months of this continual back and forth, but this was paying dues, and they knew it. The clubs stunk of vomit, stale beer, and cheap perfume. Their roadies—Jake, Larry, Stu, and Marvin—in Gina's mind, had the worst job, breaking down the equipment for the night. They too had their own posse of females who waited long nights to say they were "with the band."

Gina and Trevor wondered if it was this bad now, what would it be like when they finally got that record deal? Could it be worse?

Some nights after gigs, they would find a nearby diner, have something to eat, and drive home. Most work nights the band got home around two in the morning.

Some nights upon arriving home, they would notice a car easing silently along the private driveway. How did they get in? One night, Gina told Trevor to wait. They parked at the carriage house and watched a car drive around the back to Mario's private entrance. Not the first time Gina thought she heard cars, but this was a validation that her father conducted his "business" late at night. No onlookers.

Gina remarked to Trevor, "We pretend we don't see anything. That's how I was raised. But now I'm actually seeing what we were never meant to notice."

Every evening when they got home Gina needed to get the club off her body, so no matter how tired they were, Trevor always wanted to make love to Gina in the shower. They would go to sleep clean and satisfied.

WEDDING BLUES

FRANNY LEFT A MESSAGE on the answering machine. "Gina love don't forget we have MaryAnn's bridal shower. What were you planning to get her? She has a lot of unnecessary items on her registry but what can you say? Maybe buy her one of those fancy mixers—a Kitchen Aid. Get back to me. We can go together to the Fanellis'. Bye."

"Shit, shit, and shit. I can't believe it's this close." Gina had to buy an ugly lavender dress—chiffon with bell sleeves, and a hat. She was determined to change her clothes before she went to the reception. Trevor laughed at how incensed Gina got. Out of nowhere, Frankie called Trevor and asked him to be a groomsman.

"What the fuck, babe? I don't know him that well. Does that mean I have to wear some horrible tuxedo?"

Gina fell on the floor laughing hysterically. "Yes baby, it does, and I'll be laughing the whole time."

Frankie had also asked Rio to be a groomsman. "Why do I get fucked too?" Rio complained to Gina.

Gina laid it out for him. "Because we're family, that's why. You know what that means in an Italian family; it's your blood bro. No escaping it."

Gina purchased the stupid mixer and had it shipped to the Fanellis'. The day of the shower, she drove Franny in her Benz. Trevor stayed home, working on some new music. The drive over was pleasant, and Gina smoked as many of her cigarettes as she could. Franny kept waving the smoke away.

"Oh, Mom, it's not that bad. But this shower is going to be that bad. How many lingerie sets do you think she'll get? I mean it's not like her and Frankie haven't been sleeping together already, Jesus. I wouldn't be surprised if she isn't already pregnant."

Franny was shocked. "Gina Annamarie! That's terrible to say. I mean, I agree she will probably get tons of lingerie sets. Is it so unseemly?"

"Having someone pick out your lingerie is dirty and icky. I want to pick out my own lingerie. I know what Trevor likes. Why would I want someone else to buy me something I wouldn't wear?"

"Now that you mention it Gina, when can we expect you and Trevor to commit to one another? I look forward to the day I can plan my daughter's wedding."

"Hold on, Mom. Trevor and I *are* committed to each other. We don't need to be married for that. You know I could never love anyone but him, and as far as a wedding, I told you, whenever we do get married, we are going to elope to Vegas, and no one will know until we want them to."

"Gina, that's cruel. Why would you take that away from me?"

"Mom, we're here. Let's get this wedding over with before we talk about me, okay? Get ready to be underwhelmed."

The shower was as anticipated—homemade Italian dishes from relatives, a big chair for MaryAnn to sit in, and gifts galore. She must have invited every cousin and second cousin. Gina counted twenty lingerie sets from her family. Aunt Deidre could not make it—lucky her.

But Franny and Gina were fish among sharks. It was obvious that MaryAnn was marrying way above her grade. As soon as they could, they made their farewells. On the way out, many of MaryAnn's friends asked, "Don't you sing for the band Perfection?"

Gina happily admitted yes, she did. They asked her about every man in the band, first Rio, then Jeff, Trevor, and Ian. Gina responded, "Rio and Jeff are always available to many girls. Ian is quite reserved, and as far as Trevor, well he is very much taken . . . by me. So do not ever think about that again."

She gathered Franny and left. Franny looked at Gina, "What has you upset?"

"Those bitches were asking me how available Trevor was."

Franny looked worried.

Gina went on, "I told them he was taken, by me, and don't ever ask that question again."

"Gina, you have nothing to worry about. You said it—Trevor is committed to you. For heaven's sake, he has put up with you all this time."

Gina pulled up to the gate, punched the code in and drove her mother to the house. "Okay, Mom, it was so much fun, can't wait for the wedding, bye." After dropping her mother off, Gina drove down to the carriage house. Home.

Gina walked through the door and looked at Trevor. "How was the music writing?"

Trevor was proud. "I think I got a new song."

"That's phenomenal. You are so talented."

"Was it that bad?" he asked.

Gina sighed, "Yes. Can you do something? Can you take me in that bedroom and make love to me now?"

"If I have to. I mean if you insist, I'll be right there."

THOUGHTS

THE START OF THE WORKWEEK began on Monday in Roslyn. Trevor and Gina enjoyed talking to the club owner, a chatty guy from Long Island with some witty and entertaining stories of bands that played at the club. Trevor and Gina loved all the false pretenses that some of the bands had.

Everyone in Perfection wanted this, but it was a grind—same clubs, same people, same craziness, same songs. There were some new songs on the radio they were interested in covering. Rio and Trevor were writing a lot of new music and wanted Gina to play with some lyric ideas. The clubs melted into each other.

The most coveted gigs were the holiday weekends—Memorial Day, Fourth of July. Usually, a club would book a double header—two bands on one night. Pure insanity. Of course, there was Glen Island Casino on Tuesdays in the summer, where Trevor and Gina first met. They could have two bands and possibly a third downstairs.

The bands the agency signed were diverse. The trend was glam rockers—guys wearing makeup and dressing fem. Then there were the Southern rock bands. But Perfection was a true rock band. There were other pure rock bands, but Perfection was at the top. There were progressive music bands like The Thirst. Gina would try to go see them but there was always a conflict. She hoped that in the summer, they would be double-billed.

Gina still had major issues with Brian Mayfield. She saw him as a disruptor, causing trouble. Why was he here? She still did not understand the connection.

NOT A RICCI AFFAIR

IT WAS THE WEEKEND of Frankie and MaryAnn's wedding. Friday was a rehearsal dinner, which thankfully was a Ricci affair. Fifty people attended the dinner at the country club where Mario and Franny were members. The room was decorated tastefully in lavender tulle, white and blush roses, lilies of the valley, and greenery. Franny's taste was impeccable. The menu included lobster, steak, many sides, desserts, and, of course, an open bar. The Fanelli family felt like they were in wonderland.

The rehearsal was a chance for the bridal party to practice walking down the aisle. Gina and Trevor walked down together, laughing at the entire scenario. Poor Rio walked down with some cousin of MaryAnn's. The procession continued until MaryAnn and her dad walked down the pretend aisle. After the rehearsal it was time to party. Gina was going to go in hard drinking martinis and smoking some weed. Trevor and Rio joined in. Here was the opportunity to show them she did like to party—within limits. This wedding was going to be an Italian shit show. Gina, Trevor, and Rio had to hold the date, Saturday, June fourteenth—Frankie and MaryAnn's wedding. Since this was a family event, they could not get around the fact that the band would miss a weekend of work.

They did not feel good about people losing a night's pay, especially the roadies. Gina and Rio paid the band out of their own pockets. She hated the idea of paying Brian Mayfield. What did he do for them?

The next morning MaryAnn wanted all the bridesmaids to get their hair done in updo's with lots of curls. Gina was never going to get her hair done like the other bridesmaids, all MaryAnn's cousins. She skipped the salon appointment. She would claim she was too hungover to make it. What could MaryAnn do to her? Not let her walk down the aisle?

They had to be at St. Mary's at two o'clock. Gina and Trevor dressed in the ridiculous wedding attire and could not stop laughing. They rolled a joint for the ride.

They parked around the back of the church and bumped into Rio getting out of his car. "Hey, I still don't know why I'm included in this shit. I'm only a cousin."

Gina laughed. "That's right asshole, that's why." Then they all looked at each other and laughed some more.

Mario, Franny, and Ant drove up next. Franny got out of the car. "Isn't this wonderful? My family is on time. Has anyone looked inside the church yet? I can only imagine what the flowers will look like. Please save me Lord."

That made the three of them laugh even harder. They were high after all. They walked together into the church. It was decorated with an awful color of lavender with bows and ribbons and cheap carnations.

Gina thought her mother was going to cry. "Mom, remember that the Fanellis don't have your exquisite taste. Let it go."

Uncle Tony and Aunt Deidre came in. Aunt Deidre said, "Oh my Franny, I'm so sorry." Again, laughter from the three misplaced rockers.

The women decided to go to the bridal suite. MaryAnn admonished Gina. "You missed your hair appointment."

"Did I have an appointment? I'm sorry, I didn't know."

The church service was a High Mass. It took way too long, followed by an hour of wedding photos. Once that was over, there was a two-hour wait between the ceremony and reception. Gina and Trevor used the time to escape and go home to change their clothes. Rio joined in the change.

They got home and looked at themselves in ridiculous wedding garb. *We have to have sex in these getups.* Gina left the hat on, because, come on, it was funny.

They showered and put on their real clothes. Gina wore a dusty-rose velvet maxi dress with lace sleeves and matching platform shoes. Trevor wore black jeans, a crisp expensive white T-shirt, and a black leather sport coat Gina bought him a while ago.

Rio knocked at the door. "Cool, you guys are going like yourselves. Can we go together?"

Rio drove them to Huntington. The night passed as Gina knew it would—first dances, speeches, clinking glasses for the bride and groom to kiss, the Italian dance tarantella, cake-cutting. And the bouquet toss, which is always rigged for a family member or best friend to catch. To be nice, Gina asked her parents, "Can we leave now? We did all the mandatory obligations, please?"

Her Mother was resigned that this was her son's wedding. "Yes, Gina it's fine, although I did not see you and Trevor on the dance floor at all."

Gina answered, "Mom, if you want to see me dance come to Roslyn on Monday. We will dance for you and even sing. Love you both. All three of us are going home."

"Hey princess," called Mario. "I love you. Not to worry when you get married. It will be a hundred times better than this."

Gina smiled, "Okay Daddy. I look forward to it. Good night."

Rio drove to the carriage house. "Hey, can we hang out for a bit? I want to talk band business."

That intrigued both Gina and Trevor. Trevor spoke first, "What do you want to talk about, serious?"

"I'm going to try to get Sammy to book us at The Sunset for the Fourth of July weekend with The Thirst. What do you think? I think it will be packed and there'll be great music. Gina, you can hang with Matt and Stevie."

Gina's eyes got big. "Rio, if you can make that work, I'm all in."

Trevor chimed in, "I might have two new originals. We would need to practice. One is only for Gina's vocals."

"Trevor, you wrote something for me to sing. I love this guy so much."

Rio jumped in, "We have an off day tomorrow, we can practice a little."

"Rio, tomorrow is Sunday, so we don't usually get moving until the afternoon. When can you get the other guys there? Realistically." Gina had no intention of getting up early.

Rio searched his mind, "Two o'clock sounds good."

Rio went home. Gina and Trevor were tired and hungry. "What can I make you? I know you want something after all that weed we smoked. Oh, I know. How about Belgian waffles with ice cream, hot fudge, butterscotch, and whipped cream?"

"Does that have to be on waffles, or can it be on something else?"

"Like what? I don't . . . oh, I get it. Can we play after we eat?"

BAND BREAKOUT

RIO ARRANGED FOR THE BAND to play on the Fourth of July at The Sunset. The event was advertised on the radio as the hottest Fourth of July ever with two of the best bands in the Tri-State area—The Thirst and Perfection. They were also getting hourly radio drops advertising the band. The wheels were in motion and the band was gaining momentum.

The band practiced the songs Trevor wrote, each member putting their piece into the songs. Trevor gave the smoking-hot original song to Gina. He wanted to see her strut all over the stage, which would end with her singing to only him. Gina was going to slay the song and have the crowd go insane.

The Fourth of July came at The Sunset. The place had a line around the block at six thirty. The doors would open at seven. Perfection was to go on first at eight. Each band did two sets. The bands were there early to set up equipment. Usually, the roadies did the grunt work, however Perfection wanted to make sure everything went . . . well . . . perfectly.

Brian Mayfield did only one smart thing that weekend. He had Perfection T-shirts made with a picture of the band on front. The pictured showed Rio standing next to Trevor, who was sitting with Gina on his lap. Ian had a pair of sticks in his hands and Jeff stood to the side.

Brian's idea was to hand them out to the first fifty fans on line, and the group each got one. When Gina entered the club, she saw Josh setting up drums for The Thirst. She walked over and said, "Hey you, what's up big brother?"

"It's the badass bitch herself."

Gina laughed. "If anyone else said that I would kick their ass. But you, Josh, you get a pass. Is Stevie here, or Matt?"

"Not yet, but I'm sure they will find you once they get here."

"Going to be a big night. There is a line outside already. I have to catch up with Trevor."

Perfection was not sure how many of their fans were there. The Thirst was a big draw. Eight o'clock came and Perfection took the stage. Gina decided to wait till after they sang "Can't Get Enough" to play off Trevor.

"Hello Sunset! I'm Gina Poole. To my left is my cousin Rio Poole. On drums is Ian White. Playing kick-ass bass is Jeff Wainwright. And to my right is the sexiest man alive, my man Trevor McNaughton."

Gina would continue to use this sign on with only a few variations. The first set was amazing. As they were getting offstage, she saw Stevie and Matt, who weren't expecting to see Gina so full of sex appeal.

Stevie hugged her. "Well look who it is. Who would have imagined you to grow up to be the rose you are?"

The club was packed, no room to walk on the floor or even get to the bar. Perfection didn't want to wade through the crowd. They would get stopped by fans wanting to talk. The plan was to hang out in either the dressing room or onstage. Gina chose to listen to The Thirst on their stage and the waitresses brought over drinks. They played all of Gina's favorites; it brought back happy memories of watching them from the early days.

Perfection played their second set with Trevor's original rock song for Gina. It got a lot of screams from both the dudes and chicks in the crowd.

Saturday nights were always a larger crowd. The weekend was in full swing. The club was rocking, both bands had their fan bases and were up for a great show. The Thirst and Perfection brought it. It was a success. Gina even got to go to the diner with her guys and Stevie, Matt, and Josh after. They talked for hours.

After that weekend Perfection had solidified themselves as a top player in the Tri-State area.

DISCOVERED

OVER THE NEXT THREE YEARS, the band's presence became huge. The radio advertisements seemed like they were played every hour, and every club wanted a date. Sammy and Nadine Gold knew they had a great thing with Perfection and were making good money off the band.

Frankie and MaryAnn had two children—a boy and a girl. Franny was happy to be a grandmother but was waiting for Gina to have "her" grandchildren.

It was now the summer of 1978. They didn't complain about the many nights of gigs, getting home late, and having little time for family. They reminded each other it was the life they chose. It was a hard road to always walk.

During the numerous amounts of shows, Gina knew each of the band member's "girls" for a particular club. She stayed away from them. They all were playthings, not permanent.

In the last few months, Gina had noticed an incredibly attractive blonde coming to the gigs with Ian. Ian, the guy who never wanted to socialize with fans. One Friday, Gina walked over to her and introduced herself. The woman gave her name as Lisa Bloom. The two women exchanged small talk and Lisa said she was studying criminal justice at St. John's in Queens.

Gina was curious. "How did you meet Ian if I could ask? I don't mean to pry, but Ian is a private and quiet man. He doesn't socialize at the clubs."

Lisa smiled at her. "Not at all. We met at the grocery store. He didn't know how to pick out a watermelon and I showed him. After that he asked me out and told me he was a musician. I wasn't sure when I heard that, but he is a sweet soul, so I gave him a chance. He has kind of kept me under wraps for a while. He didn't know how his band members would receive me."

Gina was excited for another woman to join the crew. Not some bar slut, an actual nice woman. "That's certainly a fun and new way to meet someone. You are truly seeing them as a normal person."

Lisa was nervous around Gina. "Listen, I know you are in the band with Ian. I'm guessing you must have a tough exterior to do this for a living. Ian was truly hesitant about bringing me around. He always tells me about the craziness that goes on at the gigs. That's the right word, correct? Gigs?"

Gina assuaged her concerns. "Lisa, there is a lot that goes on, but it's not all bad. It's a lifestyle we all chose. The idea is to get a record deal, then off we go."

Lisa shyly admitted, "Yes, that was one of my concerns, I'm not sure what that means exactly. Once that happens, does it mean I'm not good enough for him?"

Gina shook her head. Are you kidding me? I'm thrilled he found a decent woman. I knew he would. Ian is such a great guy. He's not like the others, meaning my cousin and Jeff. You know Trevor and Ian have been friends for years."

"Yes, I know. Ian told me some stories from the "old days" when they got into a lot of trouble. And he told me about their addictions. He was totally honest and promised me he would never go back to anything to do with his old lifestyle. It made me trust him more since he trusted me enough to admit his faults. I know many of the girls I see around the other band members are just fluff. They aren't meaningful. I mean you can tell. But you, Gina, are different; you are a member of the band. How do you feel about the other band members having girlfriends? You have Trevor, I don't see you around too many women. You don't appear to have friends."

Gina smiled. "Lisa, it's hard, you never know if a girl wants to be your friend or get your man. So, I hope we can become good friends. I haven't had a good friend since high school. I am not easy to get along with. In this business you tend not to trust other women. But you and I have that connection now."

Gina leaned over and hugged her. "Lisa Bloom, please be my friend." Gina was kidding but she also wasn't.

Gina found out that Lisa was getting her Associate Degree as a paralegal. She was actually graduating one semester early. She doubled up on classes to finish earlier. Gina waited for Ian to introduce Lisa to Trevor and the rest of the band, the roadies, and Brian Mayfield. Trevor took a liking to Lisa right away. She was a perfect equal to Ian, cerebral and easy to talk to. Trevor was also happy that Gina had another woman to talk to.

On the evenings they had free, they went out as a foursome and did things like bowl or go to a baseball game. It only became weird if some fan recognized them.

Gina invited them to the carriage house for dinners. Lisa was also a good cook so they would each cook something for dinner and have a party. It was sweet how Lisa sat on the floor and Ian would play with her hair. It reminded Gina of how she loved playing with Trevor's hair. They were able to talk about all things Canadian—Gray Cup, hockey. Gina was happy to see Trevor open a little more of himself to her; things she never knew.

It got so serious with Ian and Lisa that Ian moved out of the Franklin Square house, and he and Lisa got their own apartment in Hempstead. The Franklin Square house now had Jeff, Kevin, Brian, and two of the roadies—Stu and Marvin.

One quiet Sunday morning, Trevor and Gina were in bed. She was going to get coffee when Trevor stopped her. "Gina, it's been three and a half years with Perfection, and before that, each of us had our own bands. Do you ever think that this is it? This is as far as we get?"

Gina leaned over and kissed his forehead. "No baby, I don't believe that. You are way too talented for this to be it. Same as Rio. You're both too talented. I think it will happen sooner than we think. But we also don't want to take the first deal. Maybe it is not the best one we can get. I don't want to jump at anything, do you?"

"No, I don't. The best is to be able to play two companies against each other."

Gina came back with coffee. "Trev, are you worried because you committed yourself here in the US and not Canada? Are you getting homesick?"

"I assure you that isn't my concern. I want to get a deal and start making our music."

"Don't we have enough for an album already?"

"We do. That's my frustration." Trevor put his head in her lap, and she stroked his hair.

"Baby, we are going to be okay. It's coming. I feel it."

"You always make me feel better, and also make me unbelievably horny first thing in the morning."

"Well, I'm glad I can take care of both those things for you."

THE DEAL

IT WAS LABOR DAY WEEKEND and there was a lot of buzz going around the clubs that several A&R guys were searching for bands to do demos with the potential to sign them to a record deal.

Perfection was scheduled to play Happy Daze in Westchester. Gina knew the owner, Bruce. He happened to be a friend of her high school boyfriend, David Shapiro.

David and Bruce's fathers were friends, so David hung out with Bruce often. Bruce had killer house parties when his father was out of town. Gina and David would drive the forty-five minutes from Long Island to Westchester to visit Bruce. Gina knew Bruce was the owner of Happy Daze, but with all that had happened to the band over the four years, she had totally forgotten.

Bruce was only too happy to book Perfection for Labor Day. Gina was excited to see her old friend. The crew was setting up for Friday night. Trevor and Gina showed up an hour and a half before they were set to start playing. Happy Daze had one big stage and two bars. Gina saw Bruce as she and Trevor walked through the club. "Gina, Gina, so good to see you, it's been years."

"It may be years, but you haven't changed at all guy. Good to be able to play your club. Sorry, Bruce, this is Trevor. He is my world."

Bruce shook his hand. "Great to meet the man who tamed Gina Ricci. Full disclosure. I want you to know that there are two A&R guys from different record companies here to watch you play. I usually get a call to comp the guys—drinks, whatever they want. I won't know who they are until they get here. They will probably show up while you are playing. I won't be able to let you know."

Gina was so excited. "Are you kidding? Knowing they will be here is enough. How crazy would it be if Perfection is discovered in your club? That would be hot."

Trevor got serious. "Bring our A game tonight for sure. And a great mix of originals and covers."

Trevor had written a song for Gina, but it wasn't polished enough yet to sing, especially tonight, but it also could be the song that would interest a record company. He would have to talk to the rest of the band, especially Gina. Would she be ready?

The band members started arriving. Trevor informed them that there would be two record company A&R guys coming. They needed to arrange their set lists to show their stage presence and original music.

Trevor looked at Gina. "Babe, you are going to have to really show that wild side to your act. That sets us apart from many bands. You are singing lead. People come to see you perform off me; we're a team and they know it. They want to see you wanting me onstage. I hate to say it that way, but you know it's the truth."

Gina looked puzzled. "Trev, we sing lead together."

Rio stepped in, "Yeah, but Gina, the audience thinks you are letting them into your private world. They dig that. You know how to make a song sexier than it is by singing with Trevor. Come on now, you really have to put it out there."

Gina started to feel the weight of a potential record deal on her back. "Hold on. You two are the guitar gurus. Guys wish they could be you, so you better smoke some guitar solos. Ian, you have to really bring the drums forward and Jeff has to have his bass elevated in the mix. The audience loves a great bass presence. We all need to perform at the maximum level. Each one of us is an important link. Perfection is all of us. We are equals in this endeavor."

Trevor pulled Gina up close. "Do you feel confident in singing the song I wrote for you? 'The Girl Behind the Song.'"

"Not really. I feel nervous. Trevor, Rio, if you think this is important, I will try to put my own fears aside. Can we not put it in the first set? I need to get my head around it. But, if we put it in the second set, I will work it out, this is for Perfection and a deal. Let's do it. Make it happen. Are you guys ready?"

Rio laughed. "We can always fake it with hard core guitar solos. You need to be on point."

It was crowded, Labor Day, summer was over. The band took to the stage and opened with one of Gina's favorites, "Love Is the Drug." She and Trevor sang it together. The next song was "Fame." Then they did "Can't Get Enough," followed by "Feel Like Makin' Love." A few people screamed, "Do it already." The band laughed. Then they started playing originals "Punch the Night" and "Music Is a Circus."

The set ended. Bruce walked up and told them he loved it. The next set would be key. Gina had to sing a song they had only rehearsed a few times. She hoped that the song would be a great fit for her voice tonight—perfect with what Trevor wrote.

The Girl Behind the Song

She sings every night the crowds adore her she moves to the beat.
And everyone loves her. The girl behind the song is a different girl.
She's sweet and wonders am I good enough.
I'm here to say I love what I do but I'm so much more, so much more.

Love me, adore me, but do you really know me, do you really know me?

If you knew me, you would know I want a regular life, with the man
I love, I'm the girl behind the song you know me, but you really don't.

I'm here to say I love what I do but I'm so much more, so much more.
Love me, adore me, but do you really know me, do you really know me.

Trevor looked at her with so much love as she sang it. Gina couldn't believe she did it, considering they didn't practice the song much in rehearsals. After the second set, the band got a drink at the bar and was approached by one of the record guys. He introduced himself as Michael Diamond from Brown Fence Records.

"It's nice to meet you all in person. You have buzz around the record companies—two lead guitarists, a great rhythm duo, and two lead vocalists. We would like to talk to you about possibly doing a demo of a couple of songs. Send it to the execs and start to promote you."

Trevor and Rio spoke up. Their main concern was maintaining the rights to the music they wrote. That was a nonstarter. Everyone knows that's where the money comes from—the rights to the songs.

Michael Diamond reassured them. "Look, I'm not here to negotiate the terms. However, I'm sure it's something that we can iron out. We would want you to start working in a recording studio in two weeks. Can you handle that?"

Trevor was enticed by the offer. "Would you be paying us if we sign and start recording? We have enough original material for an entire album, but we need to know that we will be compensated for our time if we come to an agreement."

Diamond explained, "I'm here to get you in the studio. The execs and producers will dictate that. But the label knows good talent. My experience is that we can get you a deal that will satisfy both parties."

Rio hedged. "It sounds enticing, and we would like to start recording. We know there is someone here from Pastel Cigarette. You understand if we would like to hear their proposal."

Diamond laughed. "Of course, you must do your due diligence, but I'm here to get you to record for us. Listen to their offer. I would like to leave here tonight with a commitment from Perfection. Yeah, talk to him, I know the guy. I'll wait by the bar and talk to the owner of the club."

The band walked into the dressing room not quite sure how this was going to play out. They all felt that after tonight they would be recording with some company, but which one?

The A&R rep from Pastel Cigarette knocked. Gina thought, *That' appropriate,* since she smokes pastel cigarettes. Ivan Redding came in and introduced himself. "You had two killer sets; we are interested in working with you."

This time Trevor spoke up. "We are listening. What's your proposal? We write our own music, and we want to own the royalties for the music we write. That's something we can't waiver on."

Redding was undaunted. "You know that most labels want a piece of those royalties. We would take some percentage."

Rio knew at that point where their deal was going. "Listen, we write nonstop. We have enough material to record an album right now. We all share in the writing. We aren't about sharing that with a label because we want to sign with them."

Redding was blunt. "I know that Brown Fence has already talked to you. I have no idea what he's offering, but I can't ensure that the label won't want their piece. So, if you have a better offer, maybe you should take it. I can't negotiate terms—that comes from the big guys. We would like it if you came to us. I guess you have some soul-searching to do. If you go in the other direction, we might be interested if it doesn't work out. It was nice to meet you all. Maybe we can work together or maybe not. You will be recording somewhere for sure."

After Redding walked out the door, a huge sigh came over the band. They all looked at each other. Gina spoke first. "That guy Ivan was evasive. He didn't care if we signed with them. I didn't get a great feeling. Plus, he said the label would want some of our royalties. I thought we wouldn't take a deal like that. Help me out here."

Trevor tried to sort out what both labels would do or not do. "Brown Fence isn't saying they wouldn't try to get a piece. But then again, the label wants us to record demos in two weeks. The other guy didn't give us any time frame. I know where I'm leaning. What about everyone else?"

Rio made his preference known. "I think we can work with Brown Fence. There is at least a negotiation we can have. That Ivan guy was noncommittal, and he did say Pastel Cigarette would want a piece when we write all our names on the songs. Yeah, I didn't dig that guy either. Ian, Jeff, what are your feelings?"

Ian was in his normal chill mode. "I'm going with Brown Fence. As long as we can get paid advance money, I'm in."

Jeff was the last one to comment. "Hey, Perfection, I think we have a deal! Shouldn't we find Michael Diamond?"

Gina remembered, "Oh my God, poor Lisa is out there not knowing what's going on. Let me go and get her. She is part of this now."

Ian looked crushed. "Please go get her Gina, totally slipped my mind."

Gina hurried outside to find Lisa sitting at the bar. At the other end were Bruce, and Michael Diamond.

"Lisa, Lisa come here. I'm so sorry I should have brought you with me. It looks like we have a deal for demos but I'm pretty sure they are going to like the music. I don't want to talk too loudly because their guy is talking to my friend Bruce. I'm going to let the guys talk to him. I know Trevor will do the right thing for us."

Lisa was wide-eyed, "Wow, this is really happening? I wonder how life is going to change?"

Gina stepped back. Lisa was right. How would this change things?

How would her life change? She and Trevor were solid. Nothing would come between them, not now. What about Brian Mayfield? If the band started recording an album, they would need a real manager. Maybe she could finally get rid of him.

Gina and Lisa sat with their drinks and watched the rest of the band as they talked to Michael Diamond. There were handshakes all around. He gave each of them his business card. He would let them know where they would be recording. Brown Fence Records left happy that they could get Perfection.

Ivan Redding didn't even stay to hear what their decision was. He just left his card with Bruce.

Gina ran up to Trevor and he picked her up and kissed her. "You were right, it happened. I love you so much. We get to do this together. That makes it special."

Bruce, who was in the middle of all the jubilant band members announced, "Drinks on me! I can say Perfection got their deal here at Happy Daze."

Gina gave him a hug. "Thanks friend. It was meant to be." But it was late now, they would make up the third set tomorrow.

The band, the roadies, and of course Brian all wanted to go to the diner. Gina had hoped she and Trevor could go home and celebrate privately, but she didn't want to spoil everyone else's fun. There was plenty of time to have their private moment.

They entered the Midway Diner, everyone talking excitedly. Gina lay back, soaking it all in. She wanted to remember it. Trevor noticed. "G, you okay? You are uncharacteristically quiet. You always have an opinion. What's wrong?" He put his arm around her and whispered in her ear, "I can't wait to get you home tonight."

"I want to remember this moment as the beginning, that's all." She grabbed his face and kissed him. Finally, by two o'clock, everyone headed back to the Island. Trevor drove home with Gina in the passenger seat, singing "The Girl Behind the Song."

As they walked in the door, Gina announced, "Babe, I want to wash the club off me." As she started to shampoo her hair Trevor joined her, letting the water run over his head. She faced him and wrung the water out of his hair. She touched his goatee, caressed his cheek, then put her arms around his neck and started kissing him gently, staring at his beautiful face. He took the soap and started washing her body, her neck, her breasts, all the way down her body. She then proceeded to wash him. Neither spoke a word. They rinsed the soap and the bar off their bodies.

He lifted her up and she wrapped her legs around him. Their passionate kisses, touches, and lovemaking proved once again to each other they would never be separated.

They got out of the shower, clean and satisfied. Gina put on her bathrobe and Trevor wrapped a towel around his waist. It was late, but they had nowhere to be until seven the next evening.

"G, do we have champagne or wine to celebrate?"

"Of course. Check the wine fridge."

Trevor came back to the bedroom with a bottle of Veuve Clicquot but without his towel.

"What a sight. I like the look. Come here and celebrate. Did you remember the glasses?"

"Oh, shit. I forgot. Can't we drink from the bottle like heathens?"

"We can do whatever we want. We're going to make a record."

STUDIO TIME

SINCE THE BAND GOT THEIR DEAL Friday, they still had one more night at Happy Daze. In their mind it could be the last bar performance they ever do. Perfection didn't want to think of the demo not being picked up. Sammy Gold would have to be called and told that they weren't going to be doing any more gigs, but everyone wanted to wait until the phone call came from Michael Diamond.

Two days later, Michael Diamond called Trevor and Rio to let them know that he arranged for the time in the studio and Brown Fence would be paying for the studio time. Blue Topaz Studio scheduled them on Tuesday, September twelfth, at 10:30 a.m.

Rio decided he would be the one to call Sammy Gold and tell him they were going to be recording a demo and had no time for gigs.

The band had a week off, but Trevor felt they needed to practice their material and tighten it up. After all, there would be a production crew and Kevin would be there to assist in mixing. After a few hours, the band members went their own ways to enjoy some free time. Who knew when they would have free time in the future?

Gina and Trevor went to her parents' house for dinner and shared their good news. "Mom, Trevor and I are going to do a demo next week."

Franny was excited for them. "Gina! I can't believe it. You chose a different path, and you did it."

Mario shook Trevor's hand and said, "I'm glad you will be able to take care of my daughter."

RECORDING

THE DAY FINALLY ARRIVED to get to the recording studio for Brown Fence Records. Trevor brought all four of his guitars, as did Rio. Jeff brought two bass guitars and Ian brought his own drum set, which Stu set up. Of course, Brian was there, although Gina had no idea what he could add to this session, except get coffee.

After introductions, Michael Diamond, and Lou Penn, the engineer, asked which song the band wanted to lay down to record first.

Trevor answered, "Found You," "Punch the Night," and after that they would decide what they wanted to lay down. They had gone through twenty takes of "Found You" when Lou announced, "I think we got it. You want a break and then we can work on some other material?"

Food was ordered in and, while on break, the band entertained themselves with random pieces and hit on "Gimme Shelter." Trevor had trained Gina to sing it in her range while they were messing around at home, and they easily slid into the studio. Michael Diamond silently mouthed to Lou, "Get this on tape."

When break was over, Lou asked, "What you want to play next?"

The consensus was "Punch the Night." This was more about heavy guitars, not so much vocals, but Gina sang backup to Trevor's melodic voice. Rio wasn't happy with his guitar solo. He kept adding and changing until he felt he and Trevor had the right mix of guitars. By the time that was done, it was six p.m. and Lou and Michael called it a day.

As everyone was packing up, Rio wanted to add more vocals to "Punch the Night," and said he would work on it that evening.

Ian grabbed Trevor. "Why not take our ladies to a nice place for drinks and stuff? Besides, the traffic on the LIE will be horrendous."

Trevor smiled. "Sure, I think they would like that. Where are you thinking?"

Since the studio was close to Broadway, they decided to take a cab to the Upper East Side where there were a lot of small restaurants. Lisa was excited to finally hang out in the city and just enjoy the energy around her.

They found a place called The Hole in the Wall. The guys drank beer, especially when they found out they had Labatts, a Canadian beer. The ladies had the house sangria and they ordered appetizers. Ian was extremely affectionate with Lisa, and Gina thought it was sweet and a sign this was a serious relationship.

The next day at the studio, Rio gave everyone the changes he had made to "Punch the Night." It included new drums, then Rio and Trevor would exchange guitar solos. Gina had to learn additional lyrics. She was always trying to find a good range for herself. She really could use Simon Beauvaux now. Maybe she should call him if the demos prove successful.

After five days of reworking and recording, Michael Diamond announced that he had enough to take to the executives at Brown Fence. He hinted that they had some good material. Now it was a waiting game to see if they wanted to sign the band. Diamond told them they usually meet on Thursday mornings with new talent demos, so he hoped he could let them know a decision by Friday, a week away. Everyone held their collective breath.

Everyone spent the week trying not to think about what might happen. But how could they? This was their real chance. Rio played guitar and had some ladies stop by to keep his mind off the record label. Ian and Lisa explored New York City—Central Park, Radio City Music Hall, and Broadway. Jeff practiced and partied with Stu and Marvin, who lived in the house with him. Brian Mayfield was super low-key. Maybe he knew his time was coming up.

Gina started the herb and vegetable garden that Shawn had inspired. The gardeners cleared a patch for her. Even though it was late in the season, she and Trevor went to a garden store and bought everything they could. She wanted Trevor to help her and get dirty. "Working with your hands is therapeutic," she told him. He indulged her for a while.

Gina made dinners at home and spent time with Franny and Serena. She was being a homebody. Was that who she was? Or a budding rock star? Why couldn't she be both? People do have private lives; they don't always need to be onstage.

After dinner, they snuggled on the couch and watched TV. When a commercial came on for Lucky Charms cereal, she finally realized who that bastard Brian Mayfield reminded her of—the leprechaun from Lucky Charms. She shook Trevor, "That's it! Lucky Charms—that's Mayfield's new name."

"G, seriously? Why don't you like Brian?"

"He wants to ride along in your fame. I won't have it, Lucky Charms."

THE DEAL

WHEN MICHAEL DIAMOND pitched Perfection at the Thursday meeting, the execs liked what they heard and wanted to sign them to the label. They had to work out the signing bonus, and make sure that Perfection knew the label would have the master recordings and the royalties would go to them, but the songs would be owned by the writers. Perfection wanted at least 18 percent of the royalties from their songs. They agreed. Perfection would be signed for four albums minimum. They received $69,000 for round one and a bonus of $165,000.

There was one big caveat. The producer, Tommy Whelan, who worked with the top rock bands, country singers, and R&B musicians, would only work in Los Angeles. It was a family issue—he did not want to work away from home. The band would have to relocate to Los Angeles.

Everyone was a little shocked, but they would be working with one of the hottest producers in the music industry. They couldn't refuse, so Perfection was moving to LA.

The thought of moving to LA frightened Gina. Her image of LA was women with Barbie doll bodies and bleached blonde hair. She didn't know how she would fit in as an Italian girl from Long Island.

Rio was jazzed to have a bigger playing field for himself and Jeff. Kevin had no issues moving to LA. Three out of four of the roadies—Stu, Marvin, and Jake, said yes. Then there was Brian Lucky fucking Charms, who would follow anything the band had to offer. Ian and Lisa decided to get married before they left New York.

Gina had to tell her parents they were leaving and wasn't sure how they would take it. Frankie and MaryAnn kept pumping out kids, making Franny a grandmother for the third time. Gina thought to herself, *Does he look at her, and bam, she's pregnant*?

Perfection needed to be in LA by December thirtieth, which gave them two-and-half months to figure out their individual relocation needs.

Gina and Trevor were lying in bed after making love when Gina confessed she was apprehensive. "Trev, will moving to LA change us? There are so many distractions there. I'm afraid it will change us."

"G, stop it. We are in this together forever, you know that. You aren't afraid I'm going to leave you, are you?"

"Well yes Trevor, I am. There are a ton of women prettier than me. You'll be a rock star, a magnet for every type of woman."

"You forget you will also be a rock star, a sexy one. So put that shit out of your head. Maybe *I* should worry?"

"Are you nuts? You can't say that seriously. That will never happen. But I do have to talk to my parents, please come with me. I have no idea how they will receive this news."

"Of course. We are in this together. I should be man enough to tell your father I'm taking his daughter to the other side of the country."

The next day the two of them made the drive up to her parents' house. Trevor grabbed Gina's hand as they walked in to assure her that they were a team.

Serena came out to greet them. "Princess, we haven't seen you and Trevor for a few weeks. Everything okay?"

Gina kissed her forehead. "Yes, Serena. Everything is fine. Where are my parents? In the family room?"

"Yes, they are watching TV."

Gina walked in first, "Hi you two. How are you? Trevor and I have some news, and you might not like it, so let me start with that."

Franny sighed, "Oh Gina, you're not pregnant, are you? I was hoping you would wait until marriage."

Her father spoke up, "Gina, I thought you two were smarter than that."

Gina waved them off. "No, I'm not pregnant, but Trevor and I have to move to Los Angeles. The producer will only work out of LA, some personal issue that he doesn't like to leave. So, we must, to work with this producer who is the best of the best, and he wants to work with us. I'm sorry, we have to be in California December thirtieth."

Franny got up and headed toward the phone with tears in her eyes. "You both have worked hard to get to this place. Mario, I'll call Rose and have her set me up with a realtor in Los Angeles. Do you know where you want to live? It will make house hunting so much easier."

"Mom, what are you talking about?"

"Do you think your father and I want the two of you living in some shack? No, we will plan to leave in two days and go buy a house for you."

Trevor was at a loss for words but managed to say, "It isn't necessary for you to—"

Mario spoke up. "I won't hear of it. I'll call the travel agent. We'll leave in two days."

"Gina honey, don't worry, we'll find you a lovely place. You two need to go back home and figure out where you're going to live. I'm sad that you're leaving, but your father and I understand you have this dream. Fulfill it, and then give me some grandchildren when you get married."

Gina and Trevor left the house paralyzed after what she heard, astonished. "Did they say they were buying us a house? Shit, and then throw in 'please give me grandchildren.' Way too much in one sentence."

"Trev, I guess we need to see where the studio is on a map and then go from there. Oh, my shit fuck, my Benz. I don't want to leave it behind."

This was becoming real way too fast.

"I bet your father can get the Benz to LA. If not, we'll buy another car. Let me give you a hug. Too much information going through that head of yours."

They sat at the dining room table over a map of Los Angeles in an old atlas they found in the carriage house. They found the address of the studio and hit Hollywood Hills.

"Baby, are we seriously talking about living in Hollywood?"

"G, it's close to the studio and we will probably be working late recording. We don't know how detailed this Tommy Whelan is; he could have us there late."

"Well, I need two things, my Benz and that fucking fantastic bed we sleep in every night. We will never find a bed like that."

"Those are the only two things, Gina?"

"Yeah, Trev, what else? Oh, you're a shithead; you are not even part of the discussion." She kissed him. "Without you, this means nothing. You are the only thing I really want always."

HOUSE IN HOLLYWOOD

TWO DAYS LATER, the three Riccis and one McNaughton boarded a plane to Los Angeles, first class. Gina was still nervous about this move. At least Franny would find a suitable home. Gina didn't know the cost of houses, let alone in the Hollywood Hills.

They checked in at the Beverly Hills Hotel. Franny's real estate friend had given her the name of a very reputable agent in the area.

The agent met them at the first house—a simple bungalow, with three bedrooms and two baths. Franny pronounced the house "not suitable." The kitchen and bathrooms were old and needed to be replaced. They walked through two other houses, which Franny also deemed unsuitable.

The fourth house was a bungalow with diamond pane leaded windows and a small front porch. It had the original wood floors and a huge living room with French doors that opened into a dining room. The kitchen wasn't new but updated appliances would make it acceptable; it had counter space and was open to the dining room. On the other side of the house were three bedrooms—not very big but adequate. The master bedroom had its own bathroom. It had a detached garage with a driveway, which was premium according to the agent. The backyard had a brick patio and shrubs that shielded the yard from neighbors.

The four of them sat in the car and Franny proclaimed, "I think this is the one." She turned to Trevor and Gina. "What do you think? Can you see yourselves living here? I think it's adorable. We should move on this, don't you think Mario?"

"Do you kids like the house?"

Trevor and Gina looked at each other and barely got out the words, "Yes, it's nice, but how much?"

Mario looked quizzical. "What does that matter? Your mother and I are buying you the house."

Trevor and Gina were stupefied and still wanted to know how much it cost.

Mario laughed. "You never pay the amount they ask. Always go in really low, then you get the number you want."

"But Dad, Trevor and I still want to know."

"They are asking $265,000, I'm going in at $242,000. Then if I get it for $247,000, I got a deal. That's how you negotiate, princess."

They went back to the office and a deal was negotiated, like Mario wanted. "Congratulations, you two have a house in the Hollywood Hills."

They knew the rest of the band wouldn't have it as easy as they did, so Gina asked about rentals. Kevin, Stu, Marvin, and Jake would share a house, oh and of course, Lucky Charms. Those guys would have to find a way of making a three or four bedroom house work for them.

Rio would either rent or buy himself a bachelor pad, and possibly ask Jeff to live with him. Maybe Ian and Lisa would be married and find an apartment, most likely. Gina was happy for Lisa, but it still stung a bit that she would be the one married.

Gina asked her parents if she could have her Benz brought out to LA, and she wanted the bed from the carriage house. Her father said he would arrange for the Benz, but her mother didn't understand why she wanted the bed. "Gina, we will get you new furniture. Why do you want that bed?"

"Mom, it's like a cloud. I bet you never even sat on that bed."

The papers were signed, and they could move into the house on December first. Franny took care of furnishing the house.

PREPARATIONS

IAN AND LISA would get married on November thirtieth at the courthouse in Hempstead. It would be a small ceremony—band members, Lisa's parents and sister, and Ian's parents coming in from Vancouver.

Gina and Lisa went shopping for a wedding dress. They started at Roosevelt Field, but Lisa didn't find anything she liked. It didn't have to be white, but it did have to feel special. Gina remembered a cute boutique not far from Saks, so they headed there next. They walked around the store and Lisa found a white lacy dress which fit her five-foot-seven slim frame perfectly. She looked at the price tag. "Oh, Gina, I can't afford this. It's $110.00."

Gina wanted to treat her. "Don't worry about it. Let me pay for it." But Lisa refused.

"Well, what are you willing to spend?

"Fifty, maybe sixty dollars."

Gina wasn't going to let Lisa walk out without her perfect dress and was finally able to convince Lisa to let her cover the balance as her wedding gift.

A few days later everyone gathered at the courthouse for Ian and Lisa's wedding.

Lisa looked beautiful in the lace dress and Ian was proud to be marrying her. After the ceremony they went to a private room at their favorite restaurant. The love between the couple was obvious to Gina. Trevor walked over to her at the other end of the restaurant and whispered in her ear, "Remember, we are eloping to Vegas—alone." Gina was comforted, thinking, *He really knows me.*

PACKING IT UP

THE HOLLYWOOD HILLS HOUSE closed on December first. Franny had furniture delivered but Trevor and Gina still had to pack and move what they had in the carriage house. Trevor had a moment of panic. "G, my guitars, we can't take four guitars on the plane, can we? We need to call the airline and see what we can do. I don't trust movers with my vintage guitars."

"Baby, calm down. I'll call and tell them we are part of a band and need our instruments. We may have to pay for extra luggage. But there is no way it won't be checked luggage. You're right; maybe two can come with us, but not four."

After several transfers and a wait of thirty minutes, Gina finally got an airline representative who told her they could each bring one on board and it would be stowed away, but the other two would have to go in cargo. If they wanted, they could insure the guitars. Trevor was still nervous about someone handling his coveted possessions.

"Honey, we must have some faith. It will be okay. At least they will be on the plane with us. We still have a lot of packing to do, my two closets of clothes and all the other shit I have collected through the years."

There was a knock on the door. Ant had come by to help pack. "Gina, I'm sad you're going to California. Who will I have? Mom and Dad are always off doing their business stuff and Frankie sucks. Plus, who wants to be around his kids? I know I'm their uncle, but I can't stand them. I won't have Rio either. I'll have to hang out with school friends more."

"Ant, I'm sorry love, but you are in junior high school. You have so much to look forward to. High school is around the corner, enjoy it. Don't do what I did and waste those special moments you get in high school. Dances, football games, prom. Those are events that never come back. After high school you will be going to college. Mom and Dad won't deny you like they did with me. But promise me to follow what you would like to become; don't let them influence you in what you want to study. Figure out what Ant wants to become and do it. Then, if you want, come to college in California. Don't let Mom and Dad keep you from your dreams. Stick to what you want to do. If it's California, then come."

"I've thought about it. I want to be a lawyer. Pepperdine University is in Malibu, and they have a good law program," he said hopefully.

Trevor felt bad for Ant. "Hey bro, we will be there when you're ready to come."

Ant started packing kitchen stuff. It was really Franny's, but Gina knew her mother wouldn't care if she took it. Hell, she bought them a house and furnished it; she won't miss some dishes.

In a few hours a good part of the kitchen and Gina's treasure trove of clothes, shoes, and makeup were packed. She had to leave a weeks' worth of clothing to pack in her suitcase. It will take a week or so for the movers to get to the house. Their house. Gina was still in shock that she and Trevor were on the title to a house her parents were gifting to them. It was her parents' way of letting them know, "Hurry up, get married, and have kids." But not yet; they had an album to record, and then maybe go on tour. It was all an unknown.

A few days later, the movers came to take their possessions, including the bed. Franny wanted them to stay at the house, but Gina thought it would be weird. She wanted to spend their last night in the carriage house, in the place where their love grew. They always knew it was a place of love. Being it was their last night in New York, Gina hoped they could close that chapter in the carriage house. But Trevor felt it was only fair to stay with Franny and Mario after everything they had done for them. It really wasn't asking much. "G, your parents are going to miss you. It really isn't a big deal. At least we know we will get up in time and have breakfast."

"Trev, what if they make us sleep in different rooms?"

Trevor laughed. "Is that what you're worried about? I don't think your parents have any delusions about what happens in our relationship. Ant would be happy too."

"Ugh, alright, but the car has already been shipped. How do we bring all our stuff up to the house?"

"Take what you need for the night, and we will pick everything else up when we leave for the airport."

They walked up the long driveway and into the house. They didn't realize everyone would be there: Frankie, MaryAnn, those three children, Aunt Deidre, Uncle Tony, Rio, and Ant. Serena made a spectacular dinner. There was laughter, drinking, congratulations. Everyone told Trevor, Gina, and Rio how much they would be missed, and knew they were headed for success.

Gina asked Rio, "So, when do you come out to LA?"

"In three days. My rental will be ready, then my stuff will be out in a week. I found a rancher that will hold all my stuff. I'm moving everything—my equipment and furniture. I'll stay at the Beverly Hills Hotel until all my stuff comes out. Everyone is coming out at different times. I hope we can keep track of it."

Trevor seemed a bit concerned. "We could probably use a week of practicing before we go into the studio." Trevor was acting so businesslike. Gina thought he was concerned about the producer.

It started getting late for the kids, so Frankie and MaryAnn left. Aunt Deidre and Uncle Tony followed them out. Rio hung for a bit to discuss some band checklists with Trevor.

Gina went to see her parents in the kitchen. "I can't believe I'm leaving this house. It's all I've ever known and I'm moving to a place that I'm not very fond of. I have no choice though."

Franny reassured her. "This is what you have been working toward even before you met Trevor. Now that you two are together, it's time to fly and be the best. I'm not totally sure of everything you do, but I know you do it well. Your father and I will come to visit you. It's time for you and Trevor to start your lives."

Gina teared up a bit, kissed them goodnight, and told them she would be ready in the morning. "Please don't let me forget about all our luggage still at the carriage house."

She walked back into the living room to find Trevor. "I'm tired babe, can we go to bed? Ant, I'll see you in the morning. Goodnight." They walked up the two staircases and entered Gina's childhood bedroom. Trevor had never been there. Gina locked the bedroom door and started stripping off her clothes. Then, she walked over to the dresser, pulled out a T-shirt and changed into it. Trevor got undressed, really undressed; he always slept naked.

Gina stared at him. "I love the look. Are you sleeping in my old bed like that?"

"Of course. I didn't bring pajamas."

"The door is locked. No one is going to bother us. So, what do you think of this bedroom, girly enough for you? It's not the Gina you know, but this was me a long time ago. It's weird being here on my last night in New York. Trevor, we are going to be okay, right?"

"How can we not be okay? We have a house, new furniture, and a record deal. What is going on in your head right now? Are you asking me if *we* are going to be okay? If you are, that's dumb. That's not even a discussion. We have been together for years."

Gina looked down and didn't respond.

"It's not about all the women in California again, is it? Stop. Gina, you are beautiful in my eyes, you are the most beautiful woman to me. You are also intelligent and have great business savvy. But baby, you are the only woman I want in my life. Yes, you are a sultry, seductive woman onstage. I get that, but you are my one, remember I found you, above all others. Gina, you always think I want someone other than you, but it has only been you. Come here."

She cuddled up under his arm where she felt safe. They kissed goodnight. Tomorrow they would be on their way to sunny California.

CALIFORNIA HERE WE COME

THE NEXT MORNING FRANNY, Mario, Ant, Gina, and Trevor had a big breakfast—waffles, pancakes, omelets, and lots of coffee. Serena had practically raised Gina and was saddened that she was moving to California. Gina was the easiest of the Ricci children to handle. Gina broke the silence around the table. "There are lots of flights to Los Angeles. You all can come anytime. Please don't make this a wake."

Franny spoke next. "Gina's correct. We should be celebrating the fact that she and Trevor are going to record an album. Do you know if you will travel because of the record? What do they call it? Oh yes, touring."

Trevor thought about it and answered Franny. "Well, if the record does well, yes. They would probably want us to tour with some band that's much better known than us. I could see that happening."

Ant chimed in. "Can I come when you tour? It would be fun."

Gina looked at her brother, knowing he was the last kid left in the Ricci house. "Ant, I promise you, if that happens, you can come, but who knows when that will happen." Gina knew that her parents would never let Ant go on tour with them. It made him feel better about Gina leaving.

Mario got up and started to get ready. "You guys still have stuff at the carriage house. We should start loading up and get ready to go."

Gina and Trevor said tearful goodbyes to Serena and Ant.

Trevor and Mario loaded up the luggage in the Cadillac, amazed that all of Gina's bags fit.

Gina silently stared out the window at the scenery she had taken for granted living in New York her whole life. Saying goodbye to the Miracle Mile, going past Eisenhower Park. There were many good times in that park. She could barely make out Belmont Race Track, where part of the Triple Crown is raced. Driving on the Long Island Expressway, Grand Central Parkway, took on a different feeling. Gina forgot all those times getting stuck in traffic on the roads. Every tree and exit sign was now something that would be etched in her mind. As they got closer to the airport, she could see the bridges. She could see the park where the 1964 World's Fair was, how many times had she been there. The Whitestone and Throgs Neck Bridges, if it was a clear day, you could see the beautiful NYC skyline. How many times had she gone over those bridges to see The Thirst? She had driven the highways so many times and now she didn't know when she would be back. It made her teary to think about being across the country from her parents.

She was a New York girl and leaving became a pain in her heart. Gina was always strong, but today, not so much.

They arrived at LaGuardia and checked baggage and guitars. They found their gate number and walked to the gate. It was time for the big goodbye.

Mario spoke first. "Princess, be safe and be the best Gina you can be. Remember, I love you. Trevor, please take care of my daughter, don't do anything to hurt her or I'm coming for you. I'm only kidding. But seriously, watch out for my princess."

Franny was crying. "Gina, I know you will be fine. You have gone through a lot to get here. Go get it princess. I know you will succeed higher than you ever thought." With that they said the final goodbye and walked down the jetway.

They took their seats in first class and Gina looked out the window and whispered, "Goodbye, New York, I love you," tears streaming down her face.

The flight attendant brought Gina champagne. Gina asked for a glass and a beer for Trevor.

Trevor looked at Gina as the plane took off. "Are you ready for the wildest ride you will ever be on? We are potentially going to be in the mix of bands." He grabbed her hand and kissed it. "I wouldn't want to do this with anyone but you. Remember that, always. If our life should get crazy, remind me that this is about our life together. Not the band and everything that comes with it. This doesn't mean anything without you beside me."

"I will remind you if things start to spin out of control. That's what scares me. Knowing that you care about our life—our private life—means everything. You and Me."

They napped for the next couple of hours, leaning on each other to get comfortable. Gina woke up as the plane started to descend. The young man seated next to her tapped her on the shoulder. Gina turned and answered, "Yes?"

"Are you folks with a band? I saw the guitars."

Gina thought the guy had balls to ask but didn't really mind. "Yes, we are in a band, you wouldn't know our music but one day you will. We are flying out to LA to record an album. So, remember our band's name. Perfection. Then you can tell your friends you met me when I was a nobody. It will be a good story, right?"

"I'll remember, and I hope all goes well with the album."

Gina smiled and saw that Trevor was waking up. "It won't be long until we land. We have to get a rental car, don't we?"

"I took care of it, but I don't know where the rental car company is. You may have to wait outside with our luggage until I can get you."

They disembarked the plane, got their luggage, and as Trevor expected, had to take a shuttle to get a rental car. Gina sat outside with the luggage and smoked five Sobranies. Trevor pulled up in a big sedan and they stuffed everything in and set off to find their new house.

When they pulled up, they saw Franny had already sent the painters. The house was now a soft sage color, with black shutters, and ivory-colored columns. On the front porch was an old-fashioned swing Franny had shipped from Alabama.

They opened the door to find the floors had been refinished to a nice light oak. Franny furnished the living room with two couches in deep ivory with blue-and-white paisley pillows. A Persian rug anchored the two couches. There was a heavy, knotty pine coffee table and sofa table, two Tiffany floor lamps, and a TV set. There were even knickknacks on the built-in corner cabinets in the dining room. They had a beautiful fireplace in the living room. Franny made sure they had the necessary hardware to start a fire, and on the mantel was a picture of the family. Gina and Trevor looked around their new house in disbelief that Franny had done so much. They walked through the French doors to the dining room which featured built-in china cabinets. A large round table was placed in the middle with six upholstered chairs.

In the kitchen, there was a brick floor and all new appliances. In the middle of the kitchen was a large butcher block table for food prepping.

Still stunned, they walked to the bedrooms. The master bedroom had a sleigh bed frame set up, waiting for Gina's beloved mattress to be delivered. The guest room featured a queen-sized bed with an upholstered headboard. The third bedroom contained only a desk and a chair. Gina knew Franny had not decorated that room, hoping it would be converted to a nursery soon.

Trevor was completely overwhelmed. "Your parents did all of this for us? It looks like we have lived here for years. We have nothing to do except put our clothes away. I thought the carriage house was amazing, but this is our house."

"You know when Franny Ricci does a project it's always going to be the best of the best. With that said I'm blown away; it's beautiful and we get to start our life here." She walked up to Trevor, ran her fingers through his hair, and kissed him softly. She whispered, "We have a lot of rooms to play in, and I don't mean music. I fucked up on the plane. I wanted to join the Mile High Club, but we were both knocked out. Next time."

"G, we hopefully will have many flights to take, and for you to join the club." He kissed her back.

It was time to find a grocery store and stock the kitchen. They got in the car and became starstruck seeing all the Hollywood landmarks. It was a whirlwind, but they were ready to take the next step in the band's evolution.

Gina bought all the ingredients to cook their first meal in their new home—chicken parmesan, linguine, and garlic bread. She had to buy a couple of pots, pans, and a baking dish to make dinner; their belongings weren't coming for a week. Gina cooked and cleaned. After dinner they sat on the couch and watched TV, a luxury to have the time. Gina turned to Trevor, "Is life really this easy? I'm so content. I can't believe this is our life. I know I tell you all the time but I'm so lucky to have this life, to have you. This is perfection," Gina said with emotion.

"I never thought me, this guy from Vancouver, would meet a woman like you. I was always fucking things up, but with you, I don't even know what to say either. It's so easy with you, you know me. Come here and give me some love."

Gina's eyes widened "You mean right now? I wondered when you were going to ask."

Gina got naked in a flash and sat on top of Trevor. "What's your move?" she asked.

With a throaty laugh, Trevor rolled her on her back and couldn't rip his clothes off fast enough. "I think you want me hard, don't you?"

"I want you any way you choose. How's that?"

He loved to tease her but couldn't wait any longer. As he promised, he took her hard. When he saw the way she looked at him, with so much love, he became a gentle lover.

Gina stared into his eyes, pushed back his hair, and kissed his neck, his ears, and cupped her hands around his face. "I love you Trevor McNaughton, and that will never change. I fell in love with you the first time I saw you, and every day I love you a little bit more if that's even possible."

CALI MOVES

OVER THE FOLLOWING DAYS, the rest of the band made their way west. Rio was staying in Beverly Hills until his rental became available. Kevin and the three roadies, Stu, Marvin, and Jake were the band's equipment cross-country. Jeff found a studio apartment that he said was all he needed for now. Ian and Lisa flew in and moved directly into their apartment waiting for their belongings. Gina had no idea what Brian Mayfield's living arrangements were and didn't care.

Gina invited the band members to their house for dinner. They debated which songs would be the first to be recorded, but Tommy Whelan would have the ultimate say as the producer. They enjoyed each other's company, drank wine, ate tasty food, and shared their first impressions of California living.

Christmas was a week away. How different would a California Christmas be? Lisa and Gina went Christmas shopping. They found a few kitschy stores for fun clothing. They went to a music store and Gina found a guitar that Trevor had been wanting—a Gibson Les Paul Standard Gold Top.

She told Lisa, "I'm getting this for him. He'll freak out."

Lisa looked at her. "Did you see the price? Gina, that's a lot of money."

Gina took her hand. "I never like to broadcast this, but money isn't an issue for me. I have a nice trust fund and access to my parents' money. I'm not that girl who wears fancy designer clothes, but when it comes to making my friends and Trevor happy, I don't mind spending money. Speaking of presents, what do you and Ian need? You know I'm going to get you a gift, so why not tell me?"

"Gina, stop. I couldn't. You're going to have to get us a gift that you think is appropriate."

"I love you and I hate you right now," said Gina, and Lisa laughed with her.

Gina bought Rio an acoustic guitar he had his eye on. Ian and Lisa were easy—a slow cooker and a toaster oven Lisa had mentioned she needed in passing. Jeff wanted a better amp, so that was easy. The roadies and Kevin would all get cash, and Brian Lucky Charms Mayfield also. She had already shipped gifts to her family in New York, and they had been placed under the tree by Serena. Gina promised to call as they were opening gifts in New York.

Gina bought her first Christmas tree ever. Franny always had a team decorate the Ricci estate, so she knew nothing about shopping for a tree. But she figured it out and had fun choosing the decorations. She was proud of herself; it was a first for this rich girl.

Gina and Trevor had a private Christmas Eve. She had bought him a few clothing items to fit a lead guitarist and gave those to him first. "So, now you're trying to dress me up," he said as he opened them.

"Those are trivial things. Here is your real gift." It was hard to disguise a guitar, but as he peeled off the wrapping paper, he looked at Gina with tears in his eyes. "G, you knew I was looking at this, but I never thought you would actually buy it."

"I saw it in a music store and couldn't resist. I had to buy it for you. You'll play it when we record again."

He leaned over and gave her a long kiss. "You know I'll never find a woman who cares as much as you for as long as I live. I love you."

"My gift for you doesn't compare to this, but here." Gina opened a small box that contained a necklace with three diamonds and a simple gold tag, engraved "T loves G always." Gina loved it and asked him to place it on her neck. "Trev, it's beautiful. I will never take it off."

They called their families to wish them a Merry Christmas. Gina, not forgetting Shawn, had sent him a pair of soft leather gardening gloves and gardening tools. He told her they were too nice for him. Whatever was going on between him and Trevor, she wouldn't get involved, but she liked, no she loved, Shawn and his simple lifestyle.

Gina cooked a typical Italian Christmas—turkey and lasagna. Everyone brought a dish. She missed her family in New York, but this was her family here in Los Angeles. There was much to celebrate. In just over a week, Perfection would be in the studio.

Rio's rental was ready for him to move in. Luckily all his furniture and equipment came. He worked on getting the equipment room ready so the band could practice before they went into the studio. The next day was time to rehearse at Rio's house. They went over every original song over and over. Guitar solos were tightened up and vocals were changed to add more harmonizing. They knew Tommy Whelan would rearrange songs where he felt it was needed. He was a skilled producer and Perfection knew they were lucky to collaborate with him.

December thirtieth came. Kevin and his crew of roadies went into the studio and set up the band's equipment. It was a nervous moment for Perfection. The band decided to meet and walk into the studio together, a united force.

Tommy Whelan was in his mid-forties, a decent-looking man with a great physique. He had long, slicked-back, blondish-gray hair. His hazel eyes were set in a friendly face. He had a speech prepared about how he did not want to change Perfection, only fine-tune it. He introduced his sound engineer, Maxie Wilder, saying that he worked with many R&B singers and top bands in the rock world. Maxie was an African American man in his fifties. He was Tommy's favorite sound engineer. Maxie was totally into the music he worked on. His favorite phrases were, "You got that man, it's super-hot," and "I'm digging that." In a pinch Maxie also played the saxophone.

Tommy asked the band what song they wanted to try first.

Rio chose "Punch the Night" with lots of guitar. Tommy had Trevor and Rio play their parts several times and recorded a few takes. It was a slow process, but nobody had expected it to be easy. They worked until eleven o'clock; then Tommy told the band to enjoy New Year's. He would be spending the holiday with his family. Tommy made it clear that his family would always be a priority.

A NEW YEAR

WITH NEW YEAR'S EVE AND DAY FREE, the band members went in separate directions. Rio and Jeff went clubbing. Ian and Lisa stayed home, as did Trevor and Gina. She remembered a few years ago how devastated she was not to be with Trevor, and now they couldn't be separated.

They planned a quiet dinner, followed by sitting around naked, wrapped in blankets, and watching TV. Around nine o'clock the doorbell rang. It was fucking Brian Mayfield. What the hell? Brian had a bottle with him. "Hi, Trev, I was hoping you would be home tonight. Thought we could celebrate New Year's together."

Trevor let him in and Gina shot daggers at both of them. Brian had the nerve to ask her to get three glasses for the champagne. She was burning hot with anger. She couldn't believe Trevor hadn't spoken up.

"Excuse me, Brian, I'm not understanding the *we* part. Why would you think *we* would be interested in celebrating with you? Everyone in the band is off doing their own thing. Explain to me what role you play in Perfection? And, why would Trevor and I want to celebrate with you? What instrument do you play? What music did you write? What do you do?" Gina walked into the kitchen to get the glasses and was returning to the living room when she heard Trevor's voice and stopped for a moment to hear what he would say.

Trevor was uncomfortable. He knew Gina was extremely irritated by this intrusion. Her tirade said it all. "Brian let's have one quick drink to welcome the New Year, but Gina isn't feeling well. Ya know?"

"Oh, got you. Well, let's have a drink and I'll go." Gina couldn't believe her ears. Did Trevor tell Brian she wasn't feeling

well because of her period? This was fucking nuts! Why would Trevor even allude to that?

Brian stayed for half an hour. After Trevor closed the door behind him, Gina unleashed on Trevor. "What the hell was that? Trev, really, you fucking telling him that I wasn't feeling good, because 'ya know'—meaning I was on my period. You have to be shitting me right now. You know very well I don't like him. He shows up here, unannounced, and you told him a very personal issue, which was a lie? Baby, I don't want our New Year's to be like this, but help me out, why?"

"Come on, G. I didn't know how to get him out of here. I thought that would get him out the door. I didn't think. I knew you wanted him gone. Any guy who isn't with a woman doesn't want to hear about chick issues. I knew he would go running. Come here, don't let him ruin our evening."

"Okay, you did get him to leave, so thank you. But why do you defend him? He's a snake, a weasel. I'm telling you, he is trying to get between us."

"G, he can't do that. Let's stick to our plan. Let's get naked, wrap ourselves in blankets, and watch TV. Please come on."

"Never explain any issues regarding our personal life with that snake Mayfield. Don't ever do that to me again."

"I promise," Trevor vowed. But it was a promise he wouldn't be able to keep. Brian Mayfield would soon get bolder and more disruptive to their relationship.

GETTING REAL

THE BAND WAS BACK IN THE STUDIO. Tommy Whelan came in and asked, "Do you have a manager to help with organization? There will be interviews, possible road trips—you need someone to manage that for you. I can give you a list of people who would love to work with you. But getting that worked out helps me out tremendously. I can give him a schedule for recording and touring."

Rio and Trevor agreed they needed someone to oversee all the logistics. They would interview people, but all the band members would have a say in choosing the manager. Gina had a thought, *What was Brian Mayfield's job*? He claimed he would manage the band. He had no experience and didn't even know the music business. Gina was on a mission to reduce the role of Mr. Lucky Charms.

Tommy Whelan wanted them to rehearse their cover of "Gimme Shelter." How did he know that they even covered that song? Gina asked, "Tommy, we played that song wasting time when we made the demo. How did you know that?"

Tommy laughed, "Because Michael Diamond had Lou recorded you. I heard it and it should definitely go on the album."

A little bit of panic set in for the band; they didn't even remember how they covered the song. Trevor asked Tommy if they could listen to the tape. Tommy keyed up the recording. Trevor and Gina were in sync, only Gina's voice had limitations on some of the high notes, so she and Trevor made it up as they went along. Tommy gave them the cue, "Let's do a first take and we will go from there."

The band went over the song a few times, then Tommy played it back and wanted Gina and Trevor to go over vocals. That took a few takes. The next song Tommy wanted was "Found You." He asked Trevor to write lyrics that Gina could harmonize but have a different line, as if she were answering him in the song. It took two days to get it right.

Over the next month the band recorded eight original songs plus the cover. Tommy wanted a few songs to have keyboards and chose songs he felt would jack up the background. Rio and Tommy rehearsed and figured out if they would be adding keyboards. It worked for some of the songs.

Tommy also thought "Punch the Night" and "Music Is a Circus" should have a sexy saxophone added. Maxie showed his approval by saying, "I'm digging it man." Maxie was happy to add his saxophone prowess. It gave Kevin a chance to work the recording studio mixing board.

It was getting close to the end of recording. Tommy and Maxie fine-tuned the mixes. Tommy sat everyone down and they listened to the finished product. It sounded great. That's why you get a producer who knows how to get the best out of you. Kevin learned a lot working with Maxie about how to mix the songs. Kevin was learning how to finesse a song by adding a harder drum intro or making the bass line of a song more prominent. Maxie was an amazing resource for Kevin to learn the art of sound mixing.

After they wrapped up the recording, it took forty-five days to get the finished product.

Tommy brought the subject up again. "Did you find a manager? Because you will need someone to help promote along with the record company. Promoting your album is key." Trevor told him they had decided to go with Skip Glazer, one of the names on Tommy's list.

Gina asked Tommy, "What are the next steps? What do we do now?"

"Skip and the record company are going to want to promote a single off this album. I am going to suggest 'Found You' and 'Gimme Shelter.' There is no harm in getting your original work out and marrying it with a known song. Then we drop more songs from the album as the songs get traction. The label will send copies to big stations around the country to get airtime. You will all need to get headshots done, plus group photos of the band to be sent along with your music. Brown Fence will have a release party introducing you to the public. That's where things get crazy with interviews. I'll give you the name of the photographer who does about everyone in music and film. Brown Fence and I work with the top bands in the rock business. You know who we work with, a few acts are getting ready for a fourteen-city tour. If they get you going, you could possibly be an opening act for one of them. I'm putting it out there. Getting the buzz for you is important. If they ask me for an opening act, I'll recommend Perfection. Start working on material for your next album. I think we work well together. I'll produce it."

Trevor spoke for everyone when he said, "That's a lot to digest, Tommy. I guess Skip will keep us informed about what the label wants from us."

Tommy wanted Trevor to know, "Make sure, individual shots, band, and then have a few with you and Gina. People eat that shit up that you two are a couple. Don't downplay it. I'll stay connected. Go home and get ready for a media blitz."

The band walked out proud of their work. Now the unknown waiting for a call.

Skip called the photographer that Tommy recommended and was able to get them booked the next day.

PHOTO SHOOT

GINA AND TREVOR HAD GONE clothes shopping before they left for California. The boxes arrived in time for the photo shoot. Gina was excited to unpack her new clothes, and clothing she had bought for Trevor. "Trev, should I be a sexy lady, or tone it down with jeans and a fancy shirt? I don't know. Maybe bring a little of each and have the photographer tell me the look he's going for."

"G, you're the only one who has to worry about that. Us guys are easy. We wear jeans and a shirt, even a T-shirt. A head shot is just that. It doesn't matter what we wear. Can I suggest sexy, and then maybe a little low-key sexy?"

"Trev, I love you, but you are no help. I did get you some new things that you should think of bringing. Maybe I should hire one of those people who picks out clothes for you, dresses you."

"You have done fine on your own. Here's an idea. Do you have that white dress I first saw you in?"

Gina beamed, "That's brilliant! Most definitely, especially since Tommy wants a shot of you and me. It will be meaningful to us; no one else would know the significance. See, you are handsome *and* smart. Come over here and let me kiss that beautiful face."

The band's appointment at Tabletop Photography on Fountain Avenue was for ten in the morning. Gina took five outfits in addition to "the dress." Trevor stuck with faded black jeans, T-shirts, a designer white T-shirt, and the leather jacket Gina gave him. To make Gina happy he picked a few shirts and a pair of designer jeans she bought him in her last-minute shopping spree.

Gina's red Benz had made it to California, and Trevor drove them to the photography studio in it. Ian and Lisa were already there, and Ian was nervous. "Hey, man, I don't have fancy stuff to wear. I brought jeans and tees and a hockey jersey."

Lisa was such a stable and levelheaded woman. "I told him, there's nothing to worry about. If they want you to wear something else, they have it at the studio."

Gina thought that was a good point. Rio showed up wearing his black leather pants and an incredibly old designer tee. He made it noticeably clear that his shades weren't coming off.

"Is that because you're high?" Gina asked. "That's usually why you wear sunglasses. And where did you get weed? You made a friend and didn't tell us?"

"Gina, you know I have connections everywhere. All you have to do is ask. How come you have a fucking garment bag of clothes? Do you think you're changing that often? We're in and out."

Jeff showed up, looking hungover.

"Jeff, man, I told you not to go out last night, you look like shit. And you are going to look like shit in the photos," Rio scolded.

Gina corralled the *children*. "Let's go in and do this—in and out like Rio said."

The band had no idea how long it would take. Each headshot took at least ten takes.

Gina gauged what she should wear by the way the photographer was talking to each of the band members. She wore a flowy top and let her hair fall into soft wavy curls.

Anton, the photographer, loved Rio's look. He told Ian to wear his hockey jersey. Jeff wore jeans with a button-down shirt. He wanted Trevor to look like a bad boy and told him to wear his faded jeans and an old concert T-shirt. He asked Gina if she had anything slinky. She told him there was one outfit she was holding onto for pictures with Trevor. But she did have a deep-blue velvet halter dress. Anton loved it. He positioned the band around Gina. Rio on her left, Jeff and Ian to the right, and Trevor behind her with his hands resting on her shoulders.

The studio door opened. That slimy asshole Brian Mayfield walked in like he was a band member.

Gina turned to Trevor. "What the hell Trevor? Why is he here? I know he thinks he's part of the band, but he isn't. What the fuck, man? Can we never get rid of this guy?"

Trevor tried to calm her down. "G, babe, I don't know how he found out. I didn't say a word."

"He's calculating. I see him. I don't trust him."

Anton wanted a picture of Trevor and Gina alone, so they went to the dressing room to change. "Trevor, lock the fucking door. I don't want Lucky Charms seeing me naked." Gina changed into "the dress." She made Trevor change into his "fancy" outfit she had bought him. Good thing Gina locked the door because a few minutes later the handle jiggled. Brian was trying to get in.

Gina walked out in her white crochet dress. Anton pulled up a chair and told Trevor, "You sit down. Gina, sit on his lap and look into his eyes." They tried several angles, and, finally, Gina put her arms around Trevor's neck and told Anton to take the picture.

That picture would follow the two of them for years. It was gold. Gina walked away to change, and Brian was immediately all over Trevor. She wondered if Brian was gay and in love with Trevor. That thought made her shiver.

She came out dressed in what she came in. "Hi Brian. What are you doing here?"

"Oh yeah, Skip Glazer called me to make sure everything went well at the photo shoot."

"Why would Skip call you?"

"Well, yeah he knows that I know the band and I help out."

Gina shook her head and walked away. She called out to Trevor, "Babe, come on. We have stuff to do. Remember?"

Cowed, Trevor said over his shoulder, "Hey, I'll catch you later, Brian."

Trevor caught up to Gina. "You really need to try and hide your disdain for Brian. It's not a great look for you. You're better than that."

"What should I do? Pretend that I really like him when he screws me over because he wants your time? I should bend over and take it? It is so obvious, and you can't or won't see he is trying to put a wedge between us. I don't know, maybe he's in love with you. I don't get it but if he wants to play that game with me, he will lose."

"He could never get in between us, never."

"You know what, Trevor? That's the second or third time you said that to me. I will remember that you said it. Can we have a nice lunch now? That photography session was more work than I thought."

She grabbed his face and kissed him. "I love you, that's all."

They got in the car, drove to a cute little bistro, and were seated at an outdoor table. Gina drank a few sangrias because it was hot outside, and they went right to her head.

Trevor saw an opening to put the Brian bullshit to rest. "Let's go home and take the phone off the hook and make love for the rest of the day."

Gina smirked at him. "That sounds unbelievably fantastic." Problem diverted for now.

SONGS RELEASED

THE MORNING CAME and Trevor realized he had left the phone off the hook all night. Two minutes after he put the phone back in the cradle, it rang.

It was Skip. "Trevor, I've been trying to reach you since yesterday. Was your phone working? Anyway, the label set up an interview with one of the rock radio morning shows tomorrow. This is great buzz for the band. Their listeners have been requesting 'Found You' and 'Gimme Shelter.' This is great."

Trevor was caught off guard, "What time do we need to be at this morning show? I'm guessing early."

Skip reminded him this was great exposure, and it was before the record company was officially doing their album release party.

"Okay, I'll call everyone."

Skip reminded him, "You make the music. I manage the band. You don't have to do that type of thing anymore. Everyone else already knows anyway."

Trevor hung up the phone and yelled, "G? Where are you?"

"I'm in the bedroom. What's up?" Gina walked out in her bathrobe. Trevor thought to himself, *The woman is glowing*. He knew how lucky he was to have a woman who loved him as much as she did.

"We have an interview at one of those morning rock radio shows tomorrow at eight. Can Gina Poole get herself ready for that?"

"Yes! All of us? Rio will be insane. He'll be hysterical, mostly because he won't answer questions. I guess we can expect the usual questions. Where did your inspiration come from for this song? Blah, blah. I got it. I'll be sweet. You know I'm only the chick in the band; I won't get asked any questions."

"No Gina, you're the most opinionated out of all of us. Don't hide it; bring it out. You're a badass. Be you."

Gina wasn't the type to ever be happy in the backseat. She was a force in the foundation of Perfection.

The record label was pleased the band got the interview. They were getting pre-release party buzz. It would make the release party a bigger event. They would be on air for twenty minutes, with breaks for commercials and traffic updates. The two DJs were a staple in the Los Angles morning drive. The next morning was the interview. They asked what they liked about LA. What is the transition from a New York band to being in LA like? They each had their own answer. Gina stated she will always be a New York girl no matter how many years she lives in LA. Then they segued to, "What is it like to be in a band with your boyfriend?"

"I don't like the word boyfriend. It makes our relationship sound juvenile, and we've been partners for years."

They asked her a question she dreaded. "What do you think of the groupies?"

"I hate them. They need to get their own men, not men already spoken for."

The DJs announced a contest. The first twenty people to call would win a "meet and greet" with the band at their release party. That was news to the band.

One of the DJs asked if they liked how fast things were moving. Everyone's response was a variation on, "That's rock and roll." Everybody left the station not believing that they were finally making their dream happen.

RADIO INTERVIEWS

THE RELEASE PARTY was in ten days. Gina thought should she invite her parents and Ant. Then she thought there would be too much going on for her to spend time with them. Gina wanted to know more about the meet and greet from Skip. What was the purpose? Skip explained, "Women want to say they met their favorite band member. Men want to meet you."

Wasn't that false advertising? Three of the band members were not available. Skip told her she was taking it too literally. "It's an idea. Fans want to be able to connect with you even if it is just hello."

It sounded harmless. Brown Fence Records set up a phone interview with a rock station in New York—one the band knew well. They were getting exposure on both coasts. Other stations around the country would follow since they take their cues from New York and Los Angeles.

The call was scheduled for nine thirty eastern time, which meant everybody needed to be in the same location for the call at six thirty in the morning. Rio suggested his place since he had so much equipment that would make the call easier to hear. They liked having an opportunity to talk to their fans back home. The DJ was someone they all knew because he had come to see them a couple of times. When he asked what they missed about New York, Gina answered, "everything."

Rio said, "It's different getting around LA. New York, I can take a train to get somewhere." Everyone missed New York pizza and bagels.

The DJ told them, "I love both singles and can't wait to hear the whole album. I hope we can do this again."

"For our home fans, absolutely."

Now the buzz was going to spread. Perfection was a little anxious. Skip admitted things seemed to be moving ahead of schedule. The record labels usually act more cautiously. He suggested they start shopping for something appropriate to wear to the release party. No jeans.

WHAT TO WEAR

GINA FOUND MIMI, a stylist who had a studio on Sunset Boulevard. She wanted to see some designer outfits that were classic, not fussy. She wanted Trevor to look sophisticated but not fake. She and Trevor went to Mimi's studio and saw racks and racks of designer clothes. Gina explained they needed killer outfits for their album release party. Gina immediately targeted a few dresses from a famous designer, expensive, but she didn't care; this event was important. Mimi agreed the designer would suit her well. Gina saw a dusty-rose dress with an uneven hem and tight bodice and asked to try it on. When she came out of the dressing room, she asked Trevor, "What do you think? Is it too much?"

Trevor said it was beautiful.

Mimi suggested a deep iridescent-purple dress. Gina tried that one on also. She loved both.

Mimi turned her attention to Trevor and suggested he wear a black suit jacket, black shirt, with white pants and a skinny white tie. Gina cringed at the idea, but realized Mimi knew what she was doing. When Trevor trudged out of the dressing room, he looked magnificent. Mimi told them she recently dressed a famous actor in something similar. Trevor felt out of his element; however, he understood the need to look sharp.

He admitted to Gina, "I'm okay with this, but I think it would be cooler with leather pants."

Mimi's head snapped back at him. "I have a beautiful pair of the softest leather pants straight from Paris. You're tall, I hope they're long enough for you. Let me pull them out." She returned a moment later and handed the pants to Trevor.

When he walked out of the dressing room, Gina nodded her head in appreciation. "That's it, babe. I'm a lucky lady."

Mimi walked to another rack and pulled two ties, one to match each dress Gina liked.

Gina wanted to wrap this up. "Mimi, are you loaning or renting these clothes to us, or can I buy them?"

Mimi coolly responded, "You could buy them if you had $10,000."

Gina opened her bag. "Credit card or check?"

Mimi was stunned. "Either would be fine."

Gina then advised her, "You will need to steam the garments and we will pick them up tomorrow."

Gina was concerned about Ian, Lisa, and Jeff. What would they look like? She knew Rio would be fine. Aunt Deidre had connected him with a designer. On the way home Gina mentioned that she should help Lisa find something to wear.

Trevor warned her, "You can help her find something that she can afford. Don't go offering to pay. Ian is a proud guy. He wants to know that he can take care of his wife. I know you mean well, but I've known him for years. He likes to handle his own shit. I love that you want to help Lisa, but help her with what she can afford."

"Okay, I hear you. I won't offer, but if she likes something and she's short can I—"

"G, you're generous, slow it down."

She didn't want to hurt Ian's feelings. But she would offer to take Lisa shopping.

"Trev, did they tell us where this release party is going to be? I don't remember hearing anything. Is Brown Fence hosting this? Or are we paying for this?"

"I'm fairly sure Brown Fence is handling the release party. They will be inviting promoters, radio stations, public relations people, music writers—and don't be surprised to see their top talent. You will meet bands you never thought you would meet. But remember, people are coming to see *us*."

"I wish I knew who would be there so I don't act like an excited teenager when I spot them. I guess we are one of them now. Yeah, I'm one of them. Perfection is a real band."

Trevor laughed. "Babe, are you convincing yourself?"

"Yeah, kind of. It was a dream; now it's reality. I don't know if I'm ready for this media blitz."

"Gina Ricci. You are ready. You are going to be a star, and I will be right there with you."

It could be a stratospheric change in their lives, but everything comes at a price.

PRIMPING FOR THE PARTY

MARCH 1979. Five days away from the release party Brown Fence was hosting at a new club on Sunset Boulevard. The guest list was filled with top writers, promoters, and talent. Gina hung their clothes for the evening in the spare bedroom. She looked at them every day and her head started to spin. She needed to find a makeup artist and someone to do her hair. She asked around and was given the name of a girl trying to make her way into the industry—Chante. Why not help someone who is just starting out? Someone like her.

Lisa admitted she found shopping for an outfit a bit daunting and welcomed Gina's invitation to go shopping together.

Lisa seemed a bit nervous when Gina picked her up.

"What's going on with you? You seem out of sorts, everything okay?" Gina asked.

"Honestly Gina, it's a bit scary to be part of this huge party. They are inviting other bands, big bands. I don't know how to speak to people like that."

"If it makes you feel better, neither do I. We have each other's back. Let's make a promise. If either one of us feels out of sorts, we will find the other, deal?"

"Absolutely," Lisa responded with a relieved smile.

"Great! Let's find you a dress."

Lisa landed on a dark blue chiffon dress within her budget, and Gina reassured her, "That color looks great with your complexion. You look beautiful."

BEING AVAILABLE

THERE WERE SO MANY REQUESTS for interviews, Skip had to prioritize them by value to the band. They sat down with music magazines, reviewers, and radio stations from large-market cities. The interviews became a blur, repeating the same thing every time. Gina was frequently asked, "How does it feel to be the only woman in the band?" She tried numerous ways of saying the band was a collective, not one member was more important than the other.

"What is it like singing with your boyfriend?"

Skip warned Gina to tone down her responses. "We are partners; the word 'boyfriend' is juvenile," she would answer, trying to sound as nice as possible.

They were frequently asked, "Who writes the music?"

"Everybody." Rio at one point jumped out there, "Hey man, we will show you when we play some gigs, okay? Then you can see how it all works."

The day of the party, Brown Fence sent limos to everyone's houses. Skip told Trevor and Gina they would be the last to arrive to the party. Chante was at the house doing Gina's hair and makeup. Gina asked her to do high impact makeup but to leave her wavy long hair and boost the volume.

Trevor didn't know what to do with himself. He watched TV but didn't want to take a shower with someone else in the house. Gina thought it was silly since they had their own bathroom.

Gina noticed he was looking slightly nervous. "Trev, are you okay? You look nervous. It's okay if you are, I am. We don't know what to expect. I don't think we have to sing; the album will be playing, correct?"

"I think that's the idea."

Gina had never seen Trevor so stressed out. Once Chante finished, Gina paid her, and she left. "Trevor, come here, baby. We are both nervous. It will be something new and scary if I'm being real. We can get through this, like we have for years. We are being judged, we know that. Come here."

He kneeled and put his head in her lap. She stroked his hair and kissed him. Our band is going to be the next big item, right?"

"What if we aren't that good, Gina?" he asked tearfully.

"Stop it. We will find out tonight; but we will always have each other." She wiped his tears. "You are the most handsome man in the entire world. Now come help me choose one of those amazing dresses so I can look pretty for you."

Trevor looked at the deep-purple dress and his black outfit hanging next to each other. That was the one.

Calmed down now, and with no one else in the house, Trevor got in the shower. Gina watched him from their bed, the way he washed his hair, the way he washed his body. She was enjoying every minute, aware their lives would change after that night. Gina tussled his hair dry with a hand towel. She lightly patted his entire body with the bath towel, moving in slow circles on the more responsive parts of his anatomy.

"Baby, please, I would feel so much better if you would let me have you right now," he pleaded softly.

"You've just gotten out of the shower, and I'm all made up," she responded reasonably. Quickly relenting, "You know what? Yes, take me if that puts you at ease. I want you."

She directed him to the chaise lounge in their bedroom. She dropped her bathrobe to the floor and slipped off her fancy lingerie. She sat on top of him, and pulled his head to her chest as she slowly rode him, working out his stress. "Do you feel better now?"

"Ugghhhh. Yes. Now, let's go to this party. Wear the purple. We will match better."

As they finished dressing, they could see a black limo pulling up from the bedroom window.

Trevor met the driver at the door. "Mr. and Mrs. McNaughton, I'm here to take you to the party."

"Hey, Mrs. McNaughton, let's go," Trevor called out to Gina.

"What did you say?"

"They must have told the limo driver we're married, so Mrs. McNaughton, let's go."

Gina came out of the bedroom a few minutes later. "How do I look?" she asked, uncharacteristically nervous.

"Beautiful. Sexy. Everything I love about you."

RELEASE PARTY

WHEN THEY ARRIVED at the club, there were four limos in front of them waiting to unload their passengers.

When their limo pulled up, the rest of the band was already standing on the sidewalk waiting for them to arrive. Trevor climbed out and extended his hand to Gina. Light bulbs flashed as the two of them made their way toward the club. Everyone had been instructed to stop in front of the sponsor banner to have their photos taken. Trevor and Gina already looked like they were pros. The band posed for a group shot, and each member played with the photographer for individual photos.

Skip and Tommy Whelan were there with their wives. Skip reminded them they had the meet and greet promoted by the radio station. Skip and Tommy ushered them into a small room with the twenty winners. They had to play nice, shake hands, and thank everyone for coming. The guys were interested in the best guitars and the right drums. Surprisingly, the women were drawn to Gina. "Where do get your clothes? What skin care do you use?" Gina didn't feel threatened by any of the ladies and was able to laugh with some of them. Many fans wanted their picture taken with Gina and Trevor, and they willingly obliged.

Once they entered the main room, the people, the lights, and loud house music were sensory overload. The venue was furnished with several blue sofas and large tables. In the back was a smaller room, where the famous people spent time together. Lights were flashing too brightly and too fast. The music was lowered and Benjamin Blum, Head of Operations at Brown Fence Records, introduced himself, then Tommy Whelan, the producer. Tommy then introduced Skip Glazer as the band's manager. Skip introduced each band member and brought them onstage. Rio first, Ian, Jeff, Trevor, and Gina last.

Gina stepped up to the microphone. "Thank you all for coming to our coming-out party. We're Perfection and I'm positive you will be hearing more from us in the years to come. Thank you again." Trevor took her hand and kissed her on the cheek in a gentle yet possessive gesture.

It was time to mingle with the crowd. A writer from a fashion magazine asked Gina who she was wearing. Gina was surprised by the question and replied, "a famous designer, can you guess?"

From the corner of her eye, she saw him. Fucking Lucky Charms. *Why is he here?* He had corralled Trevor in a conversation with two blonde Barbies. *He's already trying to get Trevor a hookup. No fucking way.* Gina was determined not to let her jealousy overtake her. This was Perfection's big night and nothing Brian Mayfield did would ruin it.

Trevor noticed her watching and immediately excused himself from the conversation. "G, before you go off, I had nothing to do with that."

"I know you didn't," she assured him. "It's always Brian. I'm not going to let him ruin this night."

A young guy approached them and asked them to stand together for a photo. They placed their arms around each other and posed for him. Rio rushed up to them. "Hey, this is so cool. So, you know my favorite band? They are here tonight, and they loved my guitar playing."

"Found You" began to play over the speakers.

Tiny blue lights could be seen flickering from a small patio out back, which is where Gina and Trevor found Ian and Lisa. Ian confessed, "Hey, bro, I can't go back in that room. Lisa and I didn't realize it was going to be this big. Did you see who's here? Every big band Brown Fence has under contract. I saw some of those guys in concert; this is surreal."

Trevor understood. Ian was a simple guy from Vancouver like he was. It was overwhelming. "You're now one of those guys. Ride it. No more speeches tonight, so you can relax and get a drink. Lisa, you okay?"

"I guess so. Gina, I can still count on you?"

"Yes. I'm a bit overwhelmed myself. A lot of Hollywood types, a lot of gold-digger types. Exactly how I imagined LA. I'm going to go to the bar and get myself a drink. Let's see if they even know who I am."

Gina walked up to the bar, ordered a martini, turned around, and saw the lead singer from the hottest band in the country, Brent Nolan. His band was Brown Fence Records' top talent, they lead all the music charts.

He offered up a hello. "Gina Poole. Or McNaughton? Which is it?"

"It's Poole for right now, but when I become McNaughton, nobody will know."

"Well, either way, I'm looking forward to seeing you perform. I hear you can be quite sexy, alluring onstage."

"Thank you. It's easy when you play off of the man you love, you know?"

Skip Glazer rounded up the band for a business discussion with Brown Fence and John Dunn, the promoter for White Lace Fest, and announced, "They want you to be the opening act for the Fest. Fourteen cities nationwide with a three-month commitment. It would be a great jumping-off point for Perfection."

Trevor asked, "Would our music get more national play then?"

"The idea would be to get you more airwave time in the cities you will be playing, yes." John Dunn answered.

Rio added, "It sounds great. We're interested, definitely. But we usually have a band meeting to discuss all business matters."

Gina interjected, "We need a day to discuss. I hope that is fair. We are interested and need to work out planning with Skip."

Skip knew it was a small delay tactic, but he agreed they should take a day to respond.

The McNaughtons had had enough of the party and were making their way to the door. Brian caught up with them. "Hey, where are you two going? I want to introduce you to some people. They can't wait to meet you."

Trevor was worried it would only start trouble with Gina. "No Brian. Gina and I have been here a good while, we would like to leave now."

But Brian was insistent, and Trevor gave into him. Gina was furious as she followed them to a table of noticeably young women. Brian introduced them as the new "it" couple. They said hello and told the women it was a big night and they had to go.

Their limo driver was waiting out front to take them home. There was a bottle of champagne from John Dunn chilling in the back seat with a note, "Hoping you join us."

Gina could not hold her tongue. "He moves fast, doesn't he?"

"You know what? Everything was a success. It was overwhelming, but the potential to be an opening act. Let's drink champagne on the way home. Maybe I'll get lucky."

"You got lucky earlier," Gina reminded him playfully. "You want to have a closer?"

"When I see the hottest lead singer chatting up my woman, yeah, I want a closer."

"You saw that? But you didn't hear what I told him. He was talking to the wrong woman." Gina drank her champagne and placed her hand on Trevor's crotch. "This is the only man I want. Got it?"

The champagne and Gina's swift move made Trevor even more determined to take her. "We didn't get to join the Mile High Club, but what about limo sex?"

"You're serious right now?"

"There's a privacy window I can roll up. Just please try not to be so loud."

"Oh, I'm loud? You haven't heard yourself. I'm in."

Trevor took her standard missionary, still a bit naughty though. They loved the idea that the driver might know what they were doing. He would have a story to tell.

When the limo pulled up in front of their house, they hadn't finished. Trevor quickly zipped up his pants and got out of the car while Gina rearranged her dress. He tried to give a tip to the driver, who told him it was already covered. He winked at Trevor and told him to have a good night.

They went into the house and started peeling off their formal attire. Gina stopped for a moment. "These are expensive clothes, be gentle." They stumbled to the floor in front of the fireplace. Gina could tell Trevor was ready, but offered up a little tease, backing up as he was getting ready to take her. "You know that singer you saw me talking to? He's supposed to have it all."

Trevor looked at her, puzzled. "What?"

"Yeah, women would drop down on their knees for him."

"What are you doing?"

"Hold on, that might be true, but for me," she grabbed him, "This is what I want for my whole life, please let me have it." She got teary eyed, "I mean it so deeply, no man could ever give me what you give me."

He climbed on top. "G, my God this is perfection."

"Yes. Yes, it is."

They fell asleep on the floor. Gina woke up and dragged Trevor to bed.

IT'S A DEAL

THE NEXT MORNING BROUGHT A HANGOVER. Was it the champagne or was it everything that transpired the night before? The party, the people, or the idea that they could be the opening act for two of the hottest bands in the country. Gina got up, made coffee, and brought Trevor a cup while he was still in bed. "So, what do you think the band is going to want to do about the tour? I'm shocked that this happened so fast."

Trevor sat up. "First—good morning. Kiss me, and I agree it's fast. We might have to write a few songs to go on tour, mix in some Gina kick-ass covers. I know Rio will be all in; that's a given. Jeff will be in. Ian? I'm worried a bit that this is all coming fast for him, and for Lisa. Kevin will be all in. The roadies won't care; they get to travel and work."

Gina shook her head in acknowledgment, encouraging Trevor to continue his flow of thought. "Are we truly ready? I mean opening acts usually don't get a whole lot of attention. It's an opportunity I don't think we can really pass up, especially when the label is collaborating with the promoter."

There was a knock on the door. Trevor sat up taller. "What the hell? Who's at our door this early?"

"I can guess. I'll answer it." Rio was at the door holding bags of bagels and doughnuts, wearing the same clothes from the night before.

Gina let him in. "Someone had a night. Wearing the same clothes, Rio? What's up with the breakfast? This early in the morning?"

"After you left, things got crazy. People doing lots of lines, right. Some chicks were dancing topless. It was a scene. Crazy. That's how they do it in California."

Gina placed the food on the table. "Do you want coffee? I'm guessing yes."

Trevor came into the kitchen, pulling up his sweatpants, "Thanks for breakfast, but this visit has nothing to do with you feeding us. What's going on? Other than you didn't go home last night."

"I guess we left at a suitable time. Rio said the party turned into some sort of debauchery after we left," Gina informed him.

Turning to Rio, Gina asked, "Oh, shit. Did Ian and Lisa leave before that? Do you know? That would scare them both, seeing all that batshit craziness."

Rio assured her they did, so she continued, "More importantly, we have to discuss the tour offered up to us."

Rio looked at her like she was insane. "Gina! There's no option, we fucking have to do it. This is an opportunity. We may never get another chance if we say no. We're climbing the ladder. The label will knock us off that ladder if we say no. What's up with you two? I counted you as in."

Trevor took a doughnut, while Gina took a poppy seed bagel and smeared it with lox and cream cheese.

Trevor shared what he and Gina had been discussing. "We understand that this is an opportunity, and we need to take it. However, we would need to write a few new songs. We can play them and see how the songs go over with the fans. Then we will have some songs for our next album and people will have already heard them. Great buzz for album two. My question to you is, do you feel ready?"

Rio spoke around a mouthful of doughnut. "Fuck, yeah, I'm ready to go on the road. I've been ready since I started playing. I wonder what cities, he said fourteen, right?"

Gina was already thinking ahead. "Can I stick my voice in here? We need to find someone to outfit the band. You two can't keep going onstage with those threadbare jeans. I'm not saying wearing shit that's ridiculous, just a bit more stage worthy. All bands do it."

Rio answered her. "I'm wearing what's most comfortable. I could give a shit. Gina, you're the one that has to worry about clothing."

Gina retorted, "I'll handle my shit, thank you very much. What are your thoughts about Ian? I'm not worried about Jeff."

Rio laughed, "You shouldn't be. He was in the middle of all the partying. He went in hard, motherfucker was entertaining."

Gina hoped to get an early handle on this. "We don't need Jeff being a loose cannon, partying until he can't play. You need to keep him in check. Now that I said that I realize how the concept is stupid. You will be right there."

Trevor thought for a moment. "We need to talk to Skip. Who is paying for our transportation from city to city, hotels? Is Perfection? Or since the label wants us to promote, are they picking up the tab? That's important. How are we traveling? Bus, airplane? We don't know anything."

Rio was ready to call Skip. "Do you have a speaker on your phone so we can all talk to him?"

Gina shook her head. "We do, but we haven't spoken about Ian. Last night was a bit much for him and Lisa. We have to make sure he can manage that."

Rio was exasperated. "Gina, he joined the band, he knew that this could happen, come on."

Trevor got the phone. "Let's call Skip."

Skip answered the phone without saying hello. "Trevor, I was getting ready to call you and then Rio. We need to make a major decision on the tour."

"Well, Skip, Rio is here with Gina and me. I'm putting you on speaker. We want to move forward. Ian is our only concern. He was uncomfortable last night, and touring ramps up the intensity level. Do you want to talk to him? You're the manager."

Skip sighed. "Yes, that's my job. If I have his buy in, then we're in?"

Gina spoke up. "Skip, we also want to know who is paying for transportation, hotels, all the upfront costs? The label wants us to do this to promote the album, so I believe they should incur some of the costs. Am I missing something?"

"I'll speak to Blum and Dunn," Skip managed to interject.

Gina continued, "We pay for our food, any clothes we need to buy. We know we will have to pay our road crew, but what about the transportation of our equipment? None of these are deal-breakers, but let's put it all out there."

"Agreed," added Skip.

"The label wants to promote us. They invested in us, and they reap the benefits of our sales. We do too, but come on, they win."

Skip ended the call with two points. "I'll call Ian. I don't think it will take much to convince him. He wants the band to be successful and this is part of it. I'll tell him he should bring his wife. That might help. Then, I'll work out all the points Gina mentioned. I'll have Blum and Dunn prepare the contract. We sign and we're done."

Gina had one more question. "Can we have the specific date we need to be ready? And the dates of the cities we're playing."

Skip ended with, "It will be in the contract."

Trevor had barely hung up the phone before Rio erupted with excitement. "Fuck, yeah! We're going on tour. That's some serious shit, right?"

"Yes, Rio, that's some serious shit. Don't burn out too fast," Trevor warned him. "There will be bottles of everything and any drug you want. We can have it all whenever we want. There will also be lots and lots of groupies. We can't control that, we aren't the headliners. Gina, you are going to have to come to terms with that. You have nothing to worry about."

Rio stared at her. "Gina, I have seen that side of you. When jealousy controls you, you aren't a nice person. Everyone knows that you and Trevor are a couple."

Gina smirked back at him, "Like anyone pays attention to that, Rio. It makes it more attractive. But yes, I have no control of the other bands, but I do have control over who is in our dressing room."

Rio got up to leave. "Good breakfast with you two. Do you two ever get dressed when you're home or are you always one step away from naked?"

Trevor was already closing the door. "Thanks, and goodbye."

Gina looked at Trevor. "This should be an interesting tour."

TOURING

SKIP WAS WORKING on the final details of the touring contract. A few things still needed to be worked out. Brown Fence and John Dunn, the promoter for White Lace Fest, would pay for transportation and hotels. The band would also get paid by the venue. They would receive a percentage that Skip was working on. Perfection would pay their road crew and move their equipment.

It was getting toward the end of March. The tour was to begin in April. Gina was waiting for the schedule. She needed to plan her wardrobe. The band got the itinerary:

White Lace Festival 1979

April 21	San Francisco
April 28	Seattle
May 5	Las Vegas
May 12	Phoenix
May 19	Austin
May 26	Denver
June 2	Chicago
June 9	Detroit
June 16	Atlanta
June 23	Miami

June 30	Boston
July 7	Washington, DC
July 14	New York City
July 21	Los Angeles

Gina looked at the schedule and realized there would be differences in climate, so she would need to find a stylist again, someone who worked with musicians preferably. She would ask Mimi, their stylist for the release party, to recommend someone. Mimi suggested a new stylist who dealt with a lot of rock bands. Claire Shipwell dressed both male and female musicians. Gina thought she would take Lisa with her to get her opinion.

Meanwhile, Trevor and the boys were trying to write a few songs. They wanted Gina there, but she told them, "When you have something for me to sing then I'll be there, or if you need me to write something, I'll be there. I care about my wardrobe so I'm busy."

Lisa and Gina arrived at Claire Shipwell's loft and found it filled with racks and racks of clothing. Sections were labeled "Male," "Female," "For Rent," and "For Sale." Gina only wanted to purchase the clothes. She couldn't stand the idea of putting something on her body that someone else had already worn.

Claire asked, "How do you see yourself onstage?"

Gina never really thought sexy was all she was. She wanted to dress like a rock star, she wanted to be tasteful. "Sexy not slutty."

"You can be provocative in the right jeans or leather pants, some beaded glittery tanks with part of your breasts exposed on the side, high heels, boots, platforms." She showed Gina a couple of skintight leather dresses, very skintight. For warmer weather venues, she showed her halter dresses and pants with high slits.

Gina was amassing a total wardrobe. She thought of the NYC July fourteenth performance. That was close to the date she met Trevor at Glen Island Casino. She planned to wear the dress she had on the day she fell in love with him.

For the end of the tour, they would be home in Los Angeles. Gina wanted something killer. Claire showed her a blush lace jumpsuit that would be see-through in the right lighting. There were appliqués in strategic spots. It had a high neckline and was backless. *Yes,* Gina thought, *perfect.* She reiterated that she wanted to purchase the clothing. Claire was extremely happy to add up the twenty or so items, totaling $25,459.

"Credit card or check?" Gina asked. Lisa's eyes widened, floored that Gina didn't flinch at the price tag.

On the way home, Gina asked Lisa if she was going to go on tour with Ian.

She waffled a bit, and asked Gina, "Do you think I should go?"

"You haven't had this conversation with Ian yet?"

"I've been afraid too."

"Lisa! You must ask him, see how he feels. I think he would want you to come. You settle him."

"I'm afraid he wants to go alone," Lisa sighed.

"I disagree. I think he would want his wife to be there for his first tour. I hope I'm not starting something I shouldn't."

As she dropped Lisa off, Gina told her, "Ask him. *I* would like you there, to have a friend."

When Gina arrived home, the driveway was full of cars. She hated to do it, but she parked on the grass in the front yard. She walked in and no one blinked. The men of Perfection were working on some songs.

Rio finally looked up. "We need you to throw together some lyrics. Where have you been?"

"Rio, you're not serious now. I don't report to you. I'll be happy to work up some lyrics, but can I hear the music? I need to know if it's full energy or a slow love song thing."

Trevor got up, kissed her, and asked if she was successful in finding her wardrobe. She answered yes, very. She went into the kitchen and found Brian.

"Brian, can I help you with something? You are in my kitchen."

"I'm looking for a bite to eat. The rest of them aren't hungry until they get some tunes down."

"I see. So, you thought you would go through my kitchen."

"Yeah, I had some killer leftovers you had in the fridge. I forgot you are a good cook too. I guess you are good at everything."

"Yes, Brian, I am. Consider me a woman of many talents. Don't forget that."

Trevor came into the kitchen, worried that a conversation may be going on that he would be uncomfortable with, "Hey, babe, you good? Want to sit with me and try to bang out some lyrics?"

"Sure. I love to add lyrics to your music. I most definitely can't wait to help out. Brian, you are coming."

They worked until nine o'clock.

"Lisa is going to kill me," Ian said. "I lost track of time."

Jeff said he had a late-night date, leaving Rio and Brian.

Gina called it. "You two go home. Trevor and I will work on lyrics, but I would like to run through and sing it."

Once they were alone, Gina asked Trevor, "You hungry? Brian told me you hadn't eaten. You have been working nonstop. Take a break. Come here and sit next to me. Tell me about the day."

"These guys are talking about all the shit they plan on doing on tour," he admitted. "I'm worried they will get out of control. We can't be the bad boys on the road the first time out. Ian and I can't get into that shit. I know I told you that I had some bad times with drinking a bottle of whiskey a night, taking whatever someone gave me, high to the point I would black out. I did all that with Ian. He has the same demons I do. I hope temptation doesn't nag at me. We go out—I have a beer or champagne. I can manage it. But everything, Gina, is going to be there. I don't want to start drinking like that. I'm afraid of how I might treat you. I'm a horrible drunk."

"Trev, you aren't going to do that. We will be together, unless you are telling me you would sneak it so I wouldn't know until it's too late. Is that what you're telling me? Because I'm not letting you sabotage our relationship the first chance that we have. You know you're better than this, Trevor, come on. We smoke a joint, you have no problem with that. What tips you over the edge? What? The pressure? Don't do this. Don't do this to us now."

"I'm not saying I will, but those headliners, they all party constantly. Now we have your cousin and Jeff ready to go off. I need to watch myself and I need you to be aware if I'm struggling."

"Come here my nonperfect love. I will not allow you to go there. We are a couple. Partners. You're my everything. I will not let you or anybody else destroy that. I promise you; you may hate me for it, but I'm doing it for us. Come here. Give me a kiss, then I need you to help me get a lot of clothes out of the car."

Gina was restless that night, worried about Trevor with so much temptation. She thought back to that night when he did too much cocaine and whiskey. He was a mess, and she didn't like what she saw. She thought about the night of the album release, when he drank almost the whole bottle of champagne, and they had sex in the limo. Was he being kinky, or was it the alcohol? She would try to not be judgmental if he fell. Pick him up and move on.

At three a.m. Gina was still awake so she walked out to the living room and started looking at lyrics. When Trevor got up to go to the bathroom, he noticed Gina was missing. He found her sitting on the couch, writing lyrics, and crying.

Trevor knew why. "Gina, baby, I didn't mean to scare you. I'm a better man because of you."

"I'm writing lyrics to this song so you remember your faults, but love takes that edge off. I won't let you destroy us. I want to get married. I want to have babies. I want to live a real life with you. This is great now, but twenty years from now—what are we? Two people who survived the pitfalls of living the rock and roll lifestyle? That's not what I want."

"I love you too, now let's go back to bed."

IN THE AIR

THE TOUR WAS GETTING CLOSE. Ian was bringing Lisa, and the band was going over their equipment as it was being packed into the truck. Brown Fence had a private jet, and all three bands were flying together. None of the Perfection crew had ever flown on a private jet.

Gina felt uncomfortable leaving their house empty for over three months, so she hired a house sitter—Tina Allbright, a quiet twenty-year-old woman who would come by and turn lights on and off, get the mail, and make it look like someone was living there. In Los Angeles there is always someone looking for this type of job. Rio asked her if she would do the same at his place.

Perfection wrote two new songs, but they weren't ready yet. Gina asked if they could throw in "Can't Find My Way Back Home," a soft, slow song. She also wanted to add a kick-ass song that could get the audience standing up and cheering as the band left the stage.

Trevor and Gina started packing. Gina needed her toiletries, makeup, and comfortable clothes to wear on the plane. There were two more cases to hold all her stage clothes. Trevor packed only jeans and tees, not realizing they would be invited to several parties on the road.

Gina assumed Brian Mayfield would find a way to weasel his way onto the plane. She needed to watch him around Trevor. She knew he would play to his addictions. What an asshole.

The next morning, a limo showed up at Trevor and Gina's house. Rio decided to ride with them. He noticed a bit of tension with Gina and Trevor.

Rio looked at them, "What's up with you two you? You seem nervous, something like that. We're going on tour. What's up?"

Gina was expecting the worst. "Trevor and Ian have to be careful around all the alcohol and drugs. So please watch what comes near Perfection. I need to worry about that, and honestly, I don't trust Mayfield around Trevor. He wants to see Trevor use. So yes, I am concerned." She smoked her pastel cigarettes and a joint before getting on the plane. Gina didn't care for cocaine, she didn't like the speeding feeling. Rio would do anything given to him. Why not? He had no one to answer to.

Limos were sent for the other band members, and Mayfield rode with Jeff. The limo brought them to the plane. The two headliners showed up in limos packed with people. Lots of women and guys who looked like they could be their drug connections and groupies.

Brent Nolan, the lead singer of the headline act who met Gina at the bar, threw her a look. "Well, it looks like Perfection is joining us. This will be fun. We will get to know each other well. Gina Poole, good to see you."

It made Trevor a bit jealous that this guy singled out Gina. Was he trying to piss him off? Thankfully, this was only a short flight to San Francisco. The other bands boarded first to get the best seats on the plane. Perfection was surprised they had a decent area. Gourmet food was being passed around, along with any kind of cocktail. Lisa was still in shock that she was on a private plane. Gina and Trevor found a nice wide seat that they could get comfortable in.

The pilot's voice came over the speaker and welcomed Dunn and Blum passengers. At the other end of the plane there was screaming and hollering.

Flight attendants on this plane had a good gig—good pay and the chance to meet rock stars.

After takeoff, a twenty-something guy with stringy hair made his way up the aisle to Trevor. “Hey man, I’m Tiger. If there’s anything I can get you, make sure you let me know. I got whatever you need.”

Rio and Jeff heard, and their eyes lit up. “Really?” asked Rio. “Maybe some lines would be cool.”

“Come to the back with me. I’ll hook you up.”

Gina was furious with Rio and turned to Trevor. “This is how our tour is starting. Can you believe it?”

“I told you this is big time; we haven’t been in the air long and it’s already starting. Don’t let it aggravate you.”

“We’re good, right, Trev? We’re good?”

He put his head on her shoulder. “Yes G, we’re good. No worries.”

FIRST STOP

A FLEET OF BLACK LIMOS were on the tarmac when they landed. Each driver was standing next to the car holding a sign with a band's name. Perfection had two limos assigned to them. Trevor, Gina, Ian, and Lisa climbed into one. The other limos held the partiers.

All the bands were staying at the Hyatt Regency in San Francisco. There was no need to check in. The concierge handed them their keys. A bellman took the six suitcases to their suite.

Trevor flopped on the bed. "This is almost as comfortable as the bed we have at home."

Gina didn't believe anything could be as comfortable as their bed and lay next to Trevor. "It's okay. So, what do we do now? I know what you're thinking. We can wait for later. You're so horny lately. What's up with that? I'm not complaining, but I thought we could walk around for a bit. Try to be normal."

"You realize there are fans outside the hotel, and paparazzi. Are you ready for that?"

Gina scoffed, "There's no way anyone would recognize us. You think?"

"G, there's posters around promoting the concert. We might even have to do a radio interview or something like that."

"Can we at least try? We'll wear sunglasses."

Trevor laughed, "Babe, if you want to give it a go, we'll try."

They walked out of their room and saw Brent Nolan. "Oh, shit, really my room is next to yours. Make sure you keep it down." He was laughing as he walked into his room.

Gina flicked her hair. "Don't you find him presumptuous?"

"Yes, very," Trevor agreed. "We have to spend the next three months with him."

They walked out the front entrance and right out the door. There were some fans waiting to see band members, but Gina and Trevor were safe. They walked up Embarcadero Center, enjoying the fresh air. When they came back, they ran into Ian and Lisa in the lobby.

"This is a lovely place. They have a cute bar, want to get a drink?" Ian invited.

Gina piped up, "Great idea, but just one."

The four sat at the bar with a drink and then they noticed the bar filling up with the entourage of the other bands. They were noticed. "Hey, you're in Perfection. Hi, my name is Dave. Can I buy you a drink?"

Ian answered them. "No man, we're cool, but thanks. Next time."

"Okay man, next time I got you."

"Maybe we should go back to our rooms," an uncomfortable Lisa suggested.

Gina asked, "What time is it?"

"Almost six thirty. Do you want dinner? It looks like they have nice restaurants in the hotel." Lisa had no idea how expensive the hotel was. Dinner at one of those restaurants would cost a fortune for them both.

Trevor answered Lisa. "This hotel will be crawling with groupies."

Gina suggested a different plan. "Why don't we order room service and eat in? We have a table in our room." Gina knew that room service was expensive. She didn't want Ian and Lisa to start the tour with sticker shock. She would sign for dinner in their room. Lisa loved the idea. The two couples went up to the McNaughtons' suite and ordered dinner. They enjoyed a bottle of wine and dessert. A peaceful beginning to what would be a crazy three months.

Skip Glazer stopped by to give then a rundown on how the week would roll out. "Tomorrow the truck should be here with the equipment. We want to make sure everything arrived." Looking at Trevor, "I'm guessing you brought your guitars with you. Tuesday we will walk the venue. We have to make sure our equipment rolls off the stage so the next band can set up. Wednesday, I would suggest some practice and have your set list ready. On Thursday, you have an interview with the local rock station. This is what every city on the tour will look like. The only difference will be the interviews. Those I will arrange before we get to the next city. You good with the schedule? I will let everybody know."

Trevor responded, "Yes, at least we know what we're doing." With that Lisa and Ian said good night and they'd see them tomorrow.

Skip continued after Lisa and Ian had gone. "Hey, we need to try and put a lid on Rio and Jeff. I saw what the two of them were doing on the plane. These two bands are notorious partiers. I don't want the first tour to be a drug frenzy. I'll talk to the both of them. You are with me, right?"

Gina agreed. "It should come from you, the manager. You need to manage them. I'm afraid my cousin and Jeff could go off the rails. Thank you for riding them."

Skip turned to leave. "You have a great evening; the rest of the week is work."

Gina locked the door after him and turned to Trevor. "I think he should also talk to your friend, Brian Mayfield. He is a shit stirrer. Oh, yes, I wanted to share something with you. I thought of a song we can end our set with. Do you know what will get the audience pumped? How about "Light my Fire?" You and Rio can add some guitar solos to elevate it. We can see if Kevin can get fire torches."

Trevor sat back on the bed. "I like it. We will have to see about adding fire, but I'm into it. You're going to make it very sensual, aren't you?"

Gina crawled onto the bed. "Of course I am. That's what the crowd wants, a perfect ending."

"You know what? You're a perfect ending. You are really impacting the way the band operates. I always underestimate your business savvy. I'm sorry for that." He grabbed her by her hair. "You are some sexy wench. I have to watch our friend next door. He is trying to put moves on you, did you realize that?"

"Trevor McNaughton, are you jealous? I'm the one who has a mean jealousy streak. But you, I have never given you a reason to doubt my love or commitment to you. Have I?"

"No, G, you never have, and I don't know why you love me so much, but it makes me happy."

Gina crawled up his body and pushed those beautiful blond locks off his face. She dotted sweet little kisses all over his face, then worked her way into an "I'm hungry for you" kiss. She took off his shirt and then hers. She massaged Trevor's shoulders and neck, their eyes never leaving each other. He grabbed Gina's legs from underneath her, making her laugh. "Baby let's do San Francisco. Oh, we should add 'Feel Like Makin' Love' to the set list."

And they did, all night.

Before they fell asleep, Gina filled out the room service menu for a large coffee and continental breakfast with two sides of bacon to be delivered in the morning.

Gina woke up to knocking on their door. She grabbed her robe and signed for breakfast. She rolled the cart into the room.

Trevor started to stir, "What do you have there, G? Coffee?"

"Yes, I ordered it last night. You leave it on the door, and they collect it. You didn't know that?"

"I have never stayed at fancy hotels like you have."

"Here's your coffee. Let's get a move on. I'm interested in walking the venue."

IT GETS REAL

THE BAND WALKED THE VENUE and got a feel for the stage. They checked out the backstage area as well. With three bands there would be equipment all over the place, but theirs should be easy to identify with bright pink stickers that read Perfection.

They had never played in front of this many people before, most of whom weren't coming to hear *them*.

They found a room at the hotel where they could practice. "Light My Fire" was in, and "Feel Like Makin' Love" was added to ramp up the audience. This part wasn't glamorous, just work. It's not until the concert is over that performers feel that euphoria of playing in front of thousands of fans.

Friday was sound check. All the bands were there with their sound engineers. It can take time to get the right sound. Sometimes performers sing a song to get everything correct. Perfection did three songs in their sound check to get a good sound.

That night was a restless night for most of the members of Perfection, with the exception of Rio, Jeff, and Brian. Partying with some of the ladies from the plane ride. They would be hurting the next day. The band had a meeting at ten a.m. in a private room, where they went over set lists, a few rules from the venue, minutia like that. Rio and Jeff showed up at eleven fifteen. Gina turned around and looked at Rio and Jeff with disgust. Gina couldn't help herself. "Thanks for almost screwing up the plan for tonight you two assholes. You both better reel it in." Rio laughed, "Are you going to dress down Brian?" Gina sneered, "I could give two shits about Brian and what he does. We clear?" Rio and Jeff had a few hours of rest before they needed to get to the venue. Perfection was going on at seven o'clock.

They opened with "Punch the Night," getting the crowd pumped. Gina stepped up in a skintight black leather dress and introduced the band. "Hi everyone! We are Perfection. I'm Gina Poole. To my right is my cousin, badass guitarist Rio Poole. Behind me is the guy who keeps the beat, Ian White. All the way to my left is the guy with a mean bass line, Jeff Wainwright. And next to me is, well the best of everything—guitar and vocals, the man I love, Trevor McNaughton."

The crowd was attentive and seemed familiar with their songs, which is unusual for an opening act. Was it the way Gina dressed? When she kicked it up with "Feel Like Makin' Love," the crowd was totally into it. The set ended with "Light My Fire," driving the crowd wild.

Gina walked offstage, and Brent Nolan who wasn't due onstage for an hour and a half, looked at her. "You hit that nice."

Was she going to have to listen to his remarks at every show? Maybe. They were the headliner.

The band was pumped after the show. The first stop had been a success. Skip was ecstatic.

The boys found some ladies and some coke and decided to party. They were Skip's problem.

Trevor grabbed Gina backstage and kissed her. "I'm so proud of the show you put on. Baby, you're the best. Let's get out of here before things get crazy."

Gina turned to Skip. "How did those girls get backstage to where the dressing rooms are? They don't look like they are from the plane. I thought

I made it clear from the beginning—no groupies allowed. Make sure it doesn't happen again."

Skip told her, "Gina we can't control the whole backstage. Besides, Perfection is the opening act. I wish you had that type of authority, but you don't."

Gina knew he was right. "At least make sure they aren't anywhere near our dressing rooms. Thanks, Skip."

Sunday evening, the plane would be at the airport at six thirty p.m. destined for Seattle. And so went every city, the same rhythm, different radio stations, and Perfection's music was making it on the airwaves.

Week ten was in Miami. It was sweltering—with the lights and heat off the crowd in an open-air venue, it was stifling. Some of the guys went without shirts. Gina had to find something lighter to wear. Sweat turned every outfit transparent.

GOING HOME

GINA CRIED WHEN THE PLANE was low enough for her to see the New York skyline. She was proud that she came from the greatest city in the world.

She and Trevor stayed at the carriage house instead of a hotel. They went to the big house for dinner with the entire family—Frankie and MaryAnn, their three children, Uncle Tony, Aunt Deidre, and Rio. It was a big Italian dinner with loud talking and laughter. The family didn't hold back telling Rio, Trevor, and Gina how proud they were of the band's success.

Serena cried when she saw Gina. "Princess, you come home a big star now."

Gina kissed her. "No Serena, I'm still Gina."

Trevor asked everyone if they wanted backstage passes or tickets for front row seats. Mario said he felt safer backstage instead of in the crowd with a bunch of "stoned out kids."

The band walked the venue, The Academy of Music in NYC, one that Gina knew well, as a concert goer. It was surreal to be there now as the entertainment.

Gina broke away to visit her family jeweler. She arranged for two rings to be made. The jeweler created a wedding band with a double row of pear-shaped diamonds totaling eight carats. The other band was platinum with black diamond on the top and bottom, imprinted with a guitar. The inscription inside read "G-loves-T-always."

Gina thought either she was a fool for having the rings made or one day they would use them when they eloped to Vegas.

Did the gardeners keep up my little garden? Gina wondered. She found out that Serena came down and picked the herbs for her cooking. *I'm so happy I started that.*

It was the night of the New York concert. Perfection needed to be on their A game. Not only was it an important venue, all their family and friends would be there. Gina didn't let Trevor see what she was wearing. She showed up onstage last, wearing "the dress," the one she was wearing when Trevor fell in love with her. She walked onstage and kissed him before they started "Found You." The crowd went crazy for the hometown band. For an encore, they did "Gimme Shelter" and "Light my Fire." Kevin even found fire shots that erupted when the song was finishing.

Their success that night proved that Perfection would be the headliner very soon. Her family was filled with pride. Gina was a star. The next day they were leaving for the last concert of the tour, back in LA. Everyone stayed at the hotel in the city that night.

The next morning, the limos came to take everyone to Teterboro Airport, where they boarded the private jet back to LA, their new home. The other two bands started the party early. Tiger was there pushing whatever anybody wanted. He handed Gina and Trevor a vile with two pieces of paper inside—blotter acid.

The limo dropped off Ian and Lisa first, then took Rio, Trevor, and Gina to the bungalow. The rest of the band was in another limo. Gina couldn't care less about them at this point.

THREE DAYS LATER

SKIP WANTED TO MIX UP their set list to take advantage of what they were playing. He also wanted Gina to do her rendition of "Can't Find My Way Home," taking the soft song and making it sultry.

Everyone showed up at the Hollywood Bowl. Perfection had two dressing rooms there. Chante came to do Gina's makeup. Gina wore the beige catsuit, which didn't leave much to the imagination.

When Trevor walked in to change, he said, "G, you're not wearing that are you? You're going to look naked. Not sure I want another Miami incident."

"Trev, this is the last night. Let's make it memorable. I'm not naked. Trust me, it will be okay." She kissed him. "I love you. Let's make this powerful."

Brian Mayfield knocked on their dressing room door, "Hey, there are some people who would like to meet you. Can I have them stop by?"

Gina stared daggers at him. "I told you. No groupies. We don't do that."

"But they're Playboy Bunnies. They want to say hello to both of you."

"Brian! What the fuck? Bringing bunnies into our dressing room? Are you fucking high right now? What the fuck is wrong with you? Why would I want to meet them? They want to meet Trevor and you facilitate that. You suck Brian. I won't have it. We have to be onstage in thirty minutes." Gina shot a venomous look at Trevor.

"Brian, Gina's right. We have to be onstage in thirty minutes. A quick 'hi' as we're walking out, but no one in the dressing room, okay?"

They were introduced as "LA's new band." Gina wasn't sure she liked that. She still considered them New York's band, but realized that they were an LA band also, no harm. The guys walked onstage first. Gina came out last like she always did. The crowd cheered her choice in clothing with some obscene language. But nothing fazed her.

For an encore, she chose "Light my Fire," but the band had to pump up everything; solos had to be extra. Gina danced like she was dancing for herself. The crowd cheered and yelled.

They came offstage and there he was, Brent Nolan. He pulled Trevor over and said, "That's your lady, right? You know a guy like me could win her over easily. You had better think about making it permanent or someone like me will take her away. Something to think about." He laughed.

Trevor was taken aback by his audacity. Gina was his, and she was loyal to him and the band. Trevor looked at him. "I trust Gina. Even a womanizing asshole like you could never interfere with my relationship. So, yeah, I don't think so." What kind of shit was this guy pulling? Or did he have a point about making it permanent? That's what made Trevor think.

Backstage, Skip gathered the band together. "Listen, Brown Fence wants you all in the studio soon for your next album. They are also giving you a bonus for the job you did. Congratulations. We are moving up. Thanks for letting me be part of Perfection."

BACK AT THE HILLS

IT WAS A GREAT FEELING BEING HOME after three months on the road. Trevor and Gina were going to pull the shades down, leave the phone off the hook, and sleep. They wanted to spend their time in quiet domesticity. They went to Beverly Hills and took a walk down Rodeo Drive, not thinking anyone would recognize them, but they were wrong. People started pointing and saying "hi." They didn't realize the tour made them that famous. Paparazzi began hanging out in front of their house.

That night, back at the house, Trevor remembered the blotter acid Tiger gave him. "Hey, babe, you wanna go on a trip?"

"We just got back from a three-month trip. Why would I want to go anywhere?"

Trevor held the vile up. "No, this kind of trip."

"You mean drop acid? I haven't done that since high school."

"I heard it makes sex even better."

Gina laughed at him. "You have no issues in that area. But I'm willing to see where it takes us. I'm in."

They put the paper on their tongues, and it took thirty minutes for them to realize they were tripping. They watched TV and laughed at the commercials. They put on music and slow danced.

Trevor led Gina into the bedroom. They were naked in seconds. He sat on the bed and instructed Gina to straddle him. She was more than happy to accommodate. They moved slowly, enjoying each other. The acid overstimulated every part of their bodies. Trevor turned her over, taking her from behind, moving with a passion that was overtaking every sensory part of their minds and bodies. Making love on acid was like another level of passion and seemed to last for hours. Finally, they fell asleep.

Friday, August 3, 1979, Trevor woke up before Gina and stared at her as she slept. He was bothered by what Brent Nolan said to him.

Gina began to stir. "Good morning, baby. Why are you staring at me like that? Are you still high?"

"Gina, it's time . . ."

"Trevor, you're scaring me. What do you mean it's time? What's going on in that head of yours?"

"I want to go to Vegas. I want to get married."

Gina's head was spinning. "I want to be your wife more than anything."

PLAYLIST

Good Times Bad Times Bad Times	Led Zeppelin
All Right Now	Free
American Woman	The Guess Who
All the Young Dudes	Mott the Hoople
Baba O'Riley	The Who
Stay with Me	Rod Steward and
Faces	
Angie	The Rolling Stones
I Saw the Light	Todd Rundgren
Can't Get Enough	Bad Company
Feel Like Makin' Love	Bad Company
After Midnight	Eric Clapton
Gimme Shelter	The Rolling Stones
Long Distance Runaround	Yes
Waiting*	Perfection
Found You*	Perfection
Punch the Night*	Perfection
The Girl Behind the Song*	Perfection
Love Is the Drug	Roxy Music
Fame	David Bowie
Music Is a Circus*	Perfection
Can't Find My Way Home	Blind Faith

ACKNOWLEDGMENTS

THIS HAS BEEN my maiden journey in self-publishing a book.

Foremost I'd like to acknowledge Joshua Rickelman. Without the friendship I've had with him, I would never have been introduced to the band scene of the 1970s–'80s.

I am a very lucky person to have a team who is hands down the best of the best. I would like to thank the hardest working lady I know who helped build the team, Polly Letofsky, my publishing consultant and owner of My Word Publishing. She helped me understand what I was getting into and held my hand along the way. In building my team I was introduced to my editor and another awesome woman, Maggie Mills. She understood my vision and gave me some great ideas for enhancing it I was lucky to have my next star Victoria Wolf work on my website, book cover and book layout Her work is amazing. My proofreader Cheryl Isaac did a great job in proofreading my work and also offered insightful s uggestions without changing my story. The woman who expertly tackling the tough job of marketing myself and my book(s) plus handling my social media is Mary Walewski. I have a fabulous "A" team and it will be my pleasure to work with them for my additional books in this series. How lucky can a girl be!

I'd also like to thank my closest friends who stood by me when I first decided to write *Perfection Saga* and encouraged me to keep writing: Beverly, Monica, Karen, Bekki, Casey, Christine, Jessica, Chris, Liz, Keri, and Holly have all been my rocks. Especially when I thought I was crazy in taking this all on. I know they were correct.

Lastly my family, maybe not being the most encouraging at times but understanding my dream. In the end, they believed in me.

Life is groovy.

ABOUT THE AUTHOR

BETH PELLINO-DUDZIC was born in the Bronx, NYC. She spent most of her life inWestchester County.. She received a BA in Business Administration and then moved to Honolulu, Hawaii, where her three daughters were born. She came back to Westchester to raise her girls and worked at IBM upon her return.

Although the story is fictional, it is a tribute to the author's fond memories of her time in the 1970's-80's band scene.a. The story developed over decades in her head. It was waiting to be written.

She now lives in Pike Road, Alabama, with her husband and their miniature dachshund,Truffle. Beth's favorite pastimes are cooking, baking, and everything football.